Lanigan didn't say anything. He didn't ask who Aaron Flagg was. He was trying to remember the stories: the time Noah was supposed to have beaten her up so badly that the film she was making had to be suspended for months; the Rolls-Royce he gave her for her birthday – and charged to her account; the scandal when it was discovered that he kept her and his wife in the same Beverly Hills mansion. It was hard now to know what was real and what was part of the legend, where fiction had become fact and fact fiction.

Noah said, "A woman's last love affair is with her doctor or a priest. You ever hear that? A woman's last love affair is with her doctor or a priest? If she's an actress five'll get you two it'll be with her ghostwriter, or a goddam publisher."

Peter Evans is the author of many books, including *Goodbye Baby and Amen* and the international bestseller *The Englishman's Daughter*. He is also the author of *Ari*, the biography of Aristotle Onassis. He lives in London with his wife.

And this one is for Clementine

1

As far as being a movie star, I never thought that was any great achievement. (Theodora Glass, New York Daily News, *August 3, 1948)*

Friday, September 1
Santa Aloe, West Indies

She finished her morning swim and returned to the beach. In the distance a clock struck six. Six o'clock, when it is cool and already light, is not an ungodly hour in the West Indies: studio time, she called it, although it had been a very long time since she had risen at that hour to make a movie.

Tall and slender-boned, she was naked except for a gold chain around her neck, on which hung a small gold disfigured heart. Her hair, the colour of bleached driftwood, was blunt-cut in the helmet style of the sixties. Aristocratic was the word reporters used when they wrote about her, although her skin was now a little too burnt by the sun to be truly aristocratic, and her pale lips had always been too full to be quite respectable.

She walked slowly to the top of the empty beach where a woman waited with her robe.

Theodora Glass bathed more slowly than usual that morning and thought about things she had stopped thinking about over thirty years ago. She dressed in a sleeveless white linen shirt, a white chiffon dirndl. She had her own style, being one of those women who crystallized into her own look while young, and had watched it come and go out of style many times.

She studied her face, illuminated and magnified in the make-up glass.

1

"Not bad for an old broad," she told herself.

It was not the first time she had thought of herself as being no longer young; but recognition of the fact still made her sigh. It was so cruel, not being young any more. Growing old, her Swiss gerontologist had told her, was not simply a matter of wear and tear of time: it was the expression of a complex mechanism encoded in our genes the moment we are conceived. Good bone structure, a strong jawline and high, clean-cut cheekbones had kept her skin from sagging. But the cosmetic operations Doctor Pitanguy had performed on her in Rio de Janeiro, the lenten rejuvenating shots, the collagen injections, had taken care of the lines in her neck and forehead and smoothed away the crow's feet in the fine skin below her eyes. (She regarded her body as a work of art; some restoration work now and again she regarded as a kind of philanthropy.) Her face had thinned with age, narrowing her nose and making the nostrils more sensitive, which she liked. But her chin was also beginning to sharpen as her jawbone atrophied with time (she had read somewhere that forensic experts could tell a body's age by the shape and weight of the jawbone) and she knew that in a year or so she would need a discreet implant there too.

She pushed her face nearer its reflection.

"No, not bad at all," she said aloud.

But just for a moment she saw herself as she had been fifty years ago . . .

"A face impossible to look upon," Bosley Crowther had written in the *New York Times* in 1944, "without feeling its inexorable sensuality. Yet it is no single feature, not in the smile, not in the cheek or brow, nor in the eyes or mouth, that it abides. But there it always lingers, never absent for a moment, waiting to be discovered by the camera lens, and lovingly explored in a thousand close-ups."

It was not unusual that she could remember Crowther's ancient hymn of praise. She could remember things from much further back than that. She could still see her nursery books with woodcuts of good housemothers cutting bread, and the childish calligraphy in her copybook proclaiming "My list of dolls"; she could still smell the aroma of Havanas and apricot schnapps when she snuggled in her father's arms, and hear the sound the crystal drops on the girandole candlesticks made when a wind from the Danube stirred them.

Reluctantly, as the memories of childhood crowded upon her, she picked up the tape machine.

Theodora hated microphones. Microphones always frightened her. She knew that she was beautiful and the camera loved her. Jerry Wechsler said the easiest Oscar he ever won was for lighting Theodora Glass; he invented the phrase "The girl with the bullet-proof profile". But her voice troubled her. The husky tone, the cadence and rhythm, were inimitably sensual, but her accent made her self-conscious. She knew that she sometimes said *plue* for blue, *sumsing* for something, and final d's became t's, especially when she was tired or nervous or upset. It was part of her charm and mystique, but she could not see that. She saw it only as a flaw, a weakness.

She closed her lips, inhaled through her nostrils, and produced a hum which she sustained and felt against her lips and between her slightly parted teeth. After a few moments she slowly opened her lips until the hum became a *mah* sound. Then she closed her lips again and changed the consonant to *bah*. She went quickly through several exercises, exercises she had not done since her days on the Metro lot.

She switched on the tape. Testing, she said: "Nothing in the song of the cicada intimates how soon it will die."

It had been a saying of her mother's. "Cicada Song," she said aloud, wondering whether it would make a good title for the story she was about to begin. She repeated it several times with different intonations while she searched for her reading glasses. Then with sheets of handwritten notes and diaries, she made herself comfortable on a sofa on the terrace. She closed her eyes, took a deep breath, and began:

Missy, you once told me that only to half a dozen people in all the world are the memoirs of an actress's childhood interesting: to the mother who nursed her, to her lover, and to her child,

3

perhaps, but most of all to herself . . . But dammit, Missy, I have to start some place! It's September the first, by the way. Better make a note of that. If it's going to be a day I live to regret, we might as well be exact about it!

I'll begin with basic things – Mama's name, Papa's name, some family history, stuff like that. We can check the details later, exact dates and place-names in Vienna and London before the war. I have Mama's diaries, and the notes she made for the book she was always threatening to write. How accurate this stuff is I don't know.

So let's begin, before I again talk myself out of the whole gottdam idea.

Theodora talked into the tape for almost an hour, sometimes reading from the notes, but mostly relating memories and details that came into her head. Some of the things she said were familiar facts, printed many times in articles and books about her; occasionally she surprised herself with an incident or episode that came from nowhere: the year she slept with elastic bandages over her mouth because Mama feared that her lips were becoming too sensual. (Was it this childhood nightmare that later caused her to order make-up men to paint inside the natural line of her lips to narrow the look of her mouth?) And Mama teaching her to recite Shakespeare at her knee: To be – *pause, Theodora, pause* – or not to be – *pause, again* – that is the question – *anxiety, Theodora, doubt!* – Whether 'tis nobler in the mind to suffer/The slings and arrows of outrageous fortune . . .

There was a certain pleasure in remembering old pain.

At 8.15 Missy Miller joined her for breakfast, served by a tall, black servant in a white robe. Afterwards they walked in the walled garden which Noël Coward had once described as an exercise yard and told a reporter that walking around it made him feel like a lifer. His painting of it, entitled *No Escape*, sold at Christie's after his death for $75,000; it was rumoured that Theodora had bought it and burnt it.

"I know you don't approve," Theodora said when she had

finished telling Missy about the tape, and of her decision to tell her story.

"Maybe it's not your most brilliant idea," Missy said.

"I've buried myself away too long."

"But a book will simply –"

"Bring me back from the grave?"

"Are you ready for that?" Missy said, with a worried sideways glance at Theodora. "A book could resurrect a lot of problems – for everybody, hon."

Theodora shook her head. "My friends are beginning to die, and I'm going to, sooner or later, and so will you, dearest Missy. I'd like to set a few things straight. Before it's too late."

"For a lady so passionate about privacy –"

"Find some purpose to my life – find some answers for *me*. That's worth doing, isn't it? Find an explanation for all the shit?"

"I'd rather live with doubts than have answers that might be wrong."

"Doubt is hell in the human soul," Theodora said.

The line was from one of her movies and Missy acknowledged the joke with a little smile. She liked to say that she had known Theodora for ever. But it had only been fifty years. She had been her stand-in on her first picture for Metro; their physical likeness in those days was remarkable. Later, on the strength of her resemblance to Theodora, she had starred in a string of programme pictures at Columbia, under the name Evelyn Miles. Her pictures never played Radio City Music Hall but she got plenty of publicity, cheesecake photos of her appeared on the covers of fan magazines; there was a short-lived romance with Howard Hughes, and a briefer marriage to a Latin star who had already been married four times. She saved a little money, bought a nice house in the hills above Franklin Avenue, but her pictures did nothing. Joe Mankiewicz said that Missy had everything that Theodora had except whatever the hell it was that Theodora had. And although she wept when she read it in the *Hollywood Reporter* she didn't need a Mankiewicz wisecrack to tell her the truth about herself. When Harry Cohn finally cut her loose, she got a couple of second leads, then a few smaller roles. When

Theodora offered her a job as her companion-secretary she thought of all the other girls who had had careers very much like hers, sold the house on Franklin, bade goodbye to her agent, and grabbed it without a backward glance.

She was no longer mistaken for Theodora. She still had the same slim legs and ankles, the same small wrists and gesturing hands, but she was now twelve pounds heavier than Theodora. A gash of white ran through her straight ash-blonde hair; and a nerve had died in her left eyelid causing it to droop. It made her seem habitually sad, and even when she smiled and showed her large, fine teeth the sadness was there, indelible and infinite. And although she was less than two years older than Theodora, Missy, a mother, if not by nature, by temperament and dedication, treated the star like a child. She knew her moods and her fears; she knew what to say, and what to leave unsaid. Above all, she knew what to forget.

That evening they watched one of Theodora's old movies in the small air-conditioned theatre built behind the drawing-room. Theodora never grew tired of looking at herself on the screen – "You don't need fans to admire you, you are content to admire yourself," Missy often teased her – and kept up a whispered commentary on her performance, the performance of her co-stars, the gossip and rumours that went around during the production. Missy enjoyed her comments as much as the pictures on the screen.

As the opening credits came up Theodora slipped on her horn-rimmed glasses, and settled into the deep leather armchair, curling her legs under her. Not for the first time, Missy wondered how many hours Theodora had sat in the dark looking at the beautiful girl she had been – watching a long-ago present which had become the irretrievable past. One day I'll sit down and work it out, she told herself; but even as she thought it a terrible sadness came over her and she knew she never would.

"He collected an Oscar, but this was a performance picture," Theodora began to speak in hushed tones as the director's name came on the screen. "Such a bad script, Theodora did all the work," she said, slipping into her habit of referring to herself in the third person. "Oh, this is wonderful, the way she moves her head, that *look*, Missy – she never did that look so good again . . ." It was one of her best pictures, made when she was in her prime. "I love this scene – Tynan said it was the sexiest drunk scene in the movies," she said, pronouncing it "tronk" as she did in the picture. Although it looked and sounded dated in parts, it was easy to see why the picture had become a classic and still played all over the world. "Will you look at those breasts!" she exclaimed as a Theodora untouched by time and wearing only a satin slip sat at a dressing-table brushing her hair. "Wechsler used crosslights to make them look much larger . . . Noah Swan loved it."

"I bet he did," Missy said, smiling, remembering Noah's famous quote that he had personally chosen everything Theodora wore on the screen – "from her sables to her scanties".

"He was a son of a bitch," Theodora said, as if she knew what Missy was thinking. "But I learned all I know from him."

She was quiet for almost fifteen minutes. "Oh, watch this," she ended the silence. "The way she says goodbye . . . Slowly lifts her hand, doesn't look back, no close-up, no tears, she just keeps walking . . . It's beautiful, my favourite ending . . . Did you listen to the tape?" she asked, before her long walk away from camera faded hauntingly from the screen. "You know most of the stories."

"Mama bandaging your mouth! You've never told me that! Sealed up – *shrinkwrapped* – every night! That's the most terrifying thing I ever heard."

"You think it's a good beginning?"

"Build a Hitchcock movie around a beginning like that."

"You still don't approve?"

"Summoning ghosts is a hazardous business, honey."

"Well, I have an idea."

Missy finished the red wine in her glass before she answered. "Go ahead."

"Instead of Theodora writing the book herself – instead of an autobiography – we'll commission a biography. An authorized biography. We'll keep control. We'll have the final cut, or whatever they call it with books. What do you think?"

Missy paused in the middle of lighting a cigarette, but she did not answer. She was never afraid to disagree with Theodora when she felt dissent necessary, or when disagreement was simply enjoyable or provocative, but there was something in Theodora's tone which told her that she would pay no heed to anything she said at that moment.

"Yes, I think so," Theodora continued, mistaking the silence for assent. "And I think I know exactly who could do it beautifully," she went right on with a little fluster of hurry and doggedness. "Robert Rider. What do you think? Robert Rider. Let him tell them who I was."

"But he's a novelist, Theodora. He writes thrillers."

"Why not a little suspense? Why does a biography have to be full of foregone conclusions? A biography that reads like a wonderful novel. Why not?"

"He really gets under the skin of people, Theodora."

"With his talent and –"

"Your skin?"

Theodora smiled. "You think he'd like to make my book, Missy?"

Missy got up and stood in front of the empty screen. She was serious and unsmiling, her arms folded. She wore faded jeans, neatly starched, a blue workshirt. "Rider digs deep, honey. Is that what you want? He might want to dig deeper than you'd care to have him dig. You know what I mean?"

"He understands women. He writes about women wonderfully."

"Yes, he does. And he's a wonderful storyteller, but he's also a man with a muck-rake, Theodora."

"When Noah gets wind I'm talking to him –"

"Is that it?" Missy sounded incredulous. "You want to throw a scare into Noah Swan?"

Theodora smiled. "That'd be half the fun."

Missy felt that the motive discredited Theodora. Little warning voices and bells sounded and rang in her head. "Involving Rider is one helluva risk, hon," she said quietly.

"This wouldn't be his usual kind of book."

"I hope not."

"I want an honest book done with style."

"How honest is honest, honey? You won't be dealing with some studio flack. You don't treat Robert Rider like some fancy Beverly Hills public relations outfit. Open up that closet an inch – you got skeletons in there, he'll find them."

"He's a writer. I can handle a writer."

"Writers are thieves, honey. Writers are crooks. Nobody trusts a writer."

Theodora fingered the gold heart at her throat; the gesture was always a sign that she was becoming nervous or anxious about something. The heart was worn and out of shape, teeth marks rippled the surface where it had been bitten flat as a worn penny. "I can handle a gottdam writer," she said again.

"You won't be able to treat him like just another good-looking boy with a nice thing in his pants."

"You're supposed to be my friend."

"I am."

"I'll have the final call."

"You don't hang up when he starts asking the hard questions."

"I decide what goes in my own gottdam book."

Missy took a deep breath. "Involve Rider . . . he's going to want to get into an awful lot of stuff I don't think you're going to want to get into. There's a lot of history, sweetheart . . . Noah and Barbara – *Mama* – you ready for that? Mama, Vienna . . . Your father's murder . . . Why Noah abandoned *Romeo and Juliet* . . ."

"I said, I can handle it."

"And then he starts poking around in your head," Missy continued with a careful smile. "Asking about your toilet training, how you lost your virginity . . . All those couch questions . . . Nothing would be sacred, honey."

Theodora rose and walked to the back of the small theatre and faced Missy across the rows of empty leather armchairs. She lit a cigarette, and Missy saw the small tremor in her hands. She drew on the cigarette, blew smoke towards the ceiling, giving herself

9

time to think. After a moment, she smiled solemnly at Missy, her lilac-grey eyes direct and unblinking.

"I shall not say why and how I became, at the age of fifteen, the mistress of the Earl of Craven. Whether it was love, or the severity of my father, the depravity of my own heart, or the winning arts of the noble lord, does not now much matter – or if it does, I am not in the humour to gratify curiosity in this matter." She spoke the lines slowly, the way she had spoken them in *The Diary of Harriette Wilson*.

It was the night Theodora wrote the letter to Jay Pfeiffer in London.

A professional, she always dealt through agents.

2

Noah Swan knows everybody and their skeletons. (Wall Street Journal, *November 13, 1986)*

Sunday, September 10
Washington DC

Noah Swan's eyelids flickered open. His eyes, hard and unreflecting, stared at the high ceiling. What had woken him, he knew at once, was a dream. He lay on his back, motionless in the big Louis Seize bed for nearly a minute after the dream. The muscles round his mouth were taut. A skim of sweat glistened on his bald head.

"Goddam bitch."

The loudness of his own voice in the dark startled him. He remembered reading somewhere that talking to oneself is the first sign of madness, but he wanted to confirm that he was awake. "*Goddam bitch*," he said again, louder and more vehemently.

Raising himself on one elbow he turned on the light and looked at his watch. It was five o'clock: the hour when people die, he thought. He knew that the nation's newspapers had his obituary waiting in type, but he was in no hurry to accommodate them. He worked as hard as any professional athlete to stay fit. His stress management specialist put him through a daily regime of relaxation and breathing exercises; his private yoga teacher conducted a nightly service of meditation, in which Noah visualized his arteries clearing up. Every six months in the permanent suite he kept at his own private clinic in Lexington, Virginia, he underwent plasmapheresis, to filter out of his blood any cholesterol the meditation might have missed.

He rose and walked slowly to the bathroom. The needlepoint

spray of the shower on his skin, icy cold, then steaming hot, made him shiver and grunt with satisfaction, although the hostility still stirred inside him. He shaved, cleaned his teeth, swallowed two Zyloprin tablets (a specialist in Boston had detected incipient gout), gargled with Chloraseptic liquid. He dressed slowly, with a dandy's care. He spent twenty minutes fixing a toupee to his tan scalp; the hair, white as alabaster, was the best that money could buy; a number of the beautiful women with whom he still sometimes shared his bed were taken in by it. (White human hair tends to turn yellow; Noah's hairpieces were made exclusively with the hair from the long fringes of the flanks of wild female Yak calves, found only on northern Tibetan plateaux 20,000 feet above sea level, and listed as endangered in the *Red Data Book*.)

Noah Swan had been handsome in his younger days, and a week before his eightieth birthday he was still a fine-looking man. Half an inch over six feet tall, his eyes, the colour of pine needles, still had a brittle watchfulness that the unwary mistook for a twinkle. Many years before, Theodora bit his lip so badly that a doctor had to be called to stitch it; now the scar gave a faint look of cruelty to his mouth, which women had once found sexy.

There were mornings when he secretly felt his age, but this morning he felt good. He felt sharp. He loved a fight, relished putting his abilities on the line. When he didn't have a battle on his hands his spirit was drained by boredom and black moods. "Noah Swan tests his edge on other kinds of men once in a while, just to show he can still cut off any sonofabitch's balls," said Lyndon Johnson who deeply respected machismo in a man.

And now Noah felt the return of Theodora Glass into his life beginning to restore his energies.

The penthouse of his mansion on Q Street was the nerve centre of his multinational operations. Added when the house was restored and doubled in size in 1974, it was manned twenty-four hours a day, 365 days a year, by a team of security and stock analysts, market strategists, and communications experts. With its own elevator and basement access, it was invisible from the street; few visitors to the house even guessed at its existence.

Noah lived alone in the huge house with nine servants, but only

Raoul and Marcella, a married couple who had been with him for twelve years, served his food, small portions, and saw that he took his pills. Michael Fortas, a male secretary, who had been devoted to him for even longer than Raoul and Marcella and who wore a licensed concealed sidearm, lived in a part of the house that Noah never visited.

Noah's wife had died too long ago for him to have more than a faint remembrance of her company. He thought of her once in a while, usually to assure himself that his hands were clean; whatever torment she had been through owed nothing to him, he was convinced of that. ("In the beginning of a marriage there is possibly love," he had once opined in a *Playboy* interview, which he now regretted. "Then life goes on, and it's just another deal.")

At least Barbara never gives me bad dreams, he thought. He went downstairs wondering if he *ever* dreamed of his departed wife; probably not, he concluded with satisfaction.

It was his habit and his pleasure to make his own coffee in the morning (a secret blend of mocha, Martinique and Bourbon beans, invented by Tolstoy, he told *Gourmet* magazine) in the small kitchen which served his formal study and the small dining-room, where he entertained only his closest people. While the coffee was dripping through, he read *Fortune* magazine's "Forecast for the Next Eighteen Months". Some of the predictions made him smile; occasionally he sighed with impatience. He knew things that the experts and market analysts could not even guess at.

Noah Swan's personal fortune was valued in billions. Ninth in *Forbes Four Hundred* (but the first whose fortune was self-made), he ruled an empire that included the third biggest independent oil company in the nation, a Hollywood studio, seventeen shopping malls, a pharmaceutical company, and a football team. He also owned three of the most exclusive private clinics in Europe, a chain of undertakers, nine golf courses, two horse-breeding farms (Arabians, Palominos and Appaloosas), and the largest privately-owned buffalo herd in the world.

But most of all Noah Swan owned the man who might yet be the next President of the United States.

Shortly before six he put a pot of coffee and crockery on a tray and took the elevator to the Trophy Room. He opened the shutters. The humid scent of brackish water mingled with the aroma of fresh coffee was his favourite smell in all the world: "The pure smell of Washington," he called it. "The smell of power."

At exactly six his scrambler phone rang.

"Good morning, son," he said, lifting the receiver on the first ring. "How are ya? How does it feel to be – what did that anchor dame call you? – Gulliver surrounded by political Lilliputians?"

"Feels too damn soon to have people sticking 'frontrunner' before my name, Pa," Senator Matthew Swan answered irritably; he did not put much faith in the theory of self-fulfilling prophecies.

"You came across a hundred per cent better than on the ABC show. But that smile – work on that smile, young man."

"Have you seen the *Washington Post*, Pa?"

"You mean Theodora writing her memoirs? Heard about it last night," Noah Swan said. "Charlie Considine called. Bad news travels fast, don't it? Who told you?"

Ignoring the question, Matthew said: "Is it true?"

"I don't know, son." Noah Swan filled his cup, recalling the bad dream. "We've heard these stories before. I wouldn't hang a cat on anything I read in a newspaper. On the other hand, that island of hers leaks like a sieve – and how long can she go on sitting on her fanny watching the ocean all day?"

"What does Considine think?"

"What the hell do you expect a newspaperman to think? He's probably trying to buy up the serial rights right this minute."

There was a silence on the line, except for the sound of Matthew Swan breathing deeply.

"I thought this shit was behind us, Pa," he said finally. "What's she trying to pull off here? All that stuff between you two – it was settled years ago, wasn't it?"

"Never trust the past, Matthew," his father said softly.

"Her timing's lousy." The Senator's tone had the faint querulousness of alarm.

14

"We don't need this issue right now, but it's not fatal," Noah Swan said, blowing on his coffee, trying not to let his concern show in his own voice, although the *Post*'s story had shaken him every bit as profoundly as it had Matthew. "She always had a sense of occasion," he said in the same calming tone. "How's Elizabeth?"

"She's in New York. She's fine. The girls are fine."

"You should spend more time with her. Get her with child again. A pregnant wife by your side at the Convention . . . the prospect of a new baby in the White House in November . . . Women like that."

Matthew Swan smiled. "I'll get right on to it, Pa," he said. Several seconds ticked by on the Lebbeus Bailey long case clock in the Trophy Room. "Getting back to this book thing, Pa. Theodora, Pa. We don't know what she'll get into." He chose his words with care, aware that he was not wholly in control of his feelings. It wasn't fair. What happened between Noah and Theodora, it wasn't his fight. His father's goddam past had no right, no right, to jeopardize his future like this. "I worked hard to get here, Pa. The stuff that went on back then . . . it could be a can of worms, Pa, couldn't it?"

"History always is, son."

"Whatever it is, Pa, I don't want to know, but I don't want it catching up with us like next fall, that's all I'm saying." There was a note of pleading in Matthew Swan's voice. Despite all his power and achievement, when he talked to his father he still felt the same old sense of dependency and uncertainty. Two inches taller than the old man, and stronger, he still thought of Noah as a big man, a man with dangerous secrets in him. "We're going to go through a period now where we take some heat anyway. I don't need her popping off about everything you and she got up to back when."

Noah Swan tilted back his chair and looked at the ceiling, remembering the long-ago threat: "Noah, you son of a bitch, I'm writing all this down, every mean, cruel, unfeeling word of it. And one day you'll regret it, one day, believe me, you will, all of you." They were in bed together for the last time. They had always had a good time in bed. She had the silkiest, whitest skin he'd ever known – skin the texture of trouble, he used to say. But Jesus, she was beautiful. Theodora Glass had always been worth the risk. Until now.

"What's the name again of that new ramrod Rosengarten's brought into the team? Rosy's old Company pal?"

"Lanigan. Ambrose Lanigan."

"How's he shaping up?"

"He's moving things around. Doesn't sugar-coat a thing. Ask him, he tells you. Why you asking, Pa?"

"Because we've got a problem and not a hell of a lot of time."

"Let's not start up anything that acts faster than our ability to control it, Pa."

Noah Swan paused a moment, smiling.

"Let me talk to Mr Lanigan. You stay out of it. Don't touch the tar-baby, and nothing'll stick to you." It was not spoken as a request. He took a sip of coffee. "Let Mr Lanigan start to earn his pay, Senator," he said. There was a tone of propriety back in his voice, but it allowed of no appeal.

"What you going to do, Pa?"

"I'm going to remind that bitch of the lesson of the whale: the only time you get harpooned is when you're up on the surface spouting," Noah Swan said.

It was six fifteen. In his bedroom on the second floor of his mansion in Middleburg in the heart of Virginia hunt country, Matthew Swan lit his first menthol cigarette of the day. He inhaled deeply, and tried to remember who it was who had invented the phrase "plausible deniability". Nixon? One of the Dulles brothers? Noah Swan himself? It certainly sounded like the kind of phrase his father would invent.

He opened the french windows overlooking the lake and felt the soft early fall air on his skin. He stared across the lake with a thoughtful look, a look compounded of courage, determination, and a hint of secret knowledge: it was the look he was practising for his campaign picture.

Wearing only a blue silk robe, he stood between a pair of

Chippendale mahogany tripod tables, each with its Victorian table lamp, and laden with photographs in silver frames: his mother, looking pretty and inexplicably sad at a picnic on his third birthday; his father in a ten-gallon hat riding a carousel horse; Elizabeth in a yellow bikini aboard *Seawitch II*; the twins, Camilla and Clementine, at their first communion. Pictures of himself: in a sailor suit, aged four; and twenty-three years later, the silver eagles of captaincy pinned to his shirt collar. Signed pictures of the famous: "Matt, my true friend and future President," from the highest-paid actor in Hollywood; "Always, always, a devoted fan," vowed the blonde superstar across her silicone breasts.

Rich before he was born, Matthew Swan had never worked for a living. Work at getting elected, Pa had drummed into him since he could remember. And now nobody in all of Washington did a harder or longer day's work than Senator Matthew Swan. As a junior senator his height and athletic ease had enriched his reputation as a man of action. At fifty-four (he looked ten years younger than that), some thought he looked (and sounded) like a younger Noah Swan, especially when he grinned; but it was his nose and jaw and fine blue eyes that gave his features the extra strength that made him so famously telegenic, and such an effective TV politician. He didn't have the best mind in his party, he wasn't a brilliant orator or a great parliamentarian, but on television he was a star.

His thick brown hair had been seasoned with silver highlights; worn longer than his advisers felt was presidential, it curled at the back in the Washington summer, and after he had made love. In a much reprinted interview in *Paris-Match*, conducted in perfect French, a boarding-school accomplishment, Elizabeth Averell Swan called the curls his lovelocks. Privately, with the defensive humour of a neglected wife, she called them his "poke tails". They were invaluable in her struggle to keep tabs on his infidelities.

It was six thirty. His butler arrived with coffee and grapefruit juice. "Good morning, sir. A beautiful day." His voice was as bland as only thirty-five years of Washington service could make it. "I trust you slept well, Senator?"

Matthew Swan was not listening. His mind was back on Theodora Glass, and the memoirs she was going to write.

"What am I going to find out, Pa?" he asked furiously under his breath after the butler had left the room. He was playing the morality card big in his campaign – *The Senator who submits every decision to the authority of conscience* – but he knew that morality was never his father's strong suit. The last thing he needed now was the threat of Theodora Glass disclosing some donkey's years ago Hollywood crime, some new old sin they had committed together. "What the fuck has she still got on us, Pa?" he asked unhappily.

3

Issues and ideology don't sell beans. Concentrate on the product. The product is Senator Matthew Swan. (From a memorandum to the Senator's campaign staff, from Noah Swan)

Monday, September 11
Washington DC

Ambrose Lanigan left Matthew Swan's campaign headquarters in the Old Calhoun Office building by the west basement exit on 23rd Street. The Executive Protection Service guard checked him out on his clipboard. "Muffler's spittin' up lead again, Mr Lanigan," he grinned, poking his large Irish face smelling of sweat and aftershave through the lowered window of the black 1969 Porsche Targa.

"Been better," Lanigan agreed in the tone used to impart condolences.

The guard grinned some more, his eyes behind the mirrored sunglasses scanning the interior: Detroit Tigers baseball cap, newspapers, Kleenex, paperback novel, squash racquet. "OK," he said, slapping the roof, "have a good one, sir."

Everybody in this goddam town talks in euphemisms, Lanigan thought as he turned into Virginia Avenue and the old Porsche coughed again. The purpose of a euphemism, his late father's definition came back to him, is to make anything distasteful seem less distasteful. His father had been a schoolteacher back in Kenosha, Wisconsin – the capital of Jockey underwear, he would add when he told people where he was from.

He wished he was back there now. It was not simply the heat – unusual, everybody said, for this time of year – that made him feel uncomfortable. The summons from Matthew Swan's father – the call to his unlisted home number after midnight, the insistence that he tell nobody, not even Rosengarten – seemed to him ominous.

"I am going to ask a favour of you, Mr Lanigan, and I am at a loss how to express it – perhaps you would be kind enough to drop by the house this morning at eleven o'clock, if that is convenient to you, so that we may discuss the matter?" Noah Swan had said.

Lanigan had never in his life heard an order euphemized so well.

Noah Swan's mansion, Parke Custis Place, was everything Lanigan had imagined it would be: built in the early 1800s for Martha Parke Custis, a granddaughter of Martha Washington, by William Thornton, the architect who designed the Capitol building, it was expensively preserved in its Georgian splendour (white stucco over brick, slender-columned porticoes, Palladian windows), and one of the showplaces of Georgetown.

Lanigan was greeted in the stair hall by a pale young man in a three-piece grey suit, built-up shoes, blue shirt and yellow silk tie. When he shook hands he looked away, avoiding Lanigan's eyes; this was not, as some people believed, shyness: it gave him a feeling of superiority, of being remote. "Mr Swan is expecting you," he said. "He is in the Trophy Room. Follow me, please."

Chin held high, trailing a smell of cologne, he led the way across an ice rink of white Carrara marble floor engraved with a black swan.

"My name is Michael Fortas, by the way. Mr Swan's private secretary." He was slim, with thinning grey-blond hair; his eyes had a black, horizontal pupil like the impenetrable slit in the eye of a Siamese cat. "Mr Swan says I'm the guy who runs the block," he said, glancing quickly at Lanigan. "I'm the last man he sees at night, the first one he sees in the morning."

His tone struck a curious balance of coquetry and warning. Lanigan looked impressed. He knew that nobody at headquarters liked him, nobody knew how he had got the job, but it was useful in Washington to get good grades with men like Michael Fortas.

Lanigan followed him up the grand spiral staircase, along a wide, dark-blue carpeted corridor lined with modern paintings. "Mr Swan collects abstract art, as you see. It isn't my dish of tea," Fortas said, with a vague sense of being sorely tested. "Holtzman, von Wicht, Fine, Fleischmann, Hulbeck," he pointed to each painting with his forefinger as they continued briskly along the corridor. It was like walking through a museum. "He has paintings he's forgotten he bought. The other day he discovered that he owns a whole Cistercian monastery in crates in Dallas. Ten thousand crates of Spanish cloister. I'd give all of it, and all the smart art, for a single Villon. Do you know his work? Jacques Villon?"

"I don't think so," Lanigan said.

"Deliciously limpid, but so complex, so . . . ambiguous. There is one particular canvas of his," Fortas said as they came to the last room at the end of the long corridor, "every time I look upon it I am amazed to think anyone could achieve so flawless a thing."

He looked at his watch. Satisfied they were exactly on time, he pinched the perfect tulip-knot of his tie, coughed gently against the back of his slender hand, and tapped once. "Mr Lanigan is here, sir," he announced, opening the door and standing aside for him to enter. Lanigan never heard the door close behind him.

Noah Swan's handshake was firm, not like his son's, who had to shake hands all the time and whose grip, adapted for speed, felt effeminate. "Sit down." He indicated a wing-back chair covered in leather the colour of old English riding boots. "Radio says it's another hot one out there. Some Indian summer." His tone was nostalgic and affectionate and had the flat but attractive mid-western accent of Southern California. "I've lived here since Matthew was a freshman congressman. Nothing surprises me in Washington any more. Take off your jacket if you want to. Be comfortable."

Noah Swan wore khaki pants, pink sports shirt, hand-tooled boots with cowboy heels. His steel Rolex Oyster watch was not top of the range. Lanigan remembered the claim often made in magazine profiles that he never wore a watch ("he's so rich, he makes his own time") and was disappointed that one of the popular myths about him had already been exploded. He had an easy, classless air that made him dangerously easy to talk to, and Lanigan made a note not to forget it. He kept his jacket on. "I guess you know about Washington weather, Mr Lanigan. Spent some time over at Langley when you were with the Agency, right?"

"For nine months, sir, in the fall of 1987. After my Athens tour. I was Ed Rosengarten's number two at the Office of Current Intelligence."

"And what did you do there?"

"I prepared the President's daily briefing."

"And when you left OCI?"

"I was posted to Trinidad. I was head of station there for two years."

Noah nodded. "Then you know the Caribbean well?"

"Yes, sir, I think I know it pretty well."

Noah smiled. "Tell me how you got started, Mr Lanigan. It always fascinates me how people get into your line of work."

Lanigan gave him a rundown on his career with the Central Intelligence Agency. Told with an appearance of sureness and candour, it was a well-practised piece intended to deflect questions. But now it also gave him time to feel out the situation, and to take stock of what was clearly Noah Swan's inner sanctum.

The room was redolent with achievement and acclamation. Honours, trophies, awards filled the mahogany-panelled walls and shelves; behind his desk stood the American flag on an eagle-topped staff (a gift from President Nixon, read a brass plaque, taken from the Oval Office itself). The original scripts of all Noah's movies, bound in Morocco leather and lettered in gold, filled a Georgian book press. Besides the movie accolades (three Oscars, a Thalberg award, two Golden Globes), there were tributes and awards from the Legion of Decency, the Catholic Daughters of America, the American Jewish Committee, the National Rifle Association, the NAACP, and the League of Women Voters. The Indian government had given him the Order of the Elephant; the French the Légion d'Honneur; from the Japanese he had received the Order of the Rising Sun (for his contribution "to the cultural understanding between our two countries"). There were also family photographs; and a handsome portrait of Noah himself painted some years ago by Annigoni, which hung above the fireplace.

". . . then I went briefly back to Langley again, this time with ORPA – the Methods and Forecasting Division of the Office of Regional and Political Analysis," Lanigan came to the end of his story. "That's when Ed Rosengarten asked me to join him to help restructure the Senator's field organization."

"You weren't happy at ORPA?" Noah asked sharply.

"I prefer to live on the balls of my feet," Lanigan said.

"Rosengarten's a good man."

Outlined against a mote-filled tall sunlit window, the light catching the edges of his extraordinary white hair, Noah's features were barely discernible. Lanigan guessed that he was not unaware of this.

"Rosengarten's a good man," Noah repeated. "We've got good people; we've got the pieces. But a presidential campaign is a gruelling test, you're exposed for the longest time. No candidate with any sanity declares before he has to."

He rose slowly and adjusted the louvred shutters behind him. Lanigan was grateful to be out of the sunlight, to be able to see Noah's features, to watch him thinking, feeling his way towards whatever this meeting was all about.

"A lot of names are going to jump in before the race is over. We'll let 'em chop each other up in the early primaries. Senator Swan will enter as late as possible, after Wisconsin, maybe in Pennsylvania, and he'll take the remaining primaries as a middle-of-the-road candidate whom the party respects and trusts. Waiting'll be the game," Noah said firmly.

He squeezed his eyes between his thumb and forefinger; for a moment his whole body seemed to become taut with the force of his concentration. When he spoke again, his voice had changed. It was softer, but it wasn't just that. It was less sure, less convincing, and, just for a moment, old.

"OK, the reason I asked you here . . . I have to set some history straight . . . A very long time ago . . . I guess you know this anyway – the relationship I had with Theodora Glass?"

Lanigan nodded. How could he not know? Their affair was legendary: Theodora and Noah, Noah and Theodora, the story had been told a thousand times, in books and magazines, in actors' memoirs: David Niven made it sound *risqué* and hilarious; for Bette Davis it was a romantic tragedy; Harold Robbins got a big novel (*For My Sweet Love*) and a hot mini-series out of it.

"The story's so fucking tired I'm astonished anybody's still interested," Noah said, as if reading Lanigan's mind. "She hasn't made a movie in forty years. That doesn't seem possible, does it?"

"No sir, it does not," Lanigan answered truthfully. "She's still a star."

"That's right. She's still a star," Noah Swan repeated. "They don't come along like that except once in a lifetime. And she's as big a name today as the day she made her last movie – bigger! *Nobody* has taken her place. And not just for old eggs like me. Kids worship her. TV has made her a superstar to a whole new generation. 'The Second Coming of Theodora Glass', *Time* called it. A goddam suitcase she carried in some picture – *a goddam suitcase* – fetched fifty grand at Sotheby's. Every other week a new Hollywood genius announces his intention to pay her all the money in the world to play this part, that part. But she'll never make a comeback now. Her isolation has turned her into holy fucking myth. They have even named a crater on Venus after her! And that's for real, that's no phoney-baloney stunt Aaron Flagg dreamed up for her."

Lanigan didn't say anything. He didn't ask who Aaron Flagg was. He was trying to remember the stories: the time Noah was supposed to have beaten her up so badly that the film she was making had to be suspended for months; the Rolls-Royce he gave her for her birthday – and charged to her account; the scandal when it was discovered that he kept her and his wife in the same Beverly Hills mansion. It was hard now to know what was real and what was part of the legend, where fiction had become fact and fact fiction.

Noah said, "A woman's last love affair is with her doctor or a priest. You ever hear that? A woman's last love affair is with her doctor or a priest? If she's an actress five'll get you two it'll be with her ghostwriter, or a goddam publisher."

Lanigan smiled the sort of smile distant relatives exchange at funerals. "Theodora's going to publish her memoirs?"

Noah shrugged and went over to an ancient camera which stood on a tripod by the window, its lens focused on the Henry Moore sculpture of a warrior king in the courtyard. "She has to write them first, but that's her plan." He made a sad sound, as if recognizing that he had clung too long to a belief with something shakier than reason. "I thought she'd be classier than that. I thought she'd be the one to settle for the shadow on the screen. I was wrong. It grieves me to admit it: she's like all the others.

"Isn't this beautiful?" he went on, beginning to crank the old machine. "This is the original Pathé camera with which D. W. Griffith shot *The Birth of a Nation*. My old man made a million dollars from his piece of the rental rights, 1915. Can you imagine how much a million dollars was worth in 1915?" He shook his head in awe. "He could have been on his way to becoming one of the richest men who ever lived . . . But it'd all gone by 1920. Every penny."

"That must have been some party, sir."

"I know money, Mr Lanigan. And there's never enough."

Lanigan smiled.

"People wanted my mother to write her story," he went on, in a musing voice. "My God, what a story that would have been! She said no, their private life was nobody's business but their own. And they really needed the money, believe me. She said, 'Where I come from you don't tell stories about Daddy. You don't tell tales out of school. You got a beef? Fight it out. But don't tell the whole world.' Annie Muir. One of her ancestors was said to have been the last man to die fighting for Bonnie Prince Charlie in the battle of Culloden. My own propensity to fight comes from her." He went back to his large Florentine desk, took a cigar from a silver box, and lit it without ceremony. "She was very beautiful. My father wanted to put her into movies but she would have none of it. She wasn't an actress."

25

"Actresses are big in the confession game," Lanigan said to remind Noah of why he was there, and still wondering what could possibly come out now to compare with the stories already told.

"Let me make one thing clear, Mr Lanigan. As far as I'm concerned, as far as the Senator is involved, Theodora Glass has nothing new to confess –" he cleared his throat – "no more beans to spill, no more scandal to spread."

He fixed his eyes on Lanigan's.

Lanigan waited, expressionless. He knew he had not been invited to Georgetown to discuss a non-existent problem, and he had sat through too many briefings with powerful men to believe that Noah Swan's conscience was as trouble-free as he claimed. But he admired his performance, his knowing so exactly how to ease into whatever jam it was that he needed so urgently to discuss. Listening to him lie with such ease and *savoir-faire* was a real education. It was some moments before he realized that Noah was waiting for him to say something.

"But there is a problem," Lanigan said, not making it a question, and not a statement either.

"It is the worm of politics that nothing can be done simply and above board," Noah said, beginning to smile.

"Yes, sir," Lanigan said, nodding for him to continue, his face still with no precise expression on it.

"I value caution. I fight when I have to. But nobody respects avoiding trouble more than I do." He was still smiling, ever so slightly, a smile as dangerous as a wound that will not heal. "Did you see the Gallup Poll this morning, Mr Lanigan?"

Lanigan shook his head.

Noah drew slowly on his cigar. "Senator Swan is their over-whelming frontrunner. Eighteen-point lead. People are saying he's got it sewn up, all he has to do to win is enter the race: he can't lose. But I say only them that ain't got can't lose." It was one of his favourite lines, and he acknowledged it with a brief self-deprecating grin. "I like quoting myself.

"Senator Swan's whole life has been a preparation for this campaign," he went on. "Building an organization. Picking his campaign family. Submitting to the humiliation of fund-raising:

attending every goddam rat-killing in the country, pressing the flesh, kissing babies, hugging old ladies; putting on Cherokee war bonnets, tam-o'-fucking-shanters, hats with pig snouts, skull caps, hard hats . . . Getting garlic blown in his face, smiling through rubber-chicken dinners, feigning passion for lousy kebabs, tacos . . . Food breeds crime, I swear to God . . ."

For a moment he was silent. Thoughtful. The smoke from his cigar mingled with the morning sunlight.

"Anyway, an eighteen-point lead right now has to be regarded warily. People are telling him he's gonna be President. They're asking him questions they'd ask a President. But at this stage, one mistake . . . support can bleed away real fast." He grinned. "But don't get me wrong, Mr Lanigan. I don't buy that horse manure that he's too far ahead of the parade, that he'll peak too soon, that he'll run out of gas. No, sir. But it does put him in the firing line; it makes him a target. And a sideliner, a national figure, say, who gets a little encouragement, who comes in reluctantly, could still be a problem . . ."

"And Theodora Glass could shuffle all the cards?"

"That's right," said Noah, his green eyes seemed to offer gratitude. "That's *exactly* what I'm saying. In politics nobody gets take two. That book fetches up at the wrong moment . . . If she's convincing enough and daring enough and determined enough she could make an unreal world sound very real. She wouldn't be the first, fahcrissake."

"No, sir, she wouldn't."

"I'm not saying the Senator would be gone goose for the fair. But why take the risk? The book has a little innuendo, a little suggestion here, a hint of something there, and the press start assuming things they shouldn't assume. They want to start painting it into something else . . . something more sinister, more involved."

"It was a long time ago, sir."

"One thing I've discovered in life, Mr Lanigan, is that the past is no more irrevocably past than today is irrevocably Monday."

"The timing, sir," Lanigan asked. "How much of a coincidence is that?"

Noah smiled. "The greatest of all women's pleasures is vengeance."

"Does she have something to be vengeful about?"

"You do things when you're young, Mr Lanigan . . . You don't think about the shit the future might be storing up for you." He waved his hand in the air, leaving a trail of blue smoke floating to the ceiling. "Sure, there were personal matters she was sore about . . . Matters I wouldn't want surfacing right now. I wasn't a boy scout. But she was no saint either. She did her share of sinning."

"These personal matters –"

"Are personal, Mr Lanigan."

"Dealing in secrets – that's my business, Mr Swan. I'm used to it, and I'm used to keeping my mouth shut, sir. If you want me to –"

Noah held up his hand, a gesture of apology as well as interruption. "You see, Mr Lanigan" – he drew slowly on his cigar – "nobody has time to reflect any more. People read negligently, judge precipitately . . . they have no time to ponder, no time to think things through for themselves. Now we know any book by Theodora Glass is going to get a lot of ink. The media'll eat it up. She's going to get splashed, and when you get splashed you've got a problem."

"Sir, if you will –"

"Hear me out, Mr Lanigan," Noah said, and his voice was gentle now. "The capacity of the human system for recovery is remarkable. But a candidate can *die* from innuendo. And I know how imaginative Theodora Glass can be. Movie stars always lie to the press. They lie to the press and then they believe every goddam word they read about themselves in the papers."

Lanigan smiled. "I guess no good story is ever quite true."

"I don't want to be remembered as a figment of Theodora Glass's imagination," Noah said roughly.

"Nixon said that judgement depends on who writes the history."

Noah looked at him closely. "Write my own book, you mean?"

"You could set the record straight."

"I'll never write my memoirs. When successful men start

writing their stories that's when it's all over for them."

Lanigan knew that he enjoyed drawing attention to his staying power. He was still a player, and Lanigan admired him for that.

"The primaries are a battlefield, Mr Lanigan. They shoot the wounded, you know that," Noah said, ending a silence. "The Senator's pro-family position alone . . . God almighty, he needs his father's ex-mistress shooting off her mouth like another hole in his keister."

He was walking round the room, not nervously, the pace was too deliberate for nerves, but with a look of deep thoughtfulness that Lanigan guessed was concealing a much deeper anxiety.

"If she surfaces in the run-up – if the lights go up too early . . . Well, OK, fine, Senator Swan's ready for any scrutiny. I've got nothing against people saying their piece. I'm not against candour, up to a point . . . But the press gives this sort of doo-doo such disproportionate weight, and why make his life any more difficult than it has to be? I don't want to see him hurt because of something I . . . Anyway, dammit, whatever grievances Theodora Glass may have against me, she certainly has nothing against my son. If she . . ."

Noah Swan did not finish the sentence. When he spoke again, he came straight to the point:

"What I'm saying is this, Mr Lanigan: I'd feel easier in my mind if we could get rid of this . . . irritation." He looked steadily at Lanigan. "Nip it in the bud now," he said, after a pause.

"Nip it in the bud?" Lanigan's voice, muted and unaccented, contained nothing but the words themselves; there was nothing in his eyes beyond a polite, professional look.

Noah Swan let his breath out slowly. "I need help, Mr Lanigan. I need your experience. I need your . . . expertise."

"Sir, may I ask a dumb question?"

"Go ahead."

"There must be a dozen legitimate ways to stop this book?"

"Sure there are. I've got seventy lawyers who could keep it in the deep-freeze till the ice-caps melt. But I get involved, I injunct, that's the worst possible scenario. The book's a megaseller before a single copy's printed. Even if the injunction sticks, you've still got ten thousand press boys camped on your front lawn playing at Woodward and Bernstein from hell to breakfast."

"What I was thinking, wouldn't it be prudent to –"

"All I know is that when a woman grabs your balls, Mr Lanigan, it's prudent to assume that sooner or later she's going to squeeze them."

Lanigan laughed. "Maybe she just wants to throw a scare into you, sir."

"Then she's succeeded. Coffee – something stronger?" Noah lifted a bottle of Scotch off a drinks table, and read the label: "'Specially matured and bottled in the Highlands of Scotland for Noah Swan.' If you're a whisky man, I can recommend it."

Lanigan shook his head. "I'll take a rain-check." He frowned for a moment. "Sir, does the Senator know about this meeting?"

"He does not."

"Will the Senator be told?"

"No, Mr Lanigan, he will not. This meeting, the whole of this conversation, whatever the outcome, whatever you decide, it does not go beyond this room."

"I guess it isn't the kind of thing you want to put in writing," Lanigan agreed.

"We must insulate the Senator from knowledge of any of this. But at the same time I have his complete trust, and all the authority I need. I know I'm doing what he would want done." Noah poured himself a Scotch, took it back to his desk, and sat down. "It's important we speak plainly to each other. Do you have any problem with that, Mr Lanigan?"

Lanigan shrugged. "I get nervous when people want to level with me. It usually means the shit's about to hit the fan."

Noah Swan laughed with the relief of dealing with someone who, he seemed to acknowledge, saw right through him. "I'm told that you're a lone wolf, Mr Lanigan. Don't care for committees. I respect that. Committee men are a poor contrivance for action. To do anything in this world worth a damn, we don't stand shivering on the bank, contemplating the cold and the danger, we jump right in and do it."

"But exactly what is it you expect me to –" Lanigan began.

"How you skin it is your business, Mr Lanigan. Just give it your full attention and get it finished with. I will take care of whatever you need. Money, travel cards . . . anything you need at all. We must transfer you off the Senator's payroll, of course. I'll take care of that. I promise you, you'll be very well remembered" – Noah smiled as he searched for the right phrase – "after the Inaugural."

Lanigan was wary, and embarrassed by Noah Swan's attempt to buy his loyalty. Something he had read about him came out of the recesses of his mind – *Noah Swan knows his friends down to the last itchy palm* – and he felt a sudden anger at being treated like another Washington yesser. Outwardly his resentment did not show. His lips were a thin line of self-effacement. He had the art of presenting one front while his mind worked on another. It was a fascinating invitation, he thought, although command was perhaps a better word for it.

He said, "I guess the first thing we do is find out whether or not she really is writing this book. If she isn't –".

"I've checked, and she is."

"You've spoken to her?"

"Hell, no," Noah said, with a small, bitter laugh. "We haven't spoken to one another in forty years," he added, in a manner which suggested that he had no intention of starting now.

"Then how can you be sure?"

"Missy Miller, her girlfriend, companion, whatever. She was worried that the strain would be too much for her. Theodora's always been – I guess you could call her 'highly strung'. Missy Miller consulted a specialist who just happens to be a very good friend of mine."

"So, why don't we wait and see if she is able to write it?" Lanigan asked. "If she isn't, that's the end of story."

Noah shook his head emphatically. "By the time we find that out, we'd have lost valuable months. I want this business stamped on early."

"To get this clear, sir: there's no question of your calling Miss Glass, explaining the problem, asking her – for old time's sake – to put the whole thing on the back burner?"

"All that would reveal is our own vulnerability. She'd love that!"

"OK . . ." Lanigan quickly considered the remaining options. "We look for something we can greymail her with. Something she wouldn't want made public, then we trade." He smiled apologetically. "It's crude but it's usually effective."

"Greymail? Is that what they call it now?" Noah asked dryly.

Lanigan nodded. "If that doesn't work, we try to get hold of the manuscript and kick it apart for libel, calumny, defamation, malicious gossip, inaccuracies, anything we can find that will – "

"I said no injunctions!"

"I hear what you say, sir," Lanigan said in a reasonable voice. "But what happens if you use this information to go after her privately? Keep it strictly between yourselves, no lawyers, no go-betweens, no injunctions, just you and her? You are a powerful man, Mr Swan. Spell it out for her – the hell you'll put her through if she goes ahead."

A smile came and went on Noah's face like a spasm of dark humour. "You don't know Theodora, Mr Lanigan," he said. "It wouldn't work. Just take my word for it."

Lanigan scratched the side of his lean face. He was sure now that Noah Swan was a man incapable of seeing the other side. And a rich man who harbours grudges is not only difficult but lethal. "The only option left is we play dirty pool. I don't know how far you'd be prepared to go down that route but –"

"How you skin it, sir, I repeat," Noah interrupted mildly enough to make Lanigan smile to himself, "that is your business."

"Fine," said Lanigan. He took a notebook and a pen from the inside pocket of his jacket. "That's fine with me," he continued, as he uncapped the pen, and, in his small, neat handwriting, made a note of the date and subject. "Tell me everything you think I ought to know about Theodora Glass . . ."

Noah rose and walked to the centre of the room. He turned and faced Lanigan.

"What can I tell you? It's all there in the newspaper cuttings, in the magazines and books. Unless you want me to tell you what she was like in bed, and I'm not going to tell you that. I fell in love with her. Love should be the ecstasy of a moment. It's always a mistake to try to sustain it."

"Hindsight isn't worth a damn, is it?" Lanigan said.

They talked on through lunch, chicken salad with a perfectly chilled Meursault, taken at Noah's desk, and through afternoon tea. They walked in the courtyard. Lanigan asked what he needed to ask, quietly, respectfully, sometimes backtracking to clarify a fact or to confirm a name, a date, with no sense of interrogation. Noah answered in a friendly, thoughtful, occasionally amused voice, volunteering anecdotes and gossip. He had no trouble recalling details, he seemed sure of his facts. He never changed his mind, or revised a date. But several times Lanigan noticed how he would use a reminiscence or an amusing story to change the direction of the conversation, or to head off the next question. And occasionally he used the old filibuster trick of running sentences into each other, pausing for breath at capricious moments, denying any chance to interject between the article and the noun.

He is a chess player, Ambrose Lanigan told himself: he is very good indeed.

4

Five stars who took their mother's surname:
Marilyn Monroe (father's name Mortensen);
Rita Hayworth (father's name Cansino);
Jean Harlow (father's name Carpenter);
Shelley Winters (father's name Schrift);
Theodora Glass (father's name Baron Georg
Reinhard von Tegge). (Cosmopolitan, March
1988)

11.45 p.m., same day
Washington DC

"Let me see if I've understood this right," said Kate Goldsmid, after Ambrose Lanigan had told her about his meeting with Noah Swan, and of his unease about some parts of the story told to him by the billionaire. "He takes you on board – then deliberately lies to you?"

"Maybe not flat out lying. Withholding something maybe," Lanigan said.

"Withholding something like what?" she persisted.

"I don't know. Something right off the map."

"Something he's scared might be in the book?"

Lanigan nodded. "Something so uniquely damaging, he can't even talk about it."

Some interests are furthered by the truth, but experience had taught Ambrose Lanigan that most were furthered more by hiding it, or hiding some of it. It is rare for anyone to have a single motive in any situation; singularity did not tally with the complexities of human nature. And Noah Swan was as complex a human being as he had ever met.

"Maybe I was too busy admiring his performance," he said.

"Maybe I should have taken less notes and listened more."

"If you think he's holding out on you, my advice: don't get involved," Kate said.

"I guess I like rich clients."

"Now you sound like the lawyer," she said.

"Am I crazy?"

"He wouldn't want you if you weren't the best."

"All I hear is what he wasn't saying, Kate."

"You m-mistrust his frankness, yet you also m-mistrust your mistrust," she said with the smallest stammer.

Lanigan smiled, knowing that she had summed up his old Company caution.

Kate said, "Tomorrow he'll probably have a change of heart, poo out of the whole idea."

Lanigan shook his head. "Noah Swan doesn't even *blink* until he's thought about it a dozen times."

Kate smiled. "Well, her story's got to rattle some skeletons. What's an autobiography for if it isn't to settle a few old scores? A little m-marinated rage is part of the fun. Of course Noah's getting antsy. It's going to be rough, the next few months. After Matthew's nomination the whole family's going to be put under a m-microscope – Matthew, Noah, the beautiful wife, even the perfect kids'll be in the sweatbox."

"I guess," he said.

"Think about it, Lanigan: the handsome senator from California making a big song and dance about m-moral principles, the need for a new m-moral agenda – all the whistles and bells going for him, de-da de-da . . . What could kick a hole in his bucket better than Mistress Glass reappearing on the scene with some untimely nostalgia?"

"Untimely nostalgia," Lanigan repeated with a wry smile.

"Sins of the fathers . . . who can recall, or done, undo?"

"He's scared about how much she'll exaggerate things."

"You can exaggerate only what already exists," Kate said, with her lawyer's preciseness. "It's not the same thing as lying."

" 'A beautiful Austrian kid who caught lightning in a bottle,' he called her."

"Checkout-counter revelations don't seem her style, do they?"

"He's as nervous as a cat about something."

"The most dangerous time for bad guys is when they try to clean up their act."

"You think he's a bad guy?"

"Completely good guys don't get *that* r-rich." Kate smiled. "Anyway, how does he expect you to stop her? Put her in a bag? Hit her with a rubber hose?"

He shrugged. "Most affairs end in deals of one sort or another."

"You think so?"

"Don't you?"

She hesitated. "I could make a lawyer's argument. Is that how you think our relationship will end – in a deal?"

"What's the answer?"

"I don't know the answer."

"A lawyer never asks a question without knowing the answer."

She smiled, but she really didn't know how their affair would end. "A lawyer without a precedent is a dead duck," she said.

She looked from his eyes to his mouth and looked at his mouth until he kissed her.

"Well, it sure as hell won't end in bed." She spoke softly, her mouth touching his lips which tasted of the red wine they had had with dinner at Nathan's, her favourite Washington restaurant.

"You sure of that, counsellor?"

His fingers moved beneath her T-shirt to her small naked breasts. In a little while she felt his tenderness changing towards desire.

"Sweetheart." She whispered it repeatedly: a mantra, an abetment, a need. "Sweetheart."

Her breathing quickened.

She woke believing that she had dozed only a moment. The faint streaks of early morning light streaming through the gap between the blue curtains made her smile with surprise. "You are a wonderful lover, Lanigan," she told him softly; he sighed deeply. Careful not to disturb him, she reached for her cigarettes and lighter on the bedside table. She smoked with an air of reminiscence.

It was extraordinary how good they were together. In all her life she doubted it could be so good again. She stroked his head with a gesture of protection. His dark hair, which was turning grey, still felt young. There was a look of strength in his predatory nose, and in the lines carved like wounds round his eyes and mouth. He has, she thought, a warrior's face: weathered in the winters of life.

But she also knew that at forty-seven he had become a kind of anachronism in his world. "I do not have the sure thing I used to have," he had tried to explain it to her the time he decided to leave the Company. She knew he meant that he no longer had the reflexes he might one day need to save his life. It was the nearest he ever came to telling her how dangerous his life had been, and how vulnerable he felt he had become.

It was fate how they met at a reception given by the Greek justice minister in Athens, which she would have missed had her flight to New York not been delayed twenty-four hours, and Lanigan attended only because his deputy was indisposed at the last moment and somebody from the embassy had to show. He arrived as she was leaving.

"This looks like an awful dull party," he had said. "If you don't stay a little longer I'll get so bored I'm sure to behave disgracefully, like yawn in the middle of the minister's favourite story. You don't want to be the cause of a diplomatic incident do you, Miss Goldsmid?"

It's strange how first words linger, even when they are nothing wonderful.

They had been together for five years. Still in some ways she hardly knew him at all. She never asked about his past; the past was none of her business. "I think you'd hate having somebody get really close to you," she had said to him once, and he answered: "It is hard to be close and in love. The less one knows the better." "Aren't you lonely?" she asked. "Always," he answered without self-pity.

She put out her cigarette. We'll always have Athens, she

thought. It was Lanigan's line when they said goodbye.

There had been a lot of goodbyes. They had never lived together; they had never even lived in the same city. When she lived in Washington, he lived in Athens; she moved to London, he went to Trinidad. Now he was in Washington, she had gone to New York, where she was a partner in the law firm Kilmer, Ochs, Izard and Walsh. They had probably spent longer talking to each other on the long-distance telephone than they had spent in bed together. Lanigan had told her once that he felt there were two Kate Goldsmids: the Kate he knew on the telephone, who was serious, wise, occasionally shy, and very proper; and the Kate he slept with who was none of those things and extremely carnal.

It was almost light. She studied the room. It was not large, but it was sparse and uncluttered, and the white brick walls, the corner windows, which overlooked Harbor Square, gave it an ample enough feeling. The apartment was a furnished let. Lanigan had imposed nothing of himself on the place at all: "Every flat you've ever had has been proof of your propriety and restraint," she had teased him once. Prints of nineteenth-century sailing ships in dark-green bamboo frames, a rattan chair, an unopened carton of books – even the sealed windows – seemed to be part of the enigma of his personality.

"God, it's hot," Lanigan broke in on her thoughts. "You could grow rubber in here."

"I couldn't sleep. I tried not to disturb you." She kissed his forehead and slipped out of bed in a continuous movement. "I'll make some coffee."

He watched her go through to the kitchen, admiring the litheness of her naked back. She was slender, rather tall, with muscular arms and shoulders of a tennis player. I'm a lucky fellow, he told himself and felt again the touch of wonder and alarm he always felt when he calculated the odds against their paths having crossed.

Daughter of an army doctor, Kate had lived in fifteen states and six countries as a child. One of nature's nomads, she said. She spoke German and French, even a little Russian. After graduating third in a class of a hundred and twenty at Texas

University Law School, she went to work in the Criminal Division of the Department of Justice. Six months after being assigned to a district office in Boston, where she did the gruntwork on business fraud cases, she was offered an associateship by Kilmer, Ochs, Izard and Walsh in New York. At twenty-six she won her first million-dollar verdict, the youngest lawyer in the United States to break that barrier; two years later she became only the third woman attorney ever to appear on the *Forbes* list of best-paid lawyers in the country. That year she married Frank Goldsmid. The day before their first wedding anniversary her husband, a cardiologist, died in an automobile accident. Twelve years older than Kate, he left her with an unforeseen trust fund and an unprecedented sense of despair. She had no idea that there was so much loneliness in the world.

Lanigan's was the first relationship she had been able to trust since Frank's death. Lanigan recognized her vulnerability and disappointment: grief is an attitude and he knew that she felt pain because that is what she wanted to feel, but he sensed, at a deeper level, a want of hope, her need of a new beginning. "You have reconnected me with life, Lanigan," she told him the first night they slept together.

Lanigan listened to the quiet domestic sounds of morning: the percolator bubbling, traffic reports on the kitchen radio, Kate taking a shower. In apartments all over town he imagined similar scenes taking place. He closed his eyes and wondered what it would be like to wake every morning to the same ordinary friendly family noises.

In a little while Kate returned with a tall pot of coffee, a pot of herbal tea, mugs, glasses of freshly squeezed juice. Washed with Lanigan's shampoo, her hair smelt agreeably masculine and familiar. Her blonde hair and natural pallor emphasized her dark, intelligent eyes. A small endearing scar from a childhood fall transversed the bridge of her aquiline nose. Her gentle stammer drew attention to her mouth, which Lanigan thought was the most sensual mouth he had ever known. She had learnt to use her stammer effectively, especially in court.

She wore a man's white collarless shirt; unbuttoned and several sizes too large for her, it revealed the white lace bikini panties which covered her and showed her in equal parts. She put the tray on the bed, and sat crossed-legged facing him. He liked the way her shirt stuck to her damp breasts.

"You spoil me," he said, feeling aroused by the sight of her, and making believe nothing was happening in his loins.

"Returning last night's c-compliment." She handed him his juice.

"The wine was good."

"That was fine too."

He smiled uneasily. Talking about sex embarrassed him, more so because Kate was of that generation and class that are at ease with such topics. He said, "Why couldn't you sleep, counsellor?"

"Different things."

"Want to talk about them?"

She did not wish to tell him all her night thoughts, the thoughts about him, the thoughts about herself. She said, "I was thinking about your meeting with Noah Swan."

"Yes?"

"I think he's getting into a panic over nothing. He's an old man. Times have changed since he and Theodora Glass were an item. The world is more sophisticated since Hedda and Louella were telling us who to hate and who to love. One bad word from those broads could bury a career for eternity. Do you know what Hopper called her Beverly Hills m-mansion? *The house that fear built*."

Lanigan smiled. "What about the timing? A book at this point – don't you think that's suspicious?"

"Probably the fruit of frustration, not scheming." She poured his coffee, then tea for herself. "What's your next move?"

"Talk to the lady herself, I guess."

"First you have to get to her."

"At least I know exactly where she is." He reached for his notepad on the bedside table. "Santa Aloe. Fifteen miles north-west of Trinidad, in the channel of the Dragon's Mouth, above the Gulf of Paria," he read from the notes he had made at Noah Swan's house. "The last island before you hit Venezuela. Swan

41

calls it her little rock. Not even a dot on most maps."

"I would have thought Theodora's presence would have put it on the map."

Lanigan smiled. "It's a regular tourist attraction for the pilgrims who want to worship at her shrine. Noah says she's achieved the status of a religious icon."

"Never underestimate the box-office appeal of saints and old movie stars, Lanigan. Do the pilgrims get to meet the blessed Theodora in the flesh?"

"Visitors *verboten*. A cry of faith from their cruise ships, nearest they get."

"I like the story, the way she quit Hollywood. Finished her last movie, knelt down, kissed the stage and took off, still wearing the gown in which she'd played her last scene."

"Is that true?"

"I want it to be," Kate said.

"Why'd she quit?"

"Like Garbo, nobody knows."

"Didn't Noah keep his wife and Theodora under the same roof – wasn't that one of the great scandals? Come on, counsellor, you're the movie buff."

Kate frowned. "He brought Theodora over from London, didn't he? I think his wife was pregnant . . . But it wasn't a *ménage à trois* exactly . . . Wasn't Theodora's mother there?"

"The Baroness?"

"I think she was there," Kate said, trying to remember the details yet faintly embarrassed by her recall of such trivia. "Another story was that he'd been familiar with the Baroness first – and that Theodora was his own daughter!"

"Is that possible?"

"If you believe in fatherhood at ten."

Lanigan smiled. "I don't think even Noah Swan was up to that."

"How long's she been on her little island?"

"Since the sixties. Onassis sold it to her after he bought Skorpios. She sunk a fortune in the place. A villa shipped from Italy . . . Generators, roads, pumping systems . . ."

"I'm happy only ven I haf perfection," Kate repeated one of her famous lines with a slight Viennese accent.

"How do you think she got so stinking rich?" Lanigan asked. "Her career didn't last that long. Movie stars in the forties and fifties never got the millions they get today."

Kate shrugged. "Generous lovers. Smart investments. They say she bought up a few miles of Sunset Boulevard for peanuts in the forties." She smiled. "How you going to play it over at headquarters, Lanigan?"

"Swan'll talk to Rosengarten," he said, watching Kate refill his cup. "He'll tell him he wants me to do a job for some interests of his in Trinidad."

"Rosy's not going to like it."

"Noah picks up the tabs. Rosy does what Noah wants."

"That family has a keen sense of entitlement all right," Kate said.

"Rosy'll go along."

"Poor Rosy."

"Poor Rosy's become a goddam zipper guard. Keeping Senator Swan out of strange beds is his biggest headache."

"I thought the deal was he got him into them discreetly."

Lanigan smiled.

Kate said, "A long way from Langley, Lanigan."

"Oh, not so far," he said.

He showered, shaved and dressed in less than twenty minutes. Kate was flying back to New York on the 9 a.m. shuttle, and he had things to do at Calhoun before he began his leave of absence.

"If there's anything I can do," Kate said, as he drove her out to the airport. "I'd like to help."

"I can't afford you."

"You can be one of my *pro bono* cases."

"You don't do *pro bono* cases."

"I do now. I don't just want a batch of dough and a fancy office."

"Clips on Noah Swan and Theodora would be useful. Especially the early stuff. There's an English guy in New York, an ex-reporter, Dudley Freeman, runs a research agency. He's ace on this kinda stuff." He gave her the address in Waterside Plaza. "Keep my name out of it. It wouldn't take much to trace a connection to the Swans. Tell him you're researching contract law, or something."

"I might be able to do better than that."

"Yeah?"

"It's a long shot. I went to law school with a guy who now works for Ince, Ihmsen and Meiklejohn. Big showbiz law firm. He took me to the company dinner a couple of years ago. I sat next to a little old guy who spent the evening telling me about the famous names he'd met. I'm almost certain he said Theodora had been a client."

"A lawyer?"

Kate shook her head. "A clerk. IIM's head clerk for years. But don't hold your breath. He may be dead."

He took her to the departure gate for the shuttle to La Guardia.

"Have a safe journey."

"I'll do my best."

"We'll always have Athens," he said.

5

Robert Rider spares us no detail, however small, in the make-up of his characters. His powers of observation make you thankful you are not the one he is observing. (Len Deighton, London Sunday Times, January 7, 1990)

Tuesday, September 12
London

Jay Pfeiffer dropped his Rolls-Royce in the multi-storey car park behind Berkeley Square and headed briskly for his office in Hay Hill, pausing only a moment to admire the efficiency of the team wheel-clamping a new silver BMW. Pfeiffer was a man who respected professionalism wherever he found it. Around six feet tall, thin as a rail – at seven each morning he worked out at his house in Cheyne Walk with a personal trainer – he had the perfect vanity and build for the dark Armani Black Label suits he always wore for business.

At his office he put in a call to Robert Rider in Germany. He had first met Rider two weeks after he had started his own agency in 1980. He walked into his office, one room above a delicatessen in Soho, with the manuscript of his first novel in a rucksack. "You're just out of the box, nobody's heard of me, let's make each other rich and famous, Mr Pfeiffer" – his opening line. Pfeiffer read the manuscript that night and at eight o'clock the following morning called Rider and said, "How rich and famous do you want to be?" Is there a limit, Rider asked. "Keep writing stuff like this and we might never know," Pfeiffer told him.

Rider's voice came on the line from Baden-Baden.

"Ready for some good news?" Pfeiffer greeted him without

preamble. He read him the whole of a long review of his latest novel, *The Milan Agent*, faxed from that morning's *New York Times*.

"That's more than the book deserves, Jay." Rider immediately regretted saying it, for he knew it would diminish Pfeiffer's own share of pleasure in his success. "Is it really that good?"

"What I think don't count. Frank Pleskow thinks it's the best thing you've done. What he thinks counts." Pfeiffer's voice echoed distantly, vitiated by the acoustics of the squawk box that enabled him to pace the room and hold conversations across continents. "When you due back? I don't want my principal asset wasting away."

Rider rubbed his flat stomach with the palm of his hand. Sometimes he wondered whether his lifestyle, the bouts of loneliness and isolation, had fostered a streak of unpleasant narcissism in him. "I'm back in London Friday."

"Give me the flight number." Pfeiffer searched for a pen among piles of books, manuscripts and contracts on his massive Ciancimino desk.

'Lufthansa 1644 from Stuttgart. Arrives Heathrow 8.55 a.m.," Rider told him with his habitual precision about travel arrangements.

"I'll send a car to pick you up. Let's have dinner Friday night."

Rider suggested Mario's, at nine. They shared many interests, including an appreciation of good Italian food. "*A pochi passi da Harrods,*" Pfeiffer repeated Mario's slogan, which always made them laugh. Jay Pfeiffer sounded ebullient but his eyes were unsmiling. He would never lie to Rider, he would never lie to any client, but for the first time in their relationship he was not levelling with him. And although it was simply about a matter he did not want to discuss on the telephone, it made him uneasy. He wondered whether Rider sensed it. He glanced at the picture of them together on the beach at Malibu the day they signed the CBS deal, laughing, a little drunk, their arms around each other's shoulders.

He pulled open a drawer in his desk and without touching it looked again at the letter handwritten on ash-blue opal vellum, faintly scented: a complex perfume, with a strong thread of jasmine and incense. The looped signature flowed with a simple cursive rhythm, the signature of a person old enough to have learnt the craft of handwriting, he decided the first moment he saw it; the hand of somebody capable of getting thoughts and ideas on to paper:

I am aware that those little chains that connect us to the past are being broken all the time: death and failing memory break them; the accounts of sycophants and liars break them too; and time alters gossip into fact, and fact becomes merely gossip. And with each broken link another piece of the truth, another part of the past is gone for ever. And how sad never to know why the person we once were did such and such a thing and why we loved those we loved, and why those we loved did what they did . . . Fortunately I have not yet lost track of a moment in my life, even those moments you might think I would wish to forget for ever . . . It is upon my own words that I will be judged, but be assured I do not propose a chronicle of self-love, a testament of ego . . . So much of what has happened in my life is in the public domain, but there is a part of me that nobody knows, Mr Pfeiffer. And that part is what makes the rest of my life – the things I did, the actions I took – finally comprehensible . . . I respect Mr Rider too much to expect him merely to be the keeper of the flame. Please tell him that for me. Tell him: no fictions, no evasions, only the truth. For those who loved me and made me. For those who owned me and hurt me. For myself . . .

Pfeiffer knew the letter by heart. It was as if it had been written not by Theodora Glass at all – but by one of those slightly insane, tragic, romantic women she had often played in her pictures.

But if it were genuine (and why or for what absurdity should anybody go to such lengths to fake it?) it was worth . . . the idea was worth . . . Once again that part of his brain that did the sums failed to work out a figure . . . a fortune, he concluded lamely, disturbed by his own vagueness. In his head Jay Pfeiffer carried more actuarial tables than New York Life – bestsellers by sex, by nationality, by age, by season; lemons by pros, by amateurs, by presidents, by mistresses; blockbusters by chance, by formula, by error, by hype – but he had never met a situation like this one. Nobody expected this can of worms to be opened. Ever.

He could see her face now: the arch of the eyebrows, the curve of her nostrils, that smile at camera in the memorable Eisenstaedt picture the US Post Office had put on a stamp. She had a style that was hers and no one else's. Theodora Glass was the first woman he had ever got horny about. He could still recall exactly the way she crossed and uncrossed her legs in her first Billy Wilder movie. Jesus, those *legs*. He wondered how she looked today. Except for the paparazzi shots of her – veiled with dark glasses hurrying across a New York street; half-hidden behind a newspaper at a sidewalk café in Paris; a distant silhouette sunbathing naked on Agnelli's (or was it Onassis's?) yacht; strolling beneath a parasol on her private island – she had not been photographed for what, thirty years? forty years? He calculated that she would be seventy-something now, perhaps less; she was just a kid in those early movies. She was Lolita before Nabokov invented Lolita.

Closing the drawer, he said firmly: "You're *numero uno* again, Robert." He switched off the squawk box and picked up the receiver. Inflecting his voice with intimacy and confidence, he went to work on the fiscal foreplay that worked like a charm on writers. "With the movie and serial rights, foreign sales, book club deals . . . You're going to collect quite a piece of change, my dear. Frank Pleskow's keen to get you over to New York to talk it up a little," he said, sitting back in his chair, a Marc Held combination swivel-rocking chair which he had bought at Sotheby's out of his ten per cent of the first six-figure deal he made for Rider, the first six-figure deal he had for *anyone*: the *Easy Rider* chair *Newsweek* magazine dubbed it in its cover story on Rider the week Paramount paid $5.2 million for the movie rights to his third novel.

"I think we owe it to Frank, don't you?" he went on in the offhand way he had when he particularly wanted something, and which had become familiar to Rider, who knew he was casual about nothing. "A few days, five days tops. A shot on *Good Morning America*, and –"

"No, Jay."

"It's not a trip to the dentist!"

"Have you ever sat in the Green Room at seven o'clock in the morning? Zsa Zsa Gabor on one side, Buffalo Bob and Howdy on the other?"

"I guess it's not a day at the beach either," Pfeiffer said, deciding not to push. He stretched his neck and pinched the tiny roll of beard-hidden flesh beneath his chin and wondered about taking a week at Baden-Baden himself. Perhaps after the Frankfurt Book Fair. He turned the pages of his diary as he brought Rider up to date on various foreign rights negotiations, and the mini-series deal he had made for his last book; his voice was wise and warm. They talked for twenty minutes. All the time they talked, Pfeiffer was trying to figure out Rider's mood. He was a friend but he was not an easy client: professionally he was demanding and stubborn; in matters of business he could be perverse and tricky. Publishers paid fortunes to get his books, and when they got them spent hours pleading with Pfeiffer to keep him off their backs. "Rider is a shit," one publisher, who preferred to remain anonymous, told *Vanity Fair*. "But he's a bestselling shit, with a rocket up his ass, and I don't know a publisher in the business who wouldn't beg, steal or sell his grandmother to get him on his list."

Pfeiffer came to the end of the notes he had made of the things he needed to discuss with Rider. "How far's Baden-Baden from Frankfurt, Robert?"

"By train . . . couple of hours."

Pfeiffer pencilled in five days at Brenner's Park Hotel in October. "Gotta go, my sweet. New York's on the other line. Friday, we gotta date. Put Jim Bittman on, Susan," he called through the always open door of his office even before Rider was off the line. "And, Susan, your car's been clamped, my dear."

Robert Rider lit a small *sigaro toscano* and lay back on the wide hotel bed, his left arm beneath his head, trying to put some order into his thoughts. The sound of Grace Hempel taking a shower came down the hall, and he was conscious of her scent on the pillow. Fifty-one years old, he had never been married, although he was successful with women and had been through the motions of love many times. His sensitivity was belied by his build. Heavy shoulders and muscled arms showed that he had not sat behind a typewriter all his life. His eyes, hair and eyebrows were dark; his beard was a pale auburn colour, with flecks of red in it: it was sometimes described as golden, and once, by a woman critic, as *bloodstained*. His nose had been broken, probably more than once. His voice had a faint Edinburgh accent which was regularly mistaken for Irish. Women journalists who interviewed him found him chauvinistic, and frequently found their way into his bed.

He had made peace with the loneliness of writing. Unlike other writers he knew, he was not a complete social disaster. He drank, but no longer in excess. He had a house in London, a duplex apartment in New York; the estate in Brittany – his hedge against inflation, his investment broker insisted whenever Rider suggested unloading it – and a beach house he barely visited in Malibu.

People would kill to have my problems, he decided with satisfaction. He closed his eyes and smiled, the small unvarying smile he dispensed for photographers, for talk show hosts, and strangers who asked for his autograph, a habit of his fame.

"Why is this man smiling?"

Grace Hempel was standing in the doorway, smelling of Guerlain's *Fleurs des Alpes*, Rider's favourite soap (when he was poor he had read that it was Ian Fleming's favourite soap and vowed then that one day he too would use nothing else). She compelled awe not only because she looked beautiful but because she seemed unconscious of her nakedness. Almost as tall as Rider, model thin, her hair (the colour of old Florentine gold, he had told her when he noticed the similarity in San Miniato a year before, the day they became lovers) was plastered to her small oval head.

"But such a sad smile."

"Come here," he commanded, removing the small cigar from his mouth.

A geranium-red fingernail pursued a trickle of water down her left breast to its pale tip. She smiled as the nipple came erect, embarrassed that she was so sensitive to her own touch, wondering whether Rider had noticed. "I'm wet," she said, looking down at herself. Her green eyes were flaked with amber, the whites as bright as a child's, and with the same curiosity.

"That's the way I like you," Rider said, missing nothing. He was pleased that she still had the gift of blushing.

Grace shot him with her index finger, and turned back into the bathroom. She returned wrapping a towel around her body, and sat on the bed, her square jaw resting on her knees. Beads of water glistened on her faintly freckled shoulders. She removed the bitter-scented *sigaro* from Rider's fingers and twisted it out in the ashtray balanced on his chest. As if it were a fresh wound, she touched the small, vertical scar above his left eye, which was white as fishbone in the new-looking tan. "Designer-old," she had described his face in the press release she wrote for his last book. It was written to amuse him, but it had been used in almost every piece written about him since.

"Was that Jay on the blower? What news from Londinium?"

"Susie's been clamped again." He gripped her wrist. "And you are a very tactile person." He spoke gently, calmly; she knew he was irritated. He had been on edge since they arrived in Germany.

"Jay called to tell you about Susie's parking problems?"

"He said the New York reviews are pretty good."

"Pretty good? That's all? Pretty good?"

"The *Times* says it's better than *Unrecorded Deaths*."

"Darling, that's marvellous." She moved the ashtray to the bedside table, put her head on his shoulder. She was not embarrassed that a part of what she loved in him was success. "Then why the sad smile?"

"I live in a limbo of tenable dissatisfaction," he said.

"Tenable dissatisfaction," she repeated ambiguously.

51

"Not with you."

They smiled at each other, their faces close. They kissed. Her lips were soft and tasted faintly of the wheatgerm in her sunscreen. He moved his hand beneath the towel. She was still moist from the shower. She closed her eyes.

"That's good," she said after a long moment. "That's nice."

"The devil also finds mischief for hands that have not yet learnt how to be idle."

"He does," Grace said in a dreamy voice. She was always amazed how well he knew her body, how well he was able to match his sense of time to hers. "He does." Her thighs parted by degrees, acceding to the sensations he was making her feel. "He does, he does, oh yes" – she lifted herself up, flicked back her hair, and straddled him – "he does, so. Ride a cock horse to Banbury Cross . . ." Her voice so English, proper, disturbingly childish. "Ride a cock horse . . . Ride a cock . . . *Ride . . . Ride . . . Rider . . .*"

Her eyes opened wide, she screamed his name: an oath, an accusation, a celebration, all in a splinter of sound torn from her throat, repeated and repeated. Then it was over. She moaned, once, an animal sound, filled with contentment and complexities, and curled down on his chest.

"I screamed," she said quietly in the long stillness after the passion.

"I like you to scream."

"I sent the birds flying away, didn't I?"

"You emptied the whole forest." He stroked her hair back behind her ears. "Would you like a drink?"

"I'd like you not to move." She kissed the bite marks on his shoulder and upper arm, the slight separation between her two front teeth clearly visible in his skin.

"You have a dancer's neck." His thumb traced the thin column down to the nape, where it merged into the long, hollow sweep of her back. "I haven't been much fun the last couple of days, have I?"

"You've been funnier," she told him.

"I'll make it up to you."

"You just did."

"There are ways to tame every living creature," he said.

"*Quel monstre!*"

Minutes passed before they spoke again.

"Do you really live in . . . tenable dissatisfaction?"

"The new book isn't that good, Grace."

"The critics appear to disagree."

"The critics are wrong."

She didn't say anything; it would have been too easy to say something dumb. She had been in the business long enough, first as a PA, and now as publicity director at Rider's London publishing house, to know that success often catches a writer at his most morbid time: scared that his best ideas and inventions have been used up, some failure of nerve is understandable. She sat very still in a nest of twisted sheets.

Rider put on his bathrobe. "Frank Pleskow is pushing for a sequel to *Unrecorded Deaths*."

"What's so bad about that?"

"Sequels – there's no excitement, no risk . . . I'm getting too comfortable." He looked around the big suite. "All this bloody luxury, Grace!"

"No artist works under ideal conditions," she said, with the smallest smile.

He laughed. "Do you know how many interviews I did last year? Print, radio, television – 'A *hype*notic celeb,' a breakfast show host in Amarillo called me. I still don't know whether that was the Texas drawl or Texas humour."

"We live in the age of writer as publicist."

"It's a kind of whoredom, isn't it?"

"And you're a good old pro, Rider."

"Being a good old pro can rot a writer's mind."

"It also sells books, my dear." She studied the bedroom with narrowed eyes. "Anyway, what's wrong with a little bloody luxury?"

"The freebee suites . . . the word processors and wrist watches and whisky I'm paid to prefer. It's easy to get seduced, to get sidetracked."

"Nobody works harder than you. A few perks . . . I don't see the problem."

He shook his head. "I still don't know how good I am and I'd like to find out."

"Post-publication blahs. Don't worry about it," she said, starting for the bathroom.

"I'm a perverse, ungrateful son of a bitch," he said, smelling in her sudden movement the musk of her body mingling with the *Fleurs des Alpes*.

He woke the following morning feeling mysteriously elated. At breakfast he told Grace, "When I started my first novel I didn't know what it was going to be about or how it would end. I didn't plan it. No flow charts, no plot line, no research. All I had were a first line, my instincts and my ignorance. Just another journo who wanted to escape from the pressure of the deadline."

Grace was puzzled by this sudden explanation. He disliked talking about his work. "Is this how you plan to begin your next book?" she asked.

"I don't know," he answered slowly. "But I have that same feeling of . . . expectation, I suppose it is. A feeling that I haven't had in I forget how long. A sense that something extraordinary is about to happen, and that the process somewhere has already begun . . ."

6

Wednesday, September 13
Santa Aloe

Theodora handed the microcassette to Missy. "Talking to a machine is a soulless business."

"We are more honest with ourselves when we are alone," Missy said.

"It comes straight from the heart, anyway. Mr Rider will have to do the real work."

"Have you heard from his agent yet?"

Theodora shook her head.

"Still sure you want to go through with it?"

Theodora flicked her robe across her legs stretched in front of her in the long, straight line the camera liked best. She still had wonderful legs. "It all seems a horribly long time ago . . . But I'm beginning to understand things I did not understand before."

"It takes time to find out what really matters in all the things that happen to us," Missy said.

"Don't type it up if you think it's no gottdam good."

Missy Miller sat in the dark listening to the conspiratorial laughter of the servants as they cleared away supper on the terrace below her room. A cool night wind had blown the heat away. A smell of ocean and earth hung in the air. The terrace lights flickered out one by one; the carefree chatter stopped. Missy lit a cigarette. After a little while she made a gesture as if waving aside voices. "OK," she said aloud, reaching for the tape machine. "Talk to me, my baby."

THEODORA'S TAPE

I shall begin this story, the true story of Theodora Glass, with Baron Georg Reinhard von Tegge, my father. To me he was always simply Vati. He was born in Vienna on November 28, 1896, midway through the lifetime of the Austro-Hungarian Empire. From his first breath he moved in a privileged world of vast estates, shooting parties, and magnificent houses. It must have seemed as if the family, like the Danube itself, would go on for ever.

One interesting story about my paternal grandparents, Missy. Grandpapa was a colonel in the Imperial Army. In 1914, to rid himself for the duration of the chores of management, he sold the family sawmills and the estate in Klagenfurt, and invested the proceeds in Imperial Russian stock. In 1917, nine days after the Bolsheviks seized control in Russia, he put a gun into his mouth and squeezed both triggers. On the second anniversary of his death, a month after the remaining small estate in the South Tyrol was confiscated by the Italians under the Treaty of St Germain, my grandmother put on her bridal veil, and in the same room, with the same gun that killed grandfather, shot herself. She was forty-three years old.

(I am taking all of this from Mama's notes, Missy. I think they are reliable about the family; I hope they're not too garbled about history!)

Although most families of the old Imperial aristocracy sent their sons to the Schotten Gymnasium or to the Theresianum in Vienna, Grandmother enrolled Vati at the Jesuit College of St Ignatius Loyola at Bregenz. The Jesuits were exiles from the German Reich, and believed that union with Germany was God's will. Their faith in one Teutonic nation united in a single Empire – *Anschluss* – was drummed into every pupil.

When the war came, Vati ran away from school and, lying about his age, joined the army. I have a photograph dated December 20, 1914, one month after his eighteenth birthday, showing him in his smart new *leutnant*'s uniform, smiling and smoking a cigar, looking like a mischievous choirboy. Three weeks later he won the first Grand Cross of the Austrian Order for Conspicuous Gallantry of the war. The following year he became the youngest battalion commander in Austria. In 1917 he was wounded and captured by the Italians in the crossing of the Piave. I have a picture of him dated January 1918. He no longer looks like a choirboy.

I will try to describe him for you, Missy. He was about middle height, lean, his hair was blond and close-cropped. There was a look of hardness in the mould of his skull which made it like a Roman statue's head. His nose was straight. I never heard him raise his voice. He had a way of looking at you as if he knew the most secret things about you. Then he would smile, and his smile made him beautiful. There was kindness and sadness in his eyes, a lovely lilac-grey, like mine. I think he was a very lonely man.

He was released from the prisoner-of-war camp and returned to Vienna in 1919. Republican Austria had replaced the Imperial Empire. His allowance of twenty thousand crowns a month (bequeathed by his grandmother, when sixteen crowns bought one American dollar) had been almost wiped out by the terrible inflation; by 1922 (according to Mama's journal) eighty-three thousand crowns could not buy a single US dollar. The town house on the Löwelstrasse, all that remained of the Tegge inheritance, had been requisitioned by the authorities and divided into apartments. Vati was permitted to keep a room on the top floor.

He had used the time he spent as a prisoner to read law, and continued his studies at Vienna University. In 1923 he joined a law firm in Innsbruck. And the following winter he met my mother. There's a nice story how they met. Billy Wilder would have called it "a meet cute" scene. They were both looking at a portrait by Franz Hals in the Ferdinandeum. "I think," Mama said, to strike up a conversation with this handsome young man, "it is a big fake."

The argument between them became so heated (a convincing performance in Mama's case) Vati felt he had to apologize. He invited her to dinner.

"I'm sixteen," she warned him. She was outwardly adult, and knew she was attractive to men. "I am staying at the Grauer Bär." The Grey Bear was an inn used by young climbers with not very much money. "I shall expect you at seven o'clock," she said.

Mama had all the aloofness of old money, which was funny. Her maiden name was Gisela Verna Glass. Some years ago I found her first calling card, inscribed Gisela v. Glass. The v had been printed small, implying an abbreviation for the noble prefix *von*. It was not the only attempt to change things about herself. Born in Leopoldstadt, the Jewish district of Vienna, she was the only daughter of Paul and Hedwig Glass. They were music teachers. But she had already become a member of the Old Catholic Church when she met my father. Austria has a bad history of anti-Semitism; it was not uncommon for Jews to deny their race. Having broken with Rome, Old Catholicism was a popular choice for those who wanted to convert to Christianity. Pale-skinned, with that cloudy, lemony hair, she never looked a bit Jewish anyway.

She was seventeen years old, Vati twenty-eight, and I two months on the way when they married in 1925 in the Jesuit Church on the Universitätstrasse.

I was born at three o'clock in the morning on February 10 the following year in a house Vati had rented at the end of the Herzog Friederichstrasse, a short distance from his law office. Mama says I was born with a caul, supposed to be a good omen and a charm against drowning! So you need not worry when I swim out too far in the mornings, Missy. I will die one day, but it will not be from drowning!

Vati wanted a son, and when the doctor told Mama she had given birth to a girl, she said: *No, no! There is a mistake!* So the first words I heard in this world were words of rejection. This is why critics have never bothered me, maybe. (Are these details important, Missy? Are they interesting? I don't know. You must tell me. You once said that people want to read everything about their favourite stars. Even that Marilyn Monroe and I were born in the same year, you told me once, meant something to our fans.)

Very well, I will go on. In view of Vati's history and Mama's ambition, I suppose it was inevitable that he should go into politics. When I was three years old he entered the Chamber of Deputies on the Christian Social ticket. Chancellor Ignaz Seipel made him his political adviser.

The following years brought changes that meant little to a small child. Vati became a public figure, and newspapers began referring to Mama as "a great beauty". I think one of my earliest memories was her bringing guests to the nursery to look at me sleeping. Feigning sleep, listening to the voices singing my praises – "How long her eyelashes are . . . such beautiful ears . . ." – I would give them left and right profiles, a little sigh, a contented smile. I was the most terrible hambone, Missy.

We became well-off without becoming rich. We had a cook, a Fräulein, and a *Hausmeister*. In time, Vati succeeded in repossessing the whole of the house on Löwelstrasse (the second best street in Vienna, Mama says). The house seemed old to me, but nearly all Vienna is built of a porous brick faced with painted stone or plaster, and even a twenty-year-old building may look ancient if refacing is due. One by one the empty rooms were decorated and furnished, often with family pieces which Vati had diligently traced and recovered. I remember the pier glass in Mama's bedroom into which I gave my earliest performances! I had a good memory in those days for poems (Dante in Italian, Verlaine in French: I am showing off, but it is true). I got a governess, and tutors for music and dancing. Fred Zinnemann once told me that the important thing in Vienna at that time was music. It didn't matter what was happening in the rest of the world. The important thing was that the opera had been good the night before. When I was eight I was sent to Frau Horstenau's Academy for Young Ladies on Rauhensteingasse, next door to the house in which Mozart died. Frau Horstenau wore a fox fur round her neck and walked with a thin, ebony cane and taught me the etiquette of an age that was already dead – the distinction between asking "How is your mother?" and saying, "I hope your mother is well?" But I was not happy in a formal classroom, and

Mama took me away after my second term there, and I resumed my lessons at home.

The days were always the same. Family breakfast at seven; lessons from eight thirty to twelve; a walk in the Prater with Mama (except on Sundays, when the crowds and brass bands and steam organs gave her a headache); lunch was at exactly one thirty. Afternoons were devoted to the arts, and reading a theatrical weekly called *Die Bühne* (*The Stage*). Mama had a passion for the theatre. Had Vati been more sympathetic, perhaps she would have become an actress herself. Instead she transferred the ambition to me, and so my future was fatefully decided almost from the beginning. I was seven or eight when I began drama class. My teacher was a young stage actor named Helmuth Walther, who later became a successful movie director in Munich. It was Helmuth who got me my first screen role, in *The Little Spy*. I played a schoolgirl who discovers a plot against Napoleon. It is a charming little picture. Only one print of it now exists in the world. It is owned by a film collector in Paris who charges people a hundred dollars to see it.

I enjoyed acting. To me it was the best of games. Before Helmuth Walther, Mama taught me herself. As she brushed my hair I would recite pieces from Max Reinhardt's newest production at his theatre in der Josefstadt. We learnt duologues by heart – *Romeo and Juliet, Antony and Cleopatra*. If I blew a line, or misplaced an emphasis, Mama would hit my knuckles with the back of the hairbrush. Years later Jerry Wechsler was asked by a reporter whether I was truly perfect – surely there was some part of me Jerry had trouble lighting? He said, "I think two knuckles on her right hand might have been damaged in her childhood!" Sonofabitch, he never missed a thing!

Now I've lost my thread, Missy. Gottdammit, I've been trying so hard not to ramble . . . I hate reflections that interrupt a story . . . Anyway, yes, I was coming to the time when I was conscious that my parents were beginning to have their troubles with each other. Vati was getting caught up in the dangerous politics of the thirties. He was with the Foreign Office, and close to Chancellor Dollfuss. Mama had acquired new admirers, including some who became lovers.

One afternoon, it was winter, I returned early from a friend's birthday treat at the Café Fenstergucker. Mama was in the salon. The blinds were drawn down, and the fire had burned very low in the hearth. At first I thought she was having a megrim. She smelt of scent and perspiration, a smell indefinably disturbing, anyway. Her bodice was undone, revealing glimpses of her lovely breasts. She lay sprawled on the sofa, in her tall kid boots from Perugia's in Paris. Her skirt was up around her thighs; one of her legs was drawn up, and the other extended along the edge of the sofa. She was smoking a thin black cigarette, which I had seen only Helmuth Walther smoke before. Her hair was swept up, exposing the nape of her wonderful neck – "as thin as a governess's hatpin," I remember reading that in a newspaper and being very proud of her. I also remember even now how her pale face had a faintly translucent look in the darkened room.

"Mama, aren't you well? The fire is almost out. Aren't you cold?"

"*Liebe wintert nicht*," she said, and smiled at me with a sort of dreamy disdain. *Liebe wintert nicht* – love knows no winter. It didn't make sense to me. Then there was a sound behind the door to Vati's study. He had been in Berlin and was not expected back until the next day.

"Is Vati home early?"

Before she could answer, Helmuth Walther came through the door.

He was not a tall man, and no more than twenty-five, I imagine, although his temples had been dyed grey for a role he was playing at the Burtheater, which made him seem much older. He had a hungry face, with very light-blue eyes. Later I was told that he had been an *Eintänzer*, a gigolo, a man who lives off rich women. I remember he wore a grey suit and a silver cravat. He looked immaculate . . . only his shoelaces were undone.

"We did not expect you home so early, sweetness," he said. He looked me straight in the eye, as if trying to figure out how gullible or how smart I was. He kissed my cheek; I smelled Vati's apricot schnapps on his breath. "I have been talking to your mother about your progress. I have told her I take much pride in your accomplishment."

He gave Mama a sidelong smile that I was not meant to see.

"We dwell with more pleasure on the perfume of the flower that we have tended ourselves," he said, indulging his Viennese taste for ambiguity and intrigue.

I had until that moment believed in my parents' perfect love. It had never occurred to me that Mama had ever felt the touch of another man. I felt sick to my stomach. Years later I realized I had felt my first hurt of sexual jealousy, my first grown-up emotion.

Perhaps there was no love left between my parents by then. Although I don't think it was as simple as that. I noticed the way Vati still touched Mama's hair, the way he sometimes touched her arm when they talked. I think it was that the excitement of their love-making had passed and in passing had changed everything. But none of this I understood then. There is an old Austrian saying, *Am Abend wird man klug Fur den vergangnen Tag*. It means that in the evening we become wise about the day that has gone.

Now I am wise about many things, Missy.

Missy switched off the tape. It was almost one o'clock in the morning. She slowly poured herself a brandy and went into her bedroom and stood before the Laszlo Willinger picture of Theodora she kept on the table next to her bed. She stood looking at it for a very long moment.

"You really mean to spill the whole bibful, don't you, baby?"

There was sadness as well as anxiety in her voice.

Then she swallowed the brandy and shivered.

7

Big mistakes start real small. (Noah Swan, New York Post, October 27, 1943)

Thursday, September 14
New York City

"I'm having a f-fine old time," Kate Goldsmid said when she talked to Ambrose Lanigan in Washington. It was nine o'clock in the evening in New York, and she was still at the office. "I'm wallowing in nostalgia of the Hollywood kind. You were right: Freeman's good. Turned up some useful stuff our database people didn't have. A *Saturday Evening Post* piece from the forties, an early *New Yorker* profile. I told him I was libel-reading a manuscript, by the way."

"Make any progress with your clerk?"

"It's your lucky day, Lanigan. My friend broke a leg in Colorado and came back early. Not only is the old boy still alive – he's still working! I talked to him this evening. He lives in Jackson Heights, with his sister. He doesn't go into the office every day, but he sounds perfectly *compos mentis* – remembered exactly who I was. Or said he did. His name's Walter Rusk. I'm seeing him Friday at his office."

"You're going to his office?" Lanigan sounded alarmed.

"It's safe. He likes to work late. Apparently he's a c-character, a law unto himself at IIM. Been with the company since old Eustis Ince first hung out his shingle on Madison Avenue in the thirties, knows where all the b-bodies are buried. We have an eight o'clock date. Friday night, the place should be empty."

"Thanks, Kate."

"We still don't know whether Theodora was a client. I thought it better not to get into specifics on the phone."

"Didn't he ask why you wanted to talk to him?"

"No, but he will. Leave that to me, OK? Listen to this. This is interesting." She picked up one of the clippings arranged in neat piles across her desk. "It's undated, from the *New York Review of Books*:

> Theodora's father was a baron, a Catholic, and a diplomat; her mother a painter, a Jew, and a first cousin of the famous tragedienne Charlotte Wolters. Such mixed hereditary strains of aristocracy, religion and art produced an actress of complex and exceptional character, and must go far to explain the dual nature which is so strongly marked in Theodora – a Hollywood artist in whom originality and boldness are fused with a reclusive and anti-social temperament . . .

Etc., etc. Dual personality, reclusive habits – thought that might give you a key, some idea of what you're dealing with."

Lanigan laughed. Maybe it depressed him.

"*Women's Wear Daily* did an interesting piece, trying to figure out how she got so r-rich – a suggestion that Onassis gave her the island for services rendered. Oh, and this one I liked. From the old Leonard Lyons column. Gisela – the mother, Baroness Gisela von Tegge – once took a private tennis lesson with Baron Gottfried von Cramm, the German ace, and quit after the first set. She told him, 'There is only one place where a lady may perspire. And that most certainly is not on grass.' She sounds fun."

"Where is she now – dead, huh?"

"She was still around in the eighties. There's what looks like a paparazzi shot of her with Theodora on the island. Rather fuzzy. That's in 1986 – May," Kate told him, quickly checking the photostats systematically arranged on her desk. "But a *Boston Globe* story a year later refers to Theodora's *late* mother. A couple of other pieces have also got her deceased. I guess she's no longer with us. I wasn't particularly looking . . . Is it important?"

"Probably not. She might have been a way through to Theodora, that's all." He never failed to be impressed by Kate's efficiency and grasp of details. "Anything interesting on Noah?"

"I've got a whole bunch of stuff here. I'll have it couriered down tomorrow." She switched off the reading lamp, ran her fingers through her hair. "Shall I see you at the weekend?"

"Why don't I come to New York?"

"I'd like that."

They talked for a while and after they said goodnight, Kate put on the light and began to look for references to Gisela's death. But none of the stories in which she was mentioned in the past tense gave details of how or when she had died. Kate's feelings changed from curiosity to mild irritation. It probably meant nothing. An oversight. But it irritated her. She liked to have explanations and answers, even when the questions were not important. She liked to have facts, accurately stated. She liked to have a beginning, middle and end of things. There must have been an obituary notice some place; the mother of Theodora Glass would merit at least a couple of paragraphs somewhere.

She dialled Data Control, verified her client status, gave her personal password: *Good Vibrations*. "Baroness Gisela von Tegge," she fed her request into the computer terminal. "Socialite, mother of Hollywood actress Theodora Glass. Widow Austrian diplomat Baron Georg von Tegge. All references last five years." Fifteen minutes later the stories began to feed through on her personal printer.

There were dozens of items, mostly of short gossipy interest: recording Gisela's arrival in London or New York, Klosters or Bermuda; noting her presence at charity functions and art gallery openings; recording her departure from London or New York, Klosters or Bermuda. She had had a couple of hospitalizations for minor illnesses (probably cover stories for cosmetic surgery, Kate imagined); she'd been in a fracas with a traffic cop in upstate New York one Thanksgiving weekend; a top fashion house had sued her over an unpaid bill; and there were the familiar tabloid rumours of rifts and reconciliations with Theodora.

In December 1986 she was photographed leaving Kennedy international to join her daughter for the Christmas holidays in the Caribbean. That was the last reported sighting. After that, nothing. No reports of her death, no obituary notices, no tributes. The Baroness Gisela von Tegge had simply vanished.

It was weird.

Kate signed off.

On Friday evening, at exactly eight o'clock, Kate Goldsmid arrived at the Park Avenue offices of Ince, Ihmsen and Meiklejohn. The security man checked her name on his list, checked her credentials, and directed her to the second floor where Walter Rusk was waiting for her at the elevator. They shook hands.

"I hope I'm not too early," Kate said.

"No, no, I'm just about finished up here for tonight," he said, leading her through the firm's central filing room. His arm swept across the files and cardboard boxes stacked on the library table in the centre of the room. "I'm weeding stuff out for the shredder. Mr Meiklejohn says it's a waste of time putting old cases into the computer machines."

He showed her into a small, square, windowless cupboard of an office next to the big computer room. It contained a metal desk, a swivel chair, and, incongruously, and taking up almost half the space, an ancient rolltop desk.

"We won't be disturbed in here," he said, unaware how needless and poignant his assurance was. He made Kate sit in the swivel chair. He stood next to the desk. "What do you want to talk to me about, young lady?"

"This is strictly confidential, Mr Rusk."

"Go ahead."

"Some lawyers, a bunch of his friends, are planning a dinner for Mr Ince. A tribute dinner. Nothing's finalized yet, it won't be until next fall, so I must ask you to keep it just between the two of us for now. I've been asked to make a speech, and I hoped you might be able to help me with a few anecdotes, something personal I wouldn't get from the law journals, or by combing through old newspaper accounts of cases. It seemed to me, Mr Rusk –"

"Call me Walter. Everybody calls me Walter."

"I wondered, Walter, if there was a good show business story – something I could use to make a point of the firm's strong reputation in the entertainment field? Something amusing, a piece of gossip . . . I don't want to let any cats out of the bag, but it will be a private affair, and I think we might be a little bit . . . indiscreet."

"You mean you want to catch him with something right from the inside? You want me to be your Deep Throat?"

Kate laughed. "No, of course not, Walter. No such thing."

"I don't think I can help you, young lady."

"Oh, Walter," she said in a crestfallen voice, praying that his reluctance was simply a show of temperament, a caution expected of the old, and there to be overcome.

"Old Eustis Ince trusted me," he said sternly. "I have never betrayed that trust. Never."

"I wouldn't want you to be disloyal to IIM, Walter."

"Old Mr Ince used to say, 'You can always trust Walter.'"

"I wouldn't expect you to betray a trust, Walter. But there's usually something funny or peculiar about most cases and –"

"Especially when you got actors involved." He grinned knowingly.

"Exactly, Walter," she said, encouraged by his friendlier tone. "That's my point exactly."

"I still don't see how I could help you without –"

"A piece of history," she suggested quickly. "Nothing current. Something that couldn't possibly embarrass anybody today."

He scratched his head, pulled at his earlobe. "Well, it was old Mr Ince first got us into the show business area," he said thoughtfully.

"You mean Hollywood?"

He shook his head. "Theatre people, a lot of radio people, not many picture people at first. Floyd Gibbons, Raymond Gram Swing, H. V. Kaltenborn – I'll bet you don't remember him! Radio commentator. Clem McCarthy, another radio fella. Did all the big fights from the Garden. You'd think you were at ringside with him. Brenda Frazier. I remember her coming in all the time. The number one débutante. Pretty, pretty girl. But drank too much. Dead now . . . Get me started on those times, Miss Goldsmid, you'll think the show never goes by. I'm coming up eighty-two next July." He stood up straighter, his hand on the rolltop. "And still got milk in the coconut," he said, tapping his bald temple.

Kate looked impressed. She had got him talking, that was a start. She wasn't discouraged that he didn't mention Theodora. He had obviously said the first names that came into his head; probably names that meant something to him personally: radio stars, sports people, a girl he'd once fancied. She knew she would have to take her time with this man, go at his pace. "Have you ever thought of taking it a little easier, Walter?" she asked gently.

"Retire? Hell, no. What would I do all day?"

"I know what you mean," she said, smiling and feeling sad for him.

"Who can afford to retire these days?"

Kate had done some homework. She knew that he lived with his sister Cissy in North Queens in the same apartment building they had shared for nearly fifty years. Cissy had also worked at IIM, first as a legal secretary, later as a bookkeeper, before she retired ten years ago. Walter repeated much Kate already knew. He talked about Cissy as if she knew her well. They had always wanted to move to Douglaston, west of Little Neck, where the fine old houses were surrounded by beautiful trees. Trees were Cissy's passion, he said. Weeping willows along the bay shore, sycamores on the avenues. But they never made it to Douglaston. "When we were both travelling into the city every day, Jackson Heights was the only community outside Manhattan on the Fifth Avenue bus route. It was convenient. And when Cissy retired, well, the rents in Douglaston had gotten too rich for us. Anyway, we'd miss Jackson Heights if we moved out now. We'll leave the old apartment feet first, as the saying goes."

She let him talk. Eventually he stopped, and sighed.

"But you don't want to hear about all that." He rubbed the side of his face thoughtfully. "Maybe you should talk to Cissy. She's got a better memory for that kind of thing. Dolores del Rio, we handled her one time, but I don't think there's anything much

68

there I can think of. Xavier Cugat, he kept us busy with his
ladies . . . I remember once during the New York World's Fair
he got entangled with this swimmer in the Billy Rose aquashow, a
kid called –"

He stopped and grinned.

"*No*, I can give you something even better than that!" He had
already started out of the room, searching a ring of keys he kept
on a chain in his trouser pocket. "I'll be right back, Miss
Goldsmid."

He returned ten minutes later carrying a cardboard box filled
with files and placed it on the little metal desk. "Another week it
would have all been in the shredder: nobody's going to holler now
if we tell a tale or two out of school," he said, opening the first file
with a sense of anticipation, the way a small child unwraps an
unexpected gift. "Talking about the World's Fair did it! Oh, this
is the file – not very interesting – this is just paper on the property
the Baroness bought on –"

"The Baroness, Walter?" Kate asked quietly.

"Baroness von Tegge. Theodora Glass's mother. Wasn't any
phonus-balonus title either. She had class. A looker too. Her
husband, I think the Nazis killed him."

Kate didn't say a word. She hardly dared breathe.

He took another folder, studied it for a moment, and smiled in
recognition. "I remember this. This might be something. The
deal with Noah Swan. We had fun and games with this one." He
continued reading in a raptness something like euphoria.

"What kind of deal, Walter?" Kate asked gently after more
than a minute had gone by in silence, and only the movement of
dark veins beside his temple betraying the turmoil of his feelings.

"Oh, some diddle-damn business," he said, coming back from
somewhere deep in the past. "One of those little end of nothing
things that make lawyers rich."

She smiled encouragement. "That sounds promising."

"This was a contract between Noah Swan and the Baroness."
His hands shook as he scanned the ageing pages. "The thing of it
was . . . the Baroness agreed not to write or talk about her
private life, or her daughter's business, and so on and so

forth . . . We were still on Madison in those days. Ince, Ihmsen –
before Mr Meiklejohn became a partner. We were a family then.
We worked through the night drawing up this one . . . The
Baroness in Mr Ince's office, Noah Swan in Mr Ihmsen's . . .
everyone to-ing and fro-ing. Theodora sleeping through it all like
a little angel on the couch in the waiting-room. What would she
have been then? Thirteen? Fourteen? A stunning young woman.

"I remember in the morning, seven o'clock, we all walked over
to the Plaza for breakfast. Mr Swan ordered champagne. Mr Ince
– not the present Mr Ince, his father, *Eustis* Ince, God rest his
soul – Mr Swan's wife, Barbara, also sadly no longer with us; and
Mr Ihmsen – he went last year, aged ninety-three . . . Dammit,
who else was there? A whole tableful of people. Myself. And
Cissy must have been there. Theodora and the Baroness, of
course . . . And somebody else, there was somebody else there.
A man. And maybe another woman. I can't remember."

"Why did the World's Fair remind you –"

"October 1940. The last week of the World's Fair. The Plaza
decorated blue and orange. Official colours of the Fair. Blue and
orange. Not many people remember that, I'll bet."

"Do you know why Noah Swan wanted the muniment, Walter?" Kate asked peremptorily, like a prosecutor.

"I told you. He didn't want the Baroness getting palsy-walsy
with the press boys. She loved publicity. I remember Winchell
interviewed her in Mr Ihmsen's office one time. Mr Swan and the
Baroness never saw eye to eye about publicity, and on a lot of
things, I guess. How Theodora's career should be handled I think
was at the heart of the problem. She was on her way out to
Hollywood. The Baroness wanted one thing, Mr Swan wanted
something else. And, of course, there had been the scandal over
the picture they had abandoned in London. *Romeo and Juliet*,
wasn't it? I think people were on edge about that. But Mr Ince
was a wonderful lawyer, a great negotiator – the best I've ever
seen at getting parties locked in impossible conflicts to meet
halfway."

"But people say it was Noah who was the architect of the
Theodora mystique, don't they?" Kate said, recalling a line in

one of the pieces she had read. "Some people say he invented her."

"I guess he knew what he was doing. How much is he worth today?"

"Pick a number," said Kate.

He nodded solemnly. "Theodora Glass is the big star today because of him. He was right not to want the Baroness telling the whole world every little detail about their private lives. Today you get the whole shoot what actors get up to even behind their bedroom doors. Some things should stay private."

He took out a linen handkerchief and began polishing his pince-nez. Kate wondered whether the glasses, like the rolltop desk, were part of some deep hankering for the old days.

"Anyway," said Walter, quietly sighing, "that was at the root of it: who was going to control Theodora's career – Noah or her mother. It was really just a family wrangle but you know how footling things can get blown up out of all proportion. A man gets full of indignation at nothing at all sometimes." He wiped his leaky eyes and hooked the glasses back on to his small nose. "It was all a long time ago."

"There's nothing wrong with your memory, Walter."

"I can be kind of forgetful about some things but I remember that night . . . Breakfast at the Plaza – haven't been back since!" He found a page of figures and payment schedules and turned them round for Kate to look at. "I guess this is why the Baroness finally saw things Mr Swan's way."

"Oh my," Kate said. "Some sweetener."

"He met his match that night." He took back the ageing accounts the way a grown-up removes a dangerous object from the hands of a small child.

"When did she die, Walter?"

"The Baroness? She didn't die. We get a card from her every Christmas."

"From the Baroness? Are you sure, Walter?"

An affronted look swept across his old face. "Sure I'm sure. Every Christmas," he repeated firmly. "Arrives like clockwork, same message, same card, every year: Season's greetings from

The Baroness Gisela von Tegge. Not the warmest card we get, but she always remembers Cissy and me, and that's something in this day."

"Where does it comes from, Walter? Is there an address?"

He shook his head. "It embarrasses the hell out of us, we can never send her a card back."

"You don't still happen to have –"

"Last year's card?" he interrupted in a hopeful voice, teasing her with the childish humour of old age. "No."

Kate Goldsmid made a careful note of the conversation with Walter Rusk. It was after midnight when she finished. She called Ambrose Lanigan anyway. He answered on the first ring, as he always did when he was woken from a deep sleep. It never failed to amaze Kate. She had never known anyone become so awake as quickly as Lanigan did.

He listened in silence while she told him Rusk's story.

"It would be useful to get a look at what else is in those files," he said when she had finished.

"They're already heading for shred city, Lanigan."

"How soon?"

"Walter said Meiklejohn's office has to approbate. I don't know how long that will take. Days. Weeks. Months. I've no idea. But getting in there again without beginning to look like Mata Hari . . . Let me give it some thought." Kate smiled. "You know, Lanigan, I'm getting very, very involved with this thing."

"It could give us a line on her present whereabouts. A favourite spot somewhere, a bolt-hole . . . *if* she's still around."

"She has to be, doesn't she? The cards –"

"A standing order nobody's cancelled?"

"Possible. I still get mail addressed to Frank – but mail *from* the dead?"

"Do you think Gisela and Noah could have had something going there?"

"I thought Theodora was his patootie?"

"A little double-time with mama?"

72

"There's every kind of relationship in this world, one discovers after a while, Lanigan. You going to ask Noah about any of this stuff?"

"I don't know whether it tells us much, except that Swan and the Baroness signed some kind of contract that called for a champagne breakfast at the Plaza fifty years ago."

"Interesting to watch his reaction."

"He's a poker player, Kate. He wouldn't react if the house fell in on him."

"Still convinced he's not telling you the whole story?"

"You talked to Walter Rusk – what do you think?"

"I think I'm confused. When do you see Noah again?"

"In about six hours' time," he said, looking at his watch. "Breakfast in Georgetown. I don't think he'll be serving champagne."

"Goodnight, Lanigan," Kate said, and gently replaced the receiver.

8

Truth is never easy to get at. A writer must often do disagreeable things to find the truth of a story. Morality has no meaning at all to writers like me. I'm an utter cad in that respect. A complete shit. (Robert Rider, "Writers at Work", Paris Review Interviews, Fifth Series)

Friday, September 15
London

Jay Pfeiffer waited until the waiter had poured the Calvados before he told Robert Rider about the letter from Theodora Glass. He outlined the proposition in a tone of voice that sounded neutral, but deliberately conveyed negative vibrations. He was very good at that when he wanted to be.

"She doesn't want you to be the keeper of the flame," he quoted Theodora's line with an almost imperceptible trace of mockery as he produced the letter and lingeringly smelt its complex perfume before handing it across the table. "Read it. She's unquestionably a fan."

"What do you think, Jay?" Rider asked after he had read the vellum pages for the second time. They were seated at a table with a discreet view of the whole restaurant; a territorial man, Pfeiffer had his regular corner tables, from which he could watch everything that went on, in the best restaurants from London to Los Angeles. (In contrast, Rider disliked being recognized by head waiters and bartenders; he booked tables in other people's names, refused to go to look-at-me places. Pfeiffer accused him of "living like a spy," but he also knew it was part of what gave him his style, and made him such good copy.) "It's some invite, isn't it, Jay?" Rider said.

"By my count there have been seventeen biographies – each one claimed to be definitive, naturally. What more can be said about her, for chrissake?"

Rider smiled. "You don't think it's interesting?"

"A movie actress who's done nothing except grow old for forty years? A show business bio? You need that?"

"She's not some fading movie queen who needs a book to rekindle her career, Jay."

"I'm not saying it's not a wonderful story, Robert," Pfeiffer relented a little, but no smile. "I'm saying it's not a wonderful story for you. If it had been offered to any other client of mine I'd have grabbed it in a bang." His face observed a moment of loss. He tasted his drink, switched to his let's-get-rolling voice. "Did you talk to Frank Pleskow yet? He's going crazy in New York."

Rider nodded. "We talked this evening."

"And?"

"No," Rider said affably.

Jay Pfeiffer smiled a small smile, which he used very rarely and which could be either cajoling or unsettling, or anything he wanted it to be, according to his needs; right now it was erasing the anxiety in his eyes. "All Frank's asking for is a couple of days."

"I've had talk shows up to here, Jay. I've got nothing new to say, nothing I haven't said nine hundred times before, Jay."

"Only you know that."

Rider grinned. "You mean nobody's been listening?"

"Peter Ustinov's been telling the same stories for thirty years. People still want to watch him."

"Let's talk about Theodora Glass. Do you know, she's probably made more movies that people talk about, shot for shot, line for line, than anyone in the world? Think about it."

Pfeiffer was worried by Rider's interest. He didn't expect it to be so strong. And he was disturbed to realize that his own certainty was crumbling in the face of it. "OK," he began again, slowly. "We both accept it's an interesting situation. The timing's right. If she's serious –"

"She's already got Oscar Bookbinder on her team."

"That's serious," Pfeiffer said solemnly. He had fought many great battles with the English lawyer.

"By the sound of it, she wants to start tomorrow," Rider said, picking up her letter again. "She wants the book out for next autumn."

Pfeiffer grinned. "Actresses want everything in a hurry." His first wife had been an actress.

"That doesn't make them any the less sincere."

"OK, she's sincere and she's serious. And if she delivers half of what she's suggesting here – note, I say *if*, Robert – we must consider it. But the real question is, how much of what she says is the truth? And how much of it is something she simply believes is the truth?"

"She says she's open to all the truth about herself," Rider said quietly. "Isn't that an invitation for me to find it?"

"But how much is it a question of another ageing actress making things right in her mind?" Pfeiffer struggled with the complexity of his own feelings. Ever since he could remember publishers had been beating the bushes for this book. He had been at Twenty-One the night Charlie Sugarman at Simon & Schuster offered John Huston a Mercedes just to get him an introduction to her. But it was her book he wanted. *Theodora's* book. "It's not a Robert Rider story, is it?" Pfeiffer ended the silence before it became oppressive.

"I'd have fun with it," Rider answered.

"That still doesn't make it the right book for you. People expect certain things from a Rider book. They expect –"

"Not to be bored?"

"You're never boring, Robert."

"I bore myself, Jay. I'm in a rut. Same bag of tricks. Same old territory. You know it, and soon others are going to spot it too."

"Numbers don't lie, Robert. You want numbers?"

"I got out of newspapers because I got tired of being pushed in directions I didn't want to go," Rider said quietly.

"Nobody's pushing you, Robert."

"I really think I want to do this book, Jay. Her silence and isolation all these years . . . Don't you want to know why?

Wouldn't you like some answers, Jay?"

"Maybe people don't want answers. She's a legend. Legends are made of myths. Maybe her fans prefer the myths. Maybe they want her to remain mysterious, don't want her explained away."

"To reduce the inexplicable to the explicable, to find its reason, its law, its ground . . . Who said that? Henry James, was it?"

"You think she'll let you get that close? You think she's going to let you cut the heart out of her mystery? I don't. Remoteness, enigma, distance – that's her game, that's her stock-in-trade. That stuff is oxygen to a woman like that. She gives up the smallest part of her private life, it's all over for her."

"Maybe she's tired. Maybe she wants to end the game."

Jay Pfeiffer looked at him hard as the lights began to dim, enclosing the restaurant in darkly luminous shadows. Rider sat very still, smoking his familiar brown cigarillo, the half-light intensifying the chiselled angles of his face, the red in his beard.

"OK," Pfeiffer said slowly. "Clearly there's a ton of money to be made out of this; and clearly I've got a client who's bored . . . But the risk is considerable, Robert. A genre novelist who embarks on a different course is asking for trouble. If you go ahead, and the book fucks up –"

"It won't fuck up."

"How long would it take to write?"

"With her cooperation, complete access . . . research, first draft, finished manuscript . . . Nine months."

"Nine months." Pfeiffer made a rapid calculation on his notepad. "Publication next autumn," he said tentatively, slowly writing OCTOBER? in block capitals.

"Theodora Glass." Rider spoke her name with excitement, but his voice was still not loud, it was not a carrying voice. "Nobody's going to call that shot. Keep the whole thing under wraps . . . build up the mystery, create an expectation . . . Tell me you're not a little bit excited, Jay?"

"I still think it's a gamble, Robert."

"How a gamble? It'll take me a month to find out whether she's serious. If she tries to screw us around, that's it. Forget it. We've lost a month."

"Theodora's back – and Rider's got her," Pfeiffer said almost to himself, a glint in his grey eyes like tarnished silver. He leaned back in his chair. "It's great casting," he said, seeming to wake from a pleasant dream.

"An event, Jay!" Rider repeated Pfeiffer's own favourite description of a big deal.

Pfeiffer drew a thoughtful ring round OCTOBER?

"You'll have fun putting the deal together."

Pfeiffer signalled the waiter to fetch the bill. "Nine months?"

"Maybe seven," Rider smiled encouragingly. He reopened Theodora's letter and reread the beguiling invitation before handing it back to Pfeiffer. "Let's do it. Let's make it happen. Call Bookbinder Monday. Get the ball rolling. I'll start checking out a few things."

With the thought of a big new deal to occupy him, Jay Pfeiffer was happy and at peace with the world. By the time he reached his Chelsea home that night, he had the numbers figured out in his head.

9

In my business, overreacting is how you stay alive. (Noah Swan, McCalls, August 1959)

11.30 p.m., Wednesday, September 20
Los Angeles

Lanigan dined on the Strip with a retired FBI Los Angeles bureau chief. When he got back to the Beverly Hills Hilton, the message light was blinking on and off. He dialled the operator. There were two messages. The first was from a contact at the Austrian embassy in Washington: Please call; the second was a blunt order from Noah Swan: *Return at once!*

He called United Airlines and booked a seat on the first flight to Washington at 7.30 the next morning.

But he resented Noah's peremptory summons. He was puzzled too. Why, a week after their meeting in Washington, at which Noah had given him a free hand, was he being recalled? Was the old man losing patience already? Did he think he could use him like a puppy to bring back his stick as soon as he whistled?

Lanigan poured a Scotch and paced slowly round the room, getting his thoughts together. He had been in Los Angeles forty-eight hours. Forty-eight hours is no time at all. Good intelligence work is gradual; good groundwork takes time. Seeking insights into human nature –

He stopped pacing. *Insights into human nature?* Who are you kidding, Lanigan? He sat down in a chair and closed his eyes. *I'm here in California* – he let the words form deliberately in his mind, as if they were spoken aloud – *to get the dirt on Theodora Glass*.

He sipped his drink, and smiled. Information is power, and power is a force in every situation. It was almost the first thing they taught you at The Farm. "Blackmail, gentlemen," he recalled the lecture on the use of secret knowledge, "is a businesslike expression of power."

He opened his portable typewriter. "Notes/interview Frank Maris," he typed quickly with two fingers, adding the date and place.

Two hours later he stopped typing, counted the seventeen pages of single-spaced notes and wondered what he'd got. Maris had been in Hollywood throughout the forties. The FBI's chief liaison man with studio security, an important role in the war years, when Hollywood played a big part in the nation's morale, he probably knew more about the dark side of the movie business than anyone alive. His stories were scurrilous, disrespectful, and often very funny – but what did they tell him? What did they add up to?

Lanigan read the pages again, looking for a nuanced word, a buried emotion, a connection he wasn't meant to make:

The term superstar didn't exist then, but that's what Theodora was, and Noah Swan was her creator. He was also her lover. That was an open secret out here long before it got into the papers back East. He was also supposed to be screwing her mother too. The Baroness. If just half the guys who say they screwed her are telling the truth, she must've nailed the entire *Hollywood Reporter*'s Rolodex. She was a terrific-looking dame, but crazy as a bedbug. Personally I think Noah was too smart to mess around with her. He might have been the only big potato in Hollywood who didn't screw her, as a matter of fact. Finally she went completely foofoo. Mike Romanoff told me a story . . . how she stripped off in his bar one night. He got a tablecloth over her and she was out of there so fast. You don't read those stories in the books. Because Louie Mayer knew how to bury a scandal. He could sell a movie and bury a body better than any man alive. He had a similar situation with Bette Davis's sister: Bobby. She was in and out of the rubber room at Payne Whitney all the time. His own wife practically had a season ticket to the Riggs Sanatorium up in Stockbridge. Don't know what her problem was – maybe it was Louie! As soon as the Baroness started to be a handful – oh, there's a nice story. Louie puts Otto Eisler on her case: Eisler was one of the founders of the Berlin Psychoanalytic Institute who fled out here in the thirties and struck gold. Anyway, Noah thinks Louie's taking care of Otto's fees out of his own pocket, out of the goodness of his heart. Later he finds out all the bills had been loaded on to his own production costs! But Noah told a lot of stories that don't stand up. He created suspicions about his truthfulness that have lasted to this day out here. But what's truth anyway? We get older, everything changes, even the past. We get older, our memories sing another tune . . . Don't they though?

There was more, but none of it helped. It was almost two o'clock. Lanigan booked a wake-up call for six, undressed, and went to bed thinking of Kate.

Two days later Lanigan and Noah Swan sat down to breakfast in the courtyard in Georgetown. The sumac bushes had turned scarlet, although the extraordinary summer heat lingered on. Noah wore a pink sports shirt, khaki trousers, the same outfit he wore the first time Lanigan met him. He talked about stories in the morning's news, newspapers discarded around his chair. But it wasn't until his second cup of coffee that he got round to business. Issues would play a small part in the next election, he began. Personality and character would be the issue. "People don't want to read about social programmes, what to do about Nicaragua," he said. "What did you find out in LA?"

Getting to know Noah's tricks, Lanigan was ready for the unexpected question. Without mentioning Kate, he told him about Walter Rusk. Noah listened with what appeared to be a patient smile; only it was not a smile at all but a kind of mask made with muscles that had tightened round his mouth and in his jaw.

"Walter Rusk," he said in a dry tone of voice when Lanigan finished. "No idea he was still on the hoof. Must be pushing ninety." He always exaggerated other people's ages, especially those of his contemporaries. "He tell you about the night we signed the contract?"

"Yes, sir."

"Tell me exactly what he said, Mr Lanigan."

Lanigan repeated the story Kate' had told him.

Noah nodded his head slowly. "He remembers it about right. I had to shut Gisela up. I was creating a very definite thing for Theodora, an image – that goddam aura of mystery and . . ." His voice trailed away. He looked at Lanigan across the small breakfast table, his breath smelling of coffee and strong mouthwash.

For a moment Lanigan felt he was about to tell him something important. But when he continued he merely confirmed Walter Rusk's story.

"Gisela was too damn explicit round press people. Press guys love a talky dame. A mouth and mystery don't mix. I made her an offer. She took it. That's the story. That's it. I bought her silence." He smiled again at Lanigan, but the smile was like a sudden movement of muscle he couldn't control. "She was a grabby lady, a real hog for a dollar."

"That squares with Rusk's story, sir."

"What did you expect, Mr Lanigan? There's no mystery. Don't make a mystery."

"Do you think she's dead, sir?" Lanigan asked calmly, wondering why he was treating him like the enemy.

Noah spread some marmalade on a piece of toast. "Is the Baroness dead? Newspapers say so. Death's one of the few things reporters can usually get more or less right."

Lanigan was beginning to hate his trick of avoiding answers, his oblique way of saying things, as if preparing a loophole for every sentence he uttered. "Are you telling me to forget the Baroness?" he asked.

"I'm telling you I want this book stopped," Noah said. "That's *all* I'm telling you. You're the smart apple, Mr Lanigan. But you don't seem to be making much speed."

"If you're in a car and you're lost and you go faster, you don't get home more quickly," Lanigan answered quietly. "You just get lost over a bigger area."

"I don't know why you were in California," Noah said, ignoring Lanigan's point. "Theodora's not in California. She's in the Caribbean. Been there thirty years. That's where you should be directing your attention, Mr Lanigan. That's where the answers are. Now I have a busy day, sir. You will call me as soon as you have something new to tell me."

As if he had been summoned, Michael Fortas entered the courtyard to see Lanigan to the door.

There were three messages on Lanigan's answerphone. One was from Kate, another from Ed Rosengarten; the third was from the travel agent who had been checking out flights to Trinidad. He called Kate; she was out. He called the agent and was told that there was a daily flight out of Washington at 14.00 via JFK, arriving Port of Spain thirty minutes past midnight. He booked a seat on Saturday's flight. Then the phone rang and it was his contact at the Austrian embassy whom he had asked to dig around to find out if there was anything interesting on file on Theodora. She told him that her old home in Vienna was to be bought by the government and opened as a Theodora Glass museum! Lanigan thanked her solemnly. Still grinning, he went into the kitchen, poured himself a glass of milk, and called Rosengarten, who suggested lunch at the Hay-Adams at 12.45. He did not sound happy.

Rosengarten was waiting for him at his usual table in the President Adams Room.

"Noah tells me you're off to Trinidad. What in hell you gettin' up to in Trinidad?" he asked in a furious voice as soon as Lanigan sat down.

"I can't tell you that, Rosy. Noah's business."

"And Matthew Swan is my business." His tone was still angry, but anxious too. "The old man's out of his mind taking you out of the team at this point. How long you gonna be gone, for cryin' out loud?"

"As long as it takes, I guess."

Rosengarten looked at him closely. "If it's about what I think it's about . . . Tell me straight, Lanigan. Does it in any way involve the Senator?"

"Everything Noah does involves the Senator, one way or another."

"If the sonofabitch is in some new jam –"

"Rosy, stop beating up on yourself. Noah has a problem in Port of Spain. I know the town. He's asked me to check out a couple of things down there."

"That's it?"

"That's it. End of story. Relax, you'll live longer."

Ed Rosengarten was a large, short-breathed bear of a man with stiff dark hair, shot with grey. He wore round gold-rimmed glasses, probably to make himself appear mild and scholarly. His London-made suit took twenty pounds off his appearance without hiding the fact that he was in no great cardiovascular shape; he still looked like a sixty-year-old man who chain-smoked Winstons and consumed his share of Jack Daniel's.

"Well," he said, after they had studied the menu and each settled for the *salade niçoise* and sole Americaine, with a bottle of Chassange Montrachet chosen after a short, knowledgeable discussion with the wine waiter, "anything I can do . . . anything you need . . ."

"Thanks, Rosy. I appreciate it. But it's not going to be that kind of party."

"You don't know that until the music starts."

Lanigan grinned.

"Look after yourself, ol' buddy." Rosengarten sounded calmer, but the worry stayed in his eyes all through lunch, through the fine white Burgundy, through the large glass of Remy Martin, and it was still there an hour and fifty minutes later when they said goodbye and he climbed into the chauffeured limo waiting for him on H Street.

There was another message from Kate Goldsmid on his machine when he got back to the apartment. He called her straight back.

"How ya doin', counsellor? What's on your mind?"

"I was thinking about the weekend," she said. "A Winogrand retrospective at the Guggenheim sounds interesting. What do you say? My treat."

He told her about Trinidad.

"We'll always have Athens." A Bogey lisp hid her disappointment.

He told her about his breakfast with Noah Swan, and the lunch with Rosengarten. He made them both sound more amusing than they were, playing down Noah's unpleasantness and exaggerating Rosy's suspicions. "He's convinced his boy's got a new zipper problem."

"And you're going to cover up his p-pecker tracks?"

Lanigan grinned.

"Talking of tracks, Lanigan." She said she missed him. She lowered her voice, and told him explicitly what she wanted to do to him, and what he might be interested in doing to her. It was a joke, but not completely a joke. She suggested he flew to New York that evening and caught the plane out of JFK on Saturday.

"Are you opportuning me?"

"Yes."

"On the six o'clock shuttle."

"Relax, Noah. He's just moving around, tapping his toes," Rosengarten told Noah Swan that same evening in the library of the Metropolitan Club in downtown Washington.

"He talked to the FBI guy in LA," Noah stared at Rosengarten and cracked his knuckles slowly.

"And we got to him first, right?" Rosengarten answered, smiling faintly. "Maris knew how much to say."

"But why take any risk?"

"The only way, Noah."

"Opening old wounds . . . I still think it's a big mistake."

"It was a bigger mistake pulling him out of LA. It makes you look nervous. He could start questioning your motives."

It was seven o'clock and the library was empty. Rosengarten sauntered slowly round the big room that smelt faintly of old leather and good cigars. "Let him strut his stuff," he said, not raising his voice. "That's the whole point of a BMO. Find out how secure this thing is. When Matthew announces his candidacy, ten thousand reporters'll be crawling around digging up all the shit they can find. We have to know how vulnerable we are out there."

"The book –"

"The book's a pain in the ass. We'll deal with that later."

"If she opens the bag –"

"*If* she opens the bag, we're dead," Rosengarten said roughly. But despite Noah's fears, he was convinced that Theodora wasn't going to open that particular bag. "Right now," he said, "it's only important Lanigan believes the book's the problem."

Noah frowned. "Why don't we just level with him? You trust him, don't you?"

"Trust's got nothing to do with it," Rosengarten spoke slowly. "BMOs don't work that way. We have to find out what he can dig up off his own bat. We can't help him. He has to find our weak points . . ."

"What about Walter Rusk?"

"I'll take care of Rusk," Rosengarten said. His manner was regretful, but not apologetic. "Leave Rusk to me."

"Jesus Christ," Noah said in a quiet voice.

Rosengarten said, "Settle down. Don't worry."

"I do worry, dammit," Noah said. "Tell me about this BMO business again."

"BMO – Barium Meal Operation. At its simplest: one of our own people is ordered to break into a Company operation. Only he doesn't know it's a Company operation. We monitor his progress, get a kinda X-ray picture of every move he makes. We find out whether an operation is penetrable . . . learn where it's vulnerable."

"And it works?"

Rosengarten hesitated. "We had some success with it at Langley."

"*Some* success? What the fuck does that mean? *Some success?*"

"Noah, if Lanigan can't trace anything back, nobody can." Rosengarten looked at his watch. "Now, sir, I think our table's waiting."

They took the narrow elevator upstairs to the dining-room, Noah muttering "barium meal, barium meal" under his breath, like an incantation he was trying to believe in.

10

*Once described as being part Machiavellian and
part Mephistophelean (a charge which resulted
in him being awarded a penny libel damages),
Jay Pfeiffer enjoys nothing more than pitting his
wits against someone in his own league. (Ray
Hawkey,* Observer *magazine, August 25, 1991)*

Wednesday, September 20
London

Like Jay Pfeiffer, Oscar Bookbinder – a veteran show business
lawyer who had been Theodora Glass's UK representative for
more than a quarter of a century – also had a formidable
reputation as a tough and wily negotiator. And it was not simply
Pfeiffer's own sense of gamesmanship and challenge but a mark
of respect for his guest that caused him to choose their lunch
venue with the care of a chess master.

The Savoy Hotel Restaurant was not his favourite place (its
decor – a curiously eclectic mixture of classical motifs, art deco
and kitsch – was too cloying for his taste; and the food, although
good of its kind, a shade too *nouvelle*) but he had chosen it
because the room possessed just the proper atmosphere of
understated grandeur in which to talk megabucks without appear-
ing to be rapacious. He also knew it was not one of the lawyer's
regular eating places, and that was important too.

The two men chatted amiably through the champagne and the
first course; they had many mutual friends in their overlapping
worlds, and there was no shortage of amusing gossip and those
pieces of information which men like Bookbinder and Pfeiffer file
away in that part of their brains which make them such effective
and unpredictable negotiators.

Bookbinder was conservatively dressed, with silver hair, silver-rimmed spectacles, and exceedingly bright eyes in a lean, patrician face. Born some sixty-six years ago in the East End of London, he made no attempt to keep his cockney origins out of his voice. He was very good company, and even those who feared him agreed that he had a frank and uncomplicated manner that was unusual for a lawyer of his reputation. He liked to talk man to man, and man to man he had often settled battles that would have made him infinitely richer than he undoubtedly was had he allowed them to go to court.

"Is your client going to deliver, Oscar?" Pfeiffer asked casually during the hors d'oeuvres stage of their conversation.

"I don't know," Bookbinder answered thoughtfully. "But if she wasn't utterly serious in her intent, I don't think she would have chosen your boy, do you?"

"You sound as if you disapprove of the whole idea?"

"She makes me anxious for her welfare sometimes," Bookbinder said glumly.

"Why do you think she's doing it?"

"Again, I have to tell you truthfully: I don't know."

"Care to hazard a guess?"

Bookbinder smiled. "Those who know about her do not talk; those who talk almost certainly do not know," he said.

"She wants to put the record straight?"

"Possibly."

Pfeiffer smiled. "Next year's elections in the States – a coincidence, you think?"

Bookbinder thought about it for a few moments, watching a line of barges being towed upriver in the pale autumnal sunshine. "She's been considering this book for a long time," he said, finally. "In 1974 she was talking about it. Missy Miller talked her out of it then. Why she has decided to go ahead at this precise moment, I repeat: I don't know. But, to answer your question – and I understand why you ask it – I am sure the elections in the United States are unrelated."

Both men knew that this conversation was private, an honest exchange between professional equals, and not to be used as a weapon in the serious talks that would follow. And when the paupiettes of sole arrived, Pfeiffer said pleasantly: "Well, fun though this is, Oscar, I guess we'd better start earning our keep."

"Let me restate my client's proposition," Bookbinder answered at once. And without reference to a single note, he repeated all the important points made in Theodora's letter to Pfeiffer, plus several additional conditions which the agent knew were of his own invention, thrown in to test the temperature.

Pfeiffer thought he had never seen a more professional performance. Watching him operate was an education. He had an uncanny ability to remain perfectly polite and urbane while dispossessing his face and voice of all expression; his language was precise, his words were exact and incapable of being misunderstood. He was, thought Pfeiffer, the total negotiating machine.

"We agree that your client is given exclusive and unfettered access to my client's archives, correspondence and personal reminiscences. And the copyright will be held jointly by our respective clients."

Pfeiffer nodded noncommittally, and waited for him to continue.

The lawyer tasted his fish. He was in no hurry. "Excellent," he said, judiciously, after some thoughtful mastication. He sipped his wine, dabbed his lips with his napkin. "I am instructed to suggest a seventy-five, twenty-five split."

"My client might settle for seventy-five," Pfeiffer said.

Bookbinder smiled faintly. "Twenty-five is the offer."

Pfeiffer's eyes saddened with an expression of disappointment. "Robert Rider is a top-gun novelist, Oscar. He's among the top four or five best-selling writers in the world . . . Clancy, King, Tom Harris . . . Your proposal isn't even in the ballpark."

"That's a pity," said Bookbinder. "This sauce is superb, by the way. Mushrooms, béchamel . . . a hint of white pepper?"

"I'm sorry," said Pfeiffer, as if the game were already over. "Theodora and Rider – they were a dream ticket. The English-language rights alone were worth – ten million?"

"Sterling?"

"Dollars," said Pfeiffer. "But then there would have been the foreign rights, book club rights, serial rights, movie rights – you name it."

"*You* name it, Jay."

"Plenty," Pfeiffer smiled.

"Plenty is a good place to start," Bookbinder said.

And so the bargaining began. Barely aware of what they were eating, they worked out compromises and middle ways and happy mediums until the money side was agreed: fifty-fifty. Then came the question of right of approval of the manuscript. Theodora would have the right to check it for accuracy of fact but not opinion or style, said Pfeiffer. Theodora could not be put in a position where she has no say in what is written about her – and that was not negotiable, said Bookbinder. If she wants a ghost, let her hire a hack, said Pfeiffer. The Mexican standoff lasted several minutes before Bookbinder seemed to relent a little: I'm prepared, he said, to have a clause stating that our approval will not be unreasonably withheld. Who is to judge what is reasonable or unreasonable, said the agent. And so on they went again, crossing t's, crossing bridges, dotting i's. The manuscript would be no less than a hundred and fifty thousand words long. Rider would pay his own costs to and from Santa Aloe; Theodora would provide a beach-house, food and drink, a personal cook/housekeeper and maid, word processor, Xerox and fax machines, a dune buggy and a motorboat. Rider would pay all research expenses and the cost of all illustrations demanded by the publisher over and above those pictures that would be provided from Theodora's own personal collection.

"Now all that's out of the way," Bookbinder smiled, helping himself to more coffee, "when and exactly how is the book to be written?"

"Rider will begin as soon as we've exchanged contracts. After that, I imagine it will go something like this: They'll get the basic material down on tape. As each tape is filled, a secretary will transcribe it – although Rider might prefer to do this himself."

"Why would he want to make more work for himself?"

"He can absorb the material faster and more thoroughly when

he bangs it out himself. And he's a stickler about security. Also Theodora may prefer not to involve a third party. These kind of interviews can get very personal, Oscar. The relationship between a writer and his subject, especially in this kind of deal, gets extremely close. They get into some sensitive areas. It's like a love affair. Sometimes it *is* a love affair."

"I'm sure of that," Bookbinder said gravely.

"My client isn't a skin-deep feature hack, Oscar. He's an interrogator, an inquisitor" – Pfeiffer laughed, he didn't want to scare Bookbinder off the whole deal – "a prober of people's souls!"

Bookbinder wasn't fooled by the laugh. "He shouldn't push her," he said quietly.

"He won't. He's smart. But he's going to want to show the shadows as well as the sunlight."

The lawyer nodded. "You were saying – about transcribing the tapes?"

Pfeiffer nodded. "Theodora's going to be revealing details of her life – private matters, some pretty intimate things, we hope – details that she might not wish anyone else to share . . . untreated, so to speak."

"It's a good point," Bookbinder said, although "untreated" was not the word he would have used. "Continue."

"Once the story's on paper, Rider will shape it into a first draft. Theodora will have an opportunity to make her comments. Having taken note of her suggestions, he will produce a final draft. Theodora will give her approval. And a locked room, sealed bid auction will be announced. I will agent the deal, of course," Pfeiffer said, signing the bill that had discreetly appeared on the table.

"After the deal you've screwed out of me, I must insist on it," Bookbinder said solemnly.

"Will you inform Theodora?"

"I will call her this afternoon."

"My commission comes off the top."

"I imagined it would," Bookbinder said dryly.

They made their way to the Strand lobby. "I presume Rider

will be talking to people who knew Theodora, who worked with her in the old days?"

"He'll use all the sources he can," Pfeiffer said carefully, wondering what last-minute condition Bookbinder was going to throw into the ring.

"Then he must talk to Aaron Flagg."

Pfeiffer knew the name. "Her publicist, wasn't he?"

"He was a little more than a publicist," said Bookbinder, his tone mildly rebuking. "He worked on her first film here in London in the blitz – *Romeo and Juliet* – and he worked on her last film in Hollywood. He's retired now, of course. Lives in New York. Has a beautiful place on Martha's Vineyard. If you wish, I'll write him a letter."

Pfeiffer nodded in agreement. "But it's important we keep the deal under wraps as long as we can, Oscar. Particularly we don't want Noah Swan getting early wind of it. He's a litigious bastard, and I don't think he's going to be too thrilled."

"You're right," Bookbinder said mildly.

"What we don't need is a bunch of Yank lawyers crawling all over us."

"We can trust Flagg. He fell out with Noah, most people do, eventually, they haven't spoken for years. I'll make a point to tell him to keep it under his hat. Your fellow will like him. He's an old newspaper man, like himself."

"Aaron Flagg," Pfeiffer nodded his approval, and made a note to tell Rider to put him at the top of his list of people to see.

11

Noah Swan changed my life. If I hadn't met him that day in Berlin in 1936, perhaps I would not be who I am today. I would have been an actress, that was already destiny. But I would not have been Theodora Glass. Mr Swan created her. He made her unique. My heart is awed within me when I think of all the things he did. (Theodora Glass, letter to Irene Mayer Selznick, December 2, 1949)

Wednesday night, September 20
Santa Aloe

THEODORA'S TAPE

Most of the things I am telling you now, Missy, I know to be true because I was there and heard and saw them happen, and some of it is in the history books. The rest is what Mama told me, and which of course may not be the whole truth, since Mama did not believe there was a need for truth in everyone.

If I'm to be totally honest, I don't know whether I was present the night Vati wept when he heard that poor little Dr Dollfuss had bled to death in the Ballhausplatz (because his Nazi kidnappers refused to bandage his wounds), or whether I only imagine I was because Mama told me the story so many times. This was the summer of 1934, and people who had said that the Nazis would never win power in Austria were no longer so sure.

This must have been the time Vati got a bodyguard. His name was Kleist, a former sergeant in Vati's battalion, a large, red-faced fellow with hair like a blacking-brush. He sat around the kitchen reading comic books, and constantly saying to cook, Shall we have a little snack? – *Sollen wir eine kleine Jause nehmen?*

Although I was too young to understand the significance of Kleist's presence, I remember him very clearly because he always made me laugh and clicked his heels and bowed to me every morning and sometimes pretended to skid round corners like Charlie Chaplin. I shall never forget him, and the terrible tragedy in Italy . . . But don't let me jump ahead, Missy. You must correct me when I do.

So, on the surface anyway, life on Löwelstrasse appeared to go on as always. We continued to go to Mass every Sunday morning at Mama's favourite church in the Taborstrasse. I appeared in another movie, made at the Sascha studios in Vienna. It was a small role in not a very good picture, but it caught the eye of a UFA producer, and I was asked to go to Germany to test for Thekla (a sort of German Juliet) in Schiller's *Wallenstein*. That test is now in the UCLA collection of movie memorabilia, by the way. It is very good.

Mama, you can imagine, was not happy in Berlin! She made no effort to be charming to the producers, or to flirt a little bit with the director, which she always did. She showed no interest in the script, or helping me with my lines. At night she did not go out of the hotel, but stayed with me in our room. I now know, of course: *she was terrified*. Berlin in 1936 was not a nice place to be for a woman with Mama's history. I remember the swastika flags flying in the streets, Nazi uniforms everywhere, people *Heil Hitlering* each other when they met. But I don't remember any fear. That came later.

It was an extraordinary episode, when you think about it, Missy. Mama didn't want me to get the role, and yet she agreed to go to Berlin for the test. *Why?* The sets had already been built, the producers loved my test – yet the picture was never made. *Why?*

It can only have been fate.

Why else were we drawn there, if not to meet Noah Swan?

We were all staying at the Adlon Hotel. He sent Mama flowers, the most lovely roses, and hand-made chocolates for me. Before he *was* Noah Swan he behaved like Noah Swan.

Somebody said that once. And it is true. He was only twenty-three at this time.

In a little note to Mama, sent with the flowers, he said that he had seen my test and thought I was wonderful. How he got to see the test I don't know. He was always a little mysterious – that's how he wanted to be, of course. He started inventing Noah Swan when he was thirteen years old. He told me that once. His father had been in the business and made and lost a fortune. As a child Noah had played on film lots and seemed to know everybody. He was still only fifteen when he got a job in the publicity department at Paramount. He tried his hand at a couple of screenplays which were never produced. Later he was David Selznick's assistant for a brief period. Then he went to Europe. He put a little money into a few small European pictures in return for a piece of the United Kingdom rights. He talked Max Beaverbrook into investing in some of his deals. He had great charm, and it worked just as well on men as it did on women.

We didn't meet him until we were checking out of the Adlon. He introduced himself in the lobby. He was handsome in a way that has gone out of fashion. He was tall – six feet tall – and, I have to say it: skinny – he couldn't have weighed more than 140 pounds wringing wet. He was also ungainly – is that the word, Missy? Not ungainly as if he didn't properly belong – I don't mean that – Noah Swan always knew he belonged! He was ungainly the way Gary Cooper was ungainly, and John Huston when he was young. I remember also he had fine blond-red hair brushed straight back and even to my young eyes he looked far too young for the stogie in his mouth.

He was going to London. We were returning to Vienna. We shared a limousine out to the old Kaiserhof aerodrome. I remember how his dark business suit stood out among the German uniforms that were everywhere in Berlin that summer. (The Olympics were about to start, I remember that.) I cannot recall everything that was said that day, but at the heart of it was his belief that I had a great future as an actress – *if* I were handled wisely. "She's got it. Don't throw it away," he said to Mama.

Mama resented his know-it-all attitude – she unsheathed one of her steeliest smiles for him, but I could see that she was also impressed by his knowledge of the business, and the serious way he expressed himself: "*You've got to be picky about the roles you take,*" I remember he said to me. "*You knock bits off yourself when you take a bad part.*" How did he know things like that? Who taught him such wisdom? It knocked me off my feet, but Mama thought he was patronizing us, although I don't think he knew it, because I eventually found out that he treated everyone that way.

When we said goodbye, my parting memory of him, he took hold of my chin and looked into my face for a long moment. "Good bones, great eyes . . . Lose ten pounds, lighten up your hair and" – this I remember vividly – "you'll please the goddam gods." You can hear him saying it, can't you, Missy? *You'll please the goddam gods!* Listening to those voices in my mind – Mama's voice when she was young, and Noah's voice beginning to become the voice people recognize now, the voice they imitate when they tell Noah Swan stories – so much comes back.

It was in Berlin that I first became aware of Mama's half-resentful dependence on me. "You and I are very strange creatures together," she said to me one evening in our little room at the Adlon. "Sometimes I wonder who is the finer actress, you or I?"

I didn't understand. "You're not an actress," I told her.

I remember her laugh. I can hear it.

"We all act," she said. "Once you understand that you understand a great deal."

Missy, there is so much here . . . So much I didn't know I remembered. Things come into my head *pop-pop-pop* – unbidden. And I know there are things I must soon face for which I must be strong . . . So no more tonight, Missy. Tomorrow I will be strong again . . .

12

The Baroness Gisela von Tegge had the arrogance of beauty, the arrogance of a woman who knew all her life that men and wealth would come easily to her. (Garson Kanin, Noah and Theodora)

Friday, September 22
New York City

They made love, showered, and made love again. Kate wanted him even more the second time.

"You don't make love like a lawyer," Lanigan told her afterwards.

"I cook like one," she said.

They dined at Positano's, late, after the bridge and tunnel crowd had gone. "We are both extremely hungry," she told the waiter in her best Vassar girl tone that slyly mocked the passion that had filled and shaken her voice an hour before. They dined upstairs; oysters on the half shell, and *filets de boeuf en croûte*. Kate had half a bottle of Corton Charlemagne; Lanigan sipped a Mexican lager. They both finished with her favourite *cassis sorbet*.

"I finished *Noah and Theodora*," Kate said when the coffee arrived, sensing it was the subject he was now ready to talk about.

"What's the hook between those two, Kate? After all these years, why the hell do they still hate and fear each other?"

"Do they?"

Lanigan shrugged. "How does the book end?"

"The famous exit. She walks away . . . The last great mystery."

"Everything's a fucking mystery with those two."

Kate smiled, thinking about it. "Sometimes we call things mysterious because we don't yet know the facts. They often turn out not to be mysterious at all."

"Isn't that the book that caused all the fuss a few years ago – the suggestion that she might be Matthew Swan's mother?"

"It was a rumour in Hollywood in the sixties. Kanin goes over it with a fine-tooth comb, shoots it full of holes."

"You believe him?"

"Yeah," she said thoughtfully. "He sold me."

"He was a director, wasn't he?"

"A real insider. Had a clutch on everything that happened in Tinsel Town. Never shy about letting pussycats out of the bag. Remember the book he did on Tracy and Kate Hepburn?"

Lanigan shook his head. "There's an agenda here I can't figure, Kate."

His uncertainty drew her to him. She wondered why she was becoming frightened for him. "You should read *Noah and Theodora*. The Baroness is a great character." She didn't want to get deep, not tonight. "She'd make a wonderful heroine in a novel. A great beauty, dozens of lovers. I'm surprised nobody's written a book about her."

"Noah says she's dead."

"She's sending cards from somewhere, Lanigan."

"You believe Walter Rusk's story? You'd put him on the stand?"

Now Kate's silence was a lawyer's silence, a pondering silence. "If it were a question of fact about the past . . . Yes," she said, finally, "I would. The forties are probably far more real for him than last week."

Lanigan asked for the check, but Kate had already taken care of it.

In the taxi, he said: "I'd like to talk with Rusk."

"He lives in Jackson Heights. With his sister. I certainly think you should talk to her."

"Why?"

"Women remember things differently from men."

"Cissy," Lanigan said, to show he remembered her name.

"We'll call them in the morning."

In bed, her body felt warm and familiar to him. They made love gently, slowly, with a kind of languid exhaustion, until they drifted into the deepest sleep.

Kate was standing in the doorway when he woke. He said, "Why is the party of the first part up and dressed, while the party of the second part's still in bed naked as a frog?"

"I had some reading to do. I've got coffee on."

They began calling the Rusks at ten. There was no answer, they continued calling every half-hour.

It was a lazy, sensual morning. They were both aware that once again their time together was running out. They sat and talked, read the papers; they went downstairs to the deli and bought cos lettuce, red and yellow peppers, tomatoes, fennel seeds, button mushrooms and mozzarella cheese for an Italian salad lunch. It was another bright Indian summer day, and they ate on the terrace of Kate's apartment on the river on 63rd Street. She wore a cream Chambray shirt and a silk tie with club stripes. Lanigan said she looked eighteen years old. She was the first to mention the impending parting. What time was his flight?

"Seventeen forty-five. Arrive Port of Spain midnight thirty."

"That's the godawfulest hour to arrive any place, Lanigan."

He folded the yellow lawn napkin Kate had embroidered with flowers. "Always arrive in a town by night," he said.

At two o'clock there was still no answer from the Rusks. Maybe the phone was out of order; Kate suggested they leave early and drop by the apartment on the way to Kennedy. The businesslike proposal broke the lingering sense of tristesse. They both felt it, and smiled.

The Rusks' apartment was on Eighty-second Street, north of Roosevelt Avenue. DOORBELL BROKE KNOCK, read a green ink notice stuck to the door of apartment 4A. Lanigan knocked, loudly, several times.

"You lookin' for the Rusks?" The speaker was a black man in his fifties with Bundy Building Engineer printed in yellow on the pocket of his green shirt. "If you is, they gone. Both of 'em."

"Are you a neighbour, sir?" Kate asked.

"Janitor." He jerked a thumb at the statement on his shirt. "Give no mind to this bullshine, Miss."

"Do you know when they'll be back?" Lanigan asked.

"They won't be back. They gone."

"You mean they've moved away?" Kate asked incredulously.

"Didn't say a word till the limo arrived." He produced a large bunch of keys and opened the door. They followed him into the apartment. Furniture, curtains, carpets were still there. A large old wardrobe still contained Walter's suits, heavy coats, and Cissy's things; a chest of drawers was filled up with neatly folded sweaters, pyjamas, woollen underwear. But the drawers in an old-fashioned bureau in the sitting-room were open and empty; and there was a fade mark on the wall where a small picture had been removed. Everything was spotlessly clean. The dishes had been washed and stacked in the kitchen; the beds made; a small vase of flowers stood still fresh on a sideboard. Yet the place already had an abandoned feeling. Even the bluebells on the shower curtain seemed desolate. And there was that faint inexplicable smell that gets into rooms in which people have grown old.

The janitor showed them around with a kind of stunned proprietorial air. "'Jes clean it out, Mr Pickens,' they said to me. 'Jes take anythin' you want.' They coulda handed me a boo, right?"

"Do you know where they've gone?" Lanigan asked quietly.

Pickens shook his head. "Janitors is supposed to know more about the neighbourhood than the cops do, but I tell you, I never figured Mr Rusk and Miss Rusk skyin' off."

"Do you recall anything about the limo, Mr Pickens? Was it a rental, did it have New York plates –"

"A limo's a limo. I don't notice a thing." A look of suspicion came into the janitor's gentle eyes, which were the colour of ripe plums. He looked quickly from Kate to Lanigan. "You friends of the Rusks?"

"Old friends," Lanigan said. He gave him a fifty dollar bill and

his telephone number in Washington. "If you remember anything, if you hear from them, would you call me on this number,
Mr Pickens? Leave a message on the answer machine if I'm not
in. I'll get straight back to you."

In the car, Kate said: "How did this thing get so complicated?"

"Those old file papers over at Ince Ihmsen. I'd really like to get
a look at them before they go to shred, Kate."

"Jesus, Lanigan, that won't be easy."

"Will you try?"

"Sure I will," she said uneasily.

They drove in silence for a while.

"What do you make of it, Kate?"

"They've decided to go and live somewhere warm," she said.

"How do you figure that out?"

"They left all their winter things behind," she said.

"That's not bad for an amateur," he grinned.

"OK, how about you, Sherlock. What's your theory?"

"I'll tell you when we get to know each other better," he said.

Kate laughed, but sadly, not knowing why it made her sad.
"Take good care of yourself, Lanigan," she told him when they
said goodbye.

She drove slowly back to the city.

Her sadness lingered, and troubled her.

13

Titles of nobility were banned in the Austrian Republic after World War I. Which meant you could not be listed in the telephone book. Otherwise, they were very much respected and used. (New Yorker, *May 13, 1991*)

Saturday, September 23
Santa Aloe

THEODORA'S TAPE

I have been reading Mama's Vienna journals again, and you know how sad this makes me, Missy. She records and keeps fresh everything that was cruel and dangerous and hard in her life. With all her faults, she was utterly alone with her fear and the pain.

I know what you are going to say, *If the past makes you so unhappy, forget the past, forget the goddam book*. But I can't forget, Missy. Even though I am getting into things I don't want to get into I have no choice.

So . . . the storm clouds gathered in Europe, but Vati seemed not to take them seriously. "At last we have peace," he told the German newspaper *Deutsche Allgemeine Zeitung* in 1937 when Austria signed a Treaty of Friendship with Germany. On the surface he continued to be the perfect diplomat, but he knew that the Nazis' recognition of Austria's independence would not last. Behind the scenes he was already preparing a resistance group to fight the Nazi invasion and occupation of Austria when it came.

As a cover for his activities – and an opportunity "to read the minds of those who will soon be our oppressors", Mama wrote in her journal on May 16, 1937 – the glamorous parties at Löwelstrasse continued. Sometimes press photographers waited on the sidewalk to catch the guests arriving and departing. Herr von Papen, Hitler's representative in Austria, was a frequent guest; Hermann Goering came several times. We can make a proper list for Mr Rider later, Missy.

Sometimes I was invited to meet the guests before they went into dinner. I was always uncomfortable on these occasions, not knowing what role I was expected to play. Vati wanted me simply to be his little girl, and to show me off to his friends; Mama expected me to make a kind of guest appearance, to be the child star. Shortly after the meeting with Noah in Berlin she began encouraging me, for these appearances, to wear rouge on my cheeks, and some discreet mascara.

I was eleven years old, and preferred not to be noticed at all, simply to listen to the conversations. The men discussed wine, and the calibres of hunting guns; the women seemed to talk about nothing except King Edward VIII and Mrs Simpson. Until one evening I heard a woman say to Vati, *"What are we going to do about these Jews?"* He asked what *she* would do, and she said, *"I don't know, but a pogrom here and a pogrom there is no longer the answer."*

Not long after this things started to change and somebody painted on our door, *Der ewige Jude* . . .

Ach! This is more hard than I thought, Missy. I can't go on with it tonight. I'm sorry. I did try.

14

*Noah Swan believed that there was no villainy in
the world to which fame and fortune could not
reconcile a star – and I regret to have to admit it,
he was right. (Baroness Gisela von Tegge, Life
magazine, July 1967)*

Sunday a.m., September 24
Port of Spain, Trinidad

Lanigan couldn't sleep. Because he had nothing better to do at six
thirty on a rainy Sunday morning in Trinidad, he put on the white
terrycloth hotel bathrobe and sat down at the writing desk in the
living-room of his small suite.

1. Women with grievances are natural liars – Noah Swan

he wrote at the top of a sheet of the hotel notepaper. And then he
wrote:

2. What grievances?
3. Walter/Cissy AWOL – Connection??
4. Baroness – dead or alive???

He stopped and read the short list, and smiled. He still had the
professional agent's fascination for ambiguity, for unanswered
questions. He was patient, he could live with uncertainty; amateurs reached wrong conclusions out of frustration, or sheer
exhaustion. But he also knew that time was running out. It had
been nearly two weeks since Noah Swan sent him out on this
extraordinary mission. Now here he was in the Caribbean, thirty
miles off Theodora's little rock, and he still didn't have a single
chip to bargain with.

He had nothing but threads.

He found the notes he'd made of his meeting with Frank Maris in Los Angeles. On the balcony he read the pages again. And again he could find nothing of value, nothing he could use. He hated admitting it, but perhaps Noah Swan was right to have closed him down in LA. LA was not the right place to start.

It was almost eight o'clock. He went inside, called room service, ordered coffee, croissants and juice. He took a shower, shaved and dressed. When he returned to the sitting-room a waiter was setting out his breakfast beneath a parasol on the balcony.

Over breakfast he wrote a cable to Noah Swan giving him his hotel and telephone number in Port of Spain.

He poured a second cup of coffee, and carried it to the edge of the little balcony. Ten storeys below, although the rainy season was not yet over, beach boys were raking the sand and putting out rows of sunbeds by the pool . . . like poachers laying traps for early tourists, Lanigan reflected. But his thoughts quickly turned back to Noah. Noah continued to puzzle him. He couldn't work him out at all. He wasn't sure he could trust him. And the unanswered questions were growing all the time. Why had Noah pulled him out of California so suddenly, for instance? Like so much else in this business, even when he half-admitted to himself that Noah might have been right, it made no sense at all. Would Noah pull him out of Trinidad as peremptorily, he wondered?

No, dammit! he told himself vehemently. He picked up the cable he had written and tore it into small pieces. This time he'd play it real cosy. If Noah Swan wants me out of here, he thought, as he flushed the pieces down the toilet bowl, he'll have to find me first.

At nine o'clock he called Andy Scherrer.

"You never write, you never return my calls –"

"You son of a gun!" Scherrer recognized his voice at once. "Where are you?"

"Port of Spain. The Bewick."

"The Bewick's good, a little pricey. Kate with you?"

"No."

"That's a shame. Free for lunch? Sure you are. Get your butt over here. Annie'll be pleased as the deuce."

Lanigan felt affection stir in him. "It'll be great to see you guys. Can Annie still charm up those nifty ribs?"

"Sure thing. I'll put a bottle of Vouvray on ice, just for you."

Andy Scherrer had been Lanigan's deputy in Greece. It was Scherrer's indisposition that had forced Lanigan to attend the justice minister's reception in Athens at which he and Kate first met. Now chief of station in Trinidad, Scherrer lived in Blanchisseuse, a French Creole village on the other side of Las Cuevas Bay.

Lanigan rented a Ranger pickup and took the North Coast Road, over the Saddle, the pass through the ridge which separates the valleys of Santa Cruz and Maraval. Trinidad had the best roads in the Caribbean, thanks to Pitch Lake – 105 acres of hot tar, 290 feet deep – which had not only paved the streets of the world from Lake Shore Drive to the Champs Elysées, but was also the final resting place of many Caribbean gangsters.

He was still amusing himself with these facts, stored away in some deep recess of his mind when he was station chief, as the road emerged from the rain forest and turned sharply along the edge of the range. Trees and rocks dropped into bay after bay of Caribbean sea. This was one of his favourite views in the world.

But Lanigan had other things on his mind. How much could he tell Scherrer? How much could he impose on their friendship? He desperately needed the station chief's help. But involving him even marginally in a business that deeply involved a man who might very well be the next President of the United States he knew was unfair to the CIA man. Scherrer was thirteen years older than Lanigan, and Trinidad was his last important station. Lanigan did not want to embroil him in anything that could cause him to end his career on an embarrassing note if some corner of this thing came unstuck.

These thoughts were still going round his mind when Lanigan arrived in Blanchisseuse.

Anne Scherrer hadn't changed a bit. Thin as a stic., the same boyish, honey-coloured legs, flat chest and hard little nipples jutting beneath the T-shirt; her hair, a little lighter than it had been in Athens, still worn straight and short. Lanigan suspected that Andy Scherrer was only half-kidding when he said that she appealed to the fag in him.

They lunched in the garden of their Victorian cottage (discreetly modernized and enlarged, with a studio hidden in the trees). They talked about old times, retold their favourite stories, got their familiar laughs. But Andy Scherrer was a listener, a watcher. Lanigan knew that he was watching him now, listening for a word or a hesitation that would indicate why he had come.

It rained and they hurried inside the pretty cottage. At four o'clock the rain stopped as suddenly as it came, and Scherrer suggested he and Lanigan go for a spin in his new racing dinghy. "You remember anything I taught you?"

"A port tack yacht keeps clear of a starboard tack yacht?"

"Well, we shouldn't hit anything anyway."

The station chief enjoyed the trip a lot more than Lanigan did. A strong wind came up out of nowhere, as it does at that time of year in the Caribbean, and the small boat lurched and rolled. Lanigan was grateful when they tied up in the dinghy park.

"You're not here for the tan, so let's hear what's on your mind," Scherrer said, walking back to his blue Chevrolet with its unobtrusive armour plate parked up behind the coast road.

"Santa Aloe," Lanigan said quietly.

"We haven't filed on that place since the Greek got out."

"My interest's in the present occupier."

"You're full of surprises."

"I'm a beggarman, Andy."

"What do you want?" Scherrer said, when they were in the car. His watchful eyes shifted to the rearview mirror, to the mirror on the door, then turned enquiringly to Lanigan. "What kind of merchandise are we talking about here?"

"Anything I can put on the table."

"Something to take the play away from the other side?"

"The old story," said Lanigan.

It was a conversation between men who had spent their working lives inside milieux and atmospheres of secrecy and caution, of ritualized idioms and economical responses. It made their speech sound strange, but it was a kind of bond, an idiosyncrasy of the game they played and at which they both excelled.

They sat for a few minutes without speaking.

"Stay for dinner," Scherrer ended the silence. "We'll drive into Las Cuevas. There's a new French restaurant I've been promising to take Annie to." He started the engine. "Drop by Frederick Street in the morning. Eleven o'clock. See what I can find."

Lanigan arrived at the unmarked building on Frederick Street at a minute to eleven. A tall, black secretary wearing a cream skirt three inches above the knee, pale stockings, white blouse, and an expensive scent, took him straight up to Scherrer's office on the top floor.

"I'm still pissed with you for grabbing the check," Scherrer growled with just enough warmth to pass as a welcome. He handed Lanigan a small blue file card, containing two typed nine-digit numbers. "Here's your party's current number. She changes it every six months. She's still got that Hollywood paranoia about phone numbers. The second number is Missy Miller's line. She's the hidden hand over there. Everything goes through her. Missy Miller," he repeated the name.

"There's a permanent staff of eighteen. Twelve women – couple of cooks, maids, hairdresser, a masseuse and make-up woman. There's one butler-type guy, from Martinique. An elegant sonofabitch, about seven feet tall, gay, speaks French without an accent but without any r's either. Gets up in livery on special occasions. There are two gardeners, two general duty guys, and a uniformed pistolero who provides the protection. They've all signed loyalty oaths. She also has a phobia about gossip writers and the paparazzi."

The secretary came in with a tall pot of coffee on a tray. She moved slowly, a smile on her coral-pink lips. She filled two cups, handed one to Lanigan, the other to Scherrer. She departed without a word, smiling, her high heels on the wooden floor the only sound.

"Jilly Bohlen-Williams," Scherrer said, reading his mind. "With a hyphen."

"And you said the good old days were over."

Scherrer handed him another file card. "Here's a list of some of the people she's entertained in the last three years."

Lanigan picked out the name of an English interior decorator. "Saw him on TV – doesn't know whether he's Arthur or Martha."

"You'll find quite a few of those in there," Scherrer said.

"What about Theodora?"

"Boys when she's sober, girls when she's not. That's the rumour."

Jilly Bohlen-Williams returned. "The pictures you asked for, sir." She had a Bostonian voice. "And this arrived from London." She handed Scherrer a cable thermoprinted in *Time Urgent Intelligence* red.

Lanigan watched her leave. He was not a promiscuous man, but she made him regret that he didn't have time to get to know her better.

Scherrer read the cable slowly. Then he looked at it for a long time. "This might be something for you," he said finally, handing it across his desk to Lanigan.

Lanigan read it aloud: FYI ROBERT RIDER EN ROUTE SANTA ALOE STOP NEGOTIATING ISLAND PRINCIPAL'S BIO STOP NO ACTION REQUIRED STOP INFORM LONDON STATION ARRIVAL AND DEPARTURE.

Lanigan shook his head as if to say he would never cease to be amazed at the omnipotence of the Agency. "Now you know why I'm here – and for whom, right?"

"These are the latest pictures." Scherrer ignored the question, gazing down at the photographs of Theodora spilled across his desk. "Still a piece of ass, though, ain't she?" He folded his arms behind his head. "Annie says the really great broads never get old from the waist down."

"Andy, why does Robert Rider rate TUI status?"

Scherrer looked him in the eyes. "You ever read his stuff? Spills nearly as many beans as Heinz bakes. We like to know where he is, who he sees, who he gets it from. You know the procedure." He grinned, and hit his desk with the flat of his hands. "Helluva writer though, ain't he?"

Lanigan picked up the cable and read it again. A vague and complicated feeling of anger and inadequacy stirred inside him. "I really don't need this right now."

Scherrer breathed in deeply and exhaled. He smiled gently to show he sympathized. "Somebody Up There's getting antsy about the book?"

"And that was before *this* guy showed up."

It was raining again.

That evening Ambrose Lanigan called Scherrer at his home. "I didn't ask you about the mother," he said.

"The Baroness," Scherrer said thoughtfully. "She's dead."

"That's what the papers say."

Scherrer removed the thin wire glasses which he wore to watch television, and which dug marks in the sides of his nose. "She ain't dead?"

"The clips are strange. One minute she's alive, the next she's history. But nothing in between. No reports how she died, where, when . . . You'd think there'd be some kind of story . . . details of a will, a memorial service some place . . ."

"She spent some time on Santa Aloe." Scherrer rubbed the marks in his nose, the facts gathering in his mind. "She also had her own place on one of the islands. Social bird. Titles go down big out here . . . But there's nothing deader than a dead socialite, is there?"

"But how dead is she, Andy?"

"I think she's run the good race. If she hasn't" – Scherrer tuned out the sound of a car chase in the TV movie he'd been watching – "she has to be a hundred years old, don't she?"

"She was – is – in her eighties?"

"Let me check it out," Scherrer said. "If she died in this neck of the woods, the death would have been registered. A certificate would have had to be issued."

He laughed quietly. "Unless somebody dumped her in Pitch Lake."

15

Vienna in the 1930s – a world of art, literature and fine society – a world too of terror, blackmail and perilous instability – was the seedbed of Theodora's emotions and her extraordinary talent. (Cahiers du Cinéma, *June 1977*)

I write only for myself. If what I write one day reproaches me for my weakness and mistakes, I will say: Those were bad and frightening times. (Baroness Gisela von Tegge Journal, *Vienna, July 29, 1936)*

Tuesday, September 26
Santa Aloe

THEODORA'S TAPE

This tape begins in Vienna in the summer of 1936. Most of it comes from Mama's journals, written in German. She switched to English the day we arrived in London in 1939, and except for an occasional relapse when she was angry about something, and could express herself better in her own language, or when she wanted to hide her thoughts from prying English eyes, she used English the rest of her life. Also, some of this material overlaps earlier tapes. We'll sort the timing out later, and think about how much we show to Mr Rider. I don't want *all* my cards cast up for him to see, especially about Mama. Oh, and finally, Missy: Georg, sometime simply G, is Vati. At this period he was chief of the political bureau of the Foreign Office. Mama was still passing herself off as an Old Catholic!

In the summer of 1936 Mama took me to see the handing over of the Olympic torch in the Heldenplatz, a great square between the Ringstrasse and the old Imperial Palace. We were on the official grandstand and had a wonderful view. As the torch was handed to the runner who was to carry it on the next stage to Berlin, hell broke loose. People screaming *Heil Hitler! One People, One Reich*! Bottles and bricks flying through the air. The riot had been organized by the Nazis. "Brutal, terrifying scenes," Mama wrote. "Kleist showed great courage and got us out quickly. I ruined my new Kira stockings (a gift!), and Theodora lost a shoe. How much worse it might have been without Sergeant K."

I don't remember losing a shoe. I imagine Mama's silk stockings were a gift from Helmuth Walther. Their affair was still going on. There was a deep bond between my parents, but it seems they no longer made love. "I wanted to hold G," she writes in her journal. "Neither of us seems able to make the first move any more. I know I am to blame for the distance that has come between us. It is my guilt – yet I feel no shame. What am I to do? I need what H does to me. The things he makes me feel. I cannot change. With him my body is insatiable and always available – he insists I wear no underthings when I am with him. My insanity comes out of my need for him. In passion I have betrayed my husband, and in passion I pray for his forgiveness. Last night" – this was the night of the Heldenplatz riot, Missy – "G and I talked until it was light. We should have made love."

Shortly after that we went to Berlin for the UFA test, where we met Noah. The UFA studio did not impress her – neither did Noah. She dismisses him as "a brash young American with plenty of advice on Theodora's future – free, gratis and for nothing".

We returned to Vienna. Do you remember the other evening, Missy, I said how difficult it was for me to explain what it was like in Vienna in those days, to describe the paradox of privilege and constant fear, of being pampered and yet always vigilant? Listen to this, from Mama's journal:

I am a good Foreign Office wife. In spite of my unfaithfulness and the estrangement it has brought between us, G has always taken pride in my accomplishments as a hostess. I can talk for hours without a moment's tactlessness or letting slip a single sincere opinion. But tonight I made a terrible mistake. This mistake so entirely fills my mind that I can think of nothing else. This is what sheer terror feels like. Tonight Franz von Papan came to supper (venison Ester-hazy; cherry strudel; Montrachet 1909, Château-Lafite 1913). He is now such a frequent guest, and a familiar face at morning Mass at St Stephen's, it is easy to forget what an important man he is in the Third Reich. (He has also whispered bold and affectionate things to me.) And foolishly I praised Bruno Walter, whom we saw last night conducting the Vienna Philharmonic (Beethoven's Eroica). Walter is a Jew, and an undeniable genius, and I remarked, when I should have known my interest dictated silence, that Berlin's loss was Vienna's gain.

I shall never forget the look on von P's face – as if he had seen a snake. "*Man kann Gold zu teuer kaufen*," he said in a kind of furious whisper. (In English, Missy: One can buy gold too dear.) "It is no excuse to say I was disarmed by P's sly humour – he calls Hitler "the great Austrian genius" and makes fun of his postcard collection of Austrian views – I should have been more wary. Georg has warned me not to trust this man . . .

What am I to do? Go to bed with him? To cancel one indiscretion with another? Risk a scandal to stop something worse? That is what H will urge me to do. The idea will excite him – the danger of it, the humiliation and the hurt of it . . . Sex has always been the *sine qua non* of survival for women like me, he says.

It was about this time that Noah telephoned from New York to say he was casting an important picture (wouldn't say what it was: all very mysterious) and wanted photographs of me as soon as possible. Mama insisted that I be photographed by Bernhard Hungerbach – the most expensive photographer in Vienna – at Noah's expense. Even then, Noah wanted to control everything. He sent portraits of Garbo – those wonderful Clarence Bull pictures: her face lit by candlelight, her eyelashes shadowed on her cheek – and insisted that Hungerbach use exactly the same lighting. He even called the hairdresser at the Sascha studios and told her the rinse he wanted put through my hair. I sat for Hungerbach in his studio on Friedrichstrasse. I was so nervous . . . convinced my forehead was too high, my eyes were not luminous, my fingers did not taper like Garbo's . . . Yet on that day, this is what Mama wrote, Missy:

> I have never seen my child looking prettier. I see myself in her more and more: the same gestures, the same lovely neck, the way she tilts her head when she smiles. She is almost as tall as I – as I, thank God, at twenty-seven, am still as beautiful as she. Walking in the Prater this morning (I wanted roses in her cheeks for Hungerbach today) we were asked by an elderly gentleman whether we were sisters! Yes, Theodora told him before I could answer. The wicked old spider invited us both to luncheon!

I don't remember that. I do remember having tea with Mama and Princess Zallhemberg. Have I told you this story, Missy – how she tried to talk Mama out of encouraging my career? "*To run after such a little fool as fame, a mirage, a mimic voice, a mere echo,*" she said. "*It's too absurd!*"

Does anyone talk like that any more? Anyway, Mama's heart was deaf. She was convinced I had a future, and that she was going to make it happen. About this time, at a party at the German Embassy, she met Heinrich Hoffmann, Hitler's personal photographer. He invited her to sit for him, she suggested that he photograph us together. Von Papen sent his Daimler-Benz to fetch us to the German Embassy on Metternichstrasse, and Hoffmann photographed us in a salon decorated as a winter garden. That night Mama wrote in her journal:

> Theodora looked stunning today. Hoffmann has photographed many beautiful women, and is not easily captive of a face, but I could see that even he was impressed. She isn't used to men

looking at her the way he looked at her today. It is a look she will grow to recognize many times!

By this time Hitler's troops had reoccupied the Rhineland. His next stop was Austria. Everybody knew it. Anyway, in the summer of 1937 we went to Venice for our family vacation. Italy was still considered to be a safe place. Nevertheless Otto Kleist came with us. I had become very fond of Vati's bodyguard. Although I now felt too grown-up to be amused by his Chaplin impersonations, I loved the way his eyes gleamed with mischief whenever he saw me.

A tennis match between Mama's friend Baron von Cramm and the Italian champion was the big event on the Lido that summer. Impossible to get seats together. Mama and I sat on one side of the court, Vati sat with Otto in the opposite stand.

Tennis bores me. I was more amused by the way people's heads followed the ball – like clockwork puppets. Then Otto's head stopped moving. He stared across the court at me, a fed-up grin on his big friendly face. I mouthed to him *Sollen wir eine kleine Jause nehmen?* Shall we have a little snack. He kept grinning at me. Then I saw the dark blood seeping out of his hair. Somebody else saw it at the same time and a woman began to scream . . . then another, and another . . .

I remember the blood on Vati's white jacket, which he wore for the rest of that awful day. I can hear Mama saying, "Oh Georg, what a world this has become."

We returned to Vienna that evening. On the plane, Mama kept saying, "Is this because of me? Is this because of me?" Vati said he didn't know. "In troubled times you can see little truth," he said.

The next day Mama placed a Star of David next to the crucifix that hung in the hall.

16

I shall become respectable in my old age. I shall dress in dark silks that make a gentle rustling sound as I move about my room. I shall trouble no one – but those whose secrets I keep. (Baroness Gisela von Tegge, Time *magazine, June 26, 1971)*

Thursday, September 28
Port of Spain, Trinidad

"I got this feeling I'm playing in a war-game, not in a real war," Lanigan told Kate on the phone, after she had told him the news that Baroness von Tegge's files had already been shredded at Ince, Ihmsen and Meiklejohn's.

"Andy rolling any logs?"

He told her about Robert Rider.

"Jesus," said Kate, impressed. "That's going to turn up the heat, isn't it?"

"Noah's not going to like it," Lanigan agreed in a worried voice.

"You haven't told him yet?"

"Haven't even told him I'm here."

"What about the Baroness?"

"Andy thinks she's dead."

"I'm sorry about the files," she said again. "We were twenty-four hours too late."

"Our bad luck – or somebody get there before us?"

"My guess, truthfully: plain lousy luck. It was their time to go, and they went."

"Have they heard from Walter Rusk yet?"

"IIM? Not a word."

"Don't they think it's odd? The old guy just ups and disappears . . . Isn't anybody over there concerned?"

"I told you, Walter's a law unto himself. They figure he'll turn up, or get in touch in his own good time," Kate said.

They talked longer than usual this time because Kate was going to Austin, Texas, for ten days on a difficult case, and they probably wouldn't talk again until she got back to New York.

"Goodbye, Lanigan. Oh, and listen to me: Noah has got to level with you." Kate spoke with the unconcealable impatience of anxiety. "Either he trusts you, and you do a job, or he doesn't, and you don't."

Through the rest of the afternoon Lanigan concentrated his thoughts on Theodora, trying to figure out what kind of woman she was. He wouldn't be happy until he could read her mind, and know the things she muttered in her sleep. But it was hard. She belonged to another world, another time, she came from a dimension outside his experience.

It was a hot day. Even the last showers of the rainy season felt hot. He stood at the window and drank a Coke from the minibar, watching a lonely heron exploring the empty beach. I'm getting too old for this work, he thought. He no longer had the reflexes he used to have. Was his mind less sharp too? Be patient. Concentrate. The answers would come.

At five o'clock Scherrer called and told him to be in the hotel bar at six.

After he showered and put on fresh clothes, Lanigan sealed his notes in a thick yellow envelope which he gave to the concierge to lock in the hotel safe. At ten to six he went into the bar and ordered a beer.

Scherrer arrived at six exactly.

"Well, your suspicious mind's paid off," he said, after the waitress had brought his drink to their table in an alcove lit for lovers. He took a small notebook out of his jacket pocket. "She's on St Francis. Small, private island in the Serpent's Mouth, sixty miles off Icacos Point, going west. She's in Holy Day House."

"A hotel?"

Scherrer shook his head. "Clinic . . . spa . . . sanatorium – call it what you will – but definitely only for the very rich. Barbara Hutton was there one time. Christina Onassis, the Duchess of Windsor, a couple of Gettys. Exclusive, OK?"

Lanigan smiled. "What's her problem? Drugs?"

Scherrer shrugged. "Maybe she's shooting up anti-wrinkle cream."

"Anti-wrinkle cream?"

"There's a lot of fixing going on over there . . . HRT, ERT, testicular extracts from billy goats, whatever . . . Squeeze a few more years out of the tube – it ain't immortality, but it'll do."

Lanigan grinned. "The rich want to live for ever, don't they?"

"But the Baroness seems to be a special case," Scherrer said, studying his notes again. "A permanent guest. Her own nurse, a couple of German nuns looking after her. Theodora visits her twice, three times a year. Uses her own chopper. Pilot's name, Henriksen. Henrik Henriksen, a Swede. Flies out of Piarco. Could be worth a visit." He gave him Henriksen's number, and closed his notebook. "That's it. A pebble on the pile."

"Not bad for someone who doesn't keep a file on the lady!"

"It was in the do-not-file file."

"Thanks, Andy," Lanigan said, but his gratitude was mingled with doubt about how to use the information now that he had it.

He looked tired in the bar's Chinese lantern light. Scherrer guessed that he was having trouble sleeping nights, thinking of the hours on the clock, wondering what he had forgotten to do, or what he should do next. It was the nature of the game that caused everyone in it to live with self-doubts and apprehensions, even when the breaks were going your way.

Scherrer signalled for fresh drinks. When they came, he said: "There's something else you should know, Lanigan."

Lanigan said nothing.

Scherrer took a deep breath. "In 1960 when the Agency was preparing for the Bay of Pigs invasion – I guess you were in London then – we set up a radio station, Radio Calypso, to broadcast propaganda to the Cuban people. On D-Day it switched its name to Radio Free Americas and pumped out military commands to the anti-Castro guerrillas inside Cuba."

"I remember."

"Radio Calypso was based on St Francis."

Lanigan smiled. "Small world."

"Smaller than you think. Calypso was operated by a Miami company, the Southern Star Navigation Corporation, an Agency proprietary fronted by Noah Swan. Southern Star Navigation" – Scherrer dropped his voice almost to a whisper – "remained a Company proprietary until its dissolution in the early seventies . . . when the island was bought by Swan."

"He owns St Francis! Holy Day House belongs to Noah Swan?"

"It did." Scherrer consulted his notebook again. "He sold the island and the clinic to a Swiss outfit in eighty-one. The Biddle-Biemiller Corporation, in Geneva. They own a chain of expensive clinics and health spas in Europe. The directrice is a woman named Mildred d'Erlanger. They have a reputation for protecting their clients from the press and prying eyes. A photographer was recently killed trying to get into one of their places in the South of France. He was after a deathbed picture of some rock star dying of AIDS. That gives you some idea of how conscientious these people are about security."

"I'll bear it in mind."

Scherrer lifted his glass to his lips, and put it down again. "You don't look so good."

"I think I've got a bigger problem than I realized," Lanigan said.

That night he made notes of his conversation with Scherrer, sealed them in an envelope, took them down to the hotel safe, and went to bed.

But he did not sleep.

124

17

I don't have a script, a start date or the finance, but I have found our Juliet! Her name is Theodora von Tegge, and her beauty will wring your heart. I'm going to make her the greatest movie star the world has ever seen! (Noah Swan – from a letter to Romeo and Juliet *director Émile Copeland, August 24, 1937)*

Thursday, September 28
Santa Aloe

THEODORA'S TAPE

Poor Otto Kleist was shot, and we returned to Vienna . . . Trouble with these machines, Missy, I lose the gottdam thread. Is this thing working? The spools are turning. So . . .

Otto's dead, we're back in Vienna . . . The Star of David, a crucifix, the portrait of Pope Pius XI all in a row!

What happened next is difficult to be certain about. (If only I *could* convey a thousand words with one glance, as Pauline Kael said I could, Missy!) Helmuth Walther left Mama at this point. Discovering that she was a Jew scared him off. After we returned from Venice, he cancelled their regular *cinq-à-sept* at the Sacher Hotel. "It is always lovers from whom unfaithful wives learn the lessons of betrayal," she wrote in her journal.

But she sees him again, and again. It was a physical thing. In spite of his fear, in spite of her humiliation, they could not leave each other alone. Once, when she tried to talk to him about her Catholicism, he told her: "Unfortunately, my dear, all are not huntsmen who can blow the huntsman's horn."

That crack was finally too much for Mama. She went to the synagogue in Leopoldstadt and converted back to Judaism! I'm

125

not sure that she actually did, but she writes that she did, and I want to give her the benefit of the doubt! It was a brave but foolish thing to have done, it put us both in terrible danger, but I will always love her for it.

Anyway, late one night – this was in January 1938, carnival time in Vienna – Franz von Papen arrived at the house alone . . . I will take this straight from Mama's journal, Missy:

This evening Franz P visited Löwelstrasse for the first time since we became lovers. Arrived unannounced, alone, without even his chauffeur. I have never seen him so nervous. His hands shook. He downed two stiff schnapps before he was able to speak. After making G several times check that there was no servant behind the door (Is there a spy in the house? Does he know that?) he told us that he was in fear of his life. "They are going to murder me!" he said.

"Who is going to murder you, Franz?" G asked.

"Berlin."

"Berlin?" said G incredulously. "Who in Berlin wants to kill you?"

He said the Nazis were to stage an attack on the German Embassy in which he would be shot by troops disguised as members of the Austrian Patriotic Front.

"How do you know this, Franz?" G asked.

"Thank God I still have friends at the Wilhelmstrasse," he said.

"Why should your own people want to kill you, Franz?" Georg asked patiently, as if he were dealing with a madman.

Franz said, "It will be the excuse for the Führer to send in troops to protect Germany's honour. Of course they must kill someone important," he added, with a flash of his old arrogance. "It cannot be a small outrage to provoke invasion."

He said there is a house on Teinfaltstrasse belonging to Dr Leopold Tavs in which G would find all the evidence, together with plans to torch the embassy by *agents provocateurs*. "You must order a raid at once," he said, "or I am a dead man, and your country is lost."

Can it be true? Is it a trick? One look at Franz tells me he is not lying. But if the Tavs house is raided and incriminating documents are found, G told him, it cannot be passed off without a scandal – or without suspicion falling on Franz himself.

"Do it, for God's sake," Franz said. "I will take care of the consequences in Berlin."

As he left, Franz spoke to me in the hall. "Gisela, I am pleading for my life!" There was a look of terror in his eyes. "You must persuade Georg to act at once! I will give you anything you want!" There was a stubble of grey beard on his face. I was as shocked by his beard as by his funk.

Mama has always had a talent for twisting facts to suit her purpose, Missy. But all this is true. What happened next – the police raid on the house on Teinfaltstrasse, the discovery of the Tavs documents – is in the history books. But what prompted that raid has never before now been told.

Vati had been preparing an underground resistance to the Nazi occupation and intended to stay and fight. But he planned to get Mama and me out of the country when the time came. To take care of us financially, he had been secretly selling off his art collection, smuggling it abroad . . . a couple of Fragonard wash drawings, a Jasper bowl, cameos . . . I've seen things we once owned in the Tate and in the Palais des Beaux-Arts . . . It is sad.

Anyway, a couple of months after the von Papen episode, Noah turned up in Vienna with Émile Copeland and the contracts for *Romeo and Juliet*. He wanted to start shooting in London later that year. Unfortunately, at the same time – it might have been the same day, the next day, I can't remember – Schuschnigg announced that he was to hold a plebiscite to determine whether Austria should be independent, Christian and united, or – he didn't have to say it – surrender to the Nazis.

Hitler immediately closed the border and sent the Chancellor an ultimatum to cancel the plebiscite.

Schuschnigg had no fight left. I remember his last broadcast. He would not allow Austrian blood to be shed at any price. Vati was arrested fifteen minutes after the broadcast. The radio was still playing Haydn's variations of the national anthem when they came for him, men in black leather coats. Some late snow had fallen and there was snow on their hats. I thought how rude they were not to remove their hats in the house. They said they were taking Vati to the Hotel Metropol. The Metropol was the Gestapo headquarters.

Vati was calm. At the door he embraced me. "Have faith in yourself," he said. He spoke matter-of-factly, not wishing to alarm me. But I knew something bad was happening. I tried to cling to him. I was pulled away by one of the Gestapo people. Before he got into the car Vati turned and waved his hand at me and smiled. The black limousine moved away soundlessly on the snow. Vati peered out of the little window at the back. I knew that we were looking at each other for the last time. It was Friday, March 11, 1938. The next day Hitler marched into Austria.

There was silence on the tape. Missy closed her eyes. In a little while she heard Theodora stand up and pour herself a drink and begin to walk about the room.

Missy switched off the tape.

18

*Some say she copied Greta Garbo. And maybe
she did. One always begins by imitating the best.*
(*Émile Copeland*, USA Today, *June 13, 1984*)

**Thursday, September 28
London**

Robert Rider began work on Theodora's biography as if he were
researching a novel. He borrowed books from the London
Library dealing with Austria in her childhood years; a cartogra-
pher turned up a rare large-scale map of Santa Aloe for him. At
the British Film Institute he examined over sixty books in the
English language on her life and her movies; he borrowed five
biographies, a book of collected criticism, two volumes of photographs, and a novel by Michael Korda, reputed to be the thinly
veiled true story of her life.

Tonight he was going to see a private screening of *The Classic
That Disappeared*, a ten-year-old BBC documentary on the
making and mysterious abandonment of Theodora's first big
movie, *Romeo and Juliet*. Accompanied by Grace Hempel, he
was met in the lobby of the private theatre on Audley Square by
the producer Bill Crossman, and a BBC publicist. A waiter
served champagne; a waitress followed with a tray of hot canapés.
Grace said, "I love this picture already."

"It's brilliant," the publicist said, with the faintest Australian
accent. "It won three BAFTA awards. It doesn't pull any
punches."

"I'm surprised Noah Swan never sued," Crossman said.

"I'd like to know what he thought of it," the publicity woman
said.

129

"I wouldn't," Crossman said.

They all laughed.

"How did it do in the States?" Rider asked.

"A cable company bought it, but it's never been aired," the publicist said.

"Maybe they're keeping it until Matthew Swan becomes President," Grace suggested.

"Maybe Noah Swan owns the cable company," Rider said.

They all laughed again.

Narrated by Laurence Olivier, *The Classic That Disappeared* was a compelling mixture of investigation, film history and gossip.

Romeo and Juliet began shooting at Denham studios in December 1939, three months after the start of World War II. On September 29, 1940, with less than fifty minutes completed, the production came to an abrupt and inexplicable end. "One and a half reels of film are all that remain of this extraordinary epic," intoned Olivier. "But it is enough to tantalize us with what might have been."

"It began with a lie and ended in deception," director Émile Copeland said, as he walked through the ruined sets of Verona built on the backlot of Denham, like an old general revisiting a distant battlefield. "The lie, a small one, was that shooting began on Theodora's fourteenth birthday – the age of Juliet. In fact Theodora was only thirteen when we began the picture. It made a good story for the newspapers, and it also got us round the child labour laws, which would have restricted her availability on the set."

There was a cut to a big close-up of Theodora.

Utterly still, blonde hair straight and long, her naked face possessed the luminous pallor and innocence of childhood. The camera pulled back, slowly revealing her fine gold gown, her bosom visibly bare beneath the silk. The woman-child effect was stunning. Rider had never seen anything so young so sensual. "Jesus," he said aloud.

"Noah Swan's Juliet . . . Noah Swan's Theodora," Copeland said, as the cutter's fade-cues wiped across the screen. He was now sitting alone in the old Denham projection room. He held up a sheaf of pages. "These are some of the memoranda I got from Noah. This one begins, *Anxious you remember that Theodora/ Juliet is love itself. Passion is her state of being. Out of it she has no existence. It is the soul within her soul. It is the pulse within her heart. The lifeblood in her veins . . .*"

An actor before he became a director, a dancer before he became an actor, Copeland had a waspish, theatrical manner. Ash-blond hair cut Cassius-style and expertly made-up eyes could not mask his age. Rider put him in his mid-seventies.

"Here," he continued, "on March 13, 1940, is a typical Noah telegram to me. It says, *Don't lose sight of the fact that Theodora/ Juliet and her lover are in contrast with all around them. They are all that is pure and decent in the midst of hatred and envy. Keep this aspect in sharp focus at all times.*"

Copeland smiled straight into camera. Rider sensed he was getting into his stride now. He had caught the right tone – the tone of a man who takes pleasure in the seriousness of movie-making – a tone in which to settle old scores. "I have always thought that Noah's memos to me revealed the very secrets of his soul," he said. "I have no doubt in my mind that he was always in love with Theodora. Their affair was like a Russian novel."

"How old was Swan then?" Rider asked aloud.

"Twenty-five," the publicity woman answered at once. "He's the same age as Orson Welles. Orson was shooting *Citizen Kane* at the same time."

The Classic That Disappeared was told in staccato *March of Time* style. People who had worked on the picture – actors, wardrobe and make-up people, technicians – told a piece of the story:

"We were waiting in a rainstorm at Croydon: Mr Swan, myself, a stills man, and our publicity director, Aaron Flagg. Theodora and her mother were coming in from Vienna," recalled Noah Swan's former secretary. "We'd been out to the airport three times and they hadn't been on the plane they were supposed to be on. This was 1939. Very tense. Mr Swan called it a game of tag between Viennese optimism and Nazi despotism."

Still photographs of Theodora arriving at Croydon appeared on the screen.

Aaron Flagg said, "She didn't look like a movie star. She looked tired. She looked scared. Mr Swan took my arm. 'We've got some work to do here, Aaron,' he said."

A newsreel montage of her make-up tests, costume fittings, dance classes, riding lessons and rehearsals ended with an historic piece of film discovered in Jerry Wechsler's original colour tests: a two-minute close-up without sound of Theodora gazing into deep space – "that magical world beyond the lens," said Olivier, "where stars are created" – her face slowly changing from a kind of piety to a look of erotic promise.

"Nobody taught her that look," said Aaron Flagg. "That smile is like nothing else on film. But Noah taught her how to use it. He taught her to put a premium on it. Use it, he said, when all else fails."

"She had no technique at all," said her drama coach. "Her acting was erratic, a brilliant moment followed by something unbelievably novelettish."

Juliet's soliloquy after the Friar handed her the sleeping potion came on to the screen. Placed high, the camera showed her isolation as she stalked about her boudoir, her imagination conjuring up terrible thoughts, her panic rising: "How if, when I am laid into the tomb,/I wake before the time that Romeo/Come to redeem me? There's a fearful point!/Shall I not then be stifled in the vault . . ."

She was overacting, her timing was poor, she moved awkwardly.

"After about twenty takes, Noah told Milly Copeland to shoot the whole scene in close-up," remembered Wechsler. "Until that moment he wouldn't let me go in close. I kept saying, 'She's beautiful. Let the audience see her.' But he said, 'No close-ups until we need them.' He made her do all those takes because he wanted to make her nervous. He was waiting for the moment to go in close . . . He wanted to show the fear in her eyes. It was a lousy trick to play on the kid, but it was bloody effective."

A wardrobe mistress said, "Mr Swan liked to take risks. The

see-through blouse – do you realize how daring that look was in 1940? I don't know how they expected to get it past the Hays office."

There were more scenes from the film. More anecdotes and reminiscences. Then:

"This picture of Theodora in her suite at the Dorchester Hotel appeared in *Life* magazine the week we started shooting at Denham," said Aaron Flagg, as a blow-up appeared of the young star sitting amid steamer trunks, flanked by her mother and several servants. "The caption went something like, 'When Theodora travels it's always first-class.' I was prouder of that break than anything I've ever done. Theodora and the Baroness didn't have the price of a park bench between them. If you look carefully, you can even see Noah's initials on the steamers!"

As the picture progressed, and the budget continued to escalate, days on the set would often end with Theodora in tears, and Copeland in a rage of frustration. "She was not easy," he recalled. "Anything was enough to upset her. The smell of paint made her nauseous. The sets had to be painted and aired when she wasn't around. We lost weeks airing those bloody sets!"

Listening to the anecdotes, the litany of fights and jealousies, the endless contention of egos, Rider again vowed never to become involved in the filming of one of his own books.

"*Romeo and Juliet* continued shooting into September 1940 – when the blitz came to London," Olivier said over newsreel shots of German bombers in ominous black formations, and scenes of people running to the shelters. "On the seventh, the German Luftwaffe struck at London's docks and East End. Five hundred civilians were killed.

"On September 29, the production was shut down for the last time," the actor continued over more newsreel footage of Noah and Theodora getting into a limousine outside the Savoy Hotel, and being driven off at speed. "Two days later, accompanied by Theodora and her mother, in adjoining staterooms, Noah Swan left on the SS *Samaria* for New York."

Aaron Flagg said, "The story I put out – that the picture had been suspended – was the only statement Noah ever released. He was never a guy who surrenders to calamity, and to this day I've no idea why he did what he did and that's the God's honest truth."

"The way it ended is still a bafflement to me," said Cecil Beaton, filmed wearing a straw hat in his Wiltshire garden. "One hears rumours, of course. One always does."

"Noah Swan deceived me. He deceived everyone," said Copeland, as the end credits began to roll over his lonely figure walking through the peeling remains of the backlot Verona. "I shall never, never forgive him."

The publicity woman clapped enthusiastically as the lights came up in the viewing theatre. "Thank you," Rider said to Crossman, who was sitting behind him. "Congratulations. It's a remarkable show."

"I enjoyed watching it again," Crossman said.

Rider lit a *sigaro*. "I got the feeling that Copeland could have told us more than he was saying."

"Standards and Practices made us cut a few lines."

"What were the rumours Beaton mentioned, any idea?"

"One story was that she was pregnant," the publicist said.

"Copeland more than hinted at it," Crossman said. "It was one of the lines S & P removed."

"I bet," said Rider.

19

Friday, September 29
Port of Spain, Trinidad

The morning after his meeting with Scherrer in the Bewick hotel
bar, Lanigan called Kate in New York. But she had already left
for Texas. He probably wouldn't talk to her again for a week or
more, and he wanted to tell her about the Baroness. The fact that
she was still alive would fascinate Kate. The Baroness had
become her favourite character, as if she were part of a novel she
was caught up in.

He had breakfast, walked on the beach. At nine o'clock he
dialled Henrik Henriksen's number at his office out at Piarco
airport.

"My name is Lanigan, Mr Henriksen." He was brief and to the
point. "Would it be possible to meet today?"

Theodora's pilot recognized the businesslike tone. "Do you
know Balzac's on Golden Grove Road, north of the airport?"

"I'll find it."

"I'll be there at three thirty."

Next Lanigan dialled Credit Suisse and arranged to pick up the
cash he had had wired from the Geneva fund account Noah Swan
had set up for him.

Three thirty in the afternoon is the slow time at Balzac's.
Henriksen was sitting alone at the far end of the bar. He was a

tall, slim, high-shouldered man with flaxen hair receding from his forehead. He wore octagonal sunglasses with gold wire frames, jeans, blue shirt, and a blue corduroy jacket. He hadn't shaved for several days; the blond stubble paradoxically made his pale face look boyish. He turned round on his stool and raised his hand as soon as Lanigan entered the bar.

"Mr Lanigan," he said, pronouncing it *Lonigon*.

They shook hands. Lanigan guessed he was thirty-five.

"Can I get you something?" Henriksen lifted his own glass of beer.

Lanigan asked for a Michelob.

"We'll talk in my office." Henriksen went across to a small table at the end of the empty bar and sat down with his back to the wall, like an old gunfighter. "We won't be disturbed here." Perhaps he was naturally cautious, or perhaps he had been able to tell from the tone of Lanigan's voice on the telephone that this was a matter that required discretion. "Have you been in the Port of Spain long, Mr Lanigan?" he asked, politely.

Lanigan sipped his beer. "A week or so."

"Vacation?"

"I'm a magazine writer. Freelance."

"A magazine writer. Freelance," Henriksen repeated sardonically.

"I'm trying to put something together for a piece on Theodora Glass."

"The movie queen in exile," Henriksen smiled.

"The movie queen in exile – that's not a bad title for my piece."

"It's yours." Henriksen lifted his glass. "Your journey's not been entirely wasted."

"Theodora –"

"She won't see you. Plenty of people have tried. Writers, photographers, TV people, historians, college professors . . . plenty of people. They come out here, send her messages, send her flowers – and nothing. Then they discover me. Entertain me, pump me – still they get nothing. They kick their heels for a while. Then they give up and go home." He grinned. "So don't waste your time, Mr Magazine Writer. Save your money, Freelance. It's a lost cause. Crying for the moon is the saying in your country, I think."

Lanigan took his time. He didn't push. Henriksen asked which magazines he worked for. Lanigan named a few. They talked about writers and about the stunts reporters pulled to get stories.

"The English are worst," Henriksen said in a tone heavy with Scandinavian scorn. He tapped the rim of his glass. "They try to get me to relax . . . Tell them stories out of school. 'Trust me,' they say. I trust nobody. In my line you hear a lot of things, believe me. One thing I know, one thing I learned: how to keep my trap shut."

Lanigan smiled, and said nothing.

"Nobody would believe me if I walked out today and told things I know," Henriksen said with a sudden boastfulness that had a nice ring of susceptibility in it.

Lanigan said, "I wouldn't expect you to help me for nothing."

"I understand that," Henriksen said.

Lanigan could feel something going on in Henriksen's mind. He didn't think it was resentment about being asked to betray a trust for money.

He said, "I've got an angle . . . But I need a little help to make it stand up."

He took out an envelope and placed it on the table between them.

Henriksen stared at it.

Lanigan said, "I thought something in advance . . ."

"What's the angle?"

"I want to talk with her mother."

"The Baroness?" He hid his surprise well. "She's dead. She passed on."

"I don't think so."

"A reporter's hunch?"

"She's on St Francis. Holy Day House."

"Really?" Henriksen smirked, sipped his beer. "I didn't know that."

"You know, and I know you know. You fly Theodora there two, three times a year."

Henriksen gave a bad imitation of a laugh. "Where do you get this shit anyway? Who gives you this garbage? It's unreal."

"My money's real."

"You want to visit a grave?" Divided between suspicion and the greed he always felt when journalists offered bribes, Henriksen's forefinger tapped the envelope filled with dollars. "You're prepared to wager all this on whether an old woman is alive or dead?"

Lanigan smiled, waited.

There was a sudden stillness in the air, an awareness between the two men that had nothing to do with the money on the table.

Lanigan ended the silence. "I want you to get me into Holy Day House. That's all."

Henriksen stared at the envelope.

Lanigan said, "Fifty one-hundred-dollar bills," slowly.

Henriksen lit a cigarette that he immediately stubbed out. He took a deep breath, and exhaled very slowly. Then in a tone of voice that suddenly seemed capable of telling everything, he said, "I have to fly to the island twice next week. It might be possible . . ."

Lanigan pushed the envelope towards him, nodding for him to pick it up. "We got a deal?"

"I can get you to the island," Henriksen said, slipping the money into his jacket pocket like a magician. "The problem is getting you into Holy Day House."

"How big a problem?"

"I'll need help . . . Someone on the inside."

Lanigan stared at him.

Henriksen got the message.

"No extra cost. I got a girlfriend . . . She'll help because I tell her. You can trust me."

"Sure I can," said Lanigan. "Now tell me about this girl."

20

There are forces in her which I have never come across in any other actress – in any other human being. Shall we ever know out of what past darkness such forces come? (François Truffaut, Preface to J. G. Moussy's biography, L'Histoire de Theodora G, Paris, 1980)

Saturday, September 30
Santa Aloe

THEODORA'S TAPE

In moments of despair the brain seizes up, perhaps that's why it's so hard for me to recall those awful days after the Nazis took Vati away. Wouldn't it be interesting if we could go back to relive some things, to find out what we were feeling, and thinking, and what really happened? To get things right – not to change anything, that is too much to ask, but to understand.

You once told me, Missy, that the price of happiness as we grow older is having to let go of the past. But it would be worth some pain to give a sense to some moments, to find the cause, to discover a reason why this happened, and why that happened.

A few days after Vati's arrest, officials came to the house and took an inventory of everything – my dolls, my books, my hair ribbons . . . Mama's jewellery, her underclothes, shoes, the pots of cream on her dressing-table . . . everything was written down. The most chilling thing was their politeness. They treated us with extraordinary courtesy. They even apologized when they took away our passports. It was a game they played.

Vati was imprisoned first in the Federal Court building, then in the Central Police building at the Schottenring, where he was kept for five months, and Mama was allowed to visit him. He had

139

been charged with helping enemies of the state to escape from justice, and illegally exporting capital. I don't know the truth of the first charge; there was some substance to the second, of course. Until the foreign investments were surrendered, our passports would continue to be held. Money in an account in Switzerland was returned to Vienna, but it was not enough to satisfy the Nazis.

By this time Noah was in pre-production in London, and on the anxious seat about my availability. He was totally unaware of the real peril we were in. He came to Vienna to see what was keeping us! This was before he was rich and at the top of his game, the top of his world, before he could simply buy us out of trouble.

Early in 1939 Vati was moved from Schottenring to another prison. Mama was always driven there in a closed car and we never knew where it was. It was at this prison that Vati suffered his final torture. Mama has told me this story many times, but I know that she laid it on with a trowel sometimes, so I will stick to the words she used in her journal at the time.

On February 1, 1939, she wrote:

Today I was taken not to G's cell on the third floor, but to a small ward. I almost fainted when I saw what they had done to him. His face had been smashed almost beyond recognition; his hands have been crushed and broken. Only his beautiful eyes seemed left alive. I was permitted to sit with him for an hour. He was unable to speak to me.

There is nothing more in her journal until March 23:

Major Radek arrived unannounced. Said Gestapo has given permission for me to see G again. First indication in nearly two months that he is still alive. The same forty-minute curtained automobile journey (are we going round in circles?) to the same ugly building in god-forsaken part of the city.

He has been moved to a private room which is austere, but clean. His poor face still bruised and swollen, his head shaven. He sleeps most of the time, they tell me. Doesn't seem to be like any sleep I know. After a little while he seemed to sense that I was there, and tried to speak to me. But his voice was so weak, I could barely hear a word even when I put my ear to his lips.

"I can't hear you, my darling," I told him.

"I am sixteen," he said. "I am staying at the Grauer Bär."

"That's what I told you when we first met."

He closed his eyes, and smiled. "You are still as pretty," he said, and fell back into that sleep that is not a sleep.

Radek was beckoned outside by a doctor. As if he knew that he had gone, G opened his eyes. Says he cannot take the beatings much longer; fears he will break and talk. Says I will be contacted by friends and given something to help him bear the pain. "Bring it to me as soon as you can," he says. We both know he is asking me to help him die. Sunk in misery but it would be as cowardly of me not to do it as it is cruel of him to ask.

On March 26 there are just three sentences in her journal:

11.45 this morning I kissed Georg goodbye for the last time. Did what he asked. God forgive us both.

That night after I had gone to bed, Mama came to my room and told me to get dressed. We had an important appointment, she said; it was a secret, I must hurry. I was convinced we were going to meet Vati, that we were going to be all together again. We drove to a church off Lasallestrasse. We lit candles, and prayed. Afterwards we walked. I remember bright moonlight, the city very still, like an abandoned movie set. She told me things about her family, about herself when she was a child. I had never felt so close to her before. She had never been the kind of mother who reaches out. She had always been too busy grooming me, using me.

We were halfway across a bridge – the Reichsbrücke, I think it was – when she said: "You must trust me, Theodora. We have no one else. We have only each other." She kept looking at me. At my eyes. Then she said this thing I will never forget. "The Danube is better than Dachau."

I knew then that we were both going to die. But worse than that, Missy, I accepted it. *I was thirteen years old*. I accepted it! So many people were killing themselves, you know. The *Neue Freie Presse* each morning ran announcements of people *going to the rest that they have so much longed for*. That was the code that told you it was suicide. In the first two months of the Nazi occupation nearly ten thousand people in Vienna took their own lives.

It must have been very late. Not a car went by, not a pedestrian. We stood in the middle of the bridge. I remember it had begun to snow – one of those gentle night-time falls of big, weightless flakes you sometimes get in Vienna in the early spring. Mama lifted me on to the parapet. I could hear the river in the darkness below. She took off the gold heart Vati had given her on their wedding day and fastened it around my neck. She hugged me, then I felt myself begin to topple slowly . . .

"That is not a safe place for you to be, *Liebchen*." A German soldier had come out of nowhere and lifted me down from the parapet. "Just because the moonlight is too bright in your eyes," he said, "you must not plunge into the sun."

I don't know his name, or what he looked like, although I remember the roughness of his face against mine as he held me in his arms . . . He saved our lives that night.

The tape was switched off. When it resumed, Theodora's voice was stronger, almost businesslike:

In London Noah had come up against the brick wall of bureaucracy. The British could not issue us with an entry permit without a German exit visa; the Germans would not issue an exit visa without a British entry permit. Also non-Aryans (Mama's new classification) who wished to leave the country had to get a certificate of good conduct from the police authorities. This had to be taken to the tax authorities to get another form stating that all your taxes had been paid . . . The days we spent standing in line outside police stations, in freezing waiting-rooms. The smell of those places, Missy. The stale stench of goulash and cheap cigarettes officials carried in their clothes. Mama tried everything. I once found her combing through the *Almanach de Gotha* in search of eligible Aryan husbands for us! Eventually, she put the bite on Franz von Papen. Why she didn't do it sooner is a mystery. Perhaps after Vati was arrested, and after he died, she was too scared, or too angry or simply too numb to think straight. Whether she threatened to reveal Papen's role in the Teinfaltstrasse raid, or whether it was their affair she threatened him with, I don't know. An affair with a Jew would have been bad news for von P in Berlin. Definitely, and forty-eight hours later our visas came through.

We landed in London in the rain. I took the gold heart from my neck – the heart Vati had given Mama on their wedding day – and put it back where it belonged. She wore it for the rest of her life . . .

21

My purpose is to disturb – it's the first prerogative of any writer worth his salt. (Robert Rider, Newsweek, *January 12, 1987)*

Sunday night, October 1
London

"It's been a lovely weekend," Grace Hempel said when she and Rider returned to her flat after dinner and listening to some good jazz at Smollensky's. "Thank you."

"Thank you for fixing up *The Classic That Disappeared* for me, by the way," Rider said.

She took off her coat. "Part of the service."

"It was informative, wasn't it?"

"I liked the Émile Copeland stuff."

"He has wit and wisdom."

"You'll want to get to him, I presume?"

"I think he's ready to talk his heart out, don't you?"

"Nothing's as oppressive as a fifty-year-old secret," Grace said.

"And Aaron Flagg sounded as if he might have a story to tell. Bookbinder gave Pfeiffer a number in New York. I'll try to see him on my way out to Santa Aloe."

"I'll chase up a number for Copeland in the morning."

"You're a brick, Miss Hempel."

"Not a hot brick, I trust."

"Come here."

She stood akimbo before him, a mischievous gesture, her thighs inches from his face. She drew his head towards her. He opened his mouth on to her through the thin black silk of her dress, through the finer perfumed black silk beneath.

145

"I'm having lewd thoughts . . ." he said in a muffled voice.

She was trembling.

". . . more than lewd."

"Always remember," she said, quoting Aaron Flagg quoting Noah Swan in the documentary, "the demand for a thing is in inverse ratio to its availability."

She could feel the heat of his breath on her crotch. She buckled her knees. He kissed her mouth.

"Always?"

"Not necessarily," she said in a small surrendering voice.

22

I am happy when I speak the truth. (Baroness Gisela von Tegge, Women's Wear Daily, July 30, 1984)

Sunday, October 1
Port of Spain, Trinidad

"Mr Lanigan?"

It took him several seconds to place even the gender of the soft, half-familiar voice on the phone. *The guy who runs the block!*

"This is Michael Fortas?" The precise enunciation, the mellow vowels, the little effeminate trick of making a question out of a declarative statement. "Mr Swan's private secretary?"

"So you are," Lanigan said, trying to figure how Fortas had found him.

"I must meet with you, as soon as possible?"

"I won't be back in Washington for at least a week."

"That's not a problem, Mr Lanigan. I'm here. Right here in the hotel." Fortas sounded pleased with his own cleverness. "Room nine-seventeen."

"Meet me in the coffee shop," Lanigan said in a curt voice. "Fifteen minutes."

Lanigan was baffled, and angry. How the hell did Fortas know that he was in Port of Spain, and where he was staying? Was this going to be a repeat of the California situation? Was the rug going to be pulled from under him again? Everything in his instinct and experience told him that Noah Swan's representative on earth hadn't travelled all the way to Trinidad to bring him good news.

Michael Fortas was in the coffee shop, seated at a table overlooking the tropical gardens. He didn't look like the ultra-conservative aide Lanigan had met in Georgetown. He was wearing aviator sunglasses, pink T-shirt, khaki pants and Fratelli Rossetti sneakers. A Panama hat and folding umbrella on the seat next to him completed the ensemble.

"I should warn you, Mr Lanigan," he greeted him with a smile that showed a lot of expensive American dentistry, "I don't handle compliments well."

"I'll try not to say anything that'll make you cry."

"I've ordered iced tea. Orange Pekoe?" Fortas beckoned the waitress, hinging his fingers into the palm of his hand, the way Italians wave goodbye. "You may prefer something less scenty?"

Lanigan ordered coffee.

Fortas was in no hurry to get to the purpose of his visit. "It is a pity that idleness is so frowned upon," he said, after some small-talk about his favourite vacation places. "I think I could be quite good at it, idleness, given half a chance."

"You been with Noah Swan long?"

"Oh, a tidy time," Fortas said with affable vagueness. "You come from Kenosha, Wisconsin, don't you?"

"The capital of Jockey underwear. Before you joined up with Swan what did you do?"

Fortas's smile was neither warm enough nor quick enough to hide the momentary look of uncertainty. "The past is so . . . past, don't you think?"

"So get to the point."

"Well, my goodness, you don't have to snap at me," Fortas said, sounding hurt.

"Just tell me why you're here."

"I'm just trying to be friendly."

"You're about as friendly as friendly fire, Fortas."

He blushed as if he had been paid a compliment. "Mr Swan said I was to tell you he thinks the sideshows are swallowing up the circus?"

"You've lost me, pal."

"He doesn't want you to waste time on the Baroness. She is not important. She is not meaningful. In a nutshell, Mr Lanigan, she is a sideshow."

"Are you asking me or telling me?"

Fortas shrugged his shoulders. "You ignore his wishes, his feelings get hurt. And when his feelings get hurt I get a definite feeling of unhappiness."

"You got any better ideas?"

Fortas studied him for a long moment, his thumb moving slowly across his pale lips. "Well, it's strictly your jurisdiction, of course . . . But have you ever considered how the passions – *fear* is a very good example – have such an extraordinary effect upon the mind? Fear of dental work, for example . . . how that can stop an aching tooth?"

"Go on."

"Even people who have lived all their lives beyond reproach, who have behaved with all possible caution . . . even such people must be a little mindful of the consequences. But a woman like Theodora Glass, an actress, a famous mistress . . . and who knows what else she's been and done in her time" – he glanced at Lanigan with a sort of flirtatious humour – "she must have one dark secret she's kept in lavender?"

"How do you suggest I throw a scare into her, Fortas?" Lanigan's smile was small, but with room in it for a little mockery. "Say *boo*?"

"The complicating thing here, of course, is that Mr Swan must remain discreet. Especially now, in the run-up?"

"If he knows she's got something to hide, why the hell doesn't he tell me about it, instead of sending you here with this horse manure about circuses and sideshows?"

Fortas's smile was forgiving, as if Lanigan had broken some obscure honour code. "In matters of this kind it is prudent to leave some things unsaid?"

"Why don't he ask her to postpone the book until after the election? Work something out after the election. One phone call –"

"Asking favours is not his style."

"For old time's sake?"

"It would make him terribly vulnerable, don't you think? How would it look if it became known that he was trying to stop her confessions? It could be as damaging as publication of the book itself."

"Who would know? She ain't a dame looking for publicity."

"A famous love affair is dangerous country, Mr Lanigan. The cloud that threatens every big liaison is betrayal. Sooner or later one or other of the lovers is persuaded to go public."

"This is all about her spilling their goddam pillow talk from *fifty years ago*?" Lanigan asked with irritation.

"It might start with pillow talk. But give up the smallest piece of a secret, and the rest is no longer in your power."

Lanigan was incredulous. "You're saying Theodora does know something that could –"

"Memoirs of movie actresses are numbingly trivial. I'm sure Theodora's won't be an exception. But memory is an art form and art, dear sir, is dangerously unpredictable."

"You've got a way with words, Fortas." But the answer was so pat that Lanigan knew that he had anticipated his question. He respected him for that. Fortas was a man who foresaw everything, who prepared for every move.

"Anyway, it is quite wrong to imagine that grievances mellow with age," Fortas said. "This is all about two strong-willed people on a collision course . . . Who will give way first? It looks beautiful outside. Shall we?"

They walked on the beach. Fortas was much smaller without his built-up shoes. He carried the umbrella over his shoulder, like a sawn-off shotgun. He seemed happy to continue discussing Noah and Theodora. But it was gossipy, unimportant stuff: some nice anecdotes, a few of Noah's sayings from his Hollywood years, familiar to readers of movie history. "Never let that sonofabitch back in here – unless I need him" was a quote Lanigan had heard attributed to half a dozen other studio tycoons. But "the only way to treat an actress is to keep slapping her down until she apologizes" was one he hadn't heard before. There was a good story about the time Noah insisted that Theodora play a scene with Gary Cooper, wearing nothing beneath her robe. "Who will know I'm naked beneath the robe?" she complained. "Coop will know," Swan told her, "and every man in the audience who sees his reaction when he grabs you will get the message."

"How many of those old Hollywood mogul stories are true, do you think?" Lanigan asked, remembering Kate's story of Theodora's departure from Hollywood.

"Does it matter? A man can build a whole reputation on one good piece of fiction," Fortas answered frankly for once. "What counts in life is not what happened but what other people think happened. Fiction shores up most of our lives . . . It's what makes history so interesting."

They stopped and turned back towards the hotel. Fortas shifted the umbrella to his other shoulder. The sky was cloudless, the purest blue; their shadows fell sharp and black across the sand. They had been walking for nearly an hour. Lanigan resisted asking the important questions. Questions imply doubt; a man betrays his weakness by his questions. But there were two that had to be asked, and he asked both of them together:

"How did Swan know I was here? Who told him I'd found the Baroness?"

Fortas stopped and looked at the sky.

"Did you know that Bewick is a species of swan?" he asked.

"He owns the hotel? Noah Swan owns the Bewick?"

Fortas smiled enigmatically. "Think about our conversation. Give me your thoughts in the morning. Breakfast, eight o'clock?"

The desk clerk gave Lanigan two messages. Kate Goldsmid had called from Austin; she would call again. Mr Scherrer had called, no message. And a man who refused to leave a name had called twice. Henriksen, Lanigan guessed.

He spent the afternoon in his room. Below a beach buggy, wavery in the humid air, travelled along the water's edge. A door slammed in the room above, a man and a woman laughed, then silence. After a little while the woman screamed. Her pleasure seemed to add to his isolation.

At four o'clock it began to rain. He heard the lovers moving about above. He pictured them dressing in silence, their passions all used up. He closed his eyes and thought of Kate. He wished she had been there. She would have said something wise and funny and filled him with hope.

At five he ordered tea. He drank it standing up, watching raindrops follow each other down the window. He felt conscious of time. He felt something happening, yet he, who was in the middle of it, was in the dark. The discovery that Noah owned the hotel and was reading his notes almost as soon as he deposited them in the Bewick safe made him mad at first. Now it amused him. What did it matter? Swan was merely stealing what he had already bought.

He listened to the rain, made notes, went over familiar ground, patiently searching for the links between the parts and a whole. A list of the people he wanted to talk to: Walter and Cissy Rusk, the Baroness . . . He stopped there, staring at the three names. Was there a connection? What could they possibly have in common, the Austrian aristocrat and the brother and sister from Jackson Heights? He couldn't think of a thing – except that they had all been together at a champagne breakfast at the Plaza Hotel in New York City . . . fifty years ago!

At seven, he locked his notes in his case, did fifty pushups, showered, poured a Scotch. Outside the rain had stopped. He started to call Andy Scherrer, remembered that the phone went through the Bewick switchboard, went downstairs and called from a payphone in a bar across the street.

Jilly Bohlen-Williams answered: Andy had just left for the evening. She sounded warm and friendly. He considered inviting her to dinner, but, for no good reason he could think of, decided against it. He called Henriksen's number at the airport. There was no reply; he called Balzac's.

"You've been trying to reach me," he said when Henriksen's voice came on the line above steel band music and loud voices that now filled Balzac's with the noise of happy-hour business.

"Your problem – it's solved," Henriksen shouted above the din. "Drop by my house later." He gave him the address, and directions. "'Bout nine," he said, and hung up.

23

*Secrecy has become a god in this country, and
those who have secrets travel in a kind of
fraternity.*
*(Senator J. William Fulbright, Chairman, Sen-
ate Foreign Relations Committee, 1971)*

Sunday night, October 1
Port of Spain, Trinidad

Lanigan swung his pickup off the main highway and continued
heading south on Cipriani. The rain was so hard that the wipers
could barely cope. He arrived shortly before nine. From inside
the clapboard house came the heavy muffled beat of a rock band
over the noise of the rain and the water sluicing off the roof. He
rang the bell and kept ringing until the music stopped and the
door was thrown open by a barefoot girl wearing cut-offs and an
Eric Clapton T-shirt.

"Hey! You found us! Come in! Mr Lanigan, right? Christ, this
weather! Victoria Biddulph. The one who works at HDH." She
held out her hand. "Tor." Her grip was firm and dry, like a young
man's. She led him into a spacious living-room, the white walls of
which were hung with paintings and rotogravures of World War I
biplanes. Above the brick fireplace hung a two-bladed wooden
propellor.

"Henrik's in the shower. We've just got back from Balzac's.
What can I offer you?" She stood over a table filled with drinks.
"Scotch, vodka –"

"Scotch is fine." Lanigan was grateful for the opportunity of
spending a few minutes alone with the girl on whom much now
depended. "Ice, no water."

She was not unattractive – tomboyish, thick auburn hair,

153

freckles, an overbite – but neither was she the willowy Swedish type Lanigan had imagined Henriksen would go for. She handed him his drink, poured a glass of white wine for herself. They sat opposite one another, she on a flowered sofa, he in a leather club chair.

"A magazine writer, yes?"

"Yes." He didn't elaborate. "How long have you worked at Holy Day House, Tor?"

"Oh, gosh!" She thought for a moment. "Two years. *Yonks*. I was on holiday in Mustique when I heard about it – the job at HDH. It was a chance to stay out here a little longer. I love the sun –" she stroked the tips of her fingers across the freckles on her forehead – "as you see."

"And before that?"

"Bor-*ring*," she said in a sing-song voice. "Roedean. The usual finishing school malarky in Switzerland. A bit of shorthand-typing, a bit of this, a bit of that . . . Daddy was a touch miffed when I elected to stay out here. Not at all what he had in mind."

"He had in mind what?" Lanigan had decided that she was at least five years older than he had first reckoned.

"Daddy?" She glanced in the direction of the shower. "Oh, you know, the usual Daddy things: the Season . . . then a nice respectable engagement to some jolly handsome Guards officer, or some boring Hooray Henry in the City . . . the usual English bullshit!"

"What exactly do you do at Holy Day House?"

The question made her giggle. He realized that she must also have had a few vinos at Balzac's. "I'm secretary to the senior physician. He thinks having an English sec is a bit of a status symbol. It's a hoot, really. When you're a status symbol nobody notices how really rotten your shorthand is!"

"So you two have met! Good!" Henriksen stood in the doorway, wearing a white bathrobe, towel-drying his hair. "She told you the plan?"

"Darling, we were waiting for you," she protested, going over to the drinks table and fixing him a rum and Coke.

Henriksen took the drink without thanking her. She sat next to him on the sofa, across from Lanigan, tucking her feet beneath her. "Well," she began, looking at Lanigan, "Henrik says you want to interview the Baroness . . ." She hesitated, glanced up at Henriksen. "Why don't you explain it, darling?"

"You do it."

She frowned, started again: "Normally you wouldn't have a Chinaman's chance of getting to her. However, next week there might be a way . . . Let me explain the set up over there."

"Holy Day House is a ritzy rip-off for people with more money than sense," Henriksen interrupted with a kind of resentment.

"A few of them are genuinely ill," Tor said, defensively. "Some of them are quite sick kittens, darling."

"Too much booze," Henriksen said. "Or too much dope."

Tor smiled to humour him. "We do get some thirsty souls. Some are there because they're off their feed. Others are in for cosmetic make-overs, de-da, de-da . . ."

"Which category does the Baroness fit into?" Lanigan asked.

"I'm coming to that. The cheapest accommodation is a one-bedroom suite. The most expensive a studio apartment – modelled on the bungalows at the Beverly Hills Hotel. Until nine months ago she had a bungalow on the south beach. Now she has her own wing in the old house."

"And her own walled garden," said Henriksen.

"She is completely isolated from the rest of the clinic," Tor said. "Officially, we don't even know who she is. She was admitted on a Code 9 which is complete anonymity. Although the staff refer to her as the Baroness. She has her own domestic staff, her own nursing staff – nuns, by the way. She even has her own physiotherapist."

"So you don't know whether she's genuinely –"

"A sick kitten?"

Lanigan smiled. "Or simply off her feed?"

Tor smiled too. "No, I don't. Her medical records are kept separately from those of the other patients.

"Have you seen her?"

"A few times."

"How's she looking?"

"Skinny as a griss stick. Very *chic* – can you be a *chic* recluse? She is, anyway."

"She doesn't sound fatally ill," Lanigan said.

"I don't think there's a damn thing wrong with her," Henriksen said, "except old age. She's banged up there because her daughter doesn't want to be reminded of her own goddam mortality."

Lanigan stood up and walked to the end of the room, and back again. "OK," he addressed the question to the girl. "How do I get to her?"

She stood up and took his empty glass and refilled it. "Thursday," she began, handing back his glass. "A new cardiologist checks her out. I made the arrangements last week. Dr Bayard Ramsey. From the Walter Reed Hospital in Washington. She had a mild heart attack in 1993 and has a cardiac check-up twice a year."

Lanigan nodded for her to continue.

"I'm due back at HDH on Tuesday." She looked at Henriksen. "I've had five days off for bad behaviour. If you called me – saying you are Ramsey – and told me that you'll be coming twenty-four hours earlier –"

"Get in ahead of the real Ramsey," said Henriksen, cutting to the point. "Call Tor, then call me –"

"You're flying him across?" Lanigan turned to Henriksen.

"I pick him up at Piarco International."

"Anybody on St Francis know the real Ramsey?"

"I know my boss has never met him," Tor said.

"What about the others over there? Any of the staff likely to know him?"

"I didn't conduct a poll, Mr Lanigan," she said challengingly. "How much risk are you prepared to take?"

Lanigan thought about it for a moment. "Anything else?"

"That's the plan," Henriksen said.

"What about you two – won't it make things difficult for you when they find out an imposter's been rooting around over there?"

Tor giggled. "There'll be the most frightful hoo-ha."

"What can they do about it? You'll be outta there, as you Americans say," Henriksen said.

"Henrik and I only did our jobs. We were taken in by 'Dr Ramsey' just like everyone else," Tor said.

Lanigan finished his drink. "Let's get it on," he said.

24

The main function of an intelligence service is to shield those it serves against surprise. (Walter Laqueur, World of Secrets: The Uses and Limits of Intelligence)

Monday, October 2
Port of Spain

Lanigan woke up early feeling good. The meeting with Henriksen and his girl, Victoria Biddulph, had been the first decent break he'd had since he started. He ran three miles on the beach, showered, put on a fresh tracksuit and went down to breakfast twenty minutes early.

Fortas was waiting for him.

"Enjoy your run?" Fortas greeted him. "I watched you from my window. You looked extremely fit. I don't get enough exercise in Washington. Among the misfortunes that may befall a man, the loss of health has to be one of the severest, don't you think?"

It sounded like something he had learned from a Victorian tract, Lanigan thought.

"So, have you thought about our little conversation yesterday?" Fortas asked cheerfully after they had ordered.

"I thought about it," Lanigan said, watching the waitress pour his coffee.

"And what have you decided, sir?"

"Trust me, you'll get the best I got."

Fortas shook his head. "You're not easy."

"I was hired to do a job. I was chosen because I can wipe my own nose."

"Perfectly true, sir. What you say is perfectly true. But I must ask you to see it from our principal's point of view."

"Forget about the Baroness?"

"Yes."

Lanigan shrugged his shoulders. "He don't like the way I peddle my violets, he can let me go."

"Alas, I fear that letting you go is no longer an option," Fortas said softly, ending the silence that followed Lanigan's ultimatum, and in which they felt themselves drawn together in mutual apprehension and mistrust.

"No longer an option?"

"Letting go a fellow with too much knowledge is letting loose a blind Samson . . . Surely you see that? Blind Samson is apt to wreak havoc."

"Jesus, Fortas, you ever get straight to the point?"

Fortas stared at him with disapproval. "I will ask you for the last time: is it still your intention to visit the Baroness? In spite of Mr Swan's specific wishes to the contrary?"

"Right now, she's the only shot I have."

A man and a woman were shown to the next table. The woman was much younger than the man. She had red hair and green eyes, which were shining. She asked the man what he was thinking about. And they smiled at each other. Lanigan wondered whether she was the woman he had heard making love.

Fortas said, "Mr Swan wants solutions; he doesn't want new problems."

"I do it the way I do it, or I go."

A look of bafflement touched Fortas's eyes, as if Lanigan had failed to understand a simple fact. Several moments of silence went by. Then Fortas said, "I hope you don't come to regret it."

"I have a charmed life."

"Charm is not something I would wish to trust my life to," Fortas said.

25

Death's at the bottom of everything, Martins. Leave death to the professionals. (The Third Man, *original screenplay by Graham Greene*)

Thursday, October 5
London

Robert Rider rose shortly after six, and ran in Hyde Park. When he returned Grace Hempel had gone. Except for the faint, delicious fragrance of her scent, there was no trace of her at all; no hairpins in the bed, no make-up traces on his dressing-table. She understood his fastidiousness; she respected the clandestine nature of his life. She didn't need to mark her territory. His housekeeper would never know she had ever been around. He showered, and read several chapters of the novel based on Noah and Theodora. At nine o'clock Grace called and gave him Copeland's number in the country. "I hear he's rocky," she said. "Step lively or you might miss him."

That was three days ago.

Now Rider followed the handsome young Indian up the mahogany staircase of Copeland's mansion in West Sussex. "He is *very* busy. We started shooting last week. It's a personal picture. A testamental kind of thing," the Indian said, taking Rider by the elbow, guiding him over power cables laid across the landing. "It will be the most remarkable film he's ever made."

"I hear he hasn't been well."

"He's dying, actually."

Rider couldn't tell whether the matter-of-fact tone was meant to ward off sympathy, or to discourage further questions. Before he could respond to the startling statement, he was shown into a small study.

"The *sanctum sanctorum*. Make yourself comfortable, Mr Rider. He will be with you shortly . . . He appreciates the occasional 'sir', by the way."

"How long has he got?"

The Indian shrugged fatalistically. "Weeks."

Left alone, Rider studied the room. A series of drawings of young men undressing; bookshelves of old leather volumes on religious philosophy and erotic folklore; a Victorian partners' desk piled with scripts and books, many of them on faith healing and Eastern mind-body therapies. A sweet smell of medicaments and scent in the air. He took down an 1821 edition of the Third Variorum Shakespeare.

"The Bard is best read aloud, and standing up. I have resigned myself to the fact that I shall never read Shakespeare again." Émile Copeland entered the room in a wheelchair. "Life is short: a little love, a little dreaming, and then, goodnight. I'm sorry to have kept you, Mr Rider. I am permitted to work only till midday." He wheeled himself swiftly into the centre of the room, extended a manicured but skeletal hand, and winced faintly as Rider shook it. "Time is precious. I have to use every minute. It used to be the bloody unions that called the tune, now it's the bloody quacks."

Rider was shocked by his appearance. He barely recognized him from the dandyish figure he had seen in the BBC film. His head had been shaved; his face, worn to the bone, had a luminous intensity, as if exalted by its misfortune.

"I'll try not to take up too much of your time, sir."

"We all want more time, Mr Rider. It's unlikely that it would make us any happier. You want to talk about the past. People always want to talk to me about the past . . . The future would be a very short subject in my case, of course." He smiled and his ravaged face lit up. "How may I help you?"

"I'm planning a book on Theodora Glass."

"Theodora is essential to the Hollywood myth about itself. You tamper with that at your peril!"

Rider laughed. "I saw the *Romeo and Juliet* documentary the other evening. You said some interesting things."

"The pleasures of retrospect are among the most real we possess." Copeland closed his lashless, lime-coloured eyes, either in recall or exhaustion. He was wearing make-up; his collar was lined with tissues to protect it against the pancake on his neck. "I've had regrets and disappointments in my life, an enormous number, and I've resolved most of them in my mind . . . But I have never gotten over the disappointment of not finishing that picture. It was a matter of the heart to me. The way Noah emptied his commode over it was unforgivable."

"Didn't he originally intend only to suspend production?"

"What was he going to do – complete it after the war?" Copeland opened his eyes in mock surprise. "No, my friend. Theodora was never going to be thirteen again. With the best make-up in the world – with Wechsler lighting her – he wasn't ever going to match that footage again. Time has a marvellous power of ruin, Mr Rider."

He smiled a small sad smile, as if to say, *as you can see*.

The Indian came into the room carrying glasses, a decanter, and bottles of pills on a silver tray.

"Aaah, my lunch," Copeland said. "Will you have a drink, Mr Rider – some vino?"

"Thank you."

"The Batard-Montrachet 1981," Copeland said, looking at the young Indian fondly. "No, let's splash the mazuma for our distinguished guest – *vin d'honneur* – a bottle of the Corton Charlemagne 1975. Exquisitely chilled." He banged the arms of his wheelchair with pleasure. "See to it, my boy!"

Almost at once he began telling his familiar anecdotes, saying what he wanted to say, and what he always said in interviews. Rider listened with great patience. Silence was his technique. He did not intrude when stories he had heard before rambled on; he knew that repetition sometimes revealed what it was meant to hide.

"The most hideous thing about stardom is its greed . . . Actresses have a high threshold of praise . . . Being a producer necessarily involves knavery, which is why it has such a deleterious effect on the character . . . Women pick up languages faster than men. It's all about survival. I'll bet inside a month the Sabine women were speaking Latin, with a perfect Roman accent . . . Stars believe their own publicity. Producers believe their own lies . . . If I had wanted to be remembered, I would have planted trees . . ."

He spoke with an actor's voice, a seamless monologue driven by an ageless anger. Rider listened, smiled, looked solemn, made notes.

The assistant returned with the wine, poured a little for Copeland to taste. The old man sipped, sniffed the cork, nodded his approval. Another young man brought in a plate of smoked salmon sandwiches for Rider, and a grated apple and *crème brûlée* for the director.

"Tell me about Noah," Rider said, as they ate.

"Whatever you say about him, the reverse is also true. He was cruel; he was kind. He was a cold-ass shit; he was charming. He was whatever he wanted to be. I never once experienced boredom in his company."

"Do you still believe he closed the picture down because Theodora was pregnant?" Rider asked matter-of-factly.

"I know he did," Copeland said.

"She was fourteen," Rider reminded him.

"I know how old she was." He lifted the glass of wine to his mouth, but his hand was shaking and he put it down before it spilled. "I know exactly how old she was," he said again. "She had her first period on the picture. The Baroness got the contract changed so she didn't have to work the first two days of her menstrual cycle. A director knows as much about his leading lady's inside as her gynaecologist. She was regular as clockwork. Forty-eight hours off every twenty-eight days. We built it into the schedule. Then one month she didn't exercise her rights. She missed a whole cycle. Next thing is, she's allergic to the smell of paint – to cover the morning sickness, to explain her late arrival on the set. Then we had the *crème fraiche* business."

"What was that?"

Copeland cocked his head. "She was becoming the teensiest bit . . . *zoftig*?"

"The camera is cruel on the ladies," Rider said.

"There had been some items in the press about her weight problem. Gowns having to be altered, that sort of thing. A film set is not a place for keeping secrets. Aaron Flagg put out a story about her passion for . . ." he screwed up his face in concentration, and by some fine alchemy of memory recalled the distant wording, "*truffes chocolat caraque à la crème fraiche!*"

Rider wrote it down.

Copeland had barely touched the grated apple, but continued to hold the plate in his lap. Realizing that he did not have the strength to put it down, Rider took it from him and placed it on the table.

"Aaron Flagg is more than a footnote in the Noah–Theodora story. More than a mouthpiece. He was a great ideas man. Stopped Noah fucking up more than once. Covered tracks like nobody's business. Noah's Flagg waver, I called him."

He said nothing for several minutes. Perhaps he was lost in some vision of the past, Rider thought.

Copeland ended the silence with a deep sigh. "London in 1940 . . . everybody wanted to leave town."

"Like *Casablanca*."

"She had the abortion in New York," Copeland said, missing Rider's joke. "They did a fantastic job keeping the lid on it. She was fourteen years old. Can you imagine if that had got out? It would have been the end of her –"

"And the end of Noah."

"Fuck Noah. You think I kept quiet all those years for Noah? I did it for her."

"Noah was the father?"

"Who else, my dear?" Copeland looked at his watch. "I hope I've been of some use."

"You have, sir. Thank you."

"May I ask a small favour of you, Mr Rider?"

"Of course."

"The film I am making is a little vanity – a summing up of my wretched life before these cursed flames of rage are all extinguished!"

Rider realized why he was wearing make-up: he was making a film of his last days on earth.

"I hope you don't find the idea too macabre." Copeland smiled a smile Rider imagined old embalmers dream about on dark nights. "Passions weaken but habit strengthens with age. Would you be so kind as to appear in a scene with me? Some civilized conversation . . . about life and death, perhaps!"

Rider wasn't happy about it, but he said yes anyway.

Copeland said, "Is it vanity – or something else – that causes us to be concerned with people's opinions, even when we'll exist only in name?"

"I don't know," Rider answered.

"Something else," Copeland said. "It's always something else."

26

*We are a good team – I long to know and Mr
Swan loves to teach. (Theodora Glass, Picture-
goer magazine, April 1940)*

**Thursday, October 5
Santa Aloe**

THEODORA'S TAPE

OK, losing my virginity! We'll have to think about this before we
show it to Mr Rider, Missy. But let's get it down – and think
about it.

January 1940. The nineteenth. I remember this day. London
blackout. Freezing. Snow falling in large flakes on the streets. I
wore tan slacks and a sweater beneath a mink coat borrowed
from wardrobe. We were driving back from Denham, the studio
rouge still on my nice hollow cheeks. Noah said I looked like a
pampered waif!

He was not even remotely a flirt with me but I think we both
knew or sensed that our relationship was changing. We were not
a producer and a child actress any more: he was an attractive
man, and I was becoming no longer a child. Sexual attraction
complicates relationships. Sex always makes people wary of each
other.

"Are ya happy, kid?" he said.

"We're out of Vienna. I'm happy about that," I said. I could
feel our thighs touch and move away again in the dark of the
limousine. The movement was mine, not his. "And you?" I said.
"Are you happy?"

"Oh sure," he said. "We got some good pages today."

"But you called an early wrap," I said, using his Hollywood
jargon.

167

He said, "My movie depends on you. You were beginning to look tired. Juliet must never look tired."

It was a professional judgement. It saved him time and money to stop shooting on me when I did not look at my best. But I didn't know that then. I always suspected criticism in his tone when he spoke with such blunt professionalism. I was angry that he could hurt me so easily.

"I would like to disappear and be ugly for a month," I told him.

He grinned. "No actress can live up to her publicity pictures all the time."

We'd been shooting for about four months. A closed set, no press. I was under wraps, in a cocoon, and perhaps he sensed my feeling of isolation. Anyway, that evening he invited me to dinner. It was the first time we had dined alone, without Mama (she had a chill), and without Aaron Flagg. Although Aaron I always felt good with. He was a friend I could trust and talk to.

We dined at the Savoy Grill. The wartime menu had little on it except some indefinable pilaffs. But Noah did allow me a glass of wine. He was attentive, and funny. He did everything he could to put me at ease. Told me stories about his past, his adventures in Hollywood, some slightly *risqué* stories about actresses he'd known, whose names I knew. But his little confessions I noticed always led to more questions about me.

He said, "Why are you smiling?"

I told him, "Because you tell me your secrets to find out about me."

I always surprised him, he said. I asked why he had invited me to have dinner with him. He said, "In the car coming back from the studio . . . You hinged back your head, and closed your eyes. It was such an exhausted . . . such an adult gesture. I wanted to cheer you up."

"I *am* an adult," I said.

I knew at that moment that we were going to be lovers. Maybe he did too. We talked some more, but he kept it strictly professional. He asked what I thought my biggest handicap as an actress was. I said my accent. He said, "If you become a big star you won't have an accent. People don't notice accents if a star is big enough." I said it would still limit my choice of parts. He said, "If they love you, audiences do the work for you."

"You give me hope, Noah," I told him. It was the first time I ever called him Noah.

He said, "Hope is the best thing in the world."

I said, "I'd always hoped that love would be."

I remember leaving the Grill Room. Crossing the lobby, walking slowly so as not to show my excitement.

Noah said quietly, "I could go to jail for ten years just for thinking what I'm thinking now."

In the elevator, when we reached my floor, the floor below his, I didn't move. Just stood there, stricken, my heart pounding. I remember looking into his face . . . willing him to make the next move . . .

In love everything depends on a moment, doesn't it, Missy?

He said, "Are you sure it's what you want, kid? Just say yes or no."

I took his hand. I didn't trust myself to speak.

He said, "Ever since I first saw you in Berlin I've seen this moment coming."

He was very gentle. There was no pain. Afterwards he said, "You're a fully-fledged woman now."

"Will people be able to tell?"

"Jesus," he said. "I hope not."

I seduced Noah Swan, no question of that. He could have gone to prison for what he did. But it was my idea, it was my choice. I was a month away from my fourteenth birthday.

27

*Michael Fortas does what has to be done. He carries Swan's bags, orders his shirts, fixes his appointments. But he is much more than just another Washington gofor (what other gofor has a doctorate in engineering at MIT?) and you underrate him at your peril. (*Noah Swan's Key Men, Manhattan Inc., *March 9, 1985)*

Thursday, October 5
Port of Spain

Lanigan had it all figured out at last. He felt curiously elated. He felt suddenly released from he did not know what. He put his notes into a large envelope, and sealed it with Scotch tape. He placed this envelope inside a larger envelope, which he also sealed with tape and addressed to himself c/o Andy Scherrer at the CIA station chief's home in Blanchisseuse.

He wondered why it had taken him so long to realize what Noah Swan was up to. He was used to relationships based on Byzantine secrecy and Noah's behaviour didn't surprise him. Even the fact that he was being used as a barium meal amused him. But why Noah suddenly needed to know whether the Baroness was safely buried – that fascinated him a lot. "She is not important. She is not meaningful," Fortas had told him. But clearly she had been hidden away for a reason. Because she was a risk? What kind of risk, and to whom?

He dressed slowly in the tropical-weight grey pinstripe suit he had bought the day before in an expensive menswear shop in Duke Street. It wasn't his style, but it was what he thought a distinguished Washington cardiologist would wear to visit an important patient like the Baroness von Tegge in a smart clinic like Holy Day House. The suit was as important to the deception as the blood-pressure cuff and stethoscope he had also purchased yesterday in a medical supply store on Maraval Road. He packed the cuff and stethoscope into the briefcase lent to him by Scherrer; built by the CIA's Technical Services Division, it also contained a hidden VOR camera and tape machine.

He closed the briefcase, slipped on his new jacket, and smiled at his reflection in the mirror. "Dr Bayard Ramsey, I presume?"

At Piarco International he parked in a space reserved for aircrew, and went into the main departure lounge, where he posted the envelope to himself c/o Andy Scherrer. Then, as Dr Bayard Ramsey, he presented himself at the private aircraft departure counter. A security guard checked his name on a computer screen, and dialled a number. "Tell Captain Henriksen Dr Ramsey's here. Sending him over now." He put down the phone, handed Lanigan a security clearance tag for his lapel, and pointed over his shoulder. "Take that exit to the ground floor, turn left, keeping walking. Big red 'copter shed. Have a nice trip, doc."

Henriksen, wearing a white short-sleeved shirt and perfectly pressed jeans, was supervising the loading of supplies into the hold of the pale-blue and orange Jovair, and arguing with a supervisor over several linen-wrapped carcasses of freezer meat which had not been listed on the original manifest. He was complaining that the meat took the 'copter too close to its maximum operating weight.

"Captain Henriksen?" Lanigan interrupted the argument.

Henriksen eyed Lanigan like he had never seen him before in his life. "Dr Ramsey?" he finally responded, loud enough for the crew of the provisions truck to hear. "Dr Bayard Ramsey?" he added, for good measure. "Good morning, sir." They shook hands. "You've picked a perfect day for a run out to the island, doctor," he said, looking at the dazzling-bright sapphire-blue sky through his movie star sunglasses.

After signing for the provisions, including the disputed freezer meat, and the fuel, Henriksen closed and secured the hold door, helped Lanigan into a yellow lifejacket and showed him how to inflate it in an emergency. Lanigan let himself be treated like another nervous passenger for the benefit of the mechanics and loaders who stood around. Henriksen yanked open the starboard door and ushered him into the cockpit. He slipped on his own lifejacket, pulled himself up into the pilot's seat, slammed the port door behind him. "So let's fly," he said. The 235-horsepower turboshaft engine started up with a roar that brought the entire airframe alive. The noise rose to a crescendo. Within seconds the rotor blades became an almost invisible 35-foot disc, their fierce down-draught sending a whirlwind of dust and fumes across the hot tarmac. An acrid smell of exhaust gases seeped into the cockpit. Henriksen put on a headset; went quickly through his pre-flight checks; had a brief buddy-buddy exchange with some-one in the control tower. Satisfied that the engine had run up to flight speed, he raised the pitch control lever. The angle of the blades increased to produce lift, and the machine rose slowly into the air, turned into the wind, and began a forward speed climb into the empty sky.

As they cleared the west coast of Trinidad and headed out to sea, Lanigan said: "Tell me about St Francis. I couldn't find it on the map."

Henriksen reached down into his map case and took out a navigation chart and handed it to Lanigan, who opened it and spread it across his knees.

"That's it." Henriksen jabbed his forefinger at a sickle-shaped island surrounded by depth contours and soundings, and the symbols for coral reefs and rocks, riptides and wrecks. "The only anchorage is Buccaneer Harbour," he shouted above the noise of the engine. "The whole island's not more than a thousand acres. Used to be a pirates' hole-up. Later a bunch of Franciscan monks turned it into a leper colony. Now it's a clinic for the filthy rich. Like the pirates got it back again!"

Lanigan smiled and closed his eyes.

Noah Swan's face, all but eaten away by leprosy, was grinning at him from the shore, beckoning him to come quickly . . .

Lanigan awoke with a start.

"We're almost there," Henricksen said, letting go of his arm to point through the windshield at an island on the horizon. "Jovair Golf Sierra Brava Alpha Delta to St Francis," he turned his attention to the radio. "Do you read me? Over."

A muffled thud from somewhere aft of the freight compartment sent a quiver through the whole 'copter.

The two men looked enquiringly at one another.

"Too high for a bird-strike," Henriksen said, his eyes rapidly scanning his instrument panel. The words were barely out of his mouth when the engine spluttered, stopped, started, and stopped again. The 'copter began losing altitude at a stomach-churning twenty-two feet a second; all that could be heard behind the stall-warning alarm was the beating of unpowered rotor blades and the hiss of wind streaming over the fuselage.

"Shit," Henriksen muttered under his breath, frantically hitting buttons, flicking switches.

But the engine wouldn't restart.

The needles on both the torgue-meter and gas generator gauge were falling rapidly towards zero. GEN RH and ENG OIL P signals started to flash on the central warning panel. Henriksen put a shallow pitch on the main rotor blades so that a rush of air would keep them turning, like the sails of a windmill, and produce a slight lift. In order to make a safe autorotative descent, all he had to do was get the right glide angle, maintain enough rotor rpm, and keep his nerve.

"Everything's under control," he said grimly, but more to himself than to reassure Lanigan. He pressed the transmit button. "Jovair Golf Sierra Brava Alpha Delta to St Francis. Are you eyeballing me? Over."

The radio crackled, then fell silent.

"*Fuck you doing to me?*" Henriksen shouted at the dead radio as he tried to tune it in. "*Jesus, shit,*" he said, giving up and concentrating on the controls. "Brace yourself, Magazine Writer. We're ditching." The black shadow of the 'copter skimmed across the water. "Fucking too much swell . . . not breaking white, anyway."

Lanigan kept silent, and let Henriksen handle the situation. He was a skilled aviator, he wasn't a panicker. But Lanigan understood the real danger they were in and prepared himself for the impact, while at a deeper level of his mind he thought about Noah Swan. Swan knew he was going to the island; Lanigan had spelled out his plans in the last notes he put in the hotel safe, knowing they would get back to him almost as soon as he deposited them. It was a deliberate challenge to Swan to back him or sack him. *But nobody ever defies Noah Swan and gets away with it, do they?* Images of sharks and the raw meat he had seen being loaded aboard the aircraft burst into his head. He felt his heartbeat quicken as the implications gathered in his mind.

Henriksen steered a course to the right of the island, then made a seventy degree banking turn to port. This would bring them parallel to the swell when they splashed down, and minimize the risk of the 'copter breaking its back. As soon as the altimeter showed them to be a hundred feet above the sea, Henriksen pressed the switch that would inflate the emergency flotation bags.

Nothing.

"*Shit!*" He said it over and over, as he continued to hit the switch. "*I don't believe this.*"

The 'copter hit the sea with a force that tore off the skids, fragmented the nose section, and ruptured the fuel tanks beneath the cabin floor.

"*Alas*" – Fortas's words exploded in Lanigan's head – "*letting you go is no longer an option.*"

The second explosion tore the 'copter to bits.

28

Politicians are big on the big promises. But we're seldom equal to the little sacrifices that others make for us – and they're the ones that count. (Senator Matthew Swan, Washington Post, *May 24, 1987)*

8.05 a.m., Friday, October 6
New York City

Kate Goldsmid was feeling good. Her case in Austin had gone well, and Robert Levin's improvised cadenzas in Mozart's piano concertos playing on the radio reminded her of the Ann Arbor Mozartfest she had taken Lanigan to in her quest to improve his lousy taste in music. They hadn't talked for ten days, and she missed him.

Still in her robe and pyjamas, her hair held back with an elastic band, she sat at the breakfast table reading a *Times* op-ed piece predicting that unless Matthew Swan turned out to be accident-prone, or plain unlucky, he would stay the firm favourite to win his party's presidential nomination next July. All he had to do was throw his hat in the ring.

When the phone rang she smiled and looked at her watch. She knew it would be Lanigan, and hoped he was going to tell her that he'd be back for the weekend.

She was thrown when she heard Rosengarten's voice on the line. "Rosy," she said, surprised into using the nickname only Lanigan was permitted to use. "Just reading about your man." She turned down the radio, took a sip of tea. "The *Times* says the nomination's in his pocket. Well done, you!"

"Kate, I apologize to be calling this early," Rosengarten answered, ignoring her congratulations. He spoke with deliberate slowness, his prepared-statement voice. "It's Ambrose, Kate . . ."

His use of Lanigan's first name warned her that it was something serious, and that short-circuited the shock somehow. Thinking about it later, she knew that she already knew what the answer would be when she asked, "How bad is it, Edward?"

Rosengarten couldn't trust his voice to answer, and there was just silence on the line.

Kate's steady voice made her sound braver than she felt. "What happened, Edward?"

He gave her the facts as briefly as he could. A routine flight, a sudden loss of power . . . Lanigan and the pilot both killed . . . He said the things people say when they have to break such news. The sadness, the regret, the shock. If there was anything he could do, *anything* . . .

Kate barely took in a word he said. Tears streamed out from beneath her closed eyes. She hoped he had died quickly, and that his courage had not let him down in the end. She tried not to think about the helicopter falling out of the sky. She would not ask the hour of his death. She tried to think of other things. Happier times. Kinder skies. She pictured his lovely warrior's smile.

"I want you to know, Kate, I understand what you must be going through right now." The winding-up resonance that had entered Rosengarten's tone broke in on her thoughts. "I know there's no loneliness like losing someone you love," he said.

He heard her light a cigarette.

"I know," she said, with no expression in her voice at all. "I've been there."

29

Your Theodora project is exciting. I'll die happy knowing you're on the case, and one day the truth will be told, and the world will know why my picture was sacrificed. (Émile Copeland, from a letter to Robert Rider, October 10)

7.30 p.m., Thursday, October 26
New York City

Within twenty minutes of arriving at the Regency, Rider was settled in his bath with the *Times* and a dry vodka martini. It was an idiosyncrasy of his that he only ever drank martinis in New York, and only in the bath.

He read Copeland's obit with a sense of regret, and also satisfaction that he had got to him just in time. He read the movie reviews, and an interview with a young Canadian author whose first novel was going to make her rich and famous. He almost missed the AP story below the fold on page five. Headlined *Former CIA man killed in Caribbean air crash*, it read:

The man who died when the helicopter belonging to actress Theodora Glass crashed on October 5 has been identified as Mr Ambrose Lanigan, and not, as earlier reported, Dr Bayard Ramsey of the Walter Reed Hospital, Washington DC.

An official of the Trinidad Aviation Safety Commission said that there was no immediate explanation why the confusion arose.

Mr Lanigan was a former career officer in the Central Intelligence Agency.

Mr Henrik Henriksen, a Swedish national, Miss Glass's

179

personal pilot, was also killed when the Jovair came down off the island of St Francis.

There were no other casualties.

The former Hollywood actress lives on the private Caribbean island of Santa Aloe.

Rider read it once, then again more slowly. It was the first he had heard of the accident. He hated helicopters, and he shuddered. In two weeks' time he had been due to fly from Port of Spain to Theodora's island in that same helicopter. *That could have been me in that crash*, he thought. He closed his eyes.

He woke with a start at 8.20, dressed quickly and went downstairs.

Aaron Flagg came into the lobby punctually at eight thirty. He was nothing like Rider had expected. He moved slowly, not a New York pace. A little over medium height, lightly tanned, with white hair and a white gunfighter's moustache, he wore English tweeds, Travellers' club necktie, blue-tinted glasses. There was something about him that made people turn and look when he passed.

"It's kind of you to see me," Rider said, when they were seated at a table in the grill room, after the introductions.

"How could I say no?" Flagg's voice was deep, friendly, amused. "When Oscar called and told me what you were up to, I didn't believe him. It's not Rider country, is it?"

Rider smiled. "Thought it was time I tried another tune. We'd like to keep it under wraps at this stage."

Flagg nodded. "She gonna play ball?" he asked quizzically.

"It was her idea."

"She say why she wants to stir everything up again?"

"You don't approve, Mr Flagg?" Rider asked.

Aaron Flagg shrugged. "Beats me why actresses ever want to write their memoirs."

"To be remembered?"

"You wanna be remembered be mysterious. Orson got it right. The only explanation you owe anybody is *Rosebud*. Keep the bastards guessing."

Rider laughed. They turned their attention to the menu. After they ordered, Flagg politely asked about Rider's plans.

"I'm going down to Santa Aloe in a couple of weeks. First I want to look at some of her movies. The Museum of Modern Art is arranging a few screenings for me. I want to visit the Firestone Library at Princeton, they've got some early material on her; and the Swan Collection at the Humanities Research Center at the University of Texas. Also the Wisconsin Center for Film Research, in Madison."

"You're thorough."

"I try to be."

Flagg was amused. "But you'll never get to the truth."

Rider smiled too. "If you say so."

"Nobody ever insured truth against the risk of time better than Noah Swan."

"But *you* know the truth."

Flagg gave a small self-deprecating shrug. "I was a publicist. Publicity ain't about truth. It's about what people want to believe. The anecdotes that are truest are those that never happened. Harry Cohn probably never said *I don't have ulcers – I give 'em!* It's still how people remember him. It becomes a kind of truth."

"You mean, Noah never said *Great beauties who stick around too long are what movies make character actresses out of*?"

"Oh, I know he said that. I wrote it for him. Day Theodora quit Hollywood."

Rider laughed. "I've read most of the books in the last three weeks. Didn't read that."

"A publicist's job is to be heard and not seen. Noah know about *this* book yet?"

"Jesus, I hope not. The longer he's in the dark the better."

Flagg grinned. "Say that again, scout."

Rider watched him cut his tournedos steak. The story was that he had been a rewrite man in the city room of Hearst's *Journal-American* when Noah first met him in Jimmy Glennon's saloon in 1938 and, impressed with his cynical humour, took him to London to handle the publicity for *Romeo and Juliet*. "We are

Hollywood's oldest married couple," Noah would tell reporters years later. "It's the perfect match: I'm susceptible to his suggestions, and he's mindful of my wishes!" But Flagg's strength was his ability to stand up to Noah, and keep his independence.

"I know Noah's going to squawk," Rider said, when Flagg finished chewing. "When he finds out."

"And you'd like to know how loud he's gonna squawk?"

"Will he be a problem?"

"I can only tell you he's more dangerous now he's respectable."

Rider smiled. "You mean he wasn't always respectable?"

"He's robbed a few banks."

"I wondered how he got so rich."

"There's a Spanish proverb. A man who would grow rich must buy of those who go to be hanged – and sell to those who go to be married." Flagg put down his fork and leaned back in his chair. "You probably don't remember. How Hollywood panicked when TV arrived. It was gonna be the end of movies. What did Noah do? Bought up the studios' movie libraries. Paid hundreds of thousands of dollars for pictures so old Gabby Hayes got the girl. Everybody said he was crazy. A year later he leased the same old movies – the movies the studios had almost given away – to the networks for millions. Now he's leasing the same pictures to cable, to satellite . . ."

Rider smiled. "To those who go to be married."

"Noah always had his eye on the main chance, scout. Every penny he could spare he was buying up land in Southern California in the forties, when you could buy a hundred acres for a song. I heard once that he owns a sixth of Orange County."

"That's rich."

"He got started at the right time. That great house he had up on Tower Drive cost $39,000 in forty-two."

"I imagine $39,000 was still a piece of change in 1942," Rider said.

"Not for Barbara Swan it wasn't."

"His wife had money?"

"Money and a social standing the equal of any in town. Her

father was Wendell Thiele, best contracts lawyer in the business. Died coupla days after Matthew was born. Heart attack."

"This book," Rider said carefully. "I want to get it right. I – "

"You know, I've been asked many times to write my book." Flagg's voice acquired a reminiscent tone. "Peach about my days and nights with Noah. Especially the nights. Zolotow, Bob Thomas . . . they've all been on to me. Always said hell no. Some things you take to the tomb."

He was entering the evasive stage. It would be a mistake to try to change his mind at this point. "I'd value some guidance," Rider said mildly.

"I'm retired. I have a good life. A quiet life. Why open that can of worms?"

Rider pulled his hands apart in an understanding gesture. "A few pointers."

"Haven't talked to Noah for five years. We fell out. We were always falling out . . . this time it just stuck. But we had fifty great years together. I mean *great* years. I still respect him. Still miss the son of a bitch. Love him or hate him, he was a great producer. As good as they make 'em. Milly Copeland – God rest his soul – Milly made the great remark: *Hollywood without Noah would be like the Louvre without the Mona Lisa.*"

"Trust me. I'll tell it right," Rider said gently.

Flagg looked at him for a long moment. He pushed his plate slowly away with his thumb. "Keep me outta it, OK?"

"Strictly *entre nous*."

"Where do you want to start?"

Rider smiled. "It's like archaeology . . . You start with the bones."

. . . and there are spies spying on spies. (Miles Copeland, Without Cloak or Dagger*)*

Friday, October 27
Blanchisseuse, Trinidad

The memorial service was at nine, before the heat of the day. The Scherrers had found a little graveyard next to a beautiful old wooden church on the north shore, just outside Blanchisseuse. About a dozen people were at the service: Kate Goldsmid, the Scherrers, Ed Rosengarten; two representatives from the US Embassy; Jilly Bohlen-Williams and Victoria Biddulph.

A young black priest, with a shaved head and boat shoes peeping beneath his cassock, spoke about Lanigan's qualities. He did his best, but he didn't know Lanigan, and it was too much to expect conviction. Kate had asked for a record of Leontyne Price singing Verdi's *Requiem*, which sounded honest and clear in the old church, and made up for what the valediction missed; Andy Scherrer read a passage from *Gerontion*, the T. S. Eliot poem, with its famous reference to "a wilderness of mirrors", which so well described the world in which Lanigan had lived all his adult life; the organist played the *Missa Solemnis* of Beethoven, at Annie Scherrer's request.

Rosengarten, who had succeeded in keeping Lanigan's connection with Matthew Swan from the press, had arranged brunch in his suite at the Bewick. The mourners seemed out of place, their sombre clothes intrusive against the white silk drapes, the white Carrara marble floor covered with bright African rugs, and the erotic Juergen Goerg paintings of near-naked dancers.

Apart from the Scherrers and Rosengarten, Kate knew nobody

in the room, and she was a little startled when a girl she had noticed at the church – she wore a charcoal suit with a wrapover skirt which revealed an amount of black-stockinged calf when she knelt – came across the room and introduced herself.

"My name's Victoria Biddulph – Tor," she said, with a simple factuality. "My fiancé was Henrik Henriksen . . . the pilot."

"Oh, I am sorry," Kate said, taking her hand at once.

"It was a rotten business. I hate helicopters, don't you?"

They stood in silence, neither knowing what else to say.

"Still, onwards and upwards," Tor said suddenly, with a brave surface smile. "Oh Christ, I wish I hadn't said that. I *wish* I hadn't said that." Her eyes filled with tears, and Kate realized how near the edge she was. "I always say the wrong bloody thing," she said, miserably.

"I need a drink. How about you?" Kate gently led her towards the small bar that had been set up by the window.

"It's a bit early . . . A g and t would be nice," Tor said, gratefully.

"A gin and tonic for Miss Biddulph," Kate told the barman, and asked for a white wine for herself.

"I can't sleep at night. Can you?" Tor said, taking the drink. "I have such awful thoughts . . ."

"It'll be difficult for a while," Kate said. "We both need time to mend."

"*Why?*" Why Henrik . . . why your bloke?"

At that moment the sound of Ed Rosengarten's voice interrupted their conversation:

"This is a private occasion, sir. The press has not been invited, nor is it welcome." He was talking to a small, jowly man of about forty, in a cream-coloured suit. "If you will please leave us . . ."

"But why was he using a false name?" the reporter persisted.

"It was not a false name," Rosengarten said, softly this time.

"It wasn't his name."

"Don't you listen, pal? Dr Ramsey was booked on a flight the following day. The pilot got the names confused in his log. I don't know why you're trying to make it sound like such a goddam mystery. Now, if you will excuse me, pal." Rosengarten began stabbing the reporter's chest with his index finger, pushing him back towards the door, where several security men had appeared to escort him off the premises.

Rosengarten went back to the bar, got himself a drink and went across to where Kate stood with Tor Biddulph. "The nerve of those people," he said.

"Edward – this is Victoria Biddulph," Kate said quickly. "The pilot – Mr Henriksen's fiancée."

"Of course. Andy Scherrer told me you were coming," he said, putting down his glass and taking Tor's small hands in both of his. "Please accept my condolences. It was a damn lousy business. If there's anything I can do?"

"Thank you. I'm fine," Tor said, putting up her brave front, which Kate now knew was more to do with English good manners than real fortitude.

"It was a damn lousy business," Rosengarten said again, letting go of her hands. They went over to one of the tables that were set out beneath large shades on the balcony. "You lived out here long, Miss Biddulph?" he asked, as she took the chair he had drawn out and was holding for her. "You're English, right?"

She told him her story, the way she had told it to Lanigan nine days before. But it was something more than forgetfulness that made her now omit the fact that she worked at Holy Day House. The crash had shocked her deeply. And her involvement – she could not rid her mind of the fact that she was responsible for Lanigan's presence aboard the helicopter – consumed her with guilt. The fact that she had thought it a huge lark when she entered into the conspiracy to smuggle him on to St Francis did nothing to ease her conscience. If Lanigan had not been aboard would the accident have happened? He had gone to great lengths to get to the Baroness – had somebody else gone to even greater lengths to stop him? The questions, the guilt, the apprehensions reverberated in her head. Overhearing Rosengarten's conversation with the reporter had disturbed her afresh. She did not know Rosengarten, but she knew plenty of men like him, and she knew that he had been rattled by the reporter's questions.

The brunch was not wholly a sad occasion. There was no

hypocrisy, and Kate was grateful for that. There was fond laughter as both Rosengarten and Andy Scherrer told their stories about Lanigan, and about themselves, tales of derring-do when they were all good Company men together. A few of the stories were *risqué*, some hilarious, others quite incredible. Lanigan came out of them all as a very decent man.

"He was a man totally without rancour," Scherrer said.

"Even when he knew that the risks he took far exceeded the cause," Rosengarten added.

Kate thought how sad it was that such a man should have died pursuing a movie queen. She wondered how many people at the table knew the last truth of Lanigan's life. Scherrer probably did. Rosengarten? He knew half the story; he knew that Lanigan had been down there on a mission for Noah Swan; had he guessed the rest? It was hard to tell. Sometimes he feigned a disarming foolishness – a trick Lanigan once said he had learnt from the Brits in MI6. Lanigan also said that he had lost his touch.

But watching him now, she wasn't so sure. It was always easy to misjudge men like Rosy. Put them on the stand, the ones you're sure have gone soft, they turn out to be the toughest eggs of all.

31

Noah Swan never missed a trick. When he brought Theodora Glass and her mother, Gisela, a beauty in her own right, to Hollywood in 1941, he persuaded the European Film Fund – a Hollywood charity for Nazi refugees – to support them for their first year in Tinsel Town. Paul Kohner – a big agent, and a trustee of the Fund – later suggested that he might like to repay some of the money to the charity. Noah said, "Theodora's your client – you repay the fucking money!" (David Niven, The Moon's a Balloon)

Tuesday, November 7
New York City

Rider had been busy. A day at the Firestone Library; two days at the Wisconsin Center for Film and Theatre Research. He had filled up half a dozen tapes and several notebooks with material, dug up studio memos concerning her early days in Hollywood, and seen three of her best movies at the Museum of Modern Art. But best of all, he had over fifteen hours of tape with Aaron Flagg that was pure gold. Shrewd, funny, aweless, profane, irreverent, and always in the right place at the right time, Flagg was a biographer's dream.

The evening Rider got back from Wisconsin he had dinner with Flagg at the Plaza. It was his twelfth day in New York.

"This hotel has fond memories for me," Flagg said, after the waiter had taken their order. "Where I stayed when we returned from London in 1940. Noah continued on to Hollywood, with Theodora and the Baroness. I stayed behind to organize the billboard campaign. You won't remember that. England, 1940, you had other fish to fry. We launched Theodora with a billboard blitz you wouldn't believe. Her face plastered across Manhattan. That great Lazlo Willinger shot everybody remembers. We had it blown up on Foster and Kleiser twenty-four sheets . . . Times Square, Penn Station, the old Dixie bus terminal . . . twenty bridges, eighteen tunnels . . . You couldn't get in or out of the city without seeing that face" – he moved his hand slowly in the air as if he were reading from an invisible billboard above their heads – "*Theodora Glass – The Face of the Forties*."

"That must have cost a pretty penny," Rider said.

"It got her noticed."

"Who paid? Barbara?"

"He wasn't above using her dough. He told me he borrowed $30,000 on his life insurance." He shrugged. "Anyway, it paid off. By the time they got to Hollywood there wasn't a studio in town that wasn't interested. Jack Warner, Selznick, Louie Mayer – she had those guys standing on their ears."

"Did Noah plan all this after he closed down *Romeo and Juliet*?" Rider made it sound casual, but it was the first leading question he had asked during all their hours of taping.

Flagg grinned. "I better tell you about the baby," he said. "Milly mention the baby?"

Rider nodded.

"I liked Milly. He got shafted. He worked like a bastard on that picture, and it was snatched away from him."

"He never forgave Noah."

Flagg, nodding, said: "Theodora was fourteen years old. She was pregnant. Noah was the father. That made him guilty of statutory rape, at least. The scope for scandal . . . Jesus. On top of everything else, the Baroness was some kinda Catholic, religiously opposed to abortion. No way could we finish the picture before Theodora had the kid. We all felt the trap closing. Noah was looking at a jail sentence, no doubt about that. Then Herr Hitler intervened."

"*Hitler?*"

"September 7, 1940. He launched the London blitz. Pictures

have been abandoned for a lot less!"

"What happened to the baby?"

"The pregnancy was tubal. But we didn't know that until we got to New York. If we'd known it sooner, it coulda saved us all a nightmare."

"The abortion –"

"I never heard that word used," Flagg said. "Definitely not around the Baroness."

"Copeland said the abortion was botched – that's why she's never had kids."

Flagg smiled, a little sadly. "That's what Theodora thinks too. She's convined to this day that the ectopic thing was a scam, that Noah paid off some goddamn lock-picker."

"Did he?"

Flagg shook his head. "But I understand why she thinks that."

"She never had children."

"The operation might have loused up the works. That's another story. These things happen to ladies. In the forties they did. The baby would've croaked anyway if they hadn't operated, that's a fact. Theodora too, probably."

"The Baroness –"

"The Baroness was another problem. She put the bite on Noah. I think she did it for no other reason than to rankle the shit out of him. They had a strange love-hate relationship. Till the day she got the call, she had him hearing footsteps."

"Keeping the lid on a story like that couldn't have been easy."

"There were rumours."

"There were rumours about Mary Poppins."

Flagg smiled. "Mary Poppins wasn't fourteen."

"How did Noah handle it?"

"In all the years we were together, the only business I saw get to him was that."

"Did Theodora forgive him?"

"Every actress he ever worked with fell on her ass for him."

Rider was beginning to like Aaron Flagg a lot. He enjoyed his company, especially his cynicism. Like all old-time studio publicists, there was something conspiratorial in his manner. "There can be no public praise for what we do," he said the first night they dined together. "Anything deserving of praise must be kept secret, or given to somebody else."

The following morning Flagg sent a suitcase full of memos, letters, newspaper clips, photographs and old contracts to Rider at the Regency. An accompanying note read:

Dear Robert
I looked out this bunch of stuff after dinner last night. You'll find it interesting/useless/amusing – whatever. Make whatever use of it you will. The memos will give you an inside look at Hollywood at its craziest. They'll make you laugh, if nothing else. But please do not let Theodora know I have given any of this to you. (Ditto Noah S.) It is not a question of ethics or whether my attitude in this matter is right or wrong. My concern is for you to get it right. Although I am out of her life now (Ditto N.S.) I'm still fond of her and would not like her to get the idea in her head that I am interfering or positioning myself against her or doing anything that might be inimical to her interests and ideas (I am thinking particularly of Dr Keppler's note to Noah, diagnosing her tubal pregnancy – how I came by this, and how it has survived all these years, God alone knows! The good doctor died a year or so ago loaded with honours – nobody mentioned that he was also abortionist to the stars!). Call me when you return from the famous island and let me know how our gal is looking these days. A.F.

Rider found Keppler's letter in the suitcase. Dated November 24, 1940, it was brief:

Dear Mr Swan
It is with regret that I must inform you that Miss Glass has an ectopic pregnancy. This is the implantation of a fertilized ovum somewhere other than the body of the uterus.

In this case, it is within the abdomen, which is rare. Trouble usually arises in the sixth to twelfth week.

My preliminary examination reveals that bleeding into the

abdomen walls has already begun, and may have been continuing for some time. Unless we act at once the condition will rapidly deteriorate, and severe shock may follow.

Treatment is surgical.

Rider folded the letter and replaced it with all the other treasures in the case. With a source like Aaron Flagg, he almost didn't need to talk to Theodora at all.

32

> *You cannot become a legend without self-love,*
> *and considerable self-help. There are things you*
> *must know. You must know how to reject and*
> *exploit celebrity: how to be reclusive yet not*
> *forgotten. These are secrets Theodora Glass*
> *knows better than anyone in the whole culture of*
> *celebrity. (John Pearson,* The Profession of
> Fame*)*

Wednesday, November 8
Santa Aloe

The wind pulled at the corners of Rider's eyes as the powerboat
sped across the water in a brilliant white plume of spray.

"No more whirlybirds for her," the helmsman, whose name
was Clarence, shouted in his laughing Caribbean voice above the
concert-pitch roar of the twin MerCruiser Magnum engines. "No
suh, that crock-up shook her bustin' full. Ahm happy 'bout that,"
he said, exposing his large white teeth in a wide grin. "'Cos she
got this baby instead. Yo wanna cold beer, suh?"

"Always stand a cold beer," Rider shouted back.

Clarence tossed him a Suntory from the ice chest. Forty
minutes later he pulled back on the throttles and pointed towards
the island.

She wore a white shirt, beige linen trousers cut high on the
hips, but not the dark glasses and the wide-brimmed hat Rider
had been expecting her to wear. Her hair was cut in a straight line
on a level with her jaw. Her skin, a light shade of tan, no longer
had that luminous look (he recalled Émile Copeland's remark
that her skin looked colder than the surface of Triton!).

The launch began a slow arc towards the jetty. The sun was

now directly in Rider's eyes, and she had become a black silhouette.

"Welcome to Santa Aloe." She held out her hand as he stepped ashore. "I'm Missy Miller . . . Missy, please."

It was easy to understand how she could be mistaken at a distance for Theodora. Close up, the similarity blurred in an accumulation of delicate shades of difference – the nose a little blunter, the height an illusion, the eyes not quite so wide apart – the fractions and chimeras that, blown up a thousand times on the big screen, coalesce into unforgettable beauty, or just another pretty face.

He decided to admit his mistake. "From out there – the way you hold yourself – I thought –"

"Fooling people – that was my game. Unfortunately I can't handle the close-ups any more." She ran her fingertips from her lifeless eyelid up into the swatch of white in her ash-blonde hair. It was the gesture of a woman who has abandoned all claim to physical beauty. She wore no make-up. Her hollow cheeks were criss-crossed with a thousand exquisite lines, like filigree in old vellum. On a stage she would still look stunning. "Don't worry." She laughed. "Theodora's worn much better than I. She would have been here to greet you herself, but she's got a slight migraine. Nerves. She's got the jeebies about meeting you. May I call you Robert?"

She led the way to a couple of Land Rovers parked at the end of the wooden jetty. They got into the first vehicle, Rider's bags were loaded into the second by a large, silent man in khaki cut-offs and a white T-shirt, with black Caribbean curls peeping from under his cap. "We'll go the scenic route. Show you the island, help you get your bearings. Clarence," she called over her shoulder. "You and Hatfull take Mr Rider's bags to the guest house. Tell Jassy we'll be down in a while."

They drove across the island, Missy pointing out things of interest: Theodora's favourite walks, where she swam each morning, and still rode her Arab ponies in the afternoon; where she liked to sit and paint, and strolled at sunset. Rider listened politely. It was fan stuff, and he guessed that what he was getting was a warm-up to a more important briefing. He had dealt with many women like Missy: the self-appointed guardians of the rich and famous, women with power through access, who have no power at all once that access is shared.

After a while Missy stopped the Land Rover and got out. Rider walked by her side across the dunes to where several dozen flame trees made a glade on a ridge above a small bay. Points of light glittered on the surface of the ocean where the sun touched the ripples. Missy folded her arms.

"Do you see the brilliant greenness of the shallows . . . then the sudden turquoise of the deep?"

"It's very beautiful," Rider said.

"It's also very dangerous. Perfectly safe one moment, the next . . ." She stared at him. There was something in her face that might have been accusation and might have been the glint off the sea. "I don't want Theodora to get hurt, Robert."

"You think I might hurt her?"

"There's always a line in things." She spoke slowly, with the quiet concern of a friend who has no anxiety for herself in the matter. "Sometimes you cross it without even knowing it's there."

"We discussed this in London, Missy. Everything was considered and agreed with Oscar Bookbinder."

"Movie stars are endlessly lied to."

Rider smiled. "Don't you think they know that?"

"Not after a while."

"I haven't lied to her, Missy."

"I want you to know how I feel about this."

"And I want you to say what you think. We both must. We must know where we stand."

"Let me ask you a question, Robert. Why do you want to tell her story?"

"If I don't do it, others'll go on trying."

"The grave-robbers, you mean?"

Rider shrugged. "Look what they've done to Marilyn."

"Maybe nobody else will be as clever at sniffing out things as you are."

"All it takes is time."

"I know this book is her idea. But I want you to know that I have tried, and will go on trying, to talk her out of it." She attempted a smile. "I won't stop."

"Thank you for being honest about it." He admired her loyalty and wondered what depth of envy and jealousy she'd had to overcome to reach such devotion.

"Her heart is my heart, Robert." She stood now with her face turned away from him, watching the sparkle of turquoise where the deep water was. "I'll do whatever it takes to protect her happiness."

"If you don't talk her out of it . . . will you help me to get it right?" he said with his whole attention fixed on her, knowing just how useful she could be to him, how important it was to have her on his side.

"Will I be a good loser, is that your question?"

"I don't want to have to fight you every inch of the way," he said. "I don't want you to be my enemy."

They looked at each other a moment in challenging candour.

Missy blinked first. "Let's wait and see," she said.

She turned and walked pensively back to the Land Rover. She climbed in and sat behind the wheel, not switching on the engine. "Theodora has made some tapes for you – reminiscences about her childhood, her early career, and so on," she said, staring beyond the windscreen, as if searching the distance for sight of something dangerous. "I have typed them up. She will give them to you this evening."

She stopped and looked at Rider, as if making up her mind about something.

"However, I must warn you, Robert, she's unreliable in some areas. Not about Vienna, the early stuff. I wouldn't know about that. But I saw many of the things she talks about later. The Hollywood stuff. I was involved in some of those things, and I have to tell you, she's completely flat-ass wrong about a lot of it."

She started the engine.

"Other people's experiences never seem quite so real as one's own," Rider said. "She was seeing things from a different perspective to you, Missy."

"I'm not talking perspectives, Robert. I'm not talking view-points and opinions. I'm talking facts."

Rider smiled at her vehemence. "Thank you for warning me."

They drove along a narrow road that in places was like an English country lane, fretted with leaves and broken light, and in other parts was no more than a jungle path, still slippery from the rains.

They came into a clearing. Missy stopped the Land Rover, and handed Rider a pair of binoculars. "There it is," she said proudly.

The house he looked upon was beautiful in the way that only very old things can be beautiful. Lime-washed in Pompeian pink, tall wooden louvred windows painted a tulip shade of black; the terrace, at least two hundred feet long, lined with terracotta pots of yellow roses. Even from this distance he could sense the air of great wealth lavishly used.

"There's been a building on the site since the seventeenth century. Henry Morgan built a fortress there, a sort of corporate hideaway while he was pillaging the Caribbean conquests of Spain," Missy said, over his shoulder. The voice of somebody who has been hostile, and is in the act of giving in. "He held on to the place after he gave up his pirate ways. When he became Lieutenant-Governor of Jamaica he kept his 'summer mistresses' here. Theodora swears she can still smell their scent on summer nights. Shortly before he died in 1688 he sold the house, the island, the ladies too, for all I know, to a French count. At one time, one of the Romanovs, I think it was Alexander III, owned it, and lost it in a poker game in a Paris brothel. Cornelius Vanderbilt had it for a while. He sold it the week before he killed himself at the old Glenham Hotel in New York. It must have passed through dozens of hands before that other old pirate Onassis bought it, and sold it to Theodora. Fortunately before he could do much damage."

"For a little island," Rider said, "it's lured some great legends."

Missy grinned, slammed the motor into gear. "Let's go meet the greatest legend of them all," she said.

33

I caught the very end of old Hollywood. When I was making my first movie there, Norma Shearer was making her last. She was still Thalberg's widow and Queen of the Lot. She had an orchestra play music between takes. It was a habit she couldn't shake from the silent days. (Theodora Glass in a conversation with Robert Rider)

11 p.m., Thursday, November 9
Santa Aloe

From Robert Rider's notebooks:

Impressions – first meeting (in the long room behind the tulip-black louvred windows), she seated at the far end in a willow peacock chair. Recessed spots in high ceiling illuminate her face with a downfall of soft light – suggesting celestial favour! Had situation under control to last detail. Charcoal portrait of her in Hollywood prime above mantel. On rosewood table, in silver frame, flanked by three Oscars, Willinger picture Aaron Flagg plastered across New York in 1940.

Held out *both* hands. "*I'm Theodora*" – in that famous voice. Stunning. From two feet looks forty. Made up by expert. Hair lightened at temples – gives width to brow; long neck both emphasized and discreetly covered by a red ribbon – on which hangs gold heart (curiously mangled!). Bosom firmly outlined beneath thin silk. Shadow of greasepaint above and below eyes (Confederate-grey?) gives them perilous beauty of metalled winter sky. Light perfume, can't identify. Impossible not to stare. She notices. "*This is how this old looks these days*," she said. Pushed back hair, revealing more of face. Nostrils and earlobes translucent in skilful lighting. "Your last picture could have been made yesterday," I said.

"*Well, I don't know about that.*" Says she eats right, works out every day. Swims daily (in the sea). Not too much sun. Admits she smokes too much. Taps long red nail on unopened pack of Yves Saint Laurent cigarettes on table by her side. "*These things – 1.14 mg of nicotine and 12.3 mg of tar,*" she recites, as if it is a health warning with which she tests her need. "*Missy says two packs of these are enough to keep the smile on Marlboro Man's face for a month.*"

She asked me to tell her about myself. What did my father do?

"He was a newspaperman," I told her. "He died on D-Day with the British Sixth Airborne Division, two months before I was born." Did not linger on details: stardom creates its own proprieties, stars are wrapped up in themselves like narcissistic mummies. "1944 – the year you won your second Academy Award," I reminded her, closing the door on myself.

"*Wartime Oscars tarnish so quickly,*" she said, turning the key in the lock. Says they are made of inferior alloy. "*There was a man in Burbank who restored them beautifully for a few hundred dollars, but he died . . .*"

She opened cigarettes, looked around for light. I lit it for her. "*Elegant poison.*" She blew smoke towards the ceiling. No one smokes a cigarette the way she does! Remembered how horny she used to make me as a kid.

Obviously we both trying to figure out what the other one is thinking, making first judgements. She projects sincerity – how much of it comes from her heart, how much is talent? Surprised by her next question: "*Have we started work yet? Am I to be watchful of everything I say to you?*" Not yet, I told her. But after today I said it would be better if she assumed that the meter's always running.

Dinner elegant as hell. Theodora at head of table. Missy and I either side. Black menservants in white jackets and gloves wait on us with self-effacement next to invisibility. Dining-room candle-lit, baronial. Worn-out tapestries, panels with gilding almost faded away, "*rescued*" from the house on Löwelstrasse. Perfect setting to begin journey into the past: Theodora's world of ghosts, of dead Nazis, and departed Hollywood tsars, her occasional out-of-date references (she still calls Kennedy International *Idlewild*), seem almost more palpable than the moment itself.

The two women extraordinarily close. Once or twice caught a glance between them as if they were also communicating on a separate level. Missy always asks the pertinent questions: *Do I like probing into people's lives?* Her fork poised above her *fraises à la créole*. Slowly cleaves strawberry. *Opening up their hearts . . . discovering their secrets?* Neither approval nor disapproval in her voice, but questions to remind Theodora of the risks she is taking.

"Research . . ." I pause reflectively, sip my Montrachet, decide to play the game. "It's tedious sometimes. But there are usually some surprises."

"Do people always tell you the truth?" solemnly; her eyes glitter; she knows I'm on to her game.

"Of course not," I tell her. "But part of the challenge is the possibility that you are being deceived."

"Do you know when people are lying to you?" she says.

"Not always," I admit.

"How do you get to the truth of anything?"

"You keep going," I say.

"You keep going," she repeats dully.

"They are poor explorers," I say, "that think there is no land when they can see nothing but sea."

Theodora laughs, but her fingers play nervously with the mangled gold heart at her throat. Missy knows she has pushed me as far as she dares, changes subject.

After dinner Theodora gave me tape transcripts. "*You must promise me not to read this until the morning, Robert,*" she said. "*I would not be able to sleep a wink if I thought you were reading it tonight.*"

I promised.

Slept badly, as I usually do in strange bed. Rose early with sense of expectation. Dawn breaking on the horizon, giving the first colour to the sea. Stood under cold shower for ten minutes, shaved, rang for breakfast. Wrapped myself in robe with Theodora's family crest embroidered on pocket. Six twenty – start transcripts.

On the terrace he read: *I shall begin this story, the true story of Theodora Glass, with Baron Georg Reinhard von Tegge, my father. To me he was always simply Vati . . .*

"Where do you want to begin tomorrow, Robert?" Theodora asked. He had been on the island ten days and they had fallen into the habit while walking on the beach before dinner of discussing the areas they would cover the following day.

"There are a couple of moments in your first year in Holly-wood we could develop. I'd like to know how you felt about some things," he said, as if he had only this moment thought of it. "If you could explain –"

"I can only describe what happened. The explanations I leave to you."

Rider felt as though he had been pushed away a little. "Explanations are nearly always a deception," he said.

She laughed, relented. "I feel relaxed with you, Robert."

"You sound surprised."

"You're not what I expected." The sun was low on the horizon. She wore a bandanna, gold sandals and a black gown that left her arms bare and showed her thighs. She looked like – but not quite like – the Theodora he remembered from her movies, made more than forty years ago. "Yes, I am surprised," she said, touching his beard fondly with the palm of her hand.

"Is Missy still nervous about the book?" he asked, conscious of the intimacy of her gesture.

"She still says I'm wrong to trust you," she answered matter-of-factly.

"And I thought she was growing to love me."

Theodora smiled. "She sees a menace in you, Robert."

"Doesn't that disturb you?"

Theodora shrugged. "I shall put my whole being, of which I am very weary, in your hands," she said in the self-mocking tone Rider knew she used to hide genuine feeling.

And although he also knew that she sometimes said things for effect, it meant that he had so far done nothing to alarm her. He hadn't pushed her; he hadn't pressed her, even when she contradicted herself. He had let her move at her own pace, in her own way. She was often repetitious. Sometimes she rambled and lost the point; sometimes she spoke with the urgency of confession. And sometimes he knew she was holding back on him. But he waited. He listened. He watched her eyes, and her hands. (Sometimes they told him much more than a tape could pick up.) He knew how to be patient. He would get to the truth, fill in the gaps, pin her down later.

He said, "I read the Vienna transcripts again last night. They are quite excellent, you know. They are very moving."

His praise seemed to surprise her. "I have to think a vast amount before I can find a sentence that will describe even a little bit of what I feel."

"You convey your feelings very well," he said.

"At first I was afraid to set it all down. I was afraid that if I wrote about it, if I gave away too much, I'd lose something of it for myself."

"You have an ear for the way people spoke back then."

"Mama's journals helped."

He shook his head with professional regret. "I would love to have talked to her."

"She would love to have talked to you. That's what she did best: talk."

"What was the best piece of advice she ever gave you?"

"*In love, a woman must never give herself . . . she must always get herself taken*."

"Was that good advice?"

"I found it to be so."

Rider laughed. "Were you always close?"

205

"Not always," Theodora said in a reminiscent tone, as if to herself. "She was a little . . . unpredictable, sometimes." She changed the subject, the tone of her voice. "Have you started writing anything yet?"

"Some notes."

"How long will it take, once you start?"

"The first draft, about four weeks."

"That's very fast."

"I write the way a painter paints."

"And how does a painter paint?"

"Start with a lay-in. Go after the tone and general effect. Put in only those things which are absolutely essential. When I've completed the backgrounds, I start on the figures."

"You always work that way?"

"It's the only way I can feel my way into a story . . . feel whether something is true or false."

He didn't tell her about all the books and articles he had read; he didn't tell her the things Copeland and Aaron Flagg had told him. She had no idea how much he knew. He was a secret-keeper. It gave him an edge.

They turned and walked back towards the house. She took his hand.

"How old were you?"

"How old was I when?"

"When your mother advised you to get yourself taken."

"Thirteen . . . an age when everything is ambiguous for a girl."

"In what way?"

She stopped and strolled away a few yards, then came back to him.

"In the way you are perceived, for one thing," she said, thoughtfully. "Louis B. Mayer – I was still a child to him. To Mr Swan I was already a woman. Mama used to say I was between pigtails and cocktails."

Rider smiled, recognizing the line from the biographies.

"And did you get yourself taken?" he said.

She smiled. "I was a dutiful daughter."

Still he didn't push her. They walked without speaking for a while, the twilight deepening around them. Once in a while the silence was broken by the long rollers that swept in from far out and broke languidly on the beach.

With an unconscious movement she leaned the side of her head against his shoulder. "We were on our way to Hollywood, on the Santa Fe Super Chief," she said in a dreamy voice, "when Mama gave me that piece of advice."

He said, "You travelled to Hollywood by rail?" to get it fixed in his own mind. "That was you, the Baroness . . ."

"And Noah. A few executives flew between the coasts. It took fifteen hours, via Chicago, on a UAL Sky Lounge Mainliner. But the studios considered airplanes too dangerous for stars. We took the Twentieth-Century Limited to Chicago; the Chief from there. Four days and three nights, coast to coast. Old Hollywood hands usually left the train at Pasadena – to avoid the fans, or the writs, or irate spouses at Union Station."

She was always better when she didn't know she was being taped. She talked in a steady stream of recollection, her natural defensiveness forgotten. She described the Roman columns that stretched for over half a mile along the front of the MGM studio, and her disappointment when she discovered that they were made of plaster and wood. She was funny about the commissary (the Lion's Den), with its huge mural of Louis B. Mayer – *"his bright weasel eyes behind those round wire-frame glasses watching every spoonful you ate."* She remembered the excitement at the studio when Winchell coined the word *Theodorable* in his column; and her astonishment when he took her to the Radio City Music Hall première of *Painted Moon* in his honorary NYPD patrol car, its siren screaming!

After dinner Rider returned to the guest house. He removed the miniature microphone clipped inside his shirt and connected to the recorder taped to the waistband of his trousers. He had been careful to drink little all evening, and poured himself a large whisky from a polished cut-glass decanter. Outside fireflies flickered above the dark sands. He switched on the desk lamp, collected the transcripts; he chose an apple from the large bowl of fresh fruit and cheese that was put in his room each night for what Theodora called "the three o'clock in the morning ghosts". He sat down by the open french windows and began to read.

He went backwards and forwards in time, piecing together Theodora's stories, and Missy's tales of her own brief B-picture stardom at Columbia; he fitted in Aaron Flagg's reminiscences with theirs, checked them against the Copeland tapes, and other histories of those times. By one thirty in the morning he had completed working outlines for several chapters, and was still wide awake.

"OK, Rider . . . Showtime," he said aloud, going to the word processor. "Let's see what you got here."

And not bothering about grammar, or spelling, not stopping to polish a phrase, and using his novelist's imagination to carry him over the gaps in his information (writing around his ignorance, he called it), he began to type as quickly as he could everything he knew about Theodora's first weeks in Hollywood – starting with Noah Swan's famous deal with Louis B. Mayer.

34

*Louis B. Mayer often likened people to animals.
He called Noah Swan a tiger: "dangerous, fast,
hungry – I shoulda shot the sonofabitch between
the eyes." (John Michel,* The Moguls of Hollywood*)*

1.35 a.m., Sunday, November 19
Santa Aloe

RIDER'S FIRST DRAFT, 1
January 1941. And so the great Louis B. Mayer summons Noah
to his office at the studios of Metro-Goldwyn-Mayer. It might be
assumed that Noah expects the call, for it is not an unfamiliar
situation – the young man with ambition and *chutzpah* has
something the older man with power and greed wants – and the
meeting follows a ritual pattern. Noah would enter quickly, the
way he always entered a room, a situation, your life: confident,
all-business, full of charm. It's a heady moment for him. If he
plays his hand right in the next fifteen minutes he could become
one of the most important players in town.

He must have been surprised and flattered to find that there
was nobody else at the meeting. No Eddie Mannix, Mayer's right-
hand man; no Benny Thau, the head of the studio's talent
department. No lawyers. Just Mayer and Noah. Going head to
head with Mayer had become the rite of passage that tested the
nerve and mettle of young men on the way up in Hollywood.
Noah knew that in dealing with Mayer the trick lay in staying
cool. "Taking risks," he would say later, "was part of being
young. Maybe the best part."

Mayer, fifty-six years old, is the highest salaried man in the
United States. He is as proud of that fact as he is of the studio that

209

bears his name. Below average height, mottled-pink face, thin, hard mouth, a large head of sparse white hair, heavy chest and shoulders. Neither the expensive suit nor the pale rose-coloured polish on his manicured fingernails can detract from the power of that body. It is, thinks Noah, the body of a circus strong-man.

His eyes, hard and shiny behind gold-rimmed lenses, would have followed Noah as he crosses the room and sits in one of the buttery armchairs that face his enormous desk. Watching for the first nervous gesture, waiting for a weakness he can attack. Smiling. The smile he uses on young actresses who sit on his lap and call him Uncle Louie while discussing their contracts. Like all primal species, he changes nothing that works.

He is in no hurry to get to the point. He talks about the state of the country. The picture business. His London shoemaker. Why the chopped liver at the Beverly Derby is better than the chopped liver at the Vine Street Derby. A restless man. He sits down. Stands up. Paces. Jangles coins in his trouser pockets. His office, no larger than a small ballroom, panelled in leather, is decorated in cream-coloured tones. It contains two fireplaces, big couches, twenty-foot bar and a grand piano laden with Oscars. A furled American flag hangs behind his desk; on the wall photographs – from his favourite racehorses to the Duke and Duchess of Windsor – testify to the range and grandeur of his friends and interests. On his desk are five cream-coloured telephones, the Hollywood trade papers, a family Bible, a tintype of his mother, a silver statuette of the Republican elephant, and photographs of his wife, Margaret, and their two daughters, Edith and Irene. Adjusting to the feelings of what it meant to be a major player, Noah would take all this in.

Mayer has a bewildering habit of switching subjects (and sometimes opinions) with no rhyme or reason and suddenly he says, "Saw the *Romeo and Juliet* footage. What's the girl's name again?"

"Theodora Glass," Noah tells him, knowing that pretending not to remember names is a trick Mayer uses to make people feel insecure. "She's going to be a big star," Noah says. "She looks like Garbo decided to start over."

"Garbo I got already," Mayer retorts with a gesture of impatience. "What *you* got is a problem. I hear on all sides this is a bad time for you." He speaks softly in the cantorial cadences that he knows people mimic when they tell their stories about him. "I think you got into something over your head you didn't expect to get into. You're a young man. You could be my own son – if God had given me a son – and I wanna say what's in my heart."

He knows these have been anxious months for Noah. He knows there are lawsuits. "You abandon a movie, you get trouble. But it takes moxie to gamble the whole caboodle on one actress." He admires that in a man. "But let me tell you something. My whole life is making movie stars. Louis B. Mayer *invented* the star system" – or words tantamount. "And all the billboards in the world don't make your girl a movie star. You can't *buy* stardom. *Only I, Louis B. Mayer, can make a somebody outa a nobody*. But you're a smart young fella. That's why you bring her to me. And, maybe, God willing, she can be a wonderful success for Metro-Goldwyn-Mayer."

Noah takes a deep breath. "But I haven't brought her to you, Mr Mayer."

Mayer's small eyes pop with affront. "Then why are ya here?" The sinews of his thick neck tighten into a crimson cord. "Why are ya taking up my time?" He starts to shout. "What the hell, ya walk in here –"

"You invited me, Mr Mayer."

"*I* invited you?" Mayer says, still shouting. "*I* invited *you*? What am I – the welcome wagon?"

Noah wants to laugh at Mayer's act. "Miss Koverman called me. Your secretary initiated a meeting without checking with you?" he asks solicitously.

Mayer knows his intimidation has failed.

"What we got here is a misunderstanding. I tell you what we do," he says in his fatherly voice. "Bring her in – *Theodora*, right? – bring her in. I like what I see, we test her. I like the test, we make a deal. Maybe."

What about me? Noah wants to say. Will Metro make a deal

211

with me? *Maybe?* But he crosses his legs, bounces his hand-made English shoe. "It's not that easy, Mr Mayer. Paramount, Warners . . . a lot of studios want her. Selznick has offered us a role she could kick into the stands."

"I tell you what Selznick's got. He's got nothing. I know what he's got, he's my son-in-law." He walks round his desk and grips Noah's shoulder with sincerity. "You make one picture for David and spend five years waiting for him to make up his mind what to put her in next. You don't make stars sweating for a script. You make stars with pictures. Conveyor belts make stars."

Louis B. Mayer is not an educated man, but in matters that concern his studio, nobody is wiser. He takes Noah to the window and makes him look down at the rows of studio streets teeming with life: extras in cowboy clothes, showgirls, actors in togas, a cageful of tigers.

"Seventy movies will come out of this studio in 1941," he says proudly, his arm round Noah's shoulder. "Three of them starring Theodora. We can cut a deal for both of you . . ."

Noah feels the excitement rising inside him, feels himself breathing differently. Theodora is still a month away from her fifteenth birthday. "Let me think about it, Mr Mayer," he says.

Rider printed out, read over what he had written. He had used mostly Aaron Flagg's version of that first meeting between Mayer and Noah Swan (it was a famous encounter; versions of it had appeared in a dozen books), and it was Flagg's voice he heard when he read it back. *Garbo I got already*, he spoke the line aloud, with the Yiddish rhythm and inflection Flagg had mimicked in New York. Was that the way Mayer really spoke? Or was it simply the way Flagg had told the story, adhering to the spirit of Hollywood folk memory? But hadn't Mayer had elocution lessons from the studio voice coach to improve the calibre and power of his delivery for the speaking engagements and public announcements he liked to make, and were expected of the highest-salaried man in the United States? Rider made a note to ask Flagg about it. Get the small details right, he was fond of saying, and the truth falls into place.

He closed his eyes. He tried to imagine how Theodora looked and behaved as a girl of fourteen. With so much else becoming clear to him, the young Theodora, the girl at the heart of this contest of wills between two implacable men, remained shadowy. He knew her as she was now, and he remembered her at the height of her fame. But the young Theodora – the girl Noah Swan would discover, manipulate, seduce – was an enigma to him. When did she learn the tricks he was getting to know? The way she touched his hand when he lit her cigarettes? The way she bowed her head as if in thought, but really to avoid letting him see what was in her eyes? She was still telling him only part of the story, already there were credibility gaps, and she hadn't mentioned the abortion in New York. But he would bide his time. He thought again how lucky he was to have Aaron Flagg.

He opened his eyes and peered at his watch. It was after three. From out of the moonless darkness, beyond where the lights on the veranda lit up the beach, came the slow swish of waves. He enjoyed working through the night. The discipline of it satisfied him in a way he couldn't explain. He understood things better at night.

He returned to his desk, sucked air in slowly through his nose, released it like a sigh, and continued to type.

RIDER'S FIRST DRAFT, 2
Hollywood, 1941. Noah's billboard blitz in New York, the newspaper stories of the rivalry between Mayer and Selznick, who each wanted to sign her to his own studio, were making Theodora's name famous. And still the American public hadn't seen a single frame of her on the screen. ("*Mr Swan was always in a hurry. He made me a myth before I was even a star.*") Noah knew all along that he would sign with Metro. He simply used Selznick to squeeze a juicier deal out of Mayer, according to Flagg.

Rider found the Selznick memos Flagg had given him, picked out three, and typed them in to the draft.

Mr Noah Swan   January 14, 1941
The Roosevelt Hotel
Hollywood Boulevard
Hollywood, California

Dear Noah

I call your memo a reply to mine, as it is not an answer. Let me
remind you that the essence of successful independent production is the ability to close a deal. You are not doing yourself or
Theodora any favors prevaricating like this. I know that my
offer to you is better than anything Metro can make. A
three-picture deal at David O. Selznick Productions Inc., with
your own star, her own cameraman, and with story and
director approval, is an unprecedented offer in this town. I am
puzzled by your equivocation.

> Sincerely,
> David O. Selznick

To Noah Swan   January 31, 1941
cc: Katharine Brown

Hitchcock and I looked at the *Romeo and Juliet* footage
again yesterday. He agrees with me that Theodora would be
perfect for *The Refugee*. Her child-woman look will appeal
to men, and women will not resent her (an important plus
given the "adult" nature of the story). That means strong
matinée business – women will come out afternoons to see
her. I would like you to consider this property for your first
production at David O. Selznick Productions. But I need a
decision. I will not close with anybody to play the role for a
period of ten days from today, during which time she could
talk to Hitch and me, and make a test if that is what she
wants.

> DOS

To Noah Swan   March 11, 1941
CONFIDENTIAL

Do you realize that you are behaving very badly? I hate to let
off another blast about this thing but three precious months

have gone by, and we are still getting nowhere. Just what is going on? And why do you persistently refuse to let me talk to Theodora direct? If she is not dead, I can't excuse you. Actresses do not come to Hollywood to hide. Yes, you have conducted a shrewd publicity campaign, building up her mystique and so on – it even impresses Birdwell, who is no slouch at that game himself – but sooner or later you must make up your mind, and she must make a picture.

Frankly, Noah, much of what continues to attract me to you is the hope of producing that picture at my studio. But I will not be used to butter your deal with Metro (yes, the thought has crossed my mind! As well as the suspicion that LB has been thrown way out of line by your exorbitant demands!) and unless we reach an agreement within six days from today I shall cease all interest. So let's get down to earth.

DOS

Noah signed a deal with Metro-Goldwyn-Mayer on April 23, 1941. Theodora started her first Hollywood picture, *Painted Moon*, three weeks later. The problems of the past months were for the moment forgotten, even if they had not gone away (for years Noah was pursued by someone or other trying to serve him in a lawsuit). A few weeks earlier, his son Matthew was born. Hedda Hopper broke the news in her column under the headline: *Beautiful Cygnet for Hollywood's Brave Swans*.

Five months before, Barbara Swan fell down some steps and fractured her pelvis at the home of Samuel and Frances Goldwyn. The rest of her pregnancy she was confined to bed, attended by Gershon Wedemeyer, *the* Beverly Hills physician of the forties ("More famous than half his patients, and richer than the other half," says Flagg).

Noah and Barbara had been married three days less than five years when Matthew was born on April 5. Barbara, thirty-three years old (five years older than Noah), did not suspect that her life had reached a turning point. She would never –

Rider stopped typing as he became aware of the first glimmer of dawn. He went to the window and in the distance saw Theodora coming out of the sea, naked as a bird. On the beach Missy waited for her with a robe. They kissed briefly and turned towards the house. It was a tender moment; he felt like an intruder, afraid to move until they were out of sight in case they saw him. Are they lovers? It was a thought that had not occurred to him before.

From Robert Rider's notebooks:

Aaron Flagg – part voyeur, part stool pigeon, always in the right place at the right time – remembers everything. But everybody has an angle. What's his?

35

Theodora didn't act – she just was. (Billy Wilder, New York Times *magazine, June 8, 1986)*

Wednesday, November 22
Santa Aloe

After dinner Theodora suggested they watch *Painted Moon*, her first Hollywood movie, for which she won her first Oscar. Rider sat next to her in a deep leather armchair. Missy sat two rows behind. The lights darkened, the MGM lion appeared on the screen in black and white. Theodora slipped on her glasses. "The better to see the past," she said quietly.

It was the first film she and Rider had watched together without her giving a running commentary. But she laughed aloud several times, and once or twice she caught her breath, as if she were seeing the picture for the first time.

She played Lydia Kreisky, the daughter of a Kirov ballerina who flees to France with her unborn child after her lover, a Russian nobleman, is murdered in the 1917 Revolution. Mother and daughter live a funny, impoverished and unconventional life together in Paris. The mother dies in an influenza epidemic. Lydia goes to Spain, gets caught up in the Civil War, and, with bandanna and cartridge belts criss-crossed over her chest, falls in love with a married American doctor. She also has an illegitimate baby, born the day after the doctor is killed. In the final scene, written by Noah himself to satisfy the Breen Code which insisted that wrongdoing must not go unpunished, the baby dies. Theodora's anguish as the dead infant is taken out of her arms – the scene which probably clinched the Oscar for her – is still the most famous tear-jerking ending of all time.

Watching her performance, Rider forgot that he was on a private Caribbean island, sitting next to the heroine, still beautiful over half a century on. Probably Cukor's best picture, it had played more revival dates than *Casablanca*. Theodora's perfect first-generation print was like looking at a Titian in its first freshness.

When the baby died for the umpteenth time up there on the screen, Rider felt Theodora grip his arm. "That Wechsler, isn't he something?" she whispered, to hide her emotion. "He could photograph what you were thinking."

"He'd photograph your soul," said Missy, "if he could find enough light."

The end title appeared on the screen, superimposed over a big close up of Theodora.

"It's easy to see why Mayer wanted you," Rider was the first to speak.

"LB wanted me because LB wanted everything," Theodora said, removing her glasses and slipping them into a black silk purse.

"He must have seen something in you." Rider wanted to give Mayer his due.

Theodora shrugged her shoulders. "I look at my pictures now and I wonder what all the fuss is about." She tapped a cigarette out of the packet she had taken from her purse and held it between two fingers alongside her face, waiting for a light to be offered.

"That final scene breaks my heart every time," he said, lighting her cigarette with a gold Dunhill.

"Real tears. One take," she said proudly. "We hardly discussed it at all. Cukor said, 'You know what this is about, Theodora. I want you to dig into yourself.' Then we shot it. One take."

Rider was conscious that she hadn't moved her eyes from his face. He knew that she was trying to tell whether he had understood the significance of what she was telling him. He waited.

She stood up, then walked to the empty screen and looked

back at him, her eyes sombre. "A little while before, you see, I'd lost my own baby . . ."

He didn't want to lie to her, he didn't want to feign surprise. He said nothing.

"I had an abortion in New York," she said, mistaking his silence for dumbfoundedness. "I got pregnant on *Romeo and Juliet* . . . I was a poor, simple, wanton little girl."

She repeated, more or less, the story Aaron Flagg had told him. But she told it with a simplicity that gave the episode a poignancy that Flagg's version, with all its clinical detail, didn't begin to touch. Rider was pleased she had levelled with him. He was pleased that he had waited for her to tell him about it in her own way, and in her own time.

"Cukor just let the camera stay on me and all my feelings came out. When he finally said cut, that was it. It was a risk not to shoot another take. Even when a scene is wonderful, sometimes you find there is a scratch on the film, or the lighting was not right. But Cukor knew that we could never get it so wonderful again. I would never react that way again."

"React?" Rider said quizzically.

Theodora smiled, and looked towards Missy. "I told you he was sharp."

Missy shrugged, as if she didn't want to be involved.

Theodora said: "We had several babies standing by, for retakes and so on. Before the scene, Noah came on the set with his son – "

"The baby was *Matthew Swan*?"

"Noah put him in my arms at the last moment. 'Here's your new leading man,' he said. You can imagine, I was pretty vulnerable."

"It's hard to believe they shot wonderful pictures like that in five weeks," Missy said quickly.

Theodora walked to the door. "It's late. If you want me in good form tomorrow, Robert, I must get some sleep."

"She slept badly last night," Missy said, following her out.

"Sleep is no servant of the will," Theodora said, in the strangely old-fashioned language Rider noticed she often used when she was tired, or under stress. "It has caprices of its own."

She offered him her cheek to be kissed.

The kiss was salty. He hadn't seen the tears.

From Robert Rider's notebooks:

Noah Swan – a prize shit. To have planted on Theodora his own infant son for the baby's death scene in *Painted Moon* – only weeks after she had lost their love child – to have played with her deepest emotions simply to trick a performance out of her – was an act of utter soullessness. If he had hated her very much, he could not have treated her more cruelly. This story has never been told before. A real nugget.

36

My dreams come true because I never sleep.
(Noah Swan; Wall Street Journal, *January 10,*
1990)

10.20 p.m., Wednesday, November 22
Washington DC

Seated over a whisky in the Trophy Room, Noah Swan drew a
red circle around the head of the girl in a photograph taken at
Lanigan's funeral. "Who is this?" he said, pushing the print
across his desk to Fortas.

Fortas screwed up his eyes and peered at the photograph.
"Biddulph, sir. The pilot's English girlfriend. Works at Holy Day
House. Secretary. She was in my report. Victoria Biddulph."

"Kinda young looking."

"Twenty-seven," Fortas said, returning the picture. He was
annoyed that Noah should still be asking questions about the
Lanigan business. He had done a good job; it was wrapped up
weeks ago.

"How long she been at HDH?" Noah asked, looking at the
picture again.

"Two years four months."

"Checked out her story, did ya?"

Fortas nodded. "Alpha-alpha security rating. But she has no
contact with the Baroness."

Noah stood up and walked to the window and stared out at
Moore's *Warrior King*, floodlit on its plinth against the dark
cypresses. "I distrust people on the margin of things . . . they trip
you up every time."

"Should we let her go?" Fortas said to his back.

"But not too soon." He turned away from the window. "We

221

don't want her connecting her dismissal with the accident."

"January," said Fortas, who believed in the brevity of grief.

Noah studied her photograph again. "She don't look like a kid who'll waste much time finding new pleasures."

"Rider's been on the island two weeks now," Fortas said obliquely.

"I know that," Noah said.

"Do you want me to take care of that situation?" Fortas asked politely.

"Don't worry about him," Noah said with not a very nice smile. "I've got plans for Mr Rider."

Fortas smiled too, but there was disappointment in it.

37

Noah and Theodora are perfect for each other. Everything they touch turns to gold. "There is a law forbidding us from doing anything wrong," says Noah, with a twinkle in his green, green eyes. But it does depend on what you mean by wrong, Noah, dear . . . (Sheilah Graham, syndicated columnist, North American Newspaper Alliance)

Midnight, November 23
Santa Aloe

From the Baroness's journals – 1941–2

Tower Drive, LA, September 1
We've been in new house – California-Spanish: rambly, thick-walled, red-tile roof – three months. The view – to the right, Catalina, the Pacific; the left, the pyramidal tower of City Hall – is still wondrous to my European eyes. The house was built by Mary Astor in 1930; we paid $45,600 for it – a bargain, says Noah, who knows real estate – eight bedrooms filled with the ghosts of Mary's long-gone lovers. No tennis court, but beautiful lily pond and large pool – kidney-shaped, very thirties. How long ago Vienna seems.

October 3
Rained all day. Summer over. Thank God. Thought I was going out of my mind. It was touch and go for a while there. But I have pulled myself together (with Dr Eisler's help) and Aaron Flagg has been kind and loyal. I feel happier – *safer* – when he is around. He even makes Noah – who always knows how to make me feel inadequate and uncertain – tolerable.

November 10
I am proud of Theodora – the source of my happiness and hope. But what am I myself? *I am thirty-two years old*. At two o'clock this morning I woke weeping, and with a feeling of panic. *Is it over for me?* Called Aaron and was touched that he still cares enough about me to come straight over. "What's done, and what's past changing, is past caring about," he said. We talked and talked until it was light. What secrets we share! There will always be a special feeling between us. He is right: I must learn to forget what's done.

11 p.m., December 7
My dearest daughter, let me remember this day for you:
It was noon. A warm December Sunday in Hollywood. Fragrance of laurel and eucalyptus in the air. A sense of well-being, of relief at being out of the war in Europe. I was in my room, listening to the Sunday afternoon broadcast by the New York Philharmonic: Artur Rubinstein playing the Brahms *Concerto in B-flat*. You were on a sunbed by the pool, wearing a white, one-piece bathing suit, and reading the big new bestseller *Mildred Pierce* – which you hated, but Noah insisted would help you understand modern American language. He was talking as usual on the phone. Aaron was mixing drinks, listening to a football game from the Polo Grounds in New York. The game was interrupted by a news bulletin – Pearl Harbor had been attacked by the Japanese. "Well, I guess this war is now ours as well as yours," Aaron said to me. It was exactly one week after the première of *Painted Moon*; the day before you started filming *Reunion*.

January 5, 1942
Noah is right – the war *is* good for Hollywood. Box-office receipts are up across the country. *Painted Moon* is a smash – my God, how easily I use his expressions now –

January 14
Invited to join Motion Picture Mothers, Inc. Members include:

Ethel Gumm (Judy Garland's mother), Lela Rogers (Ginger's mother), Ruth Brugh (mother of Robert Taylor), and Anna LeSueur (Joan Crawford's mother). They meet regularly to discuss their problems! Dare I tell them mine? Don't think so!

January 20
The New York film critics have given best actress award to Theodora for *Painted Moon*. Noah says promises well for next month's Academy Awards.

January 28
Hired new gardener. Armenian. V. handsome. Name Dikran (?) Talaan. Beautiful hair.

February 4
Today a publisher in New York (Bennett Cerf) has asked me to write my memoirs. Dare I? Would delicacy (or guilt) hold me back from saying the things I feel? Still too many doors I dare not open –

February 10
Theodora's sixteenth birthday. Noah's present – a tennis court (built over the lily pond), and a year's lessons from Bill Tilden. I have given her a small Dufy watercolour ($1,000). Rosenberg says its an investment – better than the Utrillos people here are buying by the yard. I shall miss the lily pond.

February 14
Fighting on Bataan going badly. For the first time Americans aware that they could lose the war. Jimmy Stewart, Robert Montgomery, Bill Holden, Ronald Reagan have enlisted. Aaron says Ty Power is planning to leave his wife *and* his boyfriend to join the marines. Ah, Hollywood heroics! Zanuck has donated his Argentine polo ponies to West Point. Hedy Lamarr offering to kiss any man who'll buy $25,000 worth of war bonds. Lana Turner's price for a kiss on the lips $50,000. Which means, says Aaron, that Lana's publicist twice as good as Hedy's!

February 15
Alone in the house today Dikran tried to kiss me. Clumsy and inexperienced, he was easy to control. Afterwards filled with the humility of his youth he wept. It was hard making a secret of my own desires watching the hard youthful body sweating before me.

February 17
Shocking news this morning – Carole Lombard is dead. Returning from a bond drive in Indiana her plane smashed into a mountain minutes after taking off from a place called Las Vegas. First reports said only that she was missing, but we all knew what had happened as soon as we heard the news flash. What a waste to obliterate so capriciously such a harmless creature. Gable is distraught. They were so in love, and married such a little while. My God, what a time –

2 a.m., February 27
Theodora collected her first Oscar at the Biltmore tonight. Noah won best picture award; Jerry Wechsler award best photography. Much wine. Fear I shall have a head tomorrow!

March 12
Dikran came to my room this morning. V. aroused. I let him kiss me again but this time I did not (could not?) stop him. He had no thought for my feelings. I loved it. There is just no other way for me. His passion, the way he forced himself upon me, lost himself in the violence of his needs, swept over me like a fever. There was no love on either of our parts. I gave him my body to take any way he wanted. But was he using me, or was I using him? He is seventeen years old. We are not cheating on a husband, or humiliating a wife. I don't think what I do is bad or evil, but I do think it's dangerous and wrong.

March 29
Perino's – dinner with Aaron. All evening I had a feeling that he was preparing to say something I didn't want to hear. Does

he know about Dikran? Finally says he's heard Bennett Cerf's asked me to write my memoirs. *Relief*. Before I could say I'd said no to Cerf, he reminded me of my deal with Noah never to talk about our private lives or anything that might harm Theodora's career. *Truth is inimical to stardom*, he said. Noah is so scared of what I know. He can never trust me. He can never relax. There's always that bullet in the chamber. He can never know when it might come round. *Truth is inimical to stardom* – Aaron is saying that to me! It cost me a great effort not to laugh. I would think about the memoirs, I lied, to brighten up my life and sow a little panic. Let Noah sweat a little. The bastard has it coming. But Aaron is in a bad spot. He adores me, but he also loves Noah and is tireless in doing what that monster wants. And Noah would like to cast me into the outer darkness –

April 1
Chasen's. Aaron says Gable is drinking heavily. Brooding about Carole's death. Unlikely he'll be in any shape to start *Night Tide* with Theodora in May. Aaron is dished – had big plans for a Glass–Gable ad campaign. Dikran's not appeared for a week. Noah said today he's fired him. No explanation and I did not ask for one –

**1 a.m., November 23,
Santa Aloe**

Theodora stopped reading. The journal stirred memories that took her from joy to apprehension – as if she did not know what was to happen next, as if the future was still random and unforeseeable.

She switched off the light, and tried to sleep.

38

*There are only two women in Hollywood with
any real class: Gisela von Tegge and myself.
(Marlene Dietrich,* New York Daily News,
December 3, 1942)

Friday, November 24
Santa Aloe

FROM AARON FLAGG TAPES
Recorded New York City, November 4
Let me tell you about Gisela – how I got into the whole of that
thing.

It's a Sunday morning, first winter of the war. Noah calls he's
gotta see me right away. I go up to the house on Coldwater
Canyon. His official residence, so to speak. He spent weekends
up there with Barbara and the kid; rest of the time he's living with
Theodora on Tower Drive. A few people knew about the
arrangement, but it hadn't gotten into any of the columns yet.
When I arrive, his face is white. The Baroness he says is humping
one of the gardeners. An Armenian kid, fifteen, sixteen years
old, hard as a young fucking oak.

This is Theodora's mother . . . Theodora's legal guardian. The
contracts, the legal paraphernalia, everything goes through her.
She's the key to everything. Getting hauled into court on a morals
rap ain't the best way to get attention in Hollywood.

"I'll handle the kid, you talk some fuckin' sense into her," he
said. "Explain this is a small town, a company town . . . A moral
town. She'll listen to you. Tell her. She's gotta pull her oar in this
thing, Aaron."

I took her to dinner. A bistro in Santa Monica. Candles,
French name for the meatloaf. I wanted to avoid the usual places.

229

This don't sound too humble but I was a good-looking kid in those days and I had my pick in that town – but an Austrian aristo was still a reach for me. Have you seen pictures of her in those days? Christ, she was beautiful. Legs from here to California; gorgeous mouth – those full, wet, carmine lips that was *the* forties look. She wore a black dress, ropes of pearls. She had this sexy way of holding her hand at her breast, palm kinda turned outwards, fingering the pearls . . .

I ordered French champagne and watched how often she came up for air. But she was in no hurry. I let her talk, and tried to figure what made her tick . . . what made her want to screw some underaged Armenian hedge trimmer . . .

She was the one who finally got down to business: why the hell were we having dinner together in a proposition joint in Santa Monica? I don't think you're looking for a big involvement here, she said. Either I wanted to find out what she was like in bed, or Noah sent me. She said she was as vain as any woman, and she'd like to think I really liked her, but her hunch was that this was Noah's idea. So why don't I say what's on Noah's mind so we can get on with our own lives?

I took a deep breath and told her we knew about the Armenian kid. I repeated the business about Hollywood's a small town, and if people wanted to play around they had t'be damn sure they didn't get caught. When I finished she said, "Everyone needs attention, Aaron. And I don't get that too often any more."

That night – I might as well come clean, it was a long time ago – I gave her a lot of attention. I was stuck on her for a while. It was never an affair. More a series of one-night stands. But we kidded ourselves for a while. "I want to marry you," she told me one time. But we both knew that wasn't going to happen. She was out to circulate – Flynn was crazy about her, Coop wanted to marry her, fahcrissake – and eventually I got shuffled outa the pack.

Rider enjoyed listening to Flagg's stories on the tapes: the insights, the self-deprecating touches. He pulled out files from a crate of material he had air-freighted from the Swan Collection at the Humanities Research Center at the University of Texas. *"Swan: Memos, letters, articles MGM 1942–3,"* read the cover on the first file he opened. He began to read, marking passages with a red highlighter. After an hour, he stopped reading and typed:

Cathy Radnitz (Noah's private secretary 1943–9) quoted in *Noah and Theodora*:

Noah's double life was amazing. He spent half the time with Barbara and Matthew on Coldwater Canyon; the other half with Theodora and the Baroness on Tower Drive. It was two years before Mr Mayer found out what was going on – or was forced to admit it. The showdown came when Theodora gave an interview to Bosley Crowther and Nick Schenck intervened. He was the president of Loew's, our parent company in New York. He sent Mr Mayer a cable . . .

Rider found the cable he had earlier discovered misfiled in a Loew's draft policy folder, and typed it up:

From: NICHOLAS M. SCHENCK
To: L. B. MAYER
MGM STUDIOS, CULVER CITY, CALIF. July 1, 1943

TOMORROW'S NYT CARRYING CROWTHER INTERVIEW HEADLINED THEODORA GROWS UP IN WHICH SHE SAYS QUOTE HOLLYWOOD PARTY SCENE IS BORING. IT TAKES ONE HUNDRED TIMES MORE IMAGINATION TO SPEND AN EVENING PLEASING ONE MAN YOU LOVE THAN TRYING TO IMPRESS ONE HUNDRED STRANGERS AT A COCKTAIL PARTY UNQUOTE. SEXUAL INNUENDO UNFORTUNATE IN VIEW RUMORS CIRCULATING HERE OF CERTAIN RELATIONSHIP. THIS NOT IMAGE WE ARE PROMOTING AND DAMAGING TO COMPANY WHICH HAS BROUGHT HER FROM

OBSCURITY TO WORLDWIDE FAME. URGE YOU
MAKE EVERY EFFORT TO SEE THAT THESE OPIN-
IONS ARE NOT REPEATED. REGARDS NICHOLAS
M. SCHENCK

FROM AARON FLAGG TAPES
Recorded New York City, November 7
I was in Noah's office when Mayer walked in the morning
Theodora's interview with Crowther broke in the *Times*. This was
1943.

"Light," he said in a quiet preacher's voice. "Light has been
thrown for me on dark places, Noah." The quiet voice he always
used when he was building up to one of his rages. "In this
country's most important newspaper I read things I don't want to
read about a young star belonging to this studio. And when I ask
questions, Howard Strickling" – Howard was his studio publicity
chief – "that fine man, Howard Strickling is bound in conscience
to tell me things I don't want to believe."

For several moments he let there be silence. He understood the
effectiveness of silence and what it could do to people. He was
very theatrical. He produced from his pocket the wire from New
York. I knew then he was getting heat from Schenck, and that
this was all tied up with the old struggle for power between New
York and the Coast, between the picturemakers and the money
people.

With New York on to it, he couldn't go on pretending he was
unaware of Noah's affair with his biggest star. He read the text
aloud, slowly, in a hurt voice – hurt was one of his specialities – he
read it from beginning to end. Some of it he repeated, shaking his
head, as if he couldn't believe what he was reading. *Movie acting
is like making love, said Miss Glass. Nobody gets it right the first
time.* He read that line twice, a tinge of purple darkening his face.

"I think she was trying to make a serious comment about movie
acting, LB," I said lamely.

"Helen Hayes, Charlie Laughton – they make serious comments about acting. Movie queens don't make serious comments
about nothing. Thinking messes up their fucking heads. What is

she now, eighteen?" Mayer directed the question at Noah.

"Seventeen, LB. You gave her a car for her birthday – the cream Cord."

"The one Connie Bennett drove in *Topper*. I remember. Cost me two grand from my own studio," he acknowledged his own generosity. "Eighteen, you say?"

"Seventeen, LB."

"And does Barbara, that sweet woman, the mother of your son, does she know what's going on – you and this girl, seventeen?"

Noah shrugged. "She thinks it'll blow over."

"Blow over! She thinks it'll blow over? Well, I think it'll blow up, that's what I think – the whole fucking thing'll blow up in all our faces!" He finally exploded, and it was awesome. A force apparently beyond his control, betraying the fury that drove him, the violence that all his life he had used to get his way. His nose swelled up, his cranberry eyes got smaller and redder. He looked like what the Hearst cartoonists made him look like after he fell out with William Randolph. "The heat's gonna come down on all of us, you dumb bastards," he screamed. "You don't even know which end of the trombone the music comes out of, neither of you. You're both stupid enough to be fucking actors. Maybe I should give you screen tests, you're so fucking stupid. You got any idea what the studio's got riding on this kid? Millions. *Millions*. We bust our balls making her a star. What thanks do I get? This is what thanks I get!"

He balled the *Times* interview in his fist and shook his fist in our faces.

"Tell her to keep her mouth shut around reporters," he turned on me again. "Not a boo –" he thew the ball of paper across the office – "*schtum*."

"It won't happen again, LB," Noah told him.

"A shut mouth don't catch flies," Mayer said.

"That's right," Noah agreed, as if he had just heard some great fucking wisdom.

"Look after yourself, or they'll piss on your grave," Mayer said looking first at Noah, then at me, as if deciding whether I was worthy of hearing such pearls.

"I shall, LB," Noah told him solemnly. He despised Mayer's tantrums, and his sentimentality but he knew it was foolish to make an enemy of him. Mayer was an asshole, but he was the asshole who ran the town, and until another asshole took his place, he was the man.

Mayer glared at me again, as if waiting for an oath of allegiance now that he had trusted me with his wisdom.

"Yes, sir," I said, joining the club.

"I love that girl." His voice was completely soft again. It was as if a storm had passed. He smiled, or rather he arranged his face in the shape of a man smiling. "I love that girl."

"I know you do, LB," Noah said soothingly.

I was wary of the sudden calm. Mayer's calm was more frightening than the rage.

He said, "I feel like a father to her – *Painted Moon*! I saw that picture five times and every time I wept. When she lost her son, I wept. I'm not ashamed. Why be ashamed? I'll see it again, I'll weep again."

"She's special, LB," Noah said. "But you always knew that."

Mayer pondered this. "Her last three pictures – you know what they earned this studio?"

"Sixteen million, LB," Noah told him.

"Fifteen-seven," Mayer said, as if a current of deep emotion were flowing through him.

"Fifteen-seven is a nice place to be, LB," Noah said.

"Isn't God good to me?" Mayer said, and there were tears in his eyes.

I guess I must have felt a little surer of myself. I said, "Did you hear that *Look* just named her the most beautiful girl in the free world, LB?"

"God made her beautiful" – his small eyes had a sort of holy fervor in them – "but Metro-Goldwyn-Mayer made her a star," he said.

He knew he wasn't going to get a better exit line than that.

39

Movie stars acquire homes to hide their whereabouts. And by the fall of 1943, in addition to the house on Tower Drive, Theodora also had a place at the beach at Malibu, and a flat in the Strathmore apartments in Westwood. The beach house haa originally been owned by Tom Mix, a cowboy star of the twenties. From the old Ocean Front road, now the Pacific Coast Highway, it appeared to be so insignificant that even fans who knew the address seldom found it, and those who did usually withdrew in the belief that they had surely made a mistake. But inside it was a palace. (Esther Crossman, Bright Star*)*

Tuesday, November 28
Santa Aloe

RIDER'S FIRST DRAFT, 3
The morning after Louie Mayer read the riot act to him, Noah rose early. From the small wardrobe he kept at the beach he picked out a tan suit, cream silk shirt, and yellow tie. He dressed with the care and attention of a man putting on a ceremonial uniform, and went down to breakfast.

Shortly after seven Theodora joined him on the terrace. It wasn't until the manservant poured her juice that she noticed the small package by her plate.

"What's this?"

"Open it."

She untied the package slowly, a child spinning out the delicious torment of anticipation. Noah watched her in silence. No one received a gift with more pleasure – and less sense of obligation. She could take tributes in her stride better than anybody he knew. Whether receiving an Academy Award or a fan's love letter, it was all the same to her. "Stardom creates habits and customs of its own," he once wrote in the *Hollywood Reporter* (or Aaron Flagg wrote it for him). "Stars are exhorted to defy ordinary society, to behave any way they will. The Hollywood myth demands a sense of élitism and edge: arrogance is a statement of success."

"For reading the small print in your contracts," he told her, when she finally extracted from the package a magnifying glass. The frame was of gold and white enamel; sapphires, rubies and emeralds entwined the handle like tiny exotic flowers on a slender stalk.

"Noah, it's beautiful."

"Eighteenth century."

She peered at him through the lens with grave, brilliant eyes. "Well, old chap, what shall we do?" she said in a British voice. "Shall we take up the chase?"

It was an opening of sorts, and Noah said casually, "Talking of the chase. Did I mention that Mayer came by the office yesterday?"

"Came by?" She lifted the magnifying glass again and eyed him with an enquiring look. She knew the rules of the studio. She knew that Mayer never paid visits to producers' offices unless there was something seriously wrong. "Mr Mayer came by your office?"

Noah smiled. "He wanted a word about the *Times* piece."

"Was he being mean? I hate those piggy eyes of his when he's being mean."

"No, he wasn't being mean." Noah poured her coffee. "A little anxious. New York's been on his back. Nick Schenck didn't like the piece."

"New York is angry with Mr Mayer because of *my* interview?"

Noah shrugged. "There's always tension between Schenck and Mayer. Some of the things you said exacerbated whatever it is they're fighting about this week."

"Why should what I say matter a damn to them?"

"It matters," Noah said a shade more seriously. "You're getting over a thousand fan items a day. Gable doesn't get that! You're a major asset, Theodora."

Theodora seemed to smile. "I didn't know that being famous was going to be such a headache."

"It's not a headache if you handle it right."

"What does Mr Mayer want me to do about it?"

"Be more discreet around newspaper people."

"This town is worse than Vienna. People scared to say what they think."

"Nobody says we can't say what we think." He grinned, and tried to lighten the conversation. "So long as it's what LB says we should think!"

"You never take me seriously."

"Sweetheart, I always take you seriously. But you got success, fame – there's a price."

"The difference between a star and a face in the crowd is fractional," she quoted one of his favourite dictums. "I'm a very lucky girl without the littlest right to complain. Yes?"

"It's how you perceive yourself," he said, anxious to move the conversation further away from Mayer.

"Sometimes I don't know who I am. I look at myself and I think, That's not me."

"Who would you like to be?"

"I don't know," Theodora answered. But sometimes she even envied Barbara Swan. Barbara had a husband, she had a child –

Rider stopped typing, and read what he had written. Almost all the dialogue came from a Theodora tape. He was pleased how well the story was falling into place, how easily the pieces fitted together. He began at last to feel a sense of control. Theodora and Noah, Aaron Flagg, Mayer, the Baroness – they were his characters now. It was the most satisfying feeling in the world.

40

It's better than being a pimp. (Harry Cohn, President, Columbia Pictures)

Thursday, November 30
Santa Aloe

FROM AARON FLAGG TAPES
Recorded New York City, October 29

Hollywood in the forties, Jesus it was booming. Four hundred new pictures a year. Fifty million Americans going to the movies every week. The studios and the cathouses never had it so good. But Claudette's was something special. She was a casting director at Republic when she got the idea that made her a millionairess a coupla times over. She specialized in girls who were dead ringers for movie stars. It was a blast getting to screw Ida Lupino, Lana Turner, spending the night with Deanna Durbin without having to listen to her sing. Even the house – it looked like Scarlett O'Hara's Tara – seemed to be part of the joke.

At that time, the place was run by a terrific-looking redhead named Suzy Auberjonois, and I still remember the look on her face when she saw us standing there. It was early, and the bar was empty. "The girls are still at prayer," she said. It was her little joke. "Women give themselves to God when the devil is through with them." She couldn't have been more than thirty, bags of class. A streak of dark greasepaint narrowed a slightly wide jaw; some skilfully blended eyeshadows hollowed the sockets of her eyes, which were flecked with changing colours, greens and golds. Her voice was low and unhurried – the voice they teach you in the best eastern schools. After a few drinks, the lamps turned low, she coulda been Paulette Goddard. Maybe she'd come to Hollywood to act.

"See if I can guess," she said, getting round to business, looking at Noah. "A girl with character . . . Stanwyck? Oberon? We have a beautiful Merle?"

He said, "I hear you signed a new girl."

She handled it well. She said, "Gentlemen who visit us are usually looking for something they're not going to get at home."

He laughed. "Why don't you let me decide what I order when I eat out?"

"I'll tell her you're here," she said.

About ten minutes later she came in and held out her hand. "Noah Swan? I'm Missy."

"I'll be damned," he said softly.

He took her hand and held it for a long moment. Noah was able to look at a woman as if imprinting on his memory every pore of her. It was a kind of rape, and a kind of devotion, and as fine an act of judgement as anything you'll ever see.

"Oh, you're good," he said, finally letting go her hand.

She said, "From you, Mr Swan, that's a great compliment."

She was about Theodora's own age. I'd been expecting somebody older. Maybe she was an inch or two shorter, and her breasts were a little heavier.

"You got everything but the voice," Noah told her.

"The voice is extra," she said.

"Is it worth it?"

"I usually slide by on the looks," she said.

Noah leaned forward and took her hand and turned it palm upward, and inhaled where a fine vein pulsed in her wrist. "You've even got the scent right."

Missy smiled. "Blue Grass."

"How do you know stuff like that?" he said.

"I was Theodora's stand-in on *Painted Moon*," she said.

"I'm sorry," he said. "I shoulda remembered."

"Nobody remembers stand-ins," she said.

We had dinner. That was the nice thing about Claudette's – you could romance the girls, get to act like Gable if you wanted. He asked her about her life – how did she land up at Claudette's?

She said, "By accident – the way I fall into most things in my life. I was working over at Monogram. Three days on a horse opera. I'd like to say it was one of my lesser jobs, but I'd be lying to you. I met Suzy Auberjonois in Joe Halff's drugstore. She told me about this place, and nobody else was breaking down my door with offers . . ."

It was a familiar Hollywood story, but she told it amusingly. Hit Hollywood at fifteen, worked in a shoe store, juggled trays in a beanery, went up to Pasadena for a while, and fell in love with a married man who wanted her to have his child, but wouldn't leave his wife. Returned to Hollywood, got a job typing for an agency supplying hostesses and snake charmers to nightclubs. One of the clients, Billy Solow, an old second assistant, and now the proprietor of Billy's Solo Room in Burbank, got her some crowd work on *The Strawberry Blonde* at Warners. A camera assistant recommended her to a friend at Metro who was looking for a stand-in for Theodora. Missy got the job – $16.50 a day – and did OK. She learned a lot just watching Theodora on the set. "It kinda stops you, the way she reads a line," she said. But she wouldn't go to bed with her Metro benefactor and when Theodora started *Reunion* Missy was out. She got a seven-year contract with six-month options with an independent producer named Moe Bonn, working out of the Hal Roach studios. She did plenty of leg art, but no movies and the contract fell at the first option. But she made some useful contacts in the business. Luck was being in the traffic, right?

Did she still want to be a star? She knew it took more than looks, she said, and more than ordinary luck, and whatever that something extra was she didn't know whether it was anything she had.

"Stardom is about deals, Missy," he told her. "Stars are supposed to be the most desirable people in the world, but most of the time they're just people who got the deals."

He always had great theories about what it takes to make a star. He said to her, "Why does oxygen unite with potassium? Why don't oxygen unite with platinum?"

"Mr Swan," she said, "the only thing I know about platinum is that touching up the roots ain't cheap."

He laughed, but I could see he was trying to figure out whether it was more profound than it sounded. He said, "I'm talking about chemistry, Missy. In chemistry, affinity is the attraction between the particles of two bodies which causes them to unite and blend. This creates a new compound from the two ingredients of which it's formed – something completely different, something completely unique. But take two bodies between whom this affinity don't exist – they can embrace till the Los Angeles river wets its bed and they won't ever blend together."

It was one of his party pieces. The chemistry of casting. Stars either exert a mutual attraction on each other, or they don't. He used it to dazzle actresses, to rib up newspaper guys. I heard him do it a hundred times . . . "If there's an affinity between the particles of two bodies they need to be brought into contract for only a moment to produce an instantaneous phenomenon – *stardom*!"

I remember Missy smiled, but like it was going to hurt. She said, "Look, I'm a whore, Mr Swan. That's what I am. I'm a whore trading on somebody else's fame. I've gone to bed with men drunk enough and crazy enough to believe I'm the real thing. You think I'm happy about that? I'm not happy about that. But that's my life."

"Then you should listen to what I got in mind," he said. "You're a looker. You got your own personality. We get the right deal – you can make it in pictures."

She said, "What's in it for you, Mr Swan?"

He said, "What's in it for me? I make myself available to people – be of assistance to people. Later, sometimes, they become available to me . . ."

I think that was the best definition of the way he operated I ever heard. She didn't know what the hell to make of him.

"Do you know Harry Cohn?" he said.

"Columbia," she said. "I wouldn't buy an apple from that s.o.b."

"You know him?"

"No, but that's what I hear," she said.

"Forget what you hear," he told her. "What you hear is off a mile. He's a bully, foul-mouthed, he'll nickel and dime you to the poorhouse, but he knows how to make pictures, and he knows star material when he sees it. I'd rather have his handshake on a deal than anybody else's signature I know.''

She said, "Mr Swan, why are you telling me this?''

"I'm going to talk to him about you," Noah told her.

Missy said, "You know what I think? I think you're crazy."

But that night she quit Claudette's anyway.

FROM AARON FLAGG TAPES
Recorded New York City, October 30
This is a coupla weeks after we saw Missy at Claudette's. Keep in mind, Columbia wasn't Metro. Columbia was Poverty Row, but Harry ruled over it like a goddam emperor. He lifted his feet on to the desk. He said, "Like the shoesies, pally? Hand-made. Fuckin' an'elope. Genuine fuckin' Arabian an'elope." That's how he talked. An actress sued him once for swearing at her and a judge ruled that his obscenities were part of his natural vocabulary and couldn't be construed as insults. He said, "Ordered twenny pairs. A whole fuckin' herda an'elopes. What the fuck, huh?"

Noah said they looked comfortable.

He said, "Like a crocheted pussy. Arabian an'elopes, the little fuckers are practically all extinc'.''

"You bought at the right time, Harry," I said, but Jesus, an entire antelope breed being wiped out to supply loafers for Harry Cohn was a melancholy thought.

It didn't worry Harry. His eyes shone with pride. His face always had this kinda barbershop finish to it. Rita Hayworth told me once that the studio barber shaved him three times a day. He took off a shoe and held it up. "Hand-fuckin'-made, yuh wouldn't believe how much, and I don't even have the elevators," he said.

"You got style, Harry," Noah told him.

"Six feet tall. Who needs fuckin' elevators?" Cohn replaced his shoe, and took his feet off the desk. "OK, down to some fuckin' business here. Wanna hear what I think about the test? Piece ashit. Worse than a piece ashit."

"Discovering Theodora don't make me Nostradamus," Noah said.

"Yuh fuckin' her?"

"No."

"What are you, a fuckin' social worker?"

Noah said, "I see something in a girl don't mean I'm playing grab-ass."

"Yuh fuckin' Theodora, yuh fuckin' your wife – give her my respects, by the way – Jesus, how much pussy do yuh need, kid? Don't yuh get tired?"

Noah said something about not looking to get a position on the deal, and Harry exploded.

"I'm so fuckin' stupid, I don't know what yuh up to?" He smashed his desk with that riding crop of his. "This is some rinky-dink outfit yuh can waltz in here – fix Columbia Pictures up with a fuckin' star hooker? Tryin'a slip the business to Harry Cohn, yuh got the wrong orders from headquarters, pally."

"You don't know what you can get away with if you don't try," Noah said, grinning that great grin of his.

Harry didn't think it was funny. "Yuh think I don't know the answers? I'm fifty-three years old. I know all the fuckin' answers, pally." He opened a drawer, took out a file, and started to read: "*Evelyn Maureen Miller, born Morristown, New Jersey, nineteen-hunnerd twenny-five. Father: James Walter Miller . . .*" He hit the report with the crop. "I got the whole tutti-frutti here, pal," he yelled triumphantly. "But it ain't just Claudette's is it, pally? Claudette's I unnerstan'. I have what they say a profoun' unnerstannin' of human nature." He smiled like a man who knew he was going to get a headache in five minutes. "How about Moe fuckin' Bonn?"

Noah said he'd told him about Moe Bonn. She'd done some tests, that's all.

Harry said, "Yuh don't think maybe she ever wiggled her ass for Moe? Jesus, I hate to put a crimp in yuh halo, kid. Moe Bonn? Dirty movies?"

"Moe Bonn's a pornographer?"

Harry shrugged. "He made dirty movies, kid. What can I

tellya? The hell of it is, she's good. Looked like she enjoyed it too."

Noah said, "You sure it was Missy?"

"She wasn't hidin' a fuckin' thing, Noah," Harry said. His anger was over. He'd had his fun. He walked to the end of the room. "Unnerstan' my situation here. I sign her, a year from now we gotta bundle invested in her and her dirty little secret gets out –"

"Crawford's dirty little secret's never gotten out," I said.

"She's got Louie to thank for that," he said. "Mayer can handle that shit . . . Tracy down with the fuckin' fish all the time . . . Garland's pills . . . Theodora's crazy mother. I can't handle that shit. And Columbia Pictures has a reputation now. We make family pictures, fahcrissake." But there was still interest in his voice. Noah spotted it too. He said, "What actress is totally untarnished, Harry?"

Harry went back to his desk. "She ain't gonna be another Theodora," he said.

"She could be another Hayworth if Hayworth steps out of line," Noah said.

We watched him select a cigar from the box on his desk. We watched him light it. We watched him blow a cloud of smoke.

Then he said, "I don't like the name, Missy – I gotta fuckin' maid called Missy."

"Change it," Noah said.

"Evelyn Miles," Harry said. "Forty-week contract, four C's a week, one-year option at six-fifty. That's the deal. Yuh wannit?"

That's how it happened. How Missy Miller became Evelyn Miles. Christ, they were interesting times, though . . .

41

Baroness von Tegge was a beautiful woman, but she couldn't compete with her daughter. It caused her a lot of grief. (Dore Schary, New York Times, June 14, 1973)

Sunday, December 3
Santa Aloe

Missy telephoned the beach house and invited herself to breakfast. "I'll be down in fifteen minutes, if you promise to be decent," she said.

Rider smiled, remembering the story of Claudette's and Moe Bonn's blue movies. If she knew what he knew! "Decent as I'm ever going to be," he said.

She arrived in less than ten minutes, dressed in white slacks and a blue gingham shirt. Rider noted how much like Theodora she held herself: the walk, the way she turned her head. Perhaps it had once been a deliberate imitation but now it was part of her own personality, he thought as she hooked her arm through his and they strolled out to the terrace.

They sat down, Rider poured the coffee.

Missy waited until he had filled her cup, and then his own. "Theodora has another migraine. She won't be able to work today. She asked me to give you this." She handed him an envelope. "I typed it up last night."

"I'm leaving on the tenth," he reminded her, taking the transcript.

"She can't help being unwell."

He felt the envelope. "There's not much here. Where does it take us to?"

"The Baroness's breakdown."

"1947? We've still got a lot of ground to cover."

"She's doing her best."

"Is she?"

"You sound upset."

"We've lost four days, Missy."

"Those migraines really knock her out."

"Is she getting second thoughts about the book?"

"I don't think so."

"Something's changed." He felt his control over the situation slipping away but he did not know what to do about it.

"Don't push her so hard. She's not a young woman any more."

"I'm not getting what she feels about anything any more."

"Sometimes when the feelings are too deep there are no memories."

"What's she hiding, Missy?"

"You expect too much, Robert."

THEODORA'S TAPE

Mama's behaviour became a problem again, this was in the fall of '47, and this time Noah and Mr Mayer arranged for her to be put into the Ober Clinic in Connecticut. Mainly devoted to "drying out" cures, it was a charming place, with swans on the lake. Although it seemed as if the patients were free to walk out of the gate if they wished, it was only a nice illusion. A lot of Hollywood people used it in those days. Maggie Mayer – LB's ex – was a regular there. Joe Mankiewicz's wife, Rosa Stradner – another Viennese – was there for a while. Mama had been there for two or three months before I was able to make the time between pictures to visit. Noah came with me. We combined the trip with a long weekend in New York.

Mama seemed fine, and was quite funny. *Verkauft's mei G'wand, i fahr in den Himmel,* she said – Sell my clothes, I'm going to heaven. I hadn't heard her say that since I was a little girl. She asked after old friends, about Noah's various projects. I had to keep reminding myself of Ober's warning – how slow and fragile her recovery still was. She read the New York papers, devoured the new books. She had enjoyed *The Loved One*. She said that Waugh made Forest Lawn sound tremendous fun. "Bury me there in my Lanvin blue!" she said. She asked about Mr Mayer. Noah said he wasn't the man he was. And she said, "*He was something in his time.*" She liked Mayer. People were always divided about him.

That weekend we saw *A Streetcar Named Desire* on Broadway. Jessica Tandy was a wonderful Blanche, but Kazan had thrown the play to Brando. He would have stolen it anyway. I said that the good young actors coming up were beginning to make me feel old. Noah said that Brando was twenty-four – two years *older* than me!

"You started young," he said.

"Young is starting to seem like a long time ago," I told him.

That was the weekend Noah learned that Mr Mayer was planning to make Dore Schary head of production. His new *dauphin*. The role he had been promising to Noah for years.

Why did Mr Mayer pass over Noah? Nobody could understand it. Some of the rumours

From Robert Rider's notebooks:

This morning's transcript short, ends abruptly. Missy insists problem is migraine and nothing more. But I seem to be losing Theodora's sense of commitment. Seems like a hundred years ago on the beach when she told me how relaxed she felt with me. Has Missy finally persuaded her that she is wrong to trust me? Frustration alleviated somewhat by fact Flagg's covered same ground. His tapes more like debriefings than interviews. Worth their weight in gold.

FROM AARON FLAGG TAPES
Recorded New York City, October 28
MGM went five mil in the red that year, 1948. This, remember, was before network TV was nationwide. But the rot set in when Mayer made Schary head of production. If he had thought very

hard for sixty years he couldn't have come up with a man more wrong for the job. Schary was a decent guy. Friendly, loyal to his staff, but he had a reputation for being an intellectual. Mayer figured he was a guy he could handle – "A guy with plenty of judgement but not much blood," that's what he told Sam Goldwyn. He knew that if he'd given the nod to Noah, Noah would've walked away with the whole studio.

This was April. Schary's set to join Metro July. It was still hush-hush. I got wind of it because I knew a girl in Bob Rubens's office in New York. Rubens, Loew's counsel, was drawing up the contract – six grand a week, two deferred, and no bonus deal. It was less than Noah was getting running his own unit. So all Schary was getting was the title. But for years Mayer had promised the job to Noah, and it rankled like shit.

One afternoon, it's early June now, Noah says we have to fly to New York that evening. He laid it out for me on the plane: we were splitting from Metro. He was gonna launch his own company with Theodora – naturally Theodora didn't know it yet! He wanted me aboard as his executive assistant, whatever the hell that meant. I took a deep breath, and said yes. I knew it was a helluva gamble – to cut Noah and Theodora loose from Metro was going to take all the wiles of Harry Houdini, who escaped for a living. The deal, which meant moving to Cohn's Columbia studios, was gonna be financed by Chase National, and Noah wanted to wrap it up before wind of Schary's appointment got out. He knew that getting passed out of the picture at Metro could make him look less of a hot proposition.

"Schary ain't got what you got," I told him.

"Well, he ain't got Theodora," he said.

The next morning we drove down to Pine Street to meet the bankers. A guy called Horace Libby, the senior vice president; Dean Willets, the director in charge of investment operations; a few others I don't remember. We were shown up to the boardroom. Libby was a young guy, thin, with a tanned, balding head, and a kinda scooped-out face. He said his bank knew a lot about Hollywood. They foreclosed on the old Fox company in Westwood. "It finished William Fox," he said.

I knew right away it would be a mistake to mess with these people.

Willets handed a file to Libby, who got down to business. "There's no start-up date for your first production," he said briskly, reading from a tagged and heavily underscored draft agreement. "But there is a date – January 1, 1949 – when Chase National participation – *Chase finance* – is triggered *bon gré, mal gré* – willy-nilly, if you prefer."

He was a patronizing bastard. Noah said, "Gentlemen, I don't know much about that French flubdub – but in the immortal words of Abraham Lincoln: You don't fertilize a field by farting through the fence."

I don't think anyone ever talked to these guys like that before. He was telling them, *Look, motherfuckers, I'm standing in the rain with you, so put up or shut up*.

His ace was Theodora, of course. And finally somebody asked about *Romeo and Juliet* – would he explain the circumstances that led to its abandonment?

He was terrific. The picture was a victim of the war, he said. "Every great general in history at some time in his career has had to make a tactical retreat when the tide turned against him." Listen, *I* believed him! He couldn't write the way he wanted to write, but he loved story-telling. He had them eating out of his hand.

He promised to negotiate the break with Metro within six months. Mayer would scream, he admitted. But the business was changing, and not even Louis B. Mayer could hold on to an unhappy star.

"Jesus, you killed those guys up there," I told him in the elevator.

He said, "You just have to tell people what they want to hear."

"Can you really spring Theodora from Metro that fast?" I asked him.

I remember his grin. "Travellers from afar can lie with impunity," he said.

42

*Barbara Swan was no innocent, she had her
share of lovers, and why the hell not? The way
Noah treated her. (Irene Mayer Selznick,*
Esquire *magazine, December 1987)*

**Sunday, December 10
Santa Aloe**

Rider stood on the jetty and read the note from Theodora. In her
distinctive handwriting, but in terms without the warmth that he
felt had grown between them in the past five weeks, she
apologized for her indisposition and regretted not being well
enough to see him off. She wished him a happy holiday, and
looked forward to his return in January.

His bags were put aboard the powerboat. Missy handed him a
manila envelope. "A few more transcripts to keep you going until
you return to us. I've pencilled in corrections of fact, but there's
not much I can do about the wrong notions she has about some
things. And this" – she kissed him on his mouth – "is from me."

"You might have shaded the last few rounds," he told her
quietly, his tone uninflected by any sign of reproach.

Clarence turned on the big MerCruiser Magnum engines. "I
told you when you came," she shouted above the sudden roar.
"I'll do anything to protect her happiness."

"Remember victory belongs to the most patient," he shouted
back, grinning.

"Happy Christmas, Robert," she called to him as the launch
sped away, but he could no longer hear her.

On the plane he read the new transcripts and made notes. After dinner, while other passengers slept, he took out a copy of *Portrait of a Hollywood Marriage* and read the note tucked inside:

Robert
Here's the Barbara Swan book I told you about. Very rare! (Few were sold; I guess the rest were deservedly pulped.) An interesting view of life inside the Swan ménage, and as accurate a picture of Barbara as anything I've read.

As always,
Aaron

A ghosted autobiography, it was published by a small publishing house in San Francisco a year after Barbara died in 1983. Contrary to expectations at the time, no shattering secrets were revealed, although she was honest about her own adulterous relationships. It was later reported that the publishing company was owned by Noah and that the book had been rewritten after her death. But that didn't make sense. If Noah owned the company and disapproved of the book why publish it at all? To squash rumours that the book was dynamite? To spread disinformation? That was possible, Rider thought – if you were into conspiracy theories.

The grainy black-and-white jacket photograph (snatched, according to Flagg, early one morning by Noah's private detective) was of Barbara leaving her lover's apartment on North Crescent Drive in Beverly Hills. The blurred movement of her small white-gloved hands raised to hide her face as she sat huddled in the back of a cab gave the picture a poignantly period look.

He opened the book at random and read:

By 1948 an unsuccessful marriage had become a deeply unhappy one, and we lived together under a flag of truce. It was worse than separation, worse than divorce, but my pride would permit no other solution. I had become forty that year. And although I knew I was still attractive, forty was never a good age for a wife to be in Hollywood. But I tried. I spent a fortune on clothes, did lunch with the girls, jumped into all the latest fads – dianetics, analysis, fortune-tellers.

The emptiness of my life came home to me suddenly one evening when Noah returned from a trip to New York with Theodora. I was in the drawing-room, waiting for George Cukor to pick me up to take me to dinner at the Goetzes. We didn't expect to meet and really had nothing to say to each other. I remember looking at my watch, and realizing that it was the Cartier Noah had bought me when we became engaged, and fixed at the hour we first met. He asked about Matthew. I told him that he was upset that his father hadn't been there for his school play. "Did you explain to him I was unavoidably detained in New York?" he said. I couldn't stand it any more. "Unavoidably detained in New York with your mistress. How do you explain that to a seven-year-old boy?"

He was calm. He never lost his temper with me, ever. He said he thought he was a good father. "Only a father can understand what is in a father's heart," he said. "You want to possess him, but you never include him," I said. I knew I was using our son to talk about us, about the distance that had come between us.

I don't know what I said, but I probably said too much. He was always intuitive about me. "Do you care for anyone else?" he asked. I recognized the tone. The tone softened with a kind of interrogator's cunning, a tone without prejudice or passion, containing neither credulity nor trust. I knew how careful I would have to be. He had a way of remembering what people said, of storing it away and using it against them later, when they least expected it.

"Do I care for anyone else?" I said. "I care for lots of people."

"But anyone special?" he asked quietly.

"Would you mind?" I said.

"Yes, I'd mind," he said. "I don't want anything to happen that might jeopardize what we have."

"What the hell *do* we have, Noah?" I asked him.

He reminded me we had Matthew. He said he didn't want anything to hurt our son.

I said, "Dostoevsky said nothing in this world is worth the tears of a child."

"You're reading Dostoevsky?" He sounded surprised.

"Dostoevsky came between dianetics and analysis," I told him.

He said, "I'm sorry, Barbara." It was the only time I ever heard him apologize in his life. It was as hard for him to apologize as it was for me to blame him. I knew that everything he ever dreamed of he had found in Theodora. I knew that they were bound together in ways that no husband and wife can ever be close. A producer and his star . . . It had happened before in Hollywood, and it would go on happening. I didn't even blame Theodora. I couldn't even hate her.

I said, "I don't expect much. I just don't want to be so bloody unhappy, Noah. I don't deserve that."

"I guess you've been planning this conversation for a long time," he said.

I said, "I didn't plan anything, Noah. I just stored up things to say."

"We've had some good times, haven't we?" he said.

"Jesus, I hope so," I said, knowing that I loved him and would always love him.

Rider closed the book, and looked at his watch. It was still on Caribbean time. He turned the hands forward to 5.15 a.m. – remembering Barbara Swan's watch for ever fixed in a happier past – and returned his thoughts to the present, and a deadline that was getting closer all the time.

43

You can close your eyes to reality, but not to memory. (Stanislaus Lec)

Thursday, December 14
Washington DC

Kate Goldsmid returned to Ambrose Lanigan's apartment for the first time since his death. She had been through it all before. Turning the key, she steeled herself against the tyranny of inanimate objects . . . a half-read novel by his bed, a book of matches from a favourite restaurant, his robe behind the bathroom door . . . The little things undo you every time, she thought.

She stood with her back against the door, her shoulders tense with held-back grief. The apartment had already broken with the past; it was no longer where they had loved and laughed and told their secrets to each other. Lanigan had owned few personal possessions he really cared about: a few books; his father's pocket watch; his mother's needlework sampler: *Rosie Malone her work aged 9 years, June 6, 1919.* He had left a short will in which he left his money to several children's charities. "Don't leave me any money, Lanigan," Kate had told him when wills were talked about last summer. "I don't need it, and it wouldn't make me any happier than I am right at this minute with you." So there were no problems . . . just the tidying up and putting away of a life, she thought.

She took a deep breath and walked through the apartment, switching on lights as she went. She gathered up the few clothes and personal belongings she had kept there and put them into a valise. She tried not to think of what she was doing as the ritual last act of her life with Lanigan.

257

But it was.

When she had finished, she poured herself a glass of his favourite Greek brandy, ran a bath, and undressed. In the bath she sipped the brandy until memories and dreams ran together in a delicious half-sleep.

The phone ringing in the bedroom startled her awake. After four rings the answer machine took care of the call. She wondered how long she had slept. A minute? An hour? The water was still warm; the smell of scented steam lingered in the air. She dried herself with one of Lanigan's big rough towels, dressed slowly. After dialling for a cab to pick her up in forty minutes, she made coffee, switched on the radio: ". . . into the ring. Still Senator Swan remains the hot ticket. If –" She changed channels. At seven the doorman called to tell her that her taxi was waiting.

She was almost out of the door when she remembered the answerphone. She went back, took out the tape and slipped it into her purse. She lingered for a moment and looked around before picking up the valise.

"Goodbye, old flat," she said softly, closing the door behind her for the last time.

44

*For all his ferocious devotion to the studio – and
that he had in full measure, since actually he
conceived the place as his – Louis B. Mayer
burned and squirmed at the deference paid to
Dore Schary as the saviour of Metro-Goldwyn-
Mayer. His tapeworm ego was revolted, and it
gnawed inside him. (Bosley Crowther, New
York Times, March 2, 1960)*

**Tuesday, December 26
West Sussex, England**

Jay Pfeiffer read the first hundred and seventy pages of Rider's
draft. "Oscar did us a real favour hooking us up with Flagg," he
said when he came to the end. The two men were in Pfeiffer's
study in his old mill house in Sussex. "Where do you go next,
storywise?"

"Complete the draft of her Hollywood years. Noah's battle to
get her away from MGM. The plot to fix Schary. I want to get
that down before I return to the island."

"On the eighth?"

Rider nodded. "Fourteen days."

"You promised the BBC a couple of days for their profile on
you," Pfeiffer reminded him.

"I know, and it's beginning to worry me."

Rider returned to London early the next morning. In the car he
slipped a tape into the cassette-player:

FROM AARON FLAGG TAPES
Recorded New York City, November 4
Noah had no secrets from me. I was his shadow. People got so

259

used to me being around, they stopped noticing I was there. If Louie Mayer was alive today and you asked him, he'd swear his life away that nobody was in his office that day but the two of them. But I was there. A shadow.

"We're a coupla vipers. Hatched from the same egg, Noah," he said. I loved it when he went Old Testament. "A coupla vipers. Recognize the kinship. We do business together."

"You made Hollywood happen, LB," Noah told him. "You're a piece of American history. Why don't I trust you?"

"I used to like you, Noah," Louie said, amiable as hell. The more he wanted something the more amiable he got. I'd never seen him so fucking amiable. He'd come straight from the studio barbershop and his face was pink and shiny from Mano's hot towels. Strange things you remember. He wore a blue tie patterned with yellow lion heads. The knot was loose and exposed a golden collar stud and under it a wattled neck that seemed to be ninety years older than the pink and pampered face above. He switched to his hurt voice. "I treated you like a son," he said.

This was eighteen months after Schary's appointment. They were shooting *An American in Paris*. Out of the window you could see the rooftops of Montmartre. Noah was telling him again how unhappy Theodora was, and pleading for her release. But she still had four years on her contract and Mayer was binding her to it. Noah was beginning to lose his temper. "Four years ain't so long," he said. "We'll still be around. Where will you be, LB?"

"Sitting right here, my friend," he said. He believed he was going to last for ever. Did he ever have moments of doubt to balance that kind of faith? I don't think so. He said, "You think my problem's keeping Theodora here? My problem's getting rid of Dore Schary." He chuckled and moved his hands in a conjuring movement in the air. "You see I'm hiding nothing."

That was the first time I realized how much power the old bastard had lost. He couldn't fire Schary because Schenck wouldn't let him. In his first year, Schary had turned a six million deficit into a small profit. He couldn't fire him, but he could fix him – with help. Revenge was nothing new to Louie, but sharing it was, and sharing it was dangerous.

"I want the cocksucker out of my hair, Noah." He smiled, and I knew why he frightened people. "And you're going to help me do it."

Noah lit a cigarette, bounced the lighter in his hand, as if trying to guess its weight, waiting for Mayer to explain.

Louie sighed. "You remind me of Irving sitting there. When he was thinking he used to swing his pocket watch . . ." His eyes filled with tears, remembering the great days with Thalberg. "He sat where you're sitting now, telling me a story – *Red-Headed Woman*. He wanted it for Harlow. I said, 'Irving, you'll go to jail. Tell the truth. It's a won'erful thing to tell the truth. Harlow, she's a platinum blonde – *that's* the truth.' He gets mad. He storms out. We make up. We make the picture. Not such a grosser. The figures, I can tell you exactly the figures: sixty-nine thousand. Not going to make us rich, but we're not complaining either. The next year I put her into *Red Dust*. Gable and Harlow. Sensational. That was Irving and I working together. I respected him. He respected me." He banged his large fist down on the desk. "Not like this Schary son of a bitch I got here now . . . He'll never fill Irving Thalberg's shoes. Never."

It was some performance. He was still the vain, proud, intolerant Louis B. Mayer. But that strain of sentimentality and self-pity that had made him such an effective manipulator of actors and situations was becoming an uncontrollable weakness in his old age. It's always sad watching an old man fighting to prove that he's not finished.

He wiped his eyes with that big handkerchief he'd pull out of his pocket like a goddam napkin from La Rue's, and got down to business. He said that Schary was planning to offer Theodora two big pictures. "I tell you with my hand on my heart" – he placed his hand on his heart – "these pictures are going to be our top grossers next year."

Noah said, "Sounds good so far, LB."

Louie said, "I want you to turn them down."

Noah looked at him and smiled. "Tell me about it, LB," he said.

"I want you to make life hell for this sonofabitch. Make impossible demands. Hold out for one year." He stood behind Noah's chair and held his shoulders between his hands in that paternal way he had. "One year from now, you both walk – with Louis B. Mayer's blessing."

Noah said, "Three years off our sentences for bad behaviour?"

Mayer chuckled. "Schary gets a reputation for not being able to deliver the talent . . . That's the deal, my boy."

It was so simple. I didn't understand then that simplicity was the gift of fanatics. It was what made Louie so dangerous and so fucking efficient.

"Schary's not going to be a sport about it," Noah said calmly.

"He'll suspend her," Louie said gleefully.

"A year with no dough. Everything's a number, LB," Noah said.

Louie shook his head. "Remember you got a friend at court. This is still Metro-Goldwyn-*Mayer*," he said.

Noah said, "My father used to say that nobody in this racket should put their faith in quid pro quos."

"Don't tell me your father. Your father died broke," Mayer said. "Do what I say, one year from now you'll both be free. No legal guns to pay, we each save ourselves a bundle. It's a good offer. Take it."

"And if you're no longer around, LB?" Noah said. It was a good point. Schary was in a strong position. "What good's your word if you're not here any more?" Noah said.

It was like Louie'd been hit in the mouth. He . . . roared. "Schary's never gonna pull the sheet over my face. I made Hollywood happen," he repeated Noah's line, unable to resist tasting it in his own mouth. "*Louis B. Mayer made Hollywood happen*," he screamed it again, like he was addressing thousands.

So, cut to the chase. The deal's made. Afterwards, I said to Noah, "I think you won some kind of victory in there." He said, "Yeah, but I wish I could have done it when the old bastard was in his prime . . . that would really have been something."

Rider switched off the tape, and began to smile.

45

Noah Swan was fearless. He stood up to Louis B. Mayer and to the big boys on Wall Street. He was the most terrifying perfectionist about what he wanted, even if it meant being occasionally unlawful. Whatever it took he had to be No. 1. I never liked the man but I admired his guts.
(James Cagney, Los Angeles Times, April 14, 1983)

Thursday, 28 December
London

RIDER'S FIRST DRAFT, 4

Halfway through the twentieth century Hollywood was caught between what it had once been and what was still to come. Noah Swan, thirty-five years old, belonged both to its past and to its future. Louis B. Mayer was at this time sixty-eight years old and belonged only to its past. Two men drawn together by a single desire to destroy a third.

In December Noah gave a party at his home in Coldwater Canyon in honour of Lord and Lady Mountbatten. It was the Hollywood social event of 1950. Two hundred and fifty guests sat at tables set for groups of ten and twenty in a marquee decorated in pink silk damask to resemble the dining-room of the old Hollywood Hotel. White orchids and lanterns were tied into the trees; the MGM studio orchestra played tunes from MGM musicals.

Flagg accompanied Theodora. They were at a table with Joe Mankiewicz and his wife, Rosa Stradner; the Edward G. Robinsons; producer Charlie Feldman, and the English actress Deborah Kerr; Harry Cohn, and the Columbia contract star, Evelyn (Missy) Miles.

Dore Schary sat at another table with his wife and a group of MGM suits. During the evening the following exchange took place between Schary and Noah:

"I want you to stop screwing me around, Noah," he said pleasantly, his voice soft so nobody else could hear.

Noah, he's smiling too, said: "It's nothing personal, Dore."

"I'm making it personal, doll," Dore said. "I know what you and Louie are up to. I know the deal he's given you. But it's not going to work. Louie's a busted flush. We can work something out. I never saw a situation where there wasn't some way out, did you?"

Noah said, "My old man told me never change livery in the middle of a war." (He had a lot of aphorisms he said he got from his father; Flagg says he made up most of them.)

Dore said, "I like Theodora. I like her as a person and I respect her as an artist. I don't want to have to suspend her, kid. Don't make me suspend her."

Noah said, "Suspension'll cost us both, Dore."

Dore said, "The studio will pay the price. How long will you be prepared to pay the cost of exacting it, Noah? You need strong nerves and a deep pocket to play games with me, doll."

"Don't threaten me, Dore," Noah said.

"I never use threats, doll," Dore told him. "Threats only put a man on his guard."

FROM AARON FLAGG TAPES
Recorded New York City, November 4
I felt sorry for Missy that night. I could tell she didn't want to be Harry's date, and she definitely didn't want to be on Theodora's table. What was it Gore Vidal said – *Theodora is the dream. Evelyn Miles is the dream hardened into reality.* That was cruel. But she never complained. She said, "I'm cast for my looks and that's what I deliver." But her performances always had a moment that was unmistakably hers, which people in the business recognized and respected. For the party, she had played down her likeness to Theodora. Maybe Theodora felt her pain. She gave Missy her number at the beach and asked her to call.

I'm getting off the point. The point is this was the night Rosa Mankiewicz, Rosa Stradner, tipped me about the photographs. It was the first we heard about them. The next morning I told Noah. He didn't believe it. He said, "Everybody knows Rosa's got problems." She'd been at the Ober Clinic with the Baroness in 1948. He said, "Somebody spins her some crazy yarn in the rubber room . . . This is how rumours start, Aaron."

"She told me she's seen them," I said, "with her own eyes."

He said, "She's Viennese, fahcrissake." He went into the bathroom and urinated noisily, like he could piss the problem away. He came out buttoning his flies. "And she drinks," he said.

"She was sober last night," I told him.

"Were you sober last night?" he said.

I warned him that photographs were always a problem. A story can be handled. A story's deniable, and it goes out with tomorrow's garbage. "But a photograph's like a bad smell, Noah. It sticks around," I said.

He told me to take care of it. That was always his answer when there was trouble: *Take care of it, Aaron. Do what you have to do*.

Gisela had her own place now on Amalfi Drive, in Santa Monica Canyon. I hadn't seen her for a year. Her face was thinner. It made her mouth look wider, and sexier – the same kind of mouth as Theodora's, only more used-looking. "You look good, Gisela," I told her. I followed her out to the patio by the pool, shaped like a half-moon. She was wearing a one-piece bathing suit. She was in her forties now, but you'd never believe it. Her legs were still great-looking. "You still a gimlet man?" she said. I said I was. "Mr Flagg will have a gimlet, Jorge," she told her houseman. "Large, *very* dry." She ordered iced tea for herself.

"There's nothing wrong with your memory," I told her.

She said, "Some things I remember better than others." Her voice was older. "But on the whole it's better to forget," she said. She asked whether I had anyone in my life. I told her no one special. She said, "The only way to get ahead in this town is through women."

"Not only in this town," I said.

"I'm glad you came," she said.

"How the hell are you?" I said.

"I'm still here," she said.

Jorge brought out the drinks.

"To old times," I said. "We had a few moments that'd be a crime to forget, didn't we?"

"It wasn't the worst thing that ever happened to me," she said.

"It ended too soon," I told her.

She shrugged. "Once the *joie de vivre*'s gone, no point going on."

"It hadn't gone out of it for me."

"It would have," she said.

I said that the excitement didn't usually go out of an affair until it stopped being a secret.

"You never told Noah about us?"

"Noah's been good to me, and I'm loyal to him . . . but there are limits," I said.

I remember she told me that the old Austrian Empire had a special decoration awarded to officers who disobeyed orders in battle, if their disobedience was reckoned to be justified.

I said, "If it's not?"

"They were shot," she said.

She was a funny lady. We talked for a long time. Jorge freshened our drinks. She still smoked Old Golds. Joe Sternberg once said that she exhaled as if her soul went up with the smoke. "I'm pleased you found your way back," she said. "We may not be in love, the way it would be nice to be in love, but let us always be friends, Aaron."

Then I guess we stopped talking, and went inside, and when I woke it was one o'clock in the morning, and she was on her side, propped on an elbow, looking at my face. Her skin glowed in the light of the bedside lamp. She asked had she changed very much since we first met in London, and I told her that she seemed a little lonelier. She smiled. She said that she had recently been looking at photographs taken at a dinner party in Vienna in 1937.

She named a bunch of people. "Everyone at that table is now dead, except me," she said.

It was the best opening I was going to get. I said she should think about publishing a book about Vienna in the thirties. With lots of pictures. I suggested we go through her photographs some time, see what she had. She said there was no time like the present.

She stood up. She didn't have a stitch on. She looked good and she knew she looked good. Faint traces of silver glistened in her hair, which she had back-scraped after our love-making. She poured two glasses of vodka, opened a cabinet and took an album from a shelf full of identical albums. She slipped on a robe and sat beside me on the bed, the album across her knees. There were pictures of her and the Baron on ski slopes, in fancy dress costumes, waving from airliner steps. She explained each picture with humour, with sadness, with perfect recall. But we got to the last page – a picture of her in a fur coat standing in the snow in Davos – still no sign of the pictures Rosa Stradner had told me about. I asked to see more, and a couple of albums later – bingo – there they were.

The first two, Theodora's sitting on a props basket, her legs tucked beneath her. Ten, eleven years old, knowing *exactly* what the photographer was doing, what he wanted. Another picture, Gisela's staring expressionless behind a veil of black lace; it probably looked cuter in the thirties. The rest were mother-and-child shots.

But what dominated all the pictures was this huge Nazi flag – a black swastika on a sea of blood – that hung in the background.

"Jesus Christ," Noah said, when I spread the pictures out across his desk, still fixed to the pages I removed from the album when she was in the shower. "Was she out of her goddam mind?"

"She told Rosa Stradner she never knew the flag was there until she saw the prints," I said. The pictures had been taken at the German Embassy in Vienna; Hoffmann probably dropped the swastika in behind them after he'd posed them. "We know she wasn't a Nazi, Noah," I said.

Peter Evans

There was no question that the pictures would be terrifically damaging if they got out.

Noah said, "Tell me Hoffmann's dead."

Unfortunately he was still alive and in business. Nazi memorabilia was a money show again. As I saw it, we had a straight choice: let sleeping dogs lie, and hope that Hoffmann would never find out what he had . . . or we made him an offer.

A couple of days later I was in Germany.

268

46

The history books – most of the memoirs you read – are bunk. If you want to understand Hollywood, study the myths. Only the myths get close to the truth. (Noah Swan, Sight and Sound, January 1956)

Saturday, December 30
London

FROM AARON FLAGG TAPES
Recorded New York City, November 5

He said, "I wondered when you'd show up" – his first words.

I said, "You *knew* I'd come?"

"Of course," he said. He never forgot a picture, he said, and I had to believe him. "You Americans are efficient. You have the earnest spirit of business, Herr Flagg. I respect that."

We were in a restaurant in the Gansemarkt in Hamburg. 1950. He was looking old and prosperous. He looked like a banker who had done well out of the war, and had every intention of doing even better out of the peace.

"I photographed all the Nazi bigshots," he said. "They *all* thought they were stars. Telling me what pictures I could use, what I must kill. Now they are all dead themselves and I am still here, and I publish whatever picture I please. So who is winning now, Herr Flagg?" He gave a short, mirthless chuckle. "I recommend rollmops, if you like the herring," he said.

I ordered meat cakes, and a beer.

The waiter returned with our order. Hoffmann lifted his glass. "*Prost*," he said cheerfully.

I sipped the beer and let him tell me the story of his life. I was patient. He'd get round to business in his own good time. He had a warm spot for Americans, he said. In 1922 an American press service commissioned him to photograph an obscure Bavarian politician – Adolf Hitler. Hitler liked his pictures, they became friends. "For the next twenty-three years, until April 1945, his final days at the Berlin Chancellery" – he paused, to let the significance of the honour sink in – "I, Heinrich Hoffmann, was the only man in the whole world permitted to photograph the Führer in public and in private."

He finished his rollmop, wiped the corners of his mouth with a little feminine gesture. "So you see, Herr Flagg, your own countrymen are responsible for my place in history. Now you will come with me." He drove me to a boatyard in the East End and stopped alongside a yacht in dry dock. "Not as large as Reichsmarschall Goering's but much prettier, I think. I am naming her *Folly*," he said. "Do you know why I am naming her *Folly*?"

"All I know is that folly is the principle of absolute unwisdom," I said. "And you don't strike me as being at all unwise, Herr Hoffmann."

That made him laugh. He said I was frank, the kind of man he liked to do business with. I followed him up the steps into the pilothouse. He pulled down the blinds, switched on a map lamp, removed a panel beneath the wheel, unlocked a small safe hidden behind it, and removed two envelopes. He opened the first one.

"Contact sheets, negatives," he said. "All are here."

I examined the contacts under the lamp. The pictures had been taken at the same session as the ones I'd removed from Gisela's albums. I turned them over. They were stamped with Hoffmann's name, the date, and a swastika. I said, "Is this everything?"

"You have my word," he said.

"And the price, Herr Hoffmann?"

He gave me the second envelope. I opened it. Inside was a collection of bills and invoices, and a bunch of estimates. I couldn't figure it out at first. Then I got it. "We settle these?"

"It is reasonable," he said.

"How much is reasonable exactly?"

"In dollars – forty-five thousand."

"Too much," I told him.

His expression didn't change. "Ah, that is a pity," he said. "Because there will be more bills before the *Folly* is finished to my satisfaction, I think."

I told him he was crazy. I guess you don't ever tell an old Nazi he's crazy, especially when he's got a fucking Luger pointing at your head. He began to collect the contacts and negs and return them to the envelope. It was like hearing the fucking hammer click. He said, "I am an artist. That does not mean I do not know the value of my work."

"We're not discussing your goddam worth as an artist, Hoffmann," I said. "What we're talking here is a down the alley shakedown."

"Blackmail?" You coulda skated on his voice. "Does a blackmailer offer receipts? Provide invoices? No, no, no, sir," he said. "This is a business arrangement. I will show a profit. You, Herr Flagg, will acquire a tax write-off. Who loses? Nobody loses."

He had it all figured. I said we had to know how much we'd be writing off before his *Folly* was shipshape. Did he have a launch date in mind? We wanted to wish him *bon* fucking *voyage*, right?

He put his head back and closed his eyes, like he was gathering up all the threads of some complex thought. "Theodora's career is worth millions," he said. "You're here because you know my photographs, if they got into unfriendly hands, could wreck that career." He said he was sure that the mighty lions of Metro-Goldwyn-Mayer were not prepared to let that happen.

"But they won't be played for suckers, Hoffmann," I told him. "You got to give them a figure, pal."

He opened his eyes, and said, "One hundred thousand dollars."

I looked at my watch. Four o'clock. 8 a.m. in California. I said I'd go back to the hotel and call my people and give him an answer before seven. I remember the phone was ringing as I unlocked the door to my room. Noah's already on the line. I told him the story. I said, "He's an old guy, Noah. But he's got big dreams."

Noah said, "A hundred grand?"

271

I said, "He waited for us to come to him. He's dangerous, Noah."

He said, "We let a fucking photographer stick us up against the wall?"

I said, "He's got the pictures, Noah."

"He's a fucking *Nazi*," he yelled.

I said, "He's a fucking Nazi who responds to money, Noah."

There was a long silence on the line. I heard him suck in his breath twelve thousand miles away, then he said quietly, "Make sure you get everything. And that better include the bastard's eternal fucking silence."

He put the phone down abruptly, as he always did when he was angry, no goodbyes.

47

*Since the beginning of Hollywood, Louis B.
Mayer had been there. At MGM, like a god,
he had not only been behind every movie, and
made every star, but he had breathed in every
wind, and thundered in every storm. He had
filled the streams and rivers, and erupted
volcanos. He had caused the earth to quake,
made oceans rage, and lightning strike. In his
smile actors witnessed glory; in his scowl was
the usher of decline. MGM, in all its length
and breadth, and in all its glory, was the
manifestation of his will, and without him the
studio would not have been, and would never
be again.* (Theodora and Garbo: Leading
Ladies, *by Jeanne Hunter*)

Sunday, December 31
London

Rider spent New Year's Eve with Grace Hempel. They had
dinner at the Lanesborough, and saw in the New Year with a
bottle of Bollinger at her Battersea apartment. She lit candles
around the room. "To *The Milan Agent*," she said. "And, of
course – to *Theodora*."

They made love on the floor, in front of the fire. She did not
completely undress, the way she knew excited him most. Later
they lay on the big tweed sofa in the firelight.

"A penny for them," she said.

"You are one of the pleasures of winter . . . like logs burning
on an open hearth . . ."

"Now the truth."

"I was thinking about Aaron Flagg."

"The man who knows so much," she said.

"The man who knows *too* much."

"What do you mean? Too much?"

"If he were one of my characters, I wouldn't trust him. *Nobody* can know that much."

"You know what you must never do with a gift horse."

"I forgot the oldest rule. My oldest rule."

She smiled. "What's your oldest rule?"

"*Errors, like straws, upon the surface flow*," he recited. "*He who would search for pearls must dive below*."

She said, "A biography has limits."

He became aware of the warmth of her unclothed belly beginning to stir furtively against his thigh. "Why should a biography have limits?" he said.

"Because it's *not* a novel." She smiled at him, acknowledging the gliding touch of their bodies, aware of what she was doing to him, and to herself. "Who was it who said that fiction is truer than history because it goes beyond . . ." She faltered, shuddered deliciously, struggled to concentrate on what she was saying. ". . . fiction can go beyond the evidence . . ."

"He who would search for pearls . . ."

". . . must dive below," Grace finished the couplet with a small gasp of pleasure.

In spite of his recent unease about some of Flagg's tapes (even when they accorded with Theodora's version of events, and the things Missy told him, they made him wary; it was as if they were almost *too* helpful) Rider continued to work with them. He had no choice: time was running out for him; if he was to complete the draft of Theodora's Hollywood years before he returned to the island he needed the background and the framework of events Flagg's stories provided. But chronology wasn't the strong point in Flagg's reminiscences, and it was some time before he found the right tape, pinpointed the section he wanted, and pushed PLAY.

FROM AARON FLAGG TAPES
Recorded New York City, October 30

. . . a banker I knew in Boston. He tipped me that Mayer was on his way out. Schenck could deal the devil outa Hoboken. I told Noah. He said, "We'll have to mend some fences, Aaron." For openers he had to make his peace with Schary – and break it to Theodora that he'd backed the wrong horse. She'd been on suspension six months, eating her money for breakfast.

See, the interest of a producer is never the same as his star's. A producer lives by deals, a star exists on dreams. The dream is dependent upon the deal, but actors don't see that. They don't see that in the beginning is the hustle. Actors are like kids. They expect their producers to be father figures, miracle workers, seers. They want to be told how great it's gonna be – the next movie, the next affair, life after death . . .

This was August. Theodora was on the sundeck. She'd never been off work so long in her life; her skin had gotten a light honey tan. I pretended to read the trades – *Missy Miles looked good enough to eat at Lucey's last night* – listening to Noah explain Louie's imminent departure. "It's just lousy, isn't it, the whole thing?" he said. But it was only a hiccup in their plans, he said. The Columbia deal wasn't gonna go away. You know what Theodora said? She said "I'll never be young again, Noah. Not the way I was." I thought she would blow her top but that's all she said.

I sensed then that she had reached the end of something important in her life. Maybe it was the limit of her will to believe him, to trust him, to be taken in by his charm. It was a turning point in their relationship. The conversation wasn't about losing a coupla good movies. It wasn't about a wasted year. It was about a lot more than that. It was as if they both recognized that they had failed each other in some way I couldn't begin to fathom.

Driving back, I said, "Think you can work something out with Schary, Noah?" He said, "He's buried Mayer, what else does he have to prove? His ego's not on the line any more. He's not going to feel challenged to hold on to Theodora to prove something to New York." I said, "He's still pissed with you." He said, "What the fuck, I'll offer him a coupla pictures." I said, "Is he going to settle for two pictures?" He said, "The alternative's what? Theodora continues to air her heels at the beach? Think about it, kid. His first week flying solo, thirty seconds over Culver City, he takes a deal like that to Schenck – gives him two big new Theodora Glass pictures to announce at the annual stockholders' meeting – he's gonna look like a goddam genius. Everybody wins." "Except Louie," I said. "Weep not for the dead, kid," he said. "That's what makes you such a hell of a swell guy," I said.

Monday, January 1,
London

Rider walked in the park. It was four thirty in the afternoon and beginning to snow. Conscious of time passing, he tried to shove the thought out of his mind that Aaron Flagg was too good to be true. Back at his flat, he called Grace and repeated his doubts. She said, "You're worried because he's giving you too many nuggets!" It was hard to explain his feelings. "I feel I'm in the right church but in the wrong pew," he said. She wanted to come over and he wanted her to, but he knew he had to work. He poured a whisky, found the tapes and transcripts he needed, and with several books he had heavily annotated, sat down at his desk to continue his journey through a time nearly fifty years ago that was a different world.

RIDER'S FIRST DRAFT, 5

The news of Mayer's abdication in August 1951 came like the shock of an earthquake to Hollywood. Dore Schary had refused to see Noah in the weeks leading up to the dethronement, but four days after the announcement he summoned him to his house in Brentwood.

It was a Saturday morning. They hadn't met face to face since December when they talked at Noah's party. Schary's living-room was filled with flowers from admirers and well-wishers and people just pleased to see the back of Louie.

Schary said, "I thought it'd be better to talk away from the studio." He wore flannels, a cashmere sweater, and blue velvet pumps on which his initials were embroidered in silver thread. "Let's not waste time going around through Dixie," he said. "We had our battles, doll. Let's bind up our wounds and get on with the business of making movies, the business we do best."

"That's why I'm here, to clear the air," Noah said.

The voices of Schary's children playing in the pool came into the room. He closed the windows, returned to the sofa, lifted his feet on to the scripts piled on the coffee table between them. "Before you start, doll, let me tell you something. MGM is not a management problem – it's a goddam war. And goddam wars are *only* about victory and defeat," he said. "Somebody always wins. Somebody always loses. You want a war, sweetheart, then war is what you got."

"Nobody goes to war if it's any way avoidable," Noah said.

Schary said, "Nobody remembers whether a war was avoidable or not avoidable, just or unjust. People only remember the winners."

"I think we can cut a deal here where we both come out like winners," Noah said.

"Tell me how we do that, doll," Schary said.

Noah told him his idea. Theodora would return to work at once. She would make a picture a year for two years. In return, Metro would cancel out the rest of her contract. "Two big pictures," Noah said, "to turn on the steam for the Schary regime. How bad can it be? In the top spot five minutes and you got Theodora back in front of the cameras, where she belongs. You're going to look an awful smart apple in New York, Dore."

Schary said, "We got a contract, Noah. A tie that binds us to one another for four more years."

"Ties are made to be untied, Dore."

"Read the contract," Schary said.

"Read the grosses," Noah said calmly. "That's the reality."

They went on like that, repeating the same objections, making the same points, stopping only when the maid brought in coffee. "I don't think Schenck will treat you kindly," Noah said after the maid had gone, "if you lose Theodora with an offer as good as this on the table."

Schary said, "*I* make the decisions, doll." He picked up the phone and held it out to Noah with both hands. "You can get her ass back in the studio with one call."

"You know that's not going to happen, Dore," Noah said, ignoring the phone.

They stared across the room at each other, too proud to back down, both caught up in the escalating threats. Schary had become pale. It could have been anger, but it was probably pressure. He was beginning to understand what pressure was. Noah was feeling the pressure too, but he could deal with it almost in a taunting way.

"You're going to kill her career, doll," Dore said with an expert look of regret, and put down the phone.

10.50 p.m., Monday, January 1
London

Rider read over the pages. They needed work, but they weren't bad for a first draft. He was still troubled by how much he was leaning on Flagg. The facts and most of the dialogue of the Schary scene came from him, although Schary had described the same meeting in his autobiography and there was nothing in Flagg's account that conflicted with Schary's version of events, except that Dore gave himself better lines. Rider looked at his watch. It was too late to call Grace and ask her to dinner. He looked out of the window and saw that the snow had settled. He made coffee and fixed himself an omelette. Afterwards he took a cold shower to wake himself up, and went back to work. He typed quickly but again most of what he wrote came out of the Flagg tapes, which continued to be filled with extraordinary nuggets and remarkable recall. Some conversations you can't recall a word, what who said to whom, but Flagg remembered everything. Rider knew that he was accepting Flagg's version of too many key events – his prejudices, his spin on things – but if he was going to complete the first draft before he returned to Santa Aloe he had no choice.

RIDER'S FIRST DRAFT, 6

Theodora had been on suspension for a year. The bankers waited; Harry Cohn waited. And Noah waited, although he continued making his own pictures for Metro.

He was staying at the St Regis in New York, preparing *The Devil Takes a Wife*. On Monday, January 28, 1952, he summoned his attorney Harlan K. Pepper to join him for breakfast, although he knew that Pepper never ate breakfast. To Pepper's astonishment, he began to quote the morals clause in Theodora's contract:

> Theodora Glass agrees to conduct herself with due regard to public conventions and morals and agrees that she will not do or commit any act or thing that will tend to degrade her in society or bring her into public hatred, contempt, scorn or ridicule, or that will tend to shock, insult or offend the community or ridicule morals or decency or prejudice the producer Metro-Goldwyn-Mayer, Loew's Inc., or the motion picture industry in general.

When he had finished, he said, "Tell me this, Harlan: if she had committed any act or thing that would tend to degrade her in society *before* she signed the contract – how would that sit in law?"

Pepper said it would depend on the nature and degree of the violation.

"If something wasn't declared . . . if an act or thing comes to light down the road . . . what happens then?" Noah asked.

Pepper said that then you entered the realm of common law, and the principle of *stare decisis* – stand by past decisions – would decide it.

Noah told him to check it out.

FROM AARON FLAGG TAPES
Recorded New York City, December 1
I'd taken Ava Gardner – we were considering her for the

society dame in *The Devil Takes a Wife* – down to the Onyx Club to hear Lena Horne. After the show, I dropped her off at the Hampshire House with a chaste kiss on the cheek; Sinatra was never far away in those days, and with plenty of time on his hands to get nasty. At the St Regis there was a message to call Noah.

I went up to his suite. As soon as I saw his grin I knew that some high-class skulduggery was at work. He said he was going to demand one final change in Theodora's Columbia deal – the removal of the morals clause.

I said that if Cohn dropped the morals clause for Theodora, he'd have Hayworth to reckon with. Rita might be a handful without a morals clause to keep her in line. Noah didn't give a shit about Cohn's problems. He said, "Harry'll do what I tell him to do, if he wants to see Theodora Glass in Gower Street." I said, "First you gotta spring her from Metro." He said that problem was solved! "*Stare decisis*," he said. "Pepper found me a precedent."

Apparently in 1937 an actress named Martita Montero signed a contract with Universal. The contract contained the standard morals clause . . . Miss Montero would conduct herself with due regard to public conventions etc., etc. Nothing in her past could be deemed to disgrace, drag in the mud the name of Universal Pictures, and so on. Two years later they discovered that Miss Montero wasn't all she seemed.

"She'd been a nun!" he said with satisfaction. I said, "They canned her for having been a *nun*?"

He said that the studio had been building her up as some hot tamale number. Another Mexican spitfire. They claimed that the revelation that she'd been a bride of Christ held them up to ridicule. I said, "How did they find out?" He said, "A priest in Boston dropped a dime on her." I said, "And now you're going to drop a dime on Theodora?" He said, "Just another caring shepherd, kid." I said, "And which particular sin of omission do you plan to expose?"

He told me he was going to leak the Hoffmann pictures. He had it all figured. He said, How many Jewish pikers out there hold Loew's scrip? Hundreds? Thousands? How are they going to feel about Theodora playing watch-the-birdy with Hitler's favourite cameraman? If Schary didn't drop her after those pictures hit the streets, he'd have the biggest stockholders' riot on his hands this business has seen.

He said he wanted me to call Crowther. He wanted to throw the pictures to the *Times*. He said it'd be a feather in Bosley's derby. I said, "You expect him to run them without any explanation . . . Like how he came by them? Or why, fahcrissake?" He said, "Tell him to keep his mouth shut." I said, "He's a newspaperman, Noah." He said, "He's a goddam critic, fahcrissake. I never met a goddam critic yet we couldn't buy."

I was stunned. He said, "OK, how would *you* handle it?"

I guess that was the moment I knew I'd been worked like a goddam piece of Play-doh. Noah could never do anything straight off the bat. Anyway, I told him to forget the *Times*. The *Times* would give the pictures credibility, and we'd need to discredit them after they'd done their job. Also we'd deliver them over the transom. I said we'd have to cut him outa the loop completely. If some corner came unstuck, lies would have to be told. He'd have to be able to deny all knowledge.

He said, "You talk as if something *will* go wrong."

I said, "The worst may happen but it may not." One thing was certain: Gisela was going to recognize the pictures, and when she did, she was going to check her albums. When she discovered the pictures missing . . . He got the point. He said, "Will she blow on us?" I said. "She's certainly gonna be mad."

That's when I suggested the break-in. Remove a few trinkets along with the albums. When the pictures were published, she'd think it was some porch-climber cashing in on his luck.

If Noah ever gave his approval, it was with no more than a look. He was the tsar of tacit understandings. He'd gotten exactly what he wanted. I could tell you that the whole thing was my idea, and that's what he wanted me to think, but Noah never moved his pieces until he had completely worked out his entire plan of campaign. *Never*.

1.57 a.m., Tuesday, January 2
London

Rider stopped the tape. He had been typing, reading transcripts and making notes for nearly fifteen hours. He lit a cigarette and stood at the window watching the snow falling. Flagg's stories squared with every fact, date and incident he had tested them against. Perhaps he sometimes exaggerated his own role in events, but Rider was sure he hadn't lied in any material way. He drew ruminatively on his cigarette, paced slowly around the room, poured another whisky, a small one.

From a steel cabinet in his study he collected a file marked *BHPD/52/Baroness Break-in* and another marked *J-Am/Pix/52*. He slid several sheets of flimsy paper out of the first file. They were smudged, badly typed carbon copies of Beverly Hills Police Department crime report sheets. He read them twice, rolled a fresh sheet of paper into his Olivetti, sipped the whisky, and began to type:

At four o'clock on the morning of February 14, 1952, several weeks after Noah and Aaron Flagg first discussed at the St Regis hotel in New York the leaking of the Heinrich Hoffmann photographs, a burglary took place at Baroness von Tegge's home on Amalfi Drive in Santa Monica Canyon. Six items were taken, and recorded by the Beverly Hills Police Department as follows:

Pratt figure of a lion, 7 inches high, the plinth with still leaf moulded border inscribed in yellow ochre *A Lion*. Chelsea figure of Cupid disguised as beggar, black hat and eye patch and scantily draped in blue; hairline crack to base. Hat brooch, arrow-shaped, gold enamel. Black mink coat (Al Teitelbaum, Beverly Hills. $2,750). Two photograph albums, green leather.

The police had a sheet on the Mexican houseboy (petty theft, being in possession of small amounts of dope) and took him in for questioning. He was released the following day; no charges were brought. On February 23, all the items except for the photographic albums were found abandoned not far from the Baroness's home in a suitcase beneath a hedge in the garden of the writer Salka Viertel. It was believed that the burglar had hidden the case, intending to collect it later. The burglary was not reported in the press.

He turned to the second file and extracted a clip from the New York *Journal-American*, dated March 19, 1952. It was a picture printed across seven columns of Theodora and the Baroness posing against a swastika backdrop. A banner headline read: THE DAY THEODORA PERFORMED FOR HITLER'S FOTOG.

48

*Noah Swan's a smart guy. I never met anyone
legit think as fast as he can. He ain't always
right, but in sports parlance, he's got a terrific
batting average. But when he's wrong – he's
clear to hell wrong. (Mike Todd, Boston Globe,
September 28, 1956)*

8.30 a.m., Tuesday, January 2
London

He slept five hours, rose, showered, made coffee, and went back
to the Olivetti.

RIDER'S FIRST DRAFT, 7

Loew's stock fell five points in the wake of the Hoffmann picture
in the *Journal-American*. As Noah predicted, hundreds of stockholders demanded Theodora's dismissal. Jewish organizations
protested in letters to Loew's president Nicholas Schenck. But
many thousands more sent letters protesting at the *Journal-
American*'s "attack" on Theodora, and her personal rating shot
up in the studio's private poll. Schary was a cautious man, or
maybe simply a weak one, and reminded of the mystique of
Theodora's fame, he did nothing. Yet his indecision was as
effective as any deliberate reprisal: it continued to stymie Noah's
hopes of an early exit from MGM and a new start at Columbia.

Two weeks later (April 1, 1952) *Daily Variety* ran a page-one
story which began:

Dore Schary, vice-president in charge of production and head
of studio operations, MGM, said last night that discussions
with Noah Swan on the future of suspended star Theodora

Glass are continuing "in good faith". Schary added that he hopes talks will be concluded "very soon" and expects that both the producer and Glass, whose last film, *Before Morning Comes*, released last fall, is Metro's standout grosser of the year, will continue their "successful ten-year tandem" at the studio.

The story appeared the morning Noah had breakfast with Chase National's Horace Libby and Dean Willets in a bungalow at the Beverly Hills Hotel. The meeting had been called by the bankers to discuss the continuing stalemate.

There was no good-natured shop talk. Libby launched straight into the problem: "We've done a lot of deal-making here, Noah," he said, "but no film-making. We've posted fifty thousand dollars in story costs alone" – he picked up that morning's *Variety* and tossed it across the table at Noah – "and you still haven't untied the knot with Metro."

Willets said, "You think you've got us so pregnant we can't pull out?" It was the first time he let his anger show.

Noah said, "It's still a good deal for Chase National."

"It *was* a good deal," Libby said. "When we renegotiated on" – he opened a folder and consulted the figures – "May 15, 1950, it still looked good. And when we re-scheduled on July 17 last year, it was acceptable. But nearly three years, Noah . . . Time brings even the most exalted reputations to a strict scrutiny."

Noah said, "Theodora's as hot now as she ever was."

Willets said they had commissioned a private poll, and comparing the figures with an MGM poll in 1947, her recognition factor had slipped eight points.

"Maybe she's already past her prime," Libby said. "Maybe we'll never see again what we've already seen."

Noah stayed calm. "Her next picture will change those numbers in a week," he said. There was a huge audience out there waiting for her next picture. The Quigley poll of theatre owners still listed her at number four, after Cooper, Wayne, and Martin and Lewis. "She hasn't been out of the top five box-office stars since 1943," he reminded them.

"Well, we've been through too much to dip our colours now," Willets said finally. "Let's not kick away the game yet."

Six days later they pulled out of the deal.

"I knew what Noah was feeling inside," Aaron Flagg would say later. "But all he said was: '*Well, kids, the jig's up.*' Theodora didn't say anything at all. She just smiled like *what's-the-use?* and went back to the beach."

THEODORA'S TAPE

I was in Noah's office when we heard the news that Chase had pulled out. It came as no surprise to me. Noah had treated them like shit. He was a great producer and wonderful with actors but he had no respect for the money people. Orson and Huston were just the same. That evening I called Dore. I said, "Mr Schary, can I come by?"

He said, "I'm always available to you, Theodora."

His office was a floor above Noah's in the Thalberg Building. It wasn't as large or as sumptuous as Mr Mayer's old office, which remained exactly as he had left it. It was like a shrine. I don't know why Dore didn't take it over when he took over the studio. Perhaps he was superstitious, perhaps he didn't want to be reminded of his predecessor. LB's reputation had grown even larger since his departure. Dore's office was like a newsroom, always filled with people – he said he concentrated better in a busy room. But he cleared everybody out for our meeting. He sat behind a large L-shaped glass table cluttered with phones, books, scripts . . . an autographed baseball bat, I remember that . . . and a bowling trophy. He had a team called the Schary Hunky-Dorys. He seemed very young after Mr Mayer.

"I'm glad you've come," he said as soon as I sat down. I'm sure he knew that the Chase deal had collapsed. But it wasn't mentioned. He was very charming. He said that there was no actress he respected and admired more.

"If you really respected me, you would let me go," I said. Mama had taught me all about the edge an actress can get from a show of naïvety.

He said that the studio had a great deal invested in me, and he couldn't let the assets walk out of the store. He called his secretary and told her to fetch my contract. She brought it in almost at once, so I guess he was well prepared. He said he didn't want to say anything that would put pressure on me without my lawyer or Noah present. "But I do want to make sure you personally understand the situation," he said.

He read the part of the contract about suspensions, how my contract would be extended for the amount of time I refused to work or was unable to work through illness, pregnancy, or whatever. He asked me if I understood that. He was treating me like a child, but that was his problem. He said he wanted to get me back to work. He said I was wasting my life and my talent buried out at the beach.

"I'm still young," I said. "Time's on my side."

"Time's never on the side of actresses," he said.

Dore can scare the shit out of you with his goddam wisdom, Ava Gardner told me once. I suddenly knew what she meant.

"You've been here making movies since you were fifteen," he said. "I want you to stay part of the family. What do I have to do to get you back to work? Maybe we could take another look at your salary?"

I said it wasn't about money.

"An actress is at her most dangerous when she doesn't care about money," he said.

He took a couple of Baccarat goblets from his bar and poured us some very good French wine. "Why don't you tell me exactly what you do want?" he said, handing me the glass.

Don't think I hadn't thought about it! I'd had plenty of time to think about it! I took a deep breath and gave him my terms: maximum two movies a year with script, director and co-star approval; no loanouts; my own exclusive hairdresser, lighting and make-up men; sole billing above the title; an Odets play I wanted the studio to buy for me; a bigger private bungalow on the lot, and a luxury dressing-room which could be hauled from stage to stage; never to work after six o'clock or be called before 8.30. Oh, yes, and twice my old salary. I think the sheer audacity of my demands tickled him. But I could hear his brain ticking away.

Figuring the cost against my value to the studio. Finally I got most of the things I asked for – except the Odets play, which was *The Country Girl*, and Paramount had already bought it for Grace Kelly.

The first picture I made after my "reinstatement" (as the trade papers reported my return) was *Out of Yesterday*. Four months after my meeting with Mr Schary it was edited, scored and ready to ship. It broke the opening-week record at the Music Hall. In London it was picked for the Royal Command Performance before the young Queen Elizabeth. My biggest box-office success since *Reunion*. It was also the first film of mine in whose preparation Noah had not been involved, and on which his name didn't appear.

He never complained. "You did what you had to. I knew you'd ask for the moon, and that Dore would give it to you" – that was all he ever said about it. People started talking about my business sense. John Houseman said I was smarter than Kate Hepburn. Some of the books say that my deal with Mr Schary was the last nail in the coffin for Noah and me. It was more complicated than that. He refused to go to England with me for the royal performance. Missy accompanied me; she had become a friend, and her own career at Columbia was starting to taper off.

Rider switched off the tape. It was midday. In fifteen minutes he had an interview with the *Times*.

49

> *LOEW'S, INC. 1540 Broadway, New York 36,*
> *NY; JUdson 2-2000. Cable: Metrofilms*
> *PRESIDENT: Nicholas M. Schenck*
> *MGM STUDIOS 10202 West Washington Boul-*
> *evard, Culver City, Calif; TExas 0-3311*
> *VICE-PRESIDENT IN CHARGE PRODUC-*
> *TION AND STUDIO OPERATIONS: Dore*
> *Schary*
> *EXECUTIVES: Dore Schary, E. J. Mannix,*
> *Ben Thau, Noah Swan, Joseph J. Cohn, Marvin*
> *Schenck, Lawrence Weingarten*
> (International Motion Picture Almanac, *1955*)

7.53 a.m., Wednesday, January 3
London

The resonance of those names, the sense of movie history in
them, even the old New York telephone exchange, satisfied
Robert Rider in a way he couldn't explain as he sat down to write
that morning. But with only four days left before he returned to
Santa Aloe he had no time to dwell on personal pleasures. "*Dore
Schary*," he said aloud and began to type.

RIDER'S FIRST DRAFT, 8

Theodora's rapprochement with the studio in 1952 was hailed as a
personal triumph for Schary. But his euphoria was shortlived.
Weeks later, the Justice Department's anti-trust laws split the
producing, distributing and exhibition phases of the corporation.
MGM pictures no longer monopolized the best dates in MGM
theatres, and the days when every Metro picture made money
were over. It was a problem Mayer never had to face, and when
Metro pictures began to fail at the box-office the blame fell on

Schary. But Schary was Schenck's man. And Schenck was the ruler of rulers. But in December 1955 at the age of seventy-four Schenck resigned, and Schary was at last exposed to his foes. "It's not enough you got Theodora back," Loew's new president Joseph Vogel warned him. "You got enemies on the board, among the stockholders, and in the studio . . . They don't say good things about you, Dore," he seized the moment with a kind of sighing malice. Vogel was not a friend.

Schary needed all the help he could get.

He called Noah Swan.

Schary Manor, the pseudo rustic-Tudor mansion in Brentwood, once the daily resort of the most celebrated and powerful men and women in Hollywood, was silent. The phone no longer rang off the hook; agents did not return Schary's calls; producers did not seek his approval. No messengers at all hours with cans of film and scripts and memos marked MOST URGENT.

Schary stood at the window and waited, his reign trembling in the balance. How like a medieval court a studio is, he thought. Producers the courtiers who owe their titles to the king, from whom they entreat favour. Men who follow the chase, and acquiesce in everything required of them; who are inordinately fond of splendour and abundance, yet know that in some dark corner of the palace their fate will be for ever decided . . .

He was fifty-one years old. Still the youngest studio head in Hollywood. Three years younger than Zanuck at Fox; fifteen years younger than Jack Warner and Harry Cohn. But the clock was ticking. "I could gauge to the second how much trouble I was in by how long Noah Swan kept me waiting," he would say later.

Darkness had fallen when Noah's limousine pulled into the drive. Schary left the window and slouched on the deep, nubby sofa, propped his feet on the coffee table, and opened a script on his lap. The doorbell rang; he picked up the phone and placed a call to Kirk Douglas in New York. Like he's in control, still in the middle of it. When Noah came into the room, he signalled him to take a seat.

"Kirk," he said, coming off the phone, shaking his head.

"Been leaving messages all day. He's off to Roma in the morning. The Presidential suite at the Excelsior. I knew him when he couldn't afford a shoeshine. I'll shut off the phones. Got some thirty-year-old bourbon that's waited long enough," he went on, speaking more quickly than ordinarily. "You heard the rumours?"

"This towns runs on rumours," Noah said blandly. "Who listens?"

"This time they're true," Dore smiled, handing him the bourbon.

"I'm sorry to hear that," Noah said politely. "We disagree about almost everything, Dore. But you made the pictures you wanted to make. You made some brave pictures. I've always respected you for that."

"I tried to make good pictures, Noah." It sounded nicely modest, but effective, a simple declaration of the purity of his motives, a caption beneath a photograph in *Newsweek*: *I just try to make good pictures*.

Noah said, "Whoever followed Louie was going to strike oil or go down the chute."

Schary knew how to contain his feelings; he used smiles to express his joy as well as his disappointments. He smiled now. "No use backing into this thing, Noah," he said. "I've made enemies at the studio. Powerful people. Now they want my head."

"Surest thing you know, Dore," Noah said sombrely, "some night you wind up alone."

"I need some heavyweights on my team," Schary said after a pause. He began walking slowly round the room, holding his drink alongside his large head, the ice cooling his temple. "Men with the clout to combat Mannix and Thau. I got the writers with me, but nobody gives a shit about writers. I need someone the suits respect, someone they fear a little bit. I'd like you aboard, Noah."

Noah didn't answer straight away. He rose from the sofa and stood looking at a portrait of Schary above the mantelpiece. It had been painted by Schary's wife, Miriam, and used to hang in his office at the studio. The likeness was a good one, but she'd caught something else: the expression in his eyes. "It was the expression of a man who knows that he will soon be found out," Noah would tell Bill Goldman many years later.

Noah turned away from the portrait. "I won't give you the stall, Dore," he told him. "Too many big guns are lined up against you. You're going to drop, Dore. You don't have a prayer."

Schary finished his drink and picked up his pipe and began to fill it from a jar of tobacco on his desk. "You should take a chance on me, Noah," he said evenly.

"This business is tough, baby," Noah said, "but it's tougher when you're dumb."

"I'm sitting on a lot of information, doll," Schary said quietly. "I kept the lid on a lot of stuff."

Noah said, "You should write a book."

"Oh, I can do much better than that," Schary said, and laughed grimly.

12.30 p.m., Wednesday, January 3
London

Grace arrived for lunch with a *caponata* salad and crusty bread from Alvaro's. She had been to the gym and her hair was still wet and sticking to her head from the shower. She wore jeans and a long-sleeved navy-blue polo sweater. She wasn't wearing a bra. Rider opened a bottle of Italian white wine.

"How was your morning?" she said.

"Five pages."

She looked impressed. "Enjoying it?"

"You don't have to enjoy it."

They talked about other things over lunch. He was grateful for her tact.

When they finished, he said, "Do you want coffee? Do you have time?"

"No," she said. "And yes."

He smiled, took her hand and led her to the bedroom.

"How far have you got?" she said.

"Schary's about to break Theodora's heart."

"Oh, don't let her heart be broken . . ." She pulled her sweater over her head, the movement languid and deliberate, her arms extended above her head, lifting her breasts, "Don't let her heart be broken . . . not yet."

Two hours later Rider went back to work. He found the page proofs of a chapter cut from Schary's 1979 autobiography, which he had discovered in a box of old MGM papers deposited at the Wisconsin Center for Film Research:

Vogel summoned me to New York. It was the day of Eisenhower's second term landslide victory. Not the best of times for old liberals like me. I knew that he was going to ask for my resignation. I also knew that without Noah Swan's backing I had no choice but to give it to him.

The morning of my departure I visited Theodora on the set of *Free Again*. The first shot of the day was in the can, and she was looking fresh and relaxed. But I knew that her hairdresser had just tightened the pin curls in her hairline, which covered the rubber bands threaded through the transparent tapes fixed behind her ears. The temporary face-lift would give her a splitting headache by lunchtime.

"It's worth the agony," I told her.

"Actresses live on a faster time-scale than ordinary mortals," she smiled, acknowledging how soon movie queens needed other people's genius to sustain their beauty.

"Not only actresses," I said. I told her my suspicions about Vogel's plans for me. We had become good friends in the past five years and I knew that her distress was genuine. "You must fight them," she said.

"I'll probably be happier if I don't," I said. We were in her mobile dressing-room which some wit had dubbed the Glass House. Furnished with genuine antiques from the prop department it was more like an elegant drawing-room than a trailer lounge. Sitting in a giltwood chair, waiting to be dressed for the next scene, she was wearing a silk robe, and, I could plainly see, little else. She recalled our successes together and made our lives sound more entwined than the bare statistics of our association might now suggest.

"I was never with you that I wasn't inspired," she said. I was deeply moved. And though my attention was focused on the showdown that loomed for me in New York, I became anxious for her. I realized how much she had grown to trust my professional judgements. And now I felt as if I were abandoning her.

I had always felt badly about the way Noah Swan had used her, but movie stars are always being used in ways they can do nothing about. But my decision to tell her the truth about Noah was forced upon me by the sense of vulnerability I saw in her that morning. I felt no bitterness towards Noah. I could never muster the outrage with which Louie Mayer responded to his enemies.

Rider stopped reading. It was natural that Schary would want to give an air of altruism to an act of revenge. But didn't he go to her dressing-room that morning determined to put the finger on Noah? Rider found the tape in which Theodora told her version of the same story. He put it into the cassette and fast-forwarded, stopping every thirty seconds to listen until he found the section he wanted:

. . . gentle voice Dore always used when he wanted to instil anxiety into a star. The rest I more or less knew, or suspected, or didn't give a damn about . . . But that Noah himself had leaked the Hoffmann picture to the newspaper . . . I felt used . . . betrayed. Dore opened his briefcase and handed me a folder. It was a private detective's report . . .

Rider smiled, and picked up the story in the Schary proofs:

It started with an ingenious scam. Noah Swan used phoney companies to buy the movie rights to a non-existent book to get the money out of MGM to pay off Hoffmann. Later Aaron Flagg (Noah's High Chamberlain) leaked the same pictures to the *Journal-American* to try to force my hand. I could never prove that Noah was behind it. But the picture had been mailed out of Chicago on a day that Flagg happened to be in the Windy City. According to his expenses, he had a meeting with the MGM publicity manager; according to the Chicago records, the publicity manager was at a sales conference in New Orleans!

The story was too libellous to publish without solid evidence and had to be cut from Schary's manuscript, and eventually forgotten. Rider went back to Theodora's tape:

. . . I said, "You must really hate me, Dore." He said he didn't hate me. He said there were a few times when he wanted to kill me! I asked him why he hadn't told New York about Noah's deal with Hoffmann. He said, "Who benefited? He was protecting Metro's investment as well as his own interests. The scale of the fraud was not so great when you consider what was at stake." I remember his smile. "Anyway," he said, "one of my own producers steals a hundred grand from under my nose – how do I explain that without looking like I don't know my ass from a hole in the ground? –"

Rider put on a sweater, poured himself a whisky and thought about where he wanted to go next.

50

Mr Mayer had gone, Schenck and Schary had gone. People were saying that Hollywood was finished. I wanted it to pass away with dignity, keeping to the last those things which made it great. But when those things went I knew I would rather go too. (Theodora Glass, in conversation with Robert Rider, December 2)

Thursday, January 4
London

Lillian Ross said in the *New Yorker* that no feud in Hollywood has ever been as destructive as the feud between Dore Schary and Noah Swan over me. It destroyed Dore's career, precipitated the decline of MGM, and marked the end of Noah's great days in Hollywood. Missy calls it the big bang theory of why I quit the movies. But there was no big bang. I'm sorry if that spoils your story, Robert. There was no showdown. I was not brave enough for that. But there was a moment when we both knew it was over for us.

Free Again was going well, although it was a difficult picture. We had a week of nights to shoot, and another three weeks in the studio. Noah came out to the house. It was a Sunday. December 1956. It was raining. He brought me flowers. The flowers were a peace offering, but I don't remember the fight. We made love. Almost everything I knew about Noah came from instinct, and as we made love I felt a spasm of sadness. I think he felt it too, because afterwards he said, "I'm sorry, Theodora."

I said, "For what?"

He said, "Everything."

299

I knew then that we had come to the end of us. Not simply the sex, but everything. It was over. We had been growing steadily apart since my deal with Schary in 1951. But our love had never seemed so precious to me as it did at that moment when I knew it had passed out of my keep for ever. I had read enough scripts to know how well silence says the things that cannot be said. I asked him to hold me. I told myself, "Now I know the first time we made love, and the last." December 1956, a date that must seem long ago to you, Robert; to me it still seems like yesterday.

I still miss him. I was lucky to have found him early – like Shearer found Thalberg, and Jennifer got Selznick. They were important men who knew how to handle a career. Noah and I went through everything that two people can go through in a lifetime, but all along I knew that our future together was limited. Oh, we talked about marriage. But it was the old story – when he wanted to, I didn't; when I did, he didn't. There were a few romances along the way. But I never slept with this one and that one. Biggest mistake you can make in Hollywood. Affairs ruin more careers in that town than bad scripts. You can waste an awful lot of time on love in Hollywood.

No one knew that the great days of Noah and Theodora were over. The lawyers began unscrambling the business deals we had together. His terms were a typical Noah mixture of generosity and selfishness. *If I don't get what I want from people, I put them on the bus* – that was one of his sayings; you must use it, Robert – and I suppose I was on the bus. I was thirty years old. A milestone in the life of an actress. But my position at MGM had never been stronger. My career was flourishing.

I didn't see or talk to Noah for several weeks after that Sunday at the beach. Then one morning there he was – *is*, as I close my eyes – waiting for me on the set. It was early – before I'd gone into make-up. He said had I seen Louella's column yet. He knew I never read her garbage. He said she was bringing up the Hoffmann picture again.

"That's a tired story," I said.

He said, "Don't you think it's time you made your peace with her?"

I said, "Why should I do that?"

He said, "There are times when pride is less desirable than sycophancy."

I said, "In your hat, Noah!" Which was about as rude as I got in those days.

I still hadn't told him that I knew he had planted the Hoffmann picture. I don't know why I didn't tell him. I want so hard to be exact, Robert, and this is difficult to explain because I'm trying to tell you things about myself which I haven't got clear in my own head even now. I couldn't ever have loved him more than I loved him when I was a child, but the days when I felt like a moon to his sun were gone, and yet, you see, although he had betrayed me terribly – it was a wound that would never, never heal – there was still so much I loved in him, there was still so very much we shared . . .

Perhaps it took me too long to understand how deeply he had hurt me, and even after I knew it, I didn't know how to deal with it. Maybe I was simply ashamed for him. I didn't want to listen to his lies. What was the point? There was no point . . .

Her voice trailed off and there was a long silence on the tape. When she spoke again her voice was strong.

That was the last time we spoke, the last words we ever said to each other face to face . . . No big bang, no *Sturm und Drang* . . . It was over. After sixteen years we never even said goodbye.

The picture wrapped. The last scene, the famous ballroom scene, when she knows she is going blind and seeing her lover for the last time, we shot on stage 18 in a single day. When it was over, I knelt down and kissed the stage, drove straight out to the airport in my studio make-up (but *not* wearing the Givenchy gown, which gets printed all the time) and boarded the next flight out to Paris.

Stayed in bed at the George Cinq for a week. Reading and sleeping and sipping champagne. Onassis sent the champagne. I hadn't even met him at that time. One of his people leaked the story about the Dom Perignon and the roses he sent me every day. He was a great user of people, Ari; another Noah. Later I spent six months on the *Christina*, the only guest, a crew of sixty-five seeing to my every need. Do you remember those *Theodora and the Flying Greek* headlines? There was a cartoon in the *Herald-Trib* of me playing dice with Ari for my soul.

I would never have been one of those actresses who goes on until the tumbril's at the door, but for a long time I continued to think that when the right part came along . . . But six months became a year, a year two and my kind of pictures were going out of fashion. One morning I woke up and discovered that ten years had slipped by and I had become a legend . . .

A good place to stop, Robert . . . before I fall asleep on you like an exhausted lover.

51

*Any resemblance to his father is confined to
Matthew Swan's firm jaw – but that's fine with
Noah, who points out "that's where the will
shows!" ("Hedda Hopper's Hollywood", Los
Angeles Times, March 19, 1959)*

Friday, January 5
London

"You order," Grace said at La Famiglia. "Something light and
aphrodisiacal." Rider ordered sole with a Venetian sauce, and a
bottle of white Frascati.

"Will you finish the draft before Tuesday?" she asked after the
waiter poured the wine.

He nodded. "Did you get a chance to look at the Barbara Swan
bio I gave you?" He kept his voice non-committal. "What you
think?"

She wrinkled her nose in concentration, and Rider imagined
that she must have had very much the same expression on her
face when she was a little girl doing her homework. "Bit
repetitious," she said. "Read like a few writing hands were
involved."

"Anything else?"

She shrugged.

"Matthew Swan was born" – he took out his notepad and
checked the date – "April 5, 1941. *Romeo and Juliet* closed down
September 29, 1940. Noah returned to the States two days later.
How could he –"

"Be Daddy?" Grace was ahead of him. "He nipped back to
California for a day. All it takes is one quickie."

"This was 1940, Grace. There was a war on. It would have

303

taken a week out of his life at least. He was Johnny at the rathole on that picture. I don't think he left it for a minute let alone a week."

Grace shrugged. "OK, Barbara came to London."

"Copeland told me he'd never met her. Wouldn't he have met her if she had been in London, even for a few days? In her book she doesn't mention any trip to London, does she?"

Grace shook her head. "Ergo?"

"I think she was having an affair, Grace."

"It's a good story – Jesus, it's a good story," she said, as the significance hit her. "If Matthew Swan runs . . . if he wins – "

"Who is the President's father?"

After dinner, they walked slowly back in the snow along the King's Road and across Battersea Bridge to Grace's apartment, trying to figure out who might be Matthew Swan's father. It was an amusing game. At the apartment, she went back to Barbara's biography.

"'From the beginning of our marriage,'" she read aloud. "'Noah was desperate to have a son. But it would be five years before I found myself, aged thirty-three, pregnant. The day I went to Dr Wedemeyer to confirm my hopes, I asked my dear friend Hedda Hopper to accompany me. Hedda broke the wonderful news in her column the next day.' She's fuzzy on dates, her age jumps about a bit. She's thirty-three one minute, twenty-nine a page later."

Rider said, "Read the bit about the fall at Goldwyn's party."

She found the paragraph. "'Shortly afterwards, I fell down some steps at a garden party at Sam Goldwyn's house and fractured my pelvis,'" she read. "'I spent the rest of my pregnancy confined to bed, attended by Wedemeyer and gloriously fussed over by everybody . . .'"

He poured a couple of brandies. "To sons and fathers," he said.

She sipped her drink. "There is another possibility," she said.

"Yeah?"

"Barbara didn't have a baby!"

Rider shook his head. "A lot of people have been down that

path. Nobody's been able to stand it up. Garson Kanin kicked it apart in *Noah and Theodora*. He talked to Barbara, Wedemeyer, Wedemeyer's nurse, Hedda Hopper, Sam Goldwyn . . . everybody."

"Kanin's a terrific gossip writer. Do you trust him as a reporter?"

"He knocked the bottom out of that rumour."

"How can you be certain?"

He sipped his brandy thoughtfully, and didn't answer.

"Wasn't he a friend of Noah Swan?" she said.

"He directed a couple of pictures for Swan in the fifties."

"Don't forget Hollywood was dealing in news management before Washington even knew what news management was."

Grace's serious tone made him hesitate. "Theodora lied about the operation in New York? She convinced me."

"She's an actress, Robert."

"When we were watching that TV footage – the interview Ed Murrow did with her in 1955 – remember you said how she always had a little laugh before she said something painful?"

"Something sad or painful."

"I played the tapes when she told me about the abortion. There it was, that little laugh. And there's Flagg's story. The doctor's letter . . . the ectopic pregnancy. The pieces fit, Grace."

She sat down, holding her brandy glass in both hands. "If Noah isn't Daddy . . . why no twitter in the dovecote? He can count, can't he?"

Rider picked up the copy of *Portrait of a Hollywood Marriage* and read, " 'Noah was desperate to have a son . . .' Who knows what manner of deals are struck in the privacy of the marital bedroom?"

Grace gave him a long look. She stood up and walked to the window and looked out at the Thames, biting her lip thoughtfully. She came back to where he was sitting on the sofa. "She was rich, connected, she really knew how to work that town. She was quite an asset. He couldn't afford to lose her . . . It was her price for turning a blind eye to his affair with Theodora?"

"It's possible, don't you think?"

There was a silence while Grace thought about it again.

"Barbara's dead. She can't tell us," she said after a pause. "Noah's not going to admit a dicky bird. Theodora? Missy Miller?"

He shook his head to both of them.

She went into the bedroom and came out slipping a robe over her cream silk chemise. "What about *The Man Who Knows Everything*?"

"If I take Sunday's Concorde, I can have an early dinner with him in New York, fly down to Miami Sunday evening, and be on a flight to the Caribbean the next morning. What do you think?"

"I think the aphrodisiac's paying off," she said, spraying a mist of Amarige de Givenchy wickedly between her thighs. "Let's go to bed."

52

It's the deaths of our friends and those we love that hurt us most, not our own. (Ambrose Lanigan, in his last letter to Kate Goldsmid)

Friday, January 5
New York City

Out of the blue Kate remembered the tape she had taken from Lanigan's answerphone. She put it into the machine and pressed PLAY. A message from his dentist's office, reminding him of an appointment; his broker wanting to talk to him about a stock; a jacket was waiting collection at the NuLook Cleaners; his dentist's office again, complaining that he had missed his appointment. Listening to the traffic of domestic trivia made her sad all over again. She was about to switch it off when a hesitant voice said:

"Mr Lanigan? You said to call. Mr Pickens, the janitor? You said if I got word about the Rusks, in 4A . . . I got an address." There was a long pause on the tape, as if Pickens was making up his mind whether to continue. "I got it right here. OK, here it is. It's 900E Harbor Tower West, Brickell Avenue." Another pause. "That's Miami Beach and that's gotta be warmer than 82nd Street Jackson Heights right now. That's all I gotta say, Mr Lanigan, except don't go tellin' anyone who give you the pointer."

Kate stood at the window and watched the night traffic on Riverside Drive. It was very cold down there. The radio said there would be snow in the morning.

She stood at the window for a long time.

Then she dialled Scherrer's number in Trinidad.

"Andy, it's awful cold in New York."

307

"We need an hour's notice," he said.

"Monday I could clear my diary for a whole week if I tried real hard."

"Try harder," he said. "Two weeks is better."

53

Only idiots trust to chance if chance hasn't been
well-prepared in advance. ("A Straight Talk
with Noah Swan", New York magazine, May
26, 1980)

Sunday, January 7
Miami

The seventeenth floor of Harbor Tower West had a view of
Miami Beach and Key Biscayne. But Cissy Rusk paid no attention to the view. Small, like her brother, whom she greatly
resembled, she slumped deep in an armchair, a travelling rug
covering her lap and legs, her eyes closed.

"She had the stroke six weeks ago, Miss Goldsmid." Walter
Rusk returned to the living-room carrying a tray of tea things. "A
mild one, according to the doctors. But at her age, what's mild?
Milk?"

"Thank you," Kate said. "Can you m-manage by yourself,
Walter? She must be a handful."

"A nurse comes in every day; maid's here twice a week. Cuban
girl." His hand shook a little, spilling tea into the saucer as he
handed Kate her cup. "Down on vacation, you say?"

"Needed a break from that New York weather," she said
easily.

"It's kind of you to look us up." He smiled at the old woman,
whose eyes had suddenly opened. "We have a visitor. From New
York. She –"

Cissy jerked forward in her chair, knocking a vase off a small
table.

"Cissy. Silly girl." He spoke kindly, but loudly, and Kate
guessed that she had been deaf before the stroke also robbed her

of her speech. He picked up the flowers and replaced them in the vase. "You don't like your pretty blooms?" he said, holding up the vase. "You want me to take them away?" He put the vase behind his back.

She stared at him with dead eyes.

"If only you could talk to me, dear."

"Is she all right, Walter?" Kate asked anxiously.

"She's fine." He wiped Cissy's forehead and the corners of her mouth. "Do you remember, dear, in New York, I told you about Miss Goldsmid? She wants to hear about the time we had breakfast at the Plaza . . . I said you remember those things so much better than I."

Cissy continued to stare at him with her dead eyes.

"I was s-surprised when I heard you'd left Queens," Kate said. "I thought perhaps you'd decided to move to Douglaston after all."

"You got a good memory. Douglaston was always the dream. But when Ince, Ihmsen and Meiklejohn suggested this place . . . Cookies?"

"IIM paid for you and Cissy to come down to Florida?" she said, shaking her head to the cookies.

He chuckled. "Those sourbellies? No, a client – or his estate did. He passed away last year. IIM handle the estate."

"That's w-wonderful, Walter. Did you know him well?"

He shrugged. "Maybe we did. I guess he knew us and liked us well enough. The estate takes care of everything. He passed away last year," he said again.

"You have no idea at all who he might have been?"

"Not the foggiest. They don't want us to know, I don't ask."

He spoke with no astonishment in his voice at all. Perhaps it was the acceptance of the aged, Kate thought. But she was puzzled that such amazing fortune had not made him curious. He seemed to have no interest in the mystery of it, or the reason behind it.

"*Wedemeyer*," he said suddenly. "That was his name. The other fella at the Plaza. And he had a young woman with him. Had a French name, but she wasn't a Frenchy."

Kate looked impressed. "You're amazing, Walter."

He smiled at his sister. "You see, it's still up there when I try," he said.

Kate sipped her tea, and tried again. "I'd be burning with curiosity, if something wonderful like this happened to me."

"I like honey, Miss Goldsmid" – he spoke softly, but with something suddenly guarded in his tone, an impending irascibility – "but I don't poke my nose into a bee's business . . . That way I don't get stung."

From across the room there came a noise like the satisfied bark of an old dog.

Monday, January 8
Miami International Airport

Half a dozen people were gathered at the first-class check-in desk when Kate arrived. She hated standing in line. She took a seat, lit a cigarette and thought about her visit to the Rusks. Although she had no idea what she expected to find out from Cissy, the meeting had been a letdown, and she felt benumbed by her own disappointment.

The check-in line moved forward. The man now at the desk was tall and looked as if he might have been a sportsman when he was younger. He had a tanned, lean face with a trimmed, auburn beard with flecks of grey and red in it. When he spoke his accent reminded her of Sean Connery. But only when she heard the clerk tell him how much she had enjoyed his last book did she realize who it was. A moment later the public relations people appeared and led him away.

"Smoking or non-smoking, Miss Goldsmid?" she was asked when she checked in, a few minutes before the flight closed.

"Has Mr Rider arrived yet?"

"Yes, he has, Miss Goldsmid," the clerk said, tagging her luggage. "He's in E3, on the aisle. Smoking section," she added, consulting the seat allocation plan on her VDU. "The window seat is free."

"Fine," Kate said. "Do I have time to buy a magazine?"

"Be quick."

She grabbed the *New Yorker* and a softback edition of *Unrecorded Deaths*.

Aboard the Boeing 747 Kate and Rider exchanged polite good-mornings. The whine of the engines became a roar, and the plane climbed steeply into the air. The engines settled into their cruising basso profundo, and with a small reassuring ping the Fasten Seatbelts/No Smoking sign was switched off. Kate opened her magazine. It was almost an hour before she took *Unrecorded Deaths* out of her bag, opened it at the beginning, and began to read. If Rider noticed what she was reading, he said nothing. When the steward handed her the lunch menu, *he* noticed at once. "I hope Mr Rider doesn't tell you how it ends," he said.

Kate looked up. "I'm sorry?"

"Your book," Rider said without fuss, taking his menu from the steward. "I'm afraid I wrote it."

She looked at its cover. "Robert Rider?"

He held out his hand.

"Kate Goldsmid," she said, shaking his hand. "It's going to sound trite saying it, but I really am a f-fan of yours."

Rider laughed. "Just promise not to ask whether any of it's autobiographical."

Lunch was served. They went through the usual small talk of travellers: favourite cities, favourite restaurants, movies they had seen. Had he come directly from London? Kate asked. He told her he had stopped off in New York for dinner. She said she thought that was very grand. What did she do? Rider asked, she told him she was a lawyer.

"For me law is a mystery where reason ends and faith begins," he said. "I always need a damn good cause to convince me to go to law."

"I'm interested in results, not c-causes," she said.

"The game's the thing for you, is it?"

She shrugged. "I'm one of those Southern Puritans – work hard, play hard, and keep out of politics."

"Where do Southern Puritans read law these days?"

"These days I don't know." She smiled. "In my day, it was Austin. Texas U Law School."

"And after that?"

"After I graduated I joined Robarts, Brown and Corry in Fort Worth. Solid, old-line firm. I mean, really c-conservative. They still had urinals in the ladies' room."

Rider laughed. "Clearly no place for an ambitious young woman."

"I wanted it all. Fast-track career, happy marriage, cellulite-free thighs." She smiled. "Well, two out of three's not bad."

"Let me guess."

"I'm a widow," she said quickly.

"Oh, I'm sorry. I take it your sojourn with Robarts and the other gentlemen of Fort Worth was brief?" he said, not dwelling on her loss.

"The urinals were a spur."

"What was your next stop?"

"I moved to Washington. Spent a c-couple of years in the Criminal Division of the Justice Department. Now I'm with Kilmer, Ochs, Izard and Walsh in New York."

"You've come a long way from Fort Worth."

"My mother died when I was three. My dad brought me up. He taught me to mend a flat, fix a fuse . . . He convinced me I could do anything I wanted to."

"He sounds like a good man. What did your late husband do?"

"He was a doctor, like my dad. May I ask *you* a question?"

"Of course."

She picked up *Unrecorded Deaths*. "Your plots turn out to be awful close to the t-truth. Is that insider trading . . . or just coincidence?"

"Pure invention is simply the talent of a deceiver," he quoted Byron, but didn't say so.

"So you limit your imagination to the p-possible . . . Is that invention, or discovery?"

"A real lawyer's question. How do you define invention?" he said, enjoying the game of words. "How do you define discovery?"

"I guess discovery is finding out something that already exists . . . Invention wasn't there until you put it there," she said. "Columbus finding America was a discovery. The application of that discovery to sell p-popcorn and jeans was an invention."

Rider laughed. "Next time I have a good cause to go to law, you'll be the first person I call."

He watched her light a cigarette. Dressed in a white tailored linen suit, with an enticing slit in the long narrow skirt, her natural pallor shone with an almost unearthly brilliance in the pure light of 35,000 feet. He liked everything about her. The gentle stammer. The way she tilted her head, letting her blonde hair swing loose across her face. Were they tricks she used in court to beguile the men in the jury? He wondered how she had spent her life since her husband died.

"Will you be staying in Trinidad long?" he asked.

"A couple of weeks."

He made a quick decision. "I'm visiting a friend on the islands. I can be in Port of Spain for a couple of days around the twentieth. Would you have dinner with me?"

"Yes, I'd like that," she said. She wrote the Scherrers' number on the back of her card. "Call me on this n-number," she said, hoping it sounded cool enough.

54

*From a message to the staff of Holy Day House:
On your happiness will depend our success, and
our reputation. We shall stand high, or the
reverse, as we act justly or unjustly by you.
(Mildred d'Erlanger, Directrice, Biddle-
Biemiller Corp., Geneva, Switzerland)*

Thursday, January 11
Holy Day House, St Francis, W.I.

Victoria Biddulph was annoyed by the brusque tone of the
letter from Geneva giving her a month's notice, and hurt that
Dr Ritchie (with whom she had had a brief affair before she got
involved with Henriksen) had not broken the news to her
himself. He was on vacation, but he must have known what
was coming.

His deputy, Dr Ettore Soffici, who had recently arrived from
the Biddle-Biemiller clinic in Florence, had not been told of her
imminent departure, nor informed of the limitations of her
security access. Married to a Venetian principessa, Soffici was a
mediocre physician, but a handsome one, and fated to earn large
fees from rich and grateful women. It was a destiny that made
him content, and rather lazy in routine matters of administration.
Tor was not surprised when he carelessly gave her Restricted
Access tapes from Alpha Sanctuary to deposit in Registry.

In her room that evening she mixed herself a planter's punch,
and slipped the Alpha Sanctuary tape into her VCR and pressed
PLAY. Sitting down she took a deep breath and watched the
images flicker on to the screen.

The Baroness was sitting in a chair in a room that Tor knew was
a recreation of the von Tegge drawing-room in Vienna. The

315

furniture was vintage Biedermeier; paintings by Waldmuller and Franz Kruger (Tor had recently typed up an itemized list for insurance purposes) hung on wine silk walls. The Baroness wore a black dress, buttoned high at the throat. Her hair was white. She did not move; even when Tor fast-forwarded the tape she remained strangely still. She reminded Tor of those manikin impersonators in store windows who never seem to draw breath.

With a shiver, she switched off the picture, rewound the tape, and replaced it in its case. The second tape was better lit, and in sharper focus. The Baroness was sitting at a desk, her pale skin as transparent as a T'ang vase. She wore a *robe de chambre*; her thin legs, like sticks really, were sheathed in pale stockings. She seemed to be deep in thought. After a few minutes she stood up and left the room. The camera picked her up in the adjoining room, talking to herself, her voice indistinct. She returned to the first room, sat down at the desk and began to write.

After a while she again stood up and said something to herself that made her laugh. She went out again, and again had a conversation with herself in the next room, then returned and placed the letter she had written in an envelope. After that she sat in the familiar trance as if all her energy had been used up.

Tor was reaching to switch off the tape when the Baroness jerked her head towards the door, smiled, and made a gesture of welcome. Tor thought she was talking to herself again. It was several moments before Theodora came into picture.

The two women spoke in English, but sometimes in German. Sometimes what they said seemed to be so painful to them that they were barely able to speak at all. They spoke softly, even the hypersensitive ribbon mikes hidden in the walls missed words, sometimes whole sentences were no more than muffled murmurs: *Blut ist dicker als Wasser . . . I have tried to pretend otherwise, Mama, but our actions are not independent of each other . . . Beruhre nicht alte Wunden . . . I know, I know . . . Böser Vogel, böses Ei . . .* Reproaches followed moments of tenderness; they accused each other, blamed each other, yet seemed to want to console and love each other too.

Tor's German was rusty. But she understood enough to know

that what was being discussed was a story so fantastic that it was almost unbelievable.

Tor checked her translation a dozen times. *Böser Vogel, böses Ei* . . . a bad bird lays a bad egg. *Beruhre nicht alte Wunden* . . . don't disturb old sores. *Blut ist dicker als Wasser*.

The force of her discovery paralysed her and she still hadn't returned the tapes to Registry, although she knew that each day that passed increased the risk of being found out. On Saturday she woke up knowing what she had to do.

The red Alpha Sanctuary label peeled off the cassette with ease. It took her less than three minutes to switch labels with a Jane Fonda workout tape.

On Monday morning she called Kate Goldsmid.

55

*Didn't Oscar Wilde say that no man's rich
enough to buy back his past? He was wrong. I
just bought it back and made it as if it had never
been. That's how rich I am. (Noah Swan, on
buying up the rights and destroying every print
of* Gloria X, *his biggest and most costly flop,*
Time, *April 26, 1963)*

Late afternoon, Monday, January 15
Blanchisseuse, Trinidad

Kate Goldsmid put down the phone. "That was Victoria Biddulph – remember the pilot's girlfriend."

"You're supposed to be on vacation. How the heck did she
track you down here?" Annie Scherrer said protectively.

"The office had my number," Kate said.

Andy Scherrer looked up from the papers he was working on.
"She say what she wants?"

"To meet me in Port of Spain on Thursday."

"Henriksen, that was her boyfriend's name," Annie said. "Did
you know he had a wife and five children in Malmö?"

"What shits men are sometimes," Kate said.

Annie had gone to bed. Scherrer went to his study and returned
with a large envelope and handed it to Kate.

"What's this?" There was something in his manner that made
her hesitate to open it.

He walked to the end of the room and rubbed the back of his
neck. He was a big man, not a giant, not tall, not fat, but big. His
white hair and craggy features reminded some people of the old
actor Spencer Tracy. He reminded Kate more of her father, and

319

she often treated him almost as though he were. "Kate, I know we both agreed to stay off the subject," he said, coming back to her. "But I have to ask you this. How much do you know about what Lanigan was up to down here when he died?"

"He was working for Noah Swan," she said matter-of-factly. "Swan was worried about the book Theodora Glass is supposed to be writing."

"Anything else?"

Her eyes narrowed thoughtfully. "I knew about Robert Rider. Lanigan told me about him the last time we spoke on the phone."

"Do you know why Lanigan was on his way to St Francis when he was killed?"

She shook her head.

"Gisela von Tegge's a patient at the clinic there, Holy Day House. Lanigan found out that –"

"Wait a minute! The *Baroness*? Theodora's *mother*? She's *alive*?"

He nodded. "Noah Swan owns the island. He owns the clinic, Kate." He shook his head slowly, calculating how much more he could say without lying to her, without admitting all his qualms. Because whatever was at the bottom of this business, it deeply involved Noah Swan, the father of the man who might yet be the next President of the United States. Some boundaries you had to respect. "Whatever's involved here, Kate . . . It's a secret somebody intends taking to the grave."

"Secrets can jump up and bite you in the ass when you least expect it, Andy," she said angrily.

He smiled. "You want something to drink?"

She shook her head. "Is the truth in here?" she said, tapping the envelope.

"They're Lanigan's case notes, Kate. He mailed them to me from the airport. He didn't trust the hotel. He found out that it was owned by Noah Swan. Things were getting back to Washington before he sent them."

"Jesus Christ," she said quietly, watching him pour himself a Jack Daniel's.

"Forget the notes . . . put them in the burn bag."

320

"Why didn't you put them in the burn bag?"

"It wasn't my call," he said sharply, hearing the accusation in the question.

She looked at him intently. "Why are you giving them to me now?"

He swirled his drink around his glass. "The call from the Biddulph girl . . . She works at Holy Day House. Lanigan was using her to get to the Baroness."

"Why didn't she say something to me at the funeral?"

Scherrer shrugged his big shoulders. "What could she say, Kate? Without her connivance Lanigan wouldn't have been aboard the chopper when it went down. Without her collusion, he might still be alive. She must have been scared half to death of what she'd gotten herself into."

He stood up, and finished his drink. "Burn the envelope, Kate," he said again. "Forget the whole business."

"And after all this forgetting – " she got to her feet – "you think that would be the end of it, Andy?"

"Let somebody else figure it out if they have to."

She kissed his cheek. "I've got a lot of thinking to do." She waved goodnight over her shoulder with the envelope, and didn't look back.

56

*Truth does more harm in the world than people
realize. (Noah Swan, Esquire, April 1959)*

**Same night
Santa Aloe**

From Robert Rider's notebooks:

Problem now serious. She's not giving a thing of herself.
Arrives promptly for sessions, but either repeats stuff we
covered weeks ago (she has weird ability to tell a story *exactly*
the same way a dozen times – *word for word*, as if scripted) or
she tells stories without point. Sometimes contradicts things
she told me a month ago, or even yesterday. Try to pin her
down, she becomes vague and evasive or tetchy. Time's not on
my side. I *have* a book but not the book she promised.

The phone rang. It was Missy, inviting herself down for a
nightcap. Ten minutes later she knocked on his door. "You don't
get many dates around here," she made a joke of her unexpected
visit. She wore a black satin parka, and jeans. She sat down,
turned out the bright table light by her side, took out a pack of
cigarettes. "Scotch. Ice, no water. Please."

Rider poured the drink, handed it to her, went into the kitchen
and returned with a bowl of ice. "Couldn't sleep?"

"Sleep is no servant of the will," she said in Theodora's accent,
filling her glass with ice. "Especially when you get to my age,"
she added in her own voice.

His lighter flared in the deep shadows in which she sat. "You're
no age, Missy," he said, lighting her cigarette.

"It's nice of you to say so." She blew a cloud of smoke out of her mouth, slowly, towards the ceiling; she still smoked the way the women she played in her movies smoked. "Seventy-two, if you're wondering."

"I know."

She pushed her hand through the streak of white in her hair. "Where are you finding out all these things?"

"Research."

"I sometimes wish that all the files in every newspaper on earth would just go up in smoke. What do you call that?"

"Spontaneous combustion?"

She shook her head. "Wishful thinking." She fixed him a steady gaze. "I'm going to miss you."

"Theodora acts as if I'm already gone. She's shut the door." He smiled. "It's what you wanted."

Missy nodded. "I never lied to you about that."

"You never did."

They were silent for a moment. "She's given you an awful lot, Robert. You've gotten into things nobody else has even got close to. What more do you want?"

"Have I missed something?" He watched her eyes. They were lovely eyes but made sad by the dead nerve in her left lid. "Why do I keep thinking I've missed something?"

"I don't think you miss a thing."

"Thank you."

"It wasn't a compliment."

"I know."

She smiled. "You've been a bright spot in our dull lives, Robert."

"Is she going to St Francis for her check-up this month?"

She nodded. "The nineteenth. It's in the contract. Two days."

"It had to be confirmed."

"It's confirmed now."

They talked about other things. She finished her drink, looked at her watch. "I'll let you go to bed, or get back to your typewriter, or whatever the hell it is writers do after midnight."

"Did you find out whatever it was you came down here to find out?"

"You always such a suspicious bastard?"

"I'm paid to be suspicious."

She started out of the room, hesitated and looked at him with her hand on the door knob. "I don't want Theodora to be hurt. I owe her everything. Without her I'd probably be just another seventy-something dress extra getting pushed around all day by shitty second assistants. And that ain't no fun at all."

"You're a loyal friend, Missy."

"I love her very much," she said, opening the door and stepping out into the night.

6.15 a.m., Tuesday, January 16
Santa Aloe

Theodora walked out of the sea naked; Missy put a robe around her shoulders. "Tell me what he said again," Theodora said, and Missy repeated her conversation with Rider.

"He sees right into people, doesn't he?" Theodora said.

"Smart as hell."

"I like him."

"I know you do."

"I should never have started any of this," Theodora said, on the edge of anger.

"You're doing the right thing now, honey," Missy told her calmly.

"Nobody understands me like you."

They walked towards the California junipers at the top of the dunes. "I love my trees," Theodora said. "I planted American trees because I love America. I know its faults and I still love it. In 1940 it took me in and gave me hope. My loyalty to America is very great, Missy. If Noah succeeds in putting Matthew into the White House –"

"Matthew is fifty-five years old, honey. If there was going to be a problem don't you think it would have shown itself by now?"

"Remember how it was with Mama? How we refused to admit the truth. Was that reticence or was it ignorance, Missy?" she said, sighing. "What is worse?"

"Don't torture yourself."

"It runs in families. It's in the blood."

"It didn't affect you."

"I was strong."

"You mustn't regret the past."

"Not the past. The future."

They reached the old burial ground. Some of Morgan's pirates, and perhaps his summer mistresses, were buried here. But it had not been used in living memory, and it was now almost impossible to read the words on the headstones; a few stray letters still resisted the winds of time, a last faint broken cry in the face of oblivion. The place had a great calm.

It was here twenty years before that Missy first heard the truth about Matthew. "There's a little bit of history I think you have the right to know," Theodora had begun. How many times had she listened to the story since? A thousand times? It had never lost its power to appal and fascinate her. The birth at 3.25 a.m. on Tower Drive – not an easy birth – screams, pain, blood-soaked sheets – Dr Wedemeyer and his nurse, Mildred d'Erlanger, afraid at first that he would not survive (the umbilical cord had tangled around his neck and reduced his oxygen supply in his struggle to be born) – the panic, the fear – nobody had considered how they would deal with a *dead* infant – but he struggled, he survived – twenty-four hours later, in the middle of the night Matthew Swan was taken to Coldwater Canyon and placed in Barbara Swan's bed. His birth was announced the following morning.

"I'm not a very good blackmailer, am I?" Theodora's voice broke into Missy's reverie. "I prayed and prayed Noah would fold when he heard about the book. And Rider."

"The battle's not over yet," Missy said in a hopeful voice.

"Perhaps I am insane."

"No."

"A tangled web, isn't it?" Theodora said with her enigmatic smile.

"Matthew hasn't declared. You still might have scared Noah off."

There was a silence and Missy knew that Theodora was

thinking about it, trying to convince herself that there was still hope. But there was no hope. Noah had called her bluff. However much Theodora may threaten him, he knew that she would never open that can of worms. She wouldn't dare. Her pride would not let her. But Rider was something else. Rider was a real threat. It seemed inconceivable that Noah would simply ignore him. Do nothing. She stood up and stared at the faint surviving letters on the tombstone. She could make out a J and an S, or perhaps it was a B. Was it a man? A mistress? A child? Old gravestones are as hard to read as Noah Swan, she thought.

"We should be getting back, honey," she said.

57

Don't ask the doctor; ask the patient. (Yiddish proverb)

Thursday, January 18
Port of Spain

At midday Kate entered Balzac's. Victoria Biddulph was waiting, the only other customer. She had lost a lot of weight since the funeral.

"It's nice to see you again, Tor," Kate said, remembering the name she had said her friends called her by. She sat down at the white iron table, on which a bottle of wine was already half-empty.

"Sorry if I sounded strange on the phone." She filled Kate's glass. "I was a bit fraught, actually."

Kate smiled, sipped the wine, said nothing.

Tor refilled her own glass. "I work at Holy Day House, on St Francis," she said as if it were something she had been rehearsing and had to say quickly. "I met your fella just before he was killed. He told me he was a writer, and wanted to meet the Baroness Gisela von Tegge. Theodora Glass's mother. She's a patient at the clinic. Only not many people know that. Your fella had a lot of charm and I was trying to help him."

"Yes," Kate said. "I know."

Tor explained the plan she and Henriksen had worked out to get Lanigan on to the island. Perhaps once she had thought it exciting, a wonderful lark, but now she recalled the details in a lifeless voice. Even when she came to the crash, and the death of her lover and Lanigan, her voice remained curiously blank.

"*Was* he a writer?"

The question surprised Kate. "Not exactly," she said.

"That's what I thought." She reached beneath the table and picked up an old blue Air Canada airline bag and put it on Kate's lap. "Take this. I've been given my marching orders at the clinic. I've still got two more weeks to go. But I'm not going back." She stared into her glass, her auburn hair hiding her face and the uncertainty in her eyes. She had never really got on with other women, and the trust she was putting in Kate was out of character and made her nervous.

"Where will you go?"

"Home."

"What will you do?"

"Try not to think about things that mess up the old top-knot."

She looked at her watch. The place was beginning to fill up. A gaggle of lunchtime drinkers had gathered at the far end of the bar. "Two hours, I'm out of this town," she said. "Not a bloody moment too soon."

In her room Kate slowly opened the Air Canada bag. Inside was a Jane Fonda workout cassette and an envelope sealed with Sellotape. She held the envelope up to the light; explored it with her fingers. On the back inscribed in an elegant black type she read *Holy Day House, St Francis, West Indies.* Inside the envelope were several photostats, the first of which was an admittance record:

Surname: von Tegge   Forename(s): Gisela   Title: Baroness
Address: Santa Aloe, W.I.   Sex: Female   Date of Birth: c. 1910
Nationality: US   Occupation: N/A   Marital Status: Widow
Religion: RC   Next of Kin: Theodora von Tegge
Relationship to Patient: Daughter   Address: As above
Telephone Number(s): Refer D'Erlanger
Referring Physician: Erskine Bone, MD, Jascha Ober Clinic
Date and time of admission: December 29, 1986; 06.49
Presenting Conditions: Bipolar Affective Disorders: Non-insulin-
dependent diabetes mellitus

Medical History: Cholecystectomy, 1975; Hip Arthroplasty (right), 1983
Allergies: None
Current Medication: Camcolit, 500 mg x 2. Salbutamol, 200 micrograms, four-hourly by aerosol inhalation
Surveillance: 24-hour
Media Enquiries: DENY
Others: Refer d'Erlanger
Mail, Outgoing and Incoming: Refer d'Erlanger
Billing: Refer d'Erlanger

Kate turned the pages at random until she came to a page marked HIGHLY CONFIDENTIAL:

On admission, patient confused and manic, with marked motor activity. Speech rapid, a mixture of English and German. She demanded to speak with Louis B. Mayer (a motion picture producer who has been dead for some years). She also wrote voluminous notes, which she insisted be sent to the Attorney-General of the United States in order "to inform him of the facts". The notes were unintelligible. Patient transferred to Suite C1 at 09.15.

Kate looked back at the admittance record, and again at the case notes. At least it explained why the Baroness had disappeared off the face of the earth after leaving Kennedy International to spend Christmas with Theodora in 1986.

She collected the Fonda tape, went downstairs and put it in the VCR. It was several moments before she realized who it was she was watching, and what she was hearing, and then the adrenalin rush of discovery shook her whole body.

She wrapped the cassette in a hand towel and put it back into the airline bag beneath a sweater and T-shirts and a pair of trainers.

She was still trying to work out what she should do when the phone rang and made her jump out of her skin.

"May I speak with Miss Goldsmid?"

She recognized his voice at once and knew then what she had to do.

58

*Only fools admit the whole truth about them-
selves. (Garson Paley*, Unrecorded Deaths, *by
Robert Rider)*

Saturday, January 20
Port of Spain

The manager, who was short and plump with black sideburns,
took Kate to Rider's suite. It was an odd feeling being inside the
hotel where Lanigan had stayed before he died. In the elevator
she closed her eyes and tried not to think of the world without
him.

Rider was in the Palm suite. "I'm glad you came," he said,
shaking her hand first, then kissing her cheek.

"Did you think I wouldn't?"

"You meet a beautiful woman on a plane, invite her to
dinner . . . it's always a presumption."

She smiled. "You do it often, do you?"

"All the time."

They looked at each other for a silent moment, acknowledging
the sexual attraction. Kate dropped her shoulder bag on the sofa
and walked round the room, inspecting the furniture while he
opened a half-bottle of Bollinger chilling in an ice-bucket.

"All genuine," he said, noticing her interest.

"This overmantel's beautiful," she said, watching his reflection
in the mirror as he filled their glasses. It was possible the suite was
bugged, but it was a risk she had already decided to take. "Then
when you're as rich as Noah Swan," she said softly, taking the
glass of champagne, "you can afford the best."

She was close enough to him to feel the sudden attention.

"Noah Swan owns this hotel?"

"Another part of the hidden empire."

His smile went and came back like a ghost, not quite there, not quite gone; it reminded her of the remoteness she had sensed in him when she first saw him in Miami.

"As a matter of fact," she went on quickly, anxious to get to the point yet nervous about how he would react to her duplicity on the plane, "when we met it wasn't an accident. I asked to be seated next to you." She lowered her voice. "I know about Theodora Glass, Robert. I know about your book."

He grabbed her wrist and took her to the bathroom and turned on all the faucets to drown their voices. "OK," he said, keeping his voice low. "Who the fuck are you, lady?"

She lit a cigarette. Quietly in a measured voice she told him the story. Told him about her relationship with Lanigan, and Lanigan's connection with Noah Swan. She told him about the Rusks, and their mysterious benefactor; and about the Baroness, whom the world believed to be dead but was still alive on the island of St Francis. She told him about Henriksen (but not about Victoria Biddulph; she would come to Tor), and how Lanigan was killed on his way to St Francis.

He said, "I read about the crash in the *Times*. I'm sorry." But all he could think was, *If the Baroness is still alive, Theodora has deliberately and systematically lied to me*. But more than that, so had Aaron Flagg. (*Till the day she died*, he remembered Flagg's words at the Plaza, telling him how the Baroness had used Theodora's abortion to blackmail Noah, *she had him hearing footsteps*.)

Kate said, "I want you to look at something." She fetched the cassette from her bag and gave it to him.

He looked at the label. "Jane Fonda?"

"Play it."

He switched on the radio, turned up the volume, and put the cassette into the VCR.

Theodora appeared on the screen. Behind her, propped up in a canopied bed was the figure of a woman not quite in focus, her features blurred. "That's the Baroness," Kate whispered, sitting down next to Rider.

He moved forward in his seat. The running time-date code in the bottom right-hand corner of the screen read: *1809 12:26.*

"How did you get this?"

"Tell you about it later," she whispered.

On the screen Theodora lit a cigarette. Then her famous voice said, "My God, Mama, sometimes I think I prefer it –"

"When I'm *crazy* – say it!" Her voice was feeble but it was more than the feebleness of old age. It was like a recording of a sound made long ago. She had that look of great fragility that old things acquire just before they crumble into dust; not only her skin but her very bones seemed to be transparent. And yet even in this ailing old woman there were still faint traces of the beauty that she had once been. Her forehead was high, her brows arched and pencilled; her nose straight, with chiselled nostrils. But her eyes, once the colour of aubergine, had faded into a filmy-purple stain. "Can't you say it? *When I'm crazy . . .*"

Theodora did not react. Kate pressed FAST-FORWARD SEARCH; the images on the screen jerked around like people in early newsreels and long since dead. "About here," she said, pressing PLAY:

Theodora was speaking in German, the Baroness interrupted in English: "Your father told me once that love was the essence of my existence . . ." Her language, like the sound of her voice, came from another time. ". . . passion was the very exigency of my soul."

"You were a whore, Mama."

The Baroness smiled, as if she had been paid a compliment. "My unfaithfulness secretly excited your father. Do you remember Helmuth Walther?" She sighed, her eyes half-closed. "What a lover he was! Vulgar and cruel but never, never boring. Once he stood me up against a wall off the Walfischgasse – lifted my skirt as if I were a common streetwalker!" She finished the story in German. "And Franz Papen," she said in English again. "The great ambassador, his little thing wouldn't stand up, but he knew how to please a woman with his tongue – and not just because of the compliments that tripped off it, my dear. His tongue –"

"*Basta!*"

"And then there was Noah . . ."

"I was hoping we'd get through this conversation without mentioning him."

"We went to bed in Berlin. The first time we met we went to bed!"

"I know, Mama," Theodora said in a quiet voice.

"He told you?"

"I always knew."

"I would have done anything he wanted me to. He had that power over me."

"Did you love him?"

"I loved him when he made love to me. In bed he was always kind."

"I know that too, Mama."

"To prefer the charms of a child!" The Baroness's head jerked angrily. "*Mit der Mutter soll beginnen, Wer die Tochter will gewinnen – Ja?*"

Theodora smiled very faintly and repeated it in English, probably because that was the language in which she now thought and dreamed: "With the mother first begin, If you would the daughter win."

"Do you think he ever felt guilty?"

"Whatever conscience he had" – Theodora paused, as if still uncertain of her feelings – "I doubt it."

"Neither one of us was every happy again."

"People like us, Mama . . . how do we ever protect ourselves from ourselves?"

They began to talk in German again but Rider didn't move, didn't say a word. It was like watching somebody who had returned from the grave. Kate stood up and walked to the window and watched the ocean. She came back and stood behind him, her arms folded.

"It gets better," she said, touching his shoulder.

The Baroness said in English, "I love you and I'm proud you're my daughter."

"I know that, Mama."

"Are you going to tell everything in the book?"

Theodora shook her head, but she looked surprised that her mother had remembered the book. Why, her look seemed to say, was she always able to remember those things best forgotten, and rarely those things best remembered? "You know I can't do that, Mama," she said. "I can only threaten. I can never tell."

The Baroness sighed. "Then there will be no revenge."

"Vati used to say that revenge is always unjust."

"So is love."

"So is love," Theodora repeated.

"He gets away with murder."

"*Rache trägt keine Frucht*," Theodora said.

"Revenge brings no fruit," Kate said over Rider's shoulder as the two women continued to speak in German again.

"*Sprechen Sie Deutsch?*" Rider asked.

"Went to school in Germany for a couple of years. This is chit-chat. But wait a minute."

Theodora began fingering the misshapen heart at her throat and Rider knew that was always a sign that she was becoming nervous or upset about something.

"Here it is," Kate said. "The Baroness says she wishes . . . I wish he'd died . . . *Adler brüten keine Tauben* – he was a tough sonofabitch – eagles don't give birth to doves . . . She wishes he'd been something at birth . . . strangled . . . I wish he'd been strangled when he was born . . . Mumble, mumble . . . *Am Tode sein* – he was on the point of death . . . a cord . . . the cord catching round his neck . . . Theodora: Don't say that. You don't mean that. The Baroness: *Gott macht gesund, und der Doktor kriegt das Geld* – God kept him alive . . . but the doctor collected the fee, the money."

Theodora played nervously with the misshapen heart. Ten seconds passed but it seemed longer than that. The Baroness leaned forward and stared at the heart.

Kate began to interpret again, her forehead creased in concentration: "The Baroness says it's hers. The heart is hers. Theodora says the Baroness gave it to her. The Baroness doesn't remember. Theodora: You gave it to me twice. In Vienna . . . on the bridge . . . *In der Klemme sein* . . . we were in a tight spot, you

337

did not know which way to turn . . . Theodora says she returned the heart back to the Baroness in London . . . Something about Vati – her father. It had been a gift from Vati to the Baroness. She says her mother gave it to her again when she came here . . . presumably the clinic. When the Baroness entered the clinic."

The Baroness closed her eyes and in a little while tears came. Theodora unclipped the heart and gave it to her. The Baroness held it to her lips.

Kate was concentrating hard. "It's difficult, she's mumbling again . . . *Kein Geld, keine Freunde mehr* – she's feeling sorry for herself: no money, no friends . . . Can't get next line, then: I did a terrible thing. I did a terrible thing. Theodora: Doesn't matter any more . . ."

The Baroness kissed the heart again.

Kate said, "This is it. The Baroness: What a sad memento of all that pain . . . all those hours . . . all my hours . . . all my hours in labour with Matthew Swan . . . Teeth marks in a heart!"

59

Senator Swan has nothing to fear from the microscopic audit running for President opens up today. Nothing in the tall grass scares us.
(Noah Swan, Los Angeles Times, *January 9*)

Saturday, January 20
Washington DC

Three hours and fifty-nine minutes after leaving London on the Concorde, he was riding through Washington in a limousine with blackened windows. No other city that he knew was as disarming as Washington. It still had the look of a town that rolled up the sidewalks after dark. He liked that. He relished deception and felt himself a part of its double life. It was beginning to snow as the limo drove into the basement entrance on Q Street that appeared to have no connection with the mansion on Parke Custis Place.

Noah Swan was waiting for him in the Trophy Room. "Rider's back on the fucking island," he told him, as soon as the greetings were out of the way.

"Noah, she's bluffing," Aaron Flagg answered calmly.

"Bookbinder say that?" asked Rosengarten, who sat in a tub armchair opposite Noah's desk.

"No. Oscar says Pfeiffer's going to New York next week to set up a deal."

"And you still think she's bluffing?" Noah said, struggling to control his voice.

"I know her," Flagg said easily.

"Fuck you know her," Noah said peevishly.

"I know her games," Flagg said amiably.

"What game is she playing now?" Noah said, still sounding ill-tempered and suspicious.

"Chicken."

"*Chicken?*" Noah looked at Rosengarten, then back at Flagg. "She thinks the book's still under fucking wraps. Rider's a big fucking secret. We're sitting here like three brass fucking monkeys. Who she think she's playing chicken *with*, Aaron?"

"She knows we're posted," Flagg said confidently.

"Think so, Aaron?" Rosengarten shifted uncomfortably in the tub armchair and undid a button on his tailored charcoal suit.

"Why'd she use Bookbinder to handle the deal?" Flagg asked evenly.

"Because he's a tough sonofabitch," Rosengarten said.

Flagg nodded. "And because she knew he'd call *me*. You taught her yourself, Noah – you gotta throw the corn where the hogs will get to it. Who better than Bookbinder to throw the corn?"

"He know she set him up?" Rosengarten asked.

"He's smart but not that smart," Flagg said.

Noah didn't look convinced.

"Noah, listen to me," Flagg said. "She knows that what she knows is potent only as long as she's sitting on it. She can only spook you with the threat of it, Noah. You've dug deep down the years because of what she knows. But she also knows once she pulls that trigger it's all over for her too." He stood up and walked to the end of the room and stared at the Annigoni portrait of Noah painted forty years ago. He hadn't changed so much, except to get richer. He turned and came back. "That was her only shot, that's as hard as she can hit you, Noah, and you took it, and you didn't blink."

Noah said, "She's never gone this far before."

"She's never felt this deeply before."

"Because Matthew's running for President, you mean?" Rosengarten said.

"She don't want him in the White House, we know that, and we know why – but she's not stupid," Flagg patiently pressed his point.

"Broads bent on revenge don't think about the cost," Noah said.

Flagg shook his head. "She ain't gonna pull that pin. Trust me."

Michael Fortas entered the room. He was wearing an English tweed jacket and a red bow tie. Nobody acknowledged his presence.

"I wish to hell I'd handled this my way," Noah said sullenly. "This whole thing could've been turned off months ago."

"You ain't going to make it better by making it worse," Flagg said, glancing at Fortas.

"She can run us off the road with a sniff of the stuff she knows," Noah growled. "How worse can it be, fahcrissake?"

"How worse can it be?" Flagg repeated in feigned astonishment. "Remember Marilyn? The crap that poured out after she was resting easy? Nobody woulda dared print half that doo-doo if Marilyn'd still been around to defend herself. They sawed off any whopper, printed any lollapaloozer. Theodora's a pain in the ass. But she's also the stopper keeping the genie in the bottle."

"What about Rider, Mr Flagg?" Fortas asked quietly, lifting his perfect eyebrows in a quizzical arch. "Are we still giving him the family jewels to sample?"

Flagg knew how to handle Fortas, and didn't rise. "A few selected pieces."

"You think that's wise, do you?" Fortas tried to ride him again.

"There are times when a man must tell half his secret in order to conceal the rest," Flagg said with a sideways glance at Noah.

"Didn't you see him in New York last week?" Rosengarten said. "What was that about?"

Flagg smiled at Fortas, who didn't smile back. "He wanted to know whether Noah was Matthew's father. I straightened him out," he said with quiet satisfaction.

Fortas coughed. It was a polite cough into the back of his hand. But it got Noah's attention and something must have passed between them because when Noah spoke again his voice had changed. It had the old bite back in it.

"You're putting a lotta faith in Rider, Aaron. Some of the stuff you've given him . . ." He took a file from his drawer, opened it and looked through it silently for a minute. "The Hoffmann deal.

341

How we got the dough outa Metro . . . What Mayer said, what I said –"

"Noah, listen to me," Flagg cut him off, holding up his palms. "The more we give him the more he'll trust us. The more we give him the less he'll try to dig out for himself."

"I don't think that's the way he does business," Fortas said.

"Counter-intelligence, Noah," Rosengarten intervened quickly. "It's like putting a virus in the bloodstream of the other side."

"We can't expect Rider to buy the tunes the old cow died of, Noah," Flagg said. "We got to hand him some fucking revelations he can hang headlines on. We got to give him some juicy bits."

"You and the Baroness, for instance?" Noah asked.

Flagg grinned. "I was only following orders."

"What Rider says is going to stick for a long time," Rosengarten cut in to stop them starting down memory lane. "We can shut this whole thing down for twenty years if we use him right."

"There's a lot at stake here," Noah said, looking at Fortas, who was shaking his head, looking at the floor.

"Aaron's done a terrific job, Noah," Rosengarten said quickly. "He's penetrated to the very heart of Rider's thinking. We're calling the shots. We're controlling the whole operation. He's our puppet, Noah. Aaron's had his hand up his ass from day one. Jesus, you can't ask for more than that."

Noah sat in silence, the doubt working in his face. "What about the Baroness?" he asked. "Lanigan proved that some determined bastard . . ."

"Rider thinks she's dead," Flagg said firmly. "The Baroness ain't a problem."

That seemed to calm Noah, although he had not shed his mistrust. "And you don't think we're giving Rider too much?"

"When you got something to hide," Rosengarten again reminded him of the tradecraft, "you give them something else – pretty baubles – to divert their attention."

"One trick needs new tricks to make it stick. I don't want to get into a Nixon position" – Noah turned the pages, glancing uneasily over the material Flagg had leaked to Rider – "having to fix one lie with another."

"It's gonna be fine, Noah," Rosengarten said. "All you gotta worry about now is the first hundred days."

Noah didn't smile. He looked across at Fortas, inviting him to say something.

"What happens if Rider smells a rat?" Fortas asked.

Aaron shook his head. "The Riders of this world are susceptible to seeing themselves in terms of their own image."

Fortas said, "And he's the smart apple author?"

"And I'm gonna make him look even smarter," Aaron Flagg said, smiling.

"Well, you smart apple sonsabitches better be right," Noah said.

60

Sometimes you have to change the truth to make it believable. (Aaron Flagg, New York Herald Tribune, March 8, 1966)

10 p.m., same night
Port of Spain

The Baroness was freeze-framed in the act of raising her hand to her mouth as if stifling a scream. "Matthew Swan's mother," Rider said softly, unable to take his eyes off the screen. The idea seemed to worry him as much as it shocked him.

Had Noah been doing a little double time with Mama? Kate remembered Lanigan's question. How long ago it seemed. She held her head between her hands. The radio was loud, the percussive effects of a steel band drowning their conversation from possible bugs. She was sitting next to Rider, and close.

He picked up the photostats, and read: *Bipolar affective disorder*.

"A manic-depressive illness." She opened her bag and took out the notes from a telephone conversation she'd had the night before with a doctor she knew in Chicago. "Mental disorder. Usually recurrent. Shaped by heredity. Episodes of mania and depression. Severe depressions. Suicide frequent outcome. Patients usually mentally normal between episodes." She spoke in a low clipped voice, reading from her notes. "Mania can develop suddenly. Sometimes shockingly. Often accompanied by delusions, and confusion. Patients often people of great talent, even genius, in the arts, politics, military leadership . . . It goes on, you get the picture."

Rider nodded, absorbing the information. "Maybe we're taking too much for granted here, Kate. Given her condition . . .

delusions, and confusion," he quoted her notes back to her.

"Plus she's old," Kate agreed. "At her age memory can play tricks." She rewound the tape. "But look at it again," she said, pressing PLAY. "This time watch Theodora . . . watch her body language."

Even when you knew it was coming, even when the surprise had gone out of it, when the Baroness said *teeth marks in a heart* it was chilling. Kate freeze-framed on Theodora's reaction.

"What do you see? *I* see acceptance. Recognition. I see despair. I don't see denial."

"Neither do I," he said.

"No doubt in my mind, Robert. She's speaking the truth."

"You said it's hereditary?"

She referred to her notes. "*Shaped* by heredity. Marked frequency of positive family histories. Predisposing genes unknown. Women tend to inherit it more often than males. Doesn't affect *every* offspring. Can skip a *whole* generation."

"So Matthew Swan could be perfectly –"

Kate shook her head. "This'll bury him. Remember Eagleton – McGovern's running mate in 1972? When the press got hold of the story that he'd been in Mayo it finished him. Finished McGovern too."

Rider was angry, although he didn't show his anger. He was angry at Theodora. He was angry at Aaron Flagg. But most of all he was angry at himself. For being taken in by their lies . . . for being so careless. He felt anger, but he also felt released. Now, he knew, he could go after the story in his own way, and on his own terms.

He ejected the tape from the VCR. "You know this is lethal?"

Kate smiled. "If you mean there are people who would kill for it . . ."

"That's exactly what I do mean, Kate."

"Yes, I know." She wasn't smiling now.

"How did you get it? Presumably you had help?"

She told him about Tor Biddulph.

"Sooner or later," he said, "somebody is going to realize it's gone missing, and they're going to come looking for it."

For the first time, Kate began to feel afraid.

"First thing we do is get the tape to someone Noah Swan can't get at. If it's all right with you, I suggest my solicitors in London."

"It's fine with me."

"I'll take it myself tomorrow. I can be back here Tuesday. As soon as the tape's secure" – he inhaled deeply – "I tell Swan what I know, what I've done, and what I plan to do."

"You'll tell him!" Kate's eyes opened wide in surprise.

"It's possible he already knows more than we think. I'll tell him that if he tries to stop me in any way, or if any harm should come to you, to Biddulph, or to me, the tape will be released to the media, along with everything else we know."

She slumped in the chair, crossing her legs, while she thought about it.

"Can you think of a better way?" he said.

She stroked her throat. The strain of whispering all evening had made her pharynx ache; the loud music was beginning to give her a headache. "I reckon in the circumstances that's all we can do," she said.

"Are you all right? You look pale."

"I am rather hungry," she said.

He laughed. "There's a French restaurant on Frederick Street. Has the best bouillabaisse in the Caribbean. I've booked a table at nine –" He looked at his watch: it was nearly midnight.

"Maybe we can grab a pizza," she said.

61

BUGS UNDER THE CHIPS?
"He's running – but not this year" is still the
official line, but Senator Matthew Swan's non-
campaign has taken him to thirty-three states
since the start of the year, and his declaration
can merely be a question of timing and tactics.
He stayed above the fray of Iowa; he kept out of
last week's unedifying contest in New Hamp-
shire. Nevertheless the longer he continues to
delay his declaration, the louder the question
will be asked: Are there any bugs under the
chips waiting to crawl out to embarrass him as a
presidential candidate? His declaration is the
only rebuttal his admirers now want to hear.
(Boston Globe, *January 20*)

12.15 a.m., Tuesday, January 23
En route to Washington DC

The private jet climbed steeply into the Colorado night sky.
"Why does the old man want me back in Washington in such a
goddam hurry, Liz?" Matthew Swan said. "I got a nasty feeling
something's coming out of the woodpile at me."

Liz smiled wearily at her husband. "Well, I'm not sorry to be
going home. I can do with the break. So can you. These
eighteen-hour days are insane for somebody who isn't campaign-
ing," she complained wryly.

Matthew Swan shook his head. "Something's wrong. I can feel
it" – he rubbed his gut – "in here."

She took his hand and placed it on her own stomach.

Matthew's smile was honed to bare essentials. "How ya
feeling?" He sounded more like his father than he wanted to. He

spread his hand affectionately across her gently swelling belly.

"Breakfast in Los Angeles, lunch in Fresno, supper in Salt Lake City – it's what every pregnant woman wants." ("Dutifully pregnant" was how she usually described her condition, to emphasize Noah's wishes in the matter.)

"Probably wants to talk about the declaration. Second thoughts about Illinois?"

"He can't delay again. I still think it was a mistake ignoring the early contests."

"Who needs Iowa in February?" he said defensively, as if he had had some say in the decision. "Getting up at five to hold a piglet while it pisses down your pants on breakfast television."

On this trip they had flown Los Angeles–San Diego–Fresno–San Francisco–Salt Lake City–Phoenix–Denver. The routine was always the same: forty-eight hours after his "warm-up" people had prepared the ground, his jet would put down and he'd appear on the ramp, Elizabeth by his side, and express surprise at the "spontaneous" welcome, the placards urging him to run: SAY "YES" MATTHEW; GO FOR IT, MATT; SWANEE HOW WE LOVE YA. He'd explain that he was in Lordsburg or Oakdale or Oshkosh, Nebraska to visit the university or the high school or his friend the mayor: ". . . a private visit to put forward some ideas I have – but, gee" – he would grin the cowboy in love kind of grin he practised in the mirror as regularly as he brushed his perfect teeth – "you kind people seem to have other ideas . . ." He'd talk about the need for peace, for jobs and self-respect, to get America moving again. Even mouthing clichés, Matthew Swan had an actor's ability to seem to be speaking from the heart. His visits were brief, tightly controlled; he never debated, never appeared on question shows. Cupping his hands as if they held a precious chalice, he would say: "This is how I *feel* about my country, our great and free and wonderful land . . . And if destiny were to put its future in my hands . . . What an honour, what a responsibility . . . But would I be worthy? But then I listen to the people and I wonder . . . do I have a choice?"

The stewardess brought Matthew a bourbon neat, and a juice for Elizabeth.

"Feeling better?" Elizabeth asked after he had taken a couple of sips. It was after midnight. They had changed into tracksuits and were alone in the front cabin, curtained-off from the team behind them.

"I'm OK."

"Want to hear something funny?"

He swivelled in his chair and smiled at her. "Make my day."

"Noah told Norman Mailer that I'm learning Norwegian to be able to read Ibsen in the original! Norman called me and asked me whether it was true."

"What did you tell him?"

"Said it was a pack of lies. Told him I was learning Norwegian because I'm going to write a biography of Sonja Henie, and plan to live in Oslo for a year and learn to ice-skate!"

Matthew laughed and some of the tiredness left his face. "You realize Mailer's going to print every word?"

Elizabeth nodded solemnly. "He asked me why a biography of Sonja Henie. I told him Noah had secretly been in love with her for years."

Matthew's eyes glittered with amusement. "Well, the old man didn't miss many."

Reassured by his humour, she said: "What's the latest on Theodora's publishing plans, by the way?"

"Noah says he's taking care of it."

"Well, that's one thing you can always trust Noah to do well: take care of things."

"Jesus, I hope so," he said.

62

*You can only believe half of what the Baroness
says, the trick of it is to know which half to
believe. (Aaron Flagg,* New York Daily News,
December 15, 1959)

6.30 a.m., same morning
Washington DC

It was snowing heavily. Noah Swan looked at his watch. "He's
landing in fifty-five minutes. Anyone want to explain how I
handle this? I tell him, what? *It's all over, son. Everything you
worked for your whole fucking life – forget it.*" He looked from
one face to the other. "That what I say?"

Nobody in the Trophy Room welcomed the question. Nobody
answered.

Rosengarten looked up at the ceiling through gold granny
glasses, trying to figure out how to get a lock on the prick who
was causing them so much trouble, and regretting that he had not
let Fortas deal with the problem his way at the start.

Fortas stood with folded arms staring out of the window at the
snow settling like a cloak on the *Warrior King*. The Baroness was
crazy in a big way, but surely Noah must have been a little crazy
too. Nobody in his right mind, with the kind of rewards at stake
that were at stake here, would have insisted on recording her
every moment. What made him do it, if not madness? Voyeur-
ism? Hate? Revenge? "I want to know what the bitch is saying
about me," he would say whenever Rosengarten tried to persuade him to terminate the surveillance. Hadn't he learned
anything from the lesson of the Watergate tapes, for God's sake?

Aaron Flagg had driven through the night from New York and
looked older than he had ever looked in his life. For years this
secret had tormented his dreams, but it had never been so real

and so close to him as it was now. Was this the day he would rid his conscience of its burden? "Exactly how much does Rider know – do we have any idea what he's got?" he asked.

"He's got everything," Fortas said, making it sound like a death sentence, and turning from the window.

"But does he have proof?" Flagg's voice was calm, but he had the look of a man trying not to listen to the sound of ice breaking beneath his own feet. "Knowledge ain't worth a hill of beans without evidence."

"He's got a tape," Rosengarten said in a flat voice. "A talkathon. A goddam gabfest, Aaron. We shoulda removed him from the fucking calendar."

"He sent a transcript," Noah said, pushing a folder across the desk. He looked old. He had barely slept. He hadn't put on his hairpiece. "It came last night with his letter."

Flagg lowered himself into a deep leather chair, opened the folder, and clenching his jaw began to read.

He read slowly, remembering Gisela the way she was over fifty years ago.

Did he have no intimation of disaster that day at the Savoy she let him catch her dressing for dinner? She was the first woman he knew who wore nothing except stockings beneath her dress. *Do you want to make love to me, Aaron?* she had asked. *Let's punish them*, she had said, to let him know she knew that Noah had become Theodora's lover too. *Let's punish them with our love*, she had said, coming towards him, laughing and naked. *You know the risks*, he had said. *The risks are part of the excitement*, she had answered. When he entered her the first time she screamed. *Do you always scream?* he had asked her afterwards. *When I don't, it will be over between us*, she had replied evenly. But she had screamed the last time too.

Flagg closed the transcript gravely, and looked at Noah, searching his face for signs.

But there was nothing in Noah's face but grief.

"How do you think Rider'll handle it, Aaron?" Rosengarten asked.

"He'll want to break it a week, ten days before publication of the book. For maximum publicity, that's what I'd do."

"A story like this'll be hard to contain for seven months," Fortas said.

"Where's Rider now?" Flagg asked.

Rosengarten looked at his watch. "He should be back in Trinidad any time now," he said.

Kate was waiting for him when he came through customs in Port of Spain. She was surprised how pleased she was to see him. He kissed her on the lips. Her response to it was deep and trusting.

"I have a limousine," she said. "I've booked a suite at the Hilton. So we can stop whispering."

The chauffeur took his bag and he settled into the back seat of the limousine with Kate. He told her what he had done in London, showed her a copy of the letter his lawyer had sent to Noah Swan.

"When will he get this?" she asked.

"He got it last night special delivery."

"You'll tell Theodora when?"

"She's expecting me back on the island tomorrow. Break it to her then."

"She's not going to like it."

"She shouldn't have lied to me, Kate."

"You have a personal contract with her?"

"Yes."

She looked worried. "You may have a problem there if she decides to fight . . . if Noah Swan gets to her."

Rider smiled and took her card out of his wallet. "I told you the next time I had a good cause go to law, you'd be the first person I call."

"What a fucking mess," Noah said violently.

There was a small heavy silence in the Trophy Room.

"Maybe it won't be as damaging as we think." Rosengarten stood up heavily and began pacing the long room. "OK, assume Rider's story breaks mid-October. We bring forward our TV push. The sixty-second spots . . . the family man, the good husband, the caring father. The winter one of the girls got sick, and he flew the Lear back from Boston in the worst snowstorm in forty years. This is a guy we can trust. A man we can depend on. A man who can take pressure." He came back to his chair and sat down, breathing hard. "We ride out seven days, ten days. After a hundred million dollar TV campaign" – he smiled his most reassuring smile – "it'll be like putting feathers back into a pillow to change his image in that time."

"But when Rider's story breaks, we –" Fortas said incredulously.

"Deny it," Rosengarten said, his smile widening. "This thing's not about truth, it's about credibility. When was the Baroness born? Nineteen-*O*-something? First question they're gonna ask: "What's Rider's source? His source, one frail old woman whose been outa touch with reality for twenty fucking years."

"If Theodora corroborates the story?"

"She won't corroborate shit. She didn't tell Rider before, she ain't gonna admit it now. She gonna confess to the whole fucking world her mother's insane . . . Admit her lover had two-timed her with her own mother? In terms of ultimate embarrassment . . ."

Rosengarten knew he'd said enough.

Noah turned to Flagg. "Aaron?"

Flagg ran his fingertips across his white gunfighter's moustache. "The problem could be the Senator."

"How the Senator?" Rosengarten snapped.

"When he learns the truth about his mother," Flagg said slowly. "When he learns he's carrying a gene that could –"

"He's gonna be upset," Rosengarten cut him off. "Drag something like this from under the bed's enough to knock anyone on their ass. But he's a pol, Aaron. He'll rationalize it. Think Jack Kennedy didn't know he had Addison's disease when he ran in sixty? That stop *him*? Hell it did!"

Noah looked across the room to Fortas. "Michael?"

"I don't think Rider's going to keep the lid on this until October," he said in a voice that was more petulant than he wanted. "And it's not going to come out neat and clean either.

It'll seep out, trickle out . . . there'll be coded hints . . ."

Noah got up and went to the window and looked out.

"The problem's timing," he went on after a long pause, "and how can we make this thing work for us? We're going to have to take the hit sooner or later. And I think the sooner the better."

"Sooner?" Rosengarten and Fortas asked together.

"*We* drop the dime." He turned and faced the room. The three men were looking at him in astonishment. "Leak the story the day before we announce," he went on undeterred. "Leak it, announce next day, day after that, start the announcement tour."

"For Chrissakes, you can't mean it –" Rosengarten started to protest, unable to believe his ears.

"Would we announce if there was a grain of truth in the story? People'll know there's no grain of truth in the story. A grain of truth in it we'd quit right there, wouldn't we?" Noah came back across the room, rubbing his hands together. "We ain't gonna shoot Niagara with something like that in the goddamn barrel, right?"

"Politically –" Rosengarten began again, and again Noah cut him off.

"Won't be about politics, Rosy. Be about family, 'bout his mother's honour, 'bout Barbara's memory. Every mother in the land's gonna be on Matthew Swan's side."

There was no response for a moment, then Rosengarten began to smile. "Leak it out . . ." he said reflectively. "Make it look like the other campaigns are behind it . . ."

"A dirty tricks stunt, that's how we close the book on this shit . . . a character assassination plot," Noah said gleefully. He had the enemy in his sights now. "Concoct some bullshit evidence we later shoot down. Rassle up some psycho sheets we shoot full of holes."

"You think we can *bluff* Rider out of his scoop?" Flagg asked quietly.

"By the time Rider gets his act together, it'll be too fucking late. His book'll be history. History's bunk, right?"

"The video?" Flagg said.

"Coupla lookalikes. Like the Sukarno porno flick Rosy cooked up for the CIA in the sixties."

"I like it," Rosengarten said, perhaps because he knew that any further protest was a waste of breath.

"Cover your tracks and don't get caught," Noah grinned. "I want to come out of this thing clean."

The telephone rang. Fortas took the call.

"The Senator's snowed in at Springfield," he said, replacing the receiver. "New ETA's 12.30, sir."

"Get me Theodora," Noah said, unwrapping his first cigar of the day. "Think it's time we had a heart to heart."

Flagg stood up, strolled over to the table filled with silver-framed photographs of Matthew Swan: Matthew with Margaret Thatcher. Matthew and Elizabeth with the Prince and Princess of Wales. Matthew with the Pope. Matthew with Michael Ovitz.

He knows nothing, and doesn't even suspect that he doesn't know, Gisela had told him many years ago. He could only guess at what secret need had urged her to shift the blame: *Why confess when another man has taken the crime on himself?* she had said, laughing, certifying her revenge against Noah's contempt.

And now even she had forgotten the truth.

He smiled to himself in his reverie. He thought, Now nobody knows what I know.

Nobody in all the world will ever know the truth of it.

He lit a cigarette and exhaled slowly, and without a backward glance walked away from the photographs of the man who was his son.

63

We all have a contract with the public – in us they see themselves or what they would like to be. They love to put us on a pedestal and worship us. But they've read the small print, and most of us haven't. So, when we get knocked off by gangsters, like Thelma did, or get hooked on booze or dope or . . . just get sold . . . the public feels satisfied. Yeah, it's a good idea to read that small print. (Clark Gable to David Niven, on hearing of the murder of the actress Thelma Todd)

Midday Tuesday, January 23
Santa Aloe

Before Theodora put down the telephone, Missy knew from the look on her face that it was serious and, although she didn't know how she knew, she knew that Rider had found out about Mama and Matthew.

"That was Noah," Theodora said quietly, replacing the receiver. "Rider called him. He's got hold of a tape. Mama and me. A conversation . . . He knows everything, Missy."

"I warned you, honey. Never try to use men like Rider. They always end up using you."

"How could I have been so stupid?"

"Darling, you're not stupid. You were in pain."

"It has eaten up my life."

"What did Noah say?"

"He'll take care of it."

"*How?*" Missy demanded nervously.

"I don't see Rider again. I must refuse to talk to him."

"But he's back tomorrow!"

359

"You'll send him away."

"You've already given him a helluva lot of stuff, honey. What about that?"

"I deny everything. Interviews, tape, book. Everything."

Missy stared at her incredulously. "He's got a contract, honey. You signed a deal –"

"We say it's a fake. Noah says we'll accuse him of copy-catting Irving somebody – the man who claimed he was writing Howard's book."

"Clifford Irving? Forget it. Rider wouldn't stoop to a stunt like that."

"Noah says we only have to sow the doubt."

"This could be the beginning of our troubles, you know that?"

"Noah is going to take care of it," Theodora said again, realizing how much she was still in his power, and recognizing too that she had had neither a sorrow nor an ecstasy that she had not shared first with him.

"Are you all right?"

"Yes, I'm all right."

"You still love him, don't you?"

"Ain't it a bitch?" Theodora smiled.

Noah looked at his watch. He had showered and fixed his hairpiece. "They'll be landing in seven minutes," he said.

"There's one more thing we should think about, Noah," Aaron Flagg said.

"Yeah?"

"Elizabeth's pregnant."

"So?"

"She might not want to risk another child when she knows the truth about the Baroness."

Noah rose slowly and went to the window and stood looking out with his hands in his pockets. "I always wanted a grandson," he said quietly.

In a little while his shoulders began to shake.

"You're right, Aaron. The risk's too much to ask."

Flagg, Rosengarten and Fortas, avoiding each other's eyes,

waited for him to overcome his disappointment. It was a side of
Noah Swan that few people had ever seen. But Aaron Flagg knew
that in his pity for Noah there was hatred too . . . not for his feet
of clay, but for using their devotion to make even his selfishness
seem noble.

"A tragic miscarriage –" Noah turned to them, suddenly
laughing his great laugh, and for a moment, just for a moment, he
looked young again, as if he had the whole world on a string again
– "that won't hurt us one little goddam bit," he said, "in the
run-up."